MURDER IN THE HAUNTED CHAMBER

BILL LEFURGY

For my wife and cats

One need not be a Chamber — to be Haunted —
One need not be a House —
The Brain has Corridors — surpassing
Material Place —

Far safer, of a midnight meeting
External Ghost
Than it's interior Confronting —
That cooler Host.

Far safer, through an Abbey gallop,
The Stones a'chase —
Than unarmed, one's a'self encounter —
In lonesome Place —

Ourself behind ourself, concealed —
Should startle most —
Assassin hid in our Apartment
Be Horror's least —

The Body — borrows a Revolver —
He bolts the Door —
O'erlooking a superior spectre —
Or More —

—Emily Dickinson

CHAPTER 1

SARAH—FRIDAY, APRIL 15, 1910, 3:00 A.M.

*A*n eerie creak sounded from deep within the dark, silent mansion.

Sarah heard the noise because, as usual, she could not sleep. Reading something light and frivolous was the only way to quiet her hyperactive mind enough to induce slumber. The book open before her, *Psychology and Perception of the Paranormal*, was suitable for that purpose.

A floorboard groaned, closer this time. Then a faint rattle as if someone had touched the doorknob. The housekeeper could be up and about, even though the woman rarely stirred at this hour.

"Hello?" No answer.

Sarah massaged her temples, exhausted. She had volunteered twelve hours a day for the past week at the Sheppard and Enoch Pratt Hospital, a treatment facility for the mentally ill. She usually put in less time, but several patients came down with typhoid fever and needed her help. One patient died—an older woman who took great comfort from Sarah's devoted attention.

She picked up reading where she left off: the deluded belief that people can communicate with the dead. "This fantasy includes encounters with 'spirits' claiming to offer advice or

1

confer criticism. The subject may talk of apparitions that appear spontaneously or via the services of so-called 'mediums.' We may attribute most such sightings to neurotic suggestibility, although we cannot rule out a serious personality disorder or even psychosis . . ."

She closed the book. After switching off the electric lamp, the bedroom glowed with the full moon's cold silver brilliance. With a shiver, she pulled up the blankets and closed her eyes.

"My sweet sister." Grace stood over the bed, wearing a pale dress. Her light hair was in a thick nighttime braid that fell over a shoulder.

"Grace. I am surprised to see you."

"I've missed you terribly, Sarah." She laughed softly and sat on the bed, light as a feather. "And yes, I know you've missed me, too. You don't need to say so."

Sarah sobbed as they embraced. "You are unchanged since we last met," she said while using the sheet to dab a wet cheek. A disturbing thought floated through her mind: she was twenty-five, and Grace was three years older. It was therefore impossible for Grace to be nineteen, as she appeared.

"And you are all grown up." Grace leaned over to wipe away more tears and stroke her hair. Her sister had exactly the right touch—a precious comfort that Sarah had dearly missed.

"I am so proud that you are a doctor with a degree from the Johns Hopkins University School of Medicine," said Grace. "It's a remarkable achievement, especially for a woman. More remarkable still is your work as a forensic pathologist on behalf of justice. All of us deeply appreciate what you are doing."

"I am determined to hold murderers accountable for their crimes." Sarah clutched her sister's hand tightly.

"You have a new opportunity in that regard. Let me show you."

She was now standing in a room looking down at a young woman lying on a bed and wearing a yellow nightgown embroidered with pink roses. "Who is this sleeping person? Why am I here?"

Grace stood close by, looking at the supine form. "She is not sleeping. She is dead—murdered. Only you can find the killer."

In an eyeblink, they were back in Sarah's bedroom. "Grace—how can I investigate the murder of an unnamed victim in an unknown location? Will you notify the police?"

"You must use your expertise to help the police solve the crime."

"I prefer to work alone. Except for Jack, of course."

"Yes, I know all about your Jack. But you must engage boldly with others if you are to solve this killing."

"Grace. Explain how you can present yourself here and communicate with me when you were murdered eight years ago. Bear in mind that I do not believe in the supernatural. I rely on tangible evidence, not on information from a dream."

"There is more to the world than you know, darling sister. Our minds are capable of experience far beyond the ordinary. Think of love, of how different it makes you feel."

"I have not loved another since your death." Sarah squeezed her sister's hand, desperate not to let her go.

"Are you sure?"

"I cannot measure my experience—"

Grace was gone, her light laughter fading into the nighttime silence.

She opened her eyes, feeling oddly certain her sister had been here. Impossible.

But for reasons Sarah could not explain or even begin to justify, she was sure the woman on that bed had been recently murdered—and that she must find the killer.

CHAPTER 2

JACK—SATURDAY, APRIL 16, 1910, 4:00 P.M.

The thundering shockwave from the foundry came every five seconds, vibrating his teeth with each metallic bang. It was enough like cannon fire to draw icy rivulets of flop sweat. Not good—his nerves were already as tight as a plug in a cider barrel.

Jack was last here at the water's edge in the Fells Point neighborhood weeks ago looking for a missing person. A client had a brother who, when drunk, had a habit of jumping into the harbor. When the brother disappeared, Jack agreed to check the wharf pilings for floaters. He found a body, but it wasn't the guy. The brother eventually turned up in jail, dazed and wearing another man's ragged clothes.

Jack's mental troubles were under control at that point. But the visions had come back.

He was nearly broke and behind on his rent. His most pressing need for money, however, was for a trip to Hot Springs, Arkansas, for its magical mineral baths. The soothing waters might finally banish the ghosts bent on driving him insane.

He'd seen a brochure for Dr. Hope's Miracle Bath Palace in Hot Springs and was sold with the promise of "radioactive waters flowing from the electric heart of the Earth," guaranteed to "cure every affliction of the body, mind, and spirit." The brochure pictured a happy customer tucked into bed, snoozing away in a "restorative, mind-healing sleep that settles nerves and reawakens joy in the despondent." He hadn't slept without nightmares for weeks and weeks. At twenty-eight, he felt like an old man on his last legs.

Jack continued down the broad wharf to a sprawling pile of oyster shells eight feet high. Straining men pushed overflowing wheelbarrows up a sloping pathway to the top. Seagulls screeched as they circled the mound looking for bits of flesh.

He took in the ramshackle collection of buildings running along the wharf's edge. It was hard to believe this dump of an oyster packing plant made so much money for its owner.

"Hey, mac," called Jack to a nearby barrow man. "Where can I find the boss?"

"Dunno," the guy kept on pushing his load without looking up, "but you can bet he's watching."

A stiff breeze blew in from the harbor. It smelled like sewage but had the virtue of pushing away the fouler stink of rotting shellfish. The waterfront stunk, but this spot was especially nasty.

"Harden? That you?"

Jack turned to see a short, fortyish man approaching. He wore an expensive suit with a yellow tie and a blue-striped shirt. A straw boater with a broad black ribbon sat on his head.

"It is if you own this place."

"I do." He thrust out a short-fingered hand. As expected, the guy's grip was like a vise.

"Had your cornflakes this morning, I see," said Jack. A short fellow always had to prove something to a taller guy.

"A buddy tells me you're a great private detective," said the man. "And if you got that son of a gun out of trouble, you surely can help me. Come on into the office and let's talk."

Jack followed as the guy strolled into the plant. The interior was dimly lit, and it took a few seconds for his eyes to adjust to the murk. Several dozen workers hunched over two long rows of slatted wooden crates, each with a tin pail hanging at the side. Nearly all the laborers were kids under the age of fourteen; many were much younger. Their small hands worked furiously to pry open oysters, scoop meat for the bucket, drop the empty shells, and reach for another mollusk. The place was damp, fetid, and much colder than outside.

"Listen up, you loafers!" yelled the owner. Nobody stopped working. "See this here detective? He's a real bastard and is going to keep an eye on you."

A huge man leaning against the wall gave a braying laugh. "You lazy dogs are in trouble now!" The guy had "FOR MAN" written in crude letters on a card stuffed into the brim of his greasy derby hat.

"Keep them working," said the owner. "We've got another load of pearlies coming in tonight."

"You got it, boss." The foreman hit a crate with a long club. The sharp thwap made Jack jump, but none of the workers missed a beat. They were a sad lot, with thin, foxy faces and scrawny bodies. The youngest kids stood with bare feet on splintery risers, their short arms straining to grab one oyster after another. Nobody spoke; nobody smiled.

Jack had nothing against hard work: after running away from home at eleven, he'd done plenty to support himself. But that was on farms in the fresh air without a club-carrying goon watching his every move. He'd also been lucky enough to finish fifth grade and learn the basics of reading and writing. These wretched kids had no shot at any education. Their minds would be forever stunted and their bodies permanently damaged—all to make one man rich.

"I was just keeping them in line," said the owner with a friendly nudge before heading through a warped door with "Office" painted in faded lettering. He dropped into a shiny leather chair. The room was a mess, with slime-green paint peeling off the walls and wooly dust balls scattered across the floor.

"I haven't taken the job," said Jack. "And if you want me to strong-arm kids, forget it."

"The thief's no kid. Have a seat."

Jack considered walking out. He didn't want to be in this place, and he sure didn't want to deal with this character. But the job was supposed to pay well. He sat down.

"Here's the deal, Harden." The man lifted the top off a cedar humidor and pulled out a fat black cigar, which he sniffed for a good five seconds before sparking it up. "Somebody stole some photographs off me."

"Dirty pictures?" This guy seemed like the type.

"No, nothing like that." The man grinned as he puffed. "Just photos of my employees hard at work."

"So?"

"So, some muckraker might think it's wrong for me to give those brats honest work to earn money for their families."

"I get it," said Jack. "You're afraid of getting dinged by the new law against child labor. Why were you ignorant enough to have those pictures in the first place?"

"Watch your mouth, pal." The owner jabbed his cigar. "I'm paying you, remember?"

"I haven't taken a dime."

"The child labor hubbub comes and goes," said the owner. "Most people don't care—law or no law. And when it comes to oysters, the newspapers only get in a tizzy about tainted product. Did you see those stories recently about how packing plant workers are sick with tuberculosis? Got customers worried about disease in their canned oysters. It's bad for business."

"Yeah," said Jack. "A real shame."

"You bet. And unfair to me. I hire kids, mostly. Young and healthy. I see anyone cough, they get fired on the spot."

"And the pictures showed how your swell operation is disease-free."

"I was going to publish a pamphlet called 'My Sanitary Oysters are Packed with Young Energy.'" The owner drew on his stogie and made the tip glow like the eye of a demon.

Jack shook his head, amazed at this guy's pickle. While it was true that press attention to child labor went up and down, nothing sold papers like a good scandal with pictures.

"Here's what I want from you, Harden. Fetch those glass negatives back to me and I'll give you a hundred dollars."

Jack stared at the ribbon of smoke rising from the smoldering cigar. This guy was in a big enough jam that he'd pay a lot more than that to get those photographs back.

"Probably a cakewalk. I got a good idea who swiped them. Fired him yesterday when I caught him coughing. I think he stole them off my desk on his way out. Low-down sneak."

"Why doesn't your gorilla foreman go get them?"

"He's my baby brother." The owner smiled. "He can get a bit too excited when smacking people around. Him killing the guy would cause problems."

"I'm supposed to deliver a beatdown, too?"

"Got to send a message not to screw with me. Look, it's easy money for you. The guy's old and won't put up a fight."

Jack stood. "Not interested."

The owner laughed and brushed ash from the desktop. "I'll give you two hundred. Final offer."

"I don't do dirty work."

"You're a private detective. That means you're already dirtier than a bum with a soap allergy."

"I can deal with dirt," said Jack. "Scum is another matter."

"Okay, you're weak-kneed." The man tossed a five-dollar gold piece on the desk. "Get lost and keep your mouth shut about what I told you."

Jack ignored the coin and walked out.

The improbable baby brother approached, his buck teeth displayed in a grin. He blocked Jack's path and poked him in the chest with the club. "Hold up, friend. I'm supposed to give you the fired guy's address."

Jack swatted at the stick and knocked it out of the man's hand. "I turned the job down. Out of my way, clown."

The man glanced at the nearby workers. "I ain't finished talking with you." He stepped close, a surly curl of the lip replacing the goofy grin.

Jack tried to brush past, but the bruiser grabbed his arm and threw a roundhouse punch. Jack blocked the swing and countered with a quick fist into the man's chin. The blow was powerful enough to drop most men, but this guy shook his head and charged with a shrill yell.

Jack's ghosts had triggers—children crying, poor sleep, even not enough coffee. For whatever reason, the screaming spectral forms, bloody and torn, chose this moment to appear in a dreamlike haze. Jack barely managed to sidestep the lunging brute.

A ghostly woman, bloody and clutching an infant, ran at Jack with a terrible shriek.

"Mister—look out for the gun!"

The young shucker's voice cut through the unearthly din, giving him just enough time to kick the foreman's hand as he fired a pistol. The gun skittered away as Jack shoved the man against an oyster crate. Everything was tinted a bright pulsing red with ghosts crowding around, screaming and moaning. Jack was ready to pound the foreman's face until it wasn't a face anymore, but the guy had tumbled backward into the crate with his big feet hanging motionless over the top.

Breathing raggedly, Jack ran out of the place, ghosts in pursuit. He kept going up the street for blocks until dropping to the curb, eyes pressed shut. Still, the bloody woman with the baby continued to shake a gory fist at him while screaming words in an unknown language.

He rocked back and forth on the curb, begging her: "I can't take anymore. Please just kill me. Kill me now."

CHAPTER 3

SARAH—SATURDAY, APRIL 16, 1910, 11:00 A.M.

*P*eople communicated with gestures and facial expressions that were impossible for her to understand. Spoken language was also impenetrably coded. When a person said, "I would love to do that," they could mean the opposite. A question might require no answer. A smile could convey a hostile intent.

Confoundingly, these cryptic modes of expression were deemed *normal*. Sarah was not normal and could not pretend to be otherwise. Dealing with people was difficult, and so she preferred solitude whenever possible.

Yet, here she was, standing in the foyer of Mrs. Beatrice Lanvale, undertaking a most arduous engagement. The woman had couched the invitation as an obligation to welcome an out-of-town guest, forcing Sarah to attend as a matter of high society etiquette. She relied on the rules of proper behavior as a lifeline to the world of others, but stress often led her to violate decorum. This was a particular issue with regard to people she disliked, such as Mrs. Lanvale.

"Sarah—are you still with me?" asked the woman. "I said your petticoat is showing—fix it. Your skirt also has a frayed waistband, but there is nothing to be done about that now.

Honestly, a young woman with so little to work with simply must present herself better."

Sarah glanced down and saw a swath of petticoat drooping over her shoes. She tugged at her skirts and managed to hide most of the offending undergarment. She began pulling at loose threads hanging from her waistband, but Mrs. Lanvale scolded her again.

"Stop. I told you to leave it alone. My guest is waiting."

"Why does this person want to see me?" Sarah balled her hands into fists so tightly they hurt.

"Miss Nightingale has heard of your detecting exploits and wants to talk. Now, stop dawdling. She's waited long enough for your grand entrance."

Sarah raised her eyes to the garish brooch hanging on her hostess's blue silk dress. Why did the woman feel compelled to make such an ostentatious display? Sarah pondered the mystery while swaying back and forth, long skirts swishing. A darting glance revealed enough space between Mrs. Lanvale and the door to permit a dash to freedom. *Must not do that,* she told herself firmly. *Must follow the rules.* She turned and moved toward the parlor and the waiting stranger.

"My goodness, hello," said a tall woman. She was about fifty, slim and elegant, with a pale face contrasting with strikingly dark hair. Her simple dress consisted of floor-length white piqué fabric with a lace collar.

Sarah stared unblinkingly into the woman's eyes. She was making a special effort lately to establish eye contact, as others seemed to regard it as polite.

Mrs. Lanvale rushed up, out of breath. "Miss Lydia Nightingale, may I present Miss Sarah Kennecott—"

"Isn't it *Doctor* Kennecott?" interrupted the visitor, who met Sarah's gaze with a serene smile.

Their hostess snickered. "Oh, yes, I suppose so—"

"I only insist on that form of address when I am working as a physician." Sarah reluctantly accepted the guest's hand before quickly dropping it. "This is a social call."

"I understand, Sarah—I hope I may call you that. And please, call me Lydia."

"Well, then." Mrs. Lanvale cleared her throat noisily. "Miss Sarah Kennecott, may I present Lydia's assistants, Mr. Luther Fuller and Miss Lucinda Pike."

Perhaps twenty-one, Mr. Fuller was dressed all in black as if for a funeral. Miss Pike was about sixty and wore a conventional day dress constructed of patterned green cotton. Both nodded simultaneously. Much to Sarah's relief, neither extended a hand.

"Let us be seated." Mrs. Lanvale dropped heavily into an armchair covered in a shiny brocade. "Niblett, we will take tea."

"Yes, madam," said the butler, who promptly departed.

Sarah sat prim in a chair near a low lacquered table populated with artless bric-a-brac, including small porcelain birds with big eyes.

The butler reappeared, pushing a cart with an elaborate tea service. "Mr. Niblett serves so beautifully," said Lydia, sitting on a sofa with an assistant on either side.

"Niblett is a genuine English butler," said Mrs. Lanvale. "He used to work for a duke."

"I was in the service of an earl, madam," said the butler in a very stiff, very proper accent.

"Doesn't matter—I pay more," said Mrs. Lanvale with a humorless titter. "That will be all, Niblett."

Sarah's thoughts wandered to blood and murder. A Hungarian scientist had recently published a paper outlining a simple portable test to differentiate the blood of humans from that of animals. If true, it would represent a remarkable advance in criminal forensics. At present, testing for human blood at a crime scene required a complex laboratory procedure. She was eager to read more about the new method—as soon as this tiresome social assignment was finished.

"Sarah," said Mrs. Lanvale. "Listen to me. I told you to try the shortbread biscuits. They are imported directly from Glasgow."

"No, thank you. Please inform me as to the purpose of this meeting."

"Watch yourself, dear." Mrs. Lanvale glared while dabbing at her downturned mouth with a napkin. "Lydia is a spirit medium and is in town for the Death as Transformation and Opportunity Spiritualism Convention. She has taken time from her busy schedule to talk with you about a missing person."

"Miss Lydia Nightingale, I reject purported clairvoyance, communication with the dead, and all other forms of so-called spiritualism." Sarah noticed her right leg churning up and down but made no effort to stop the motion. She hated surprises—Mrs. Lanvale had not mentioned spiritualism in the invitation.

Lydia smiled. "I have no wish to discuss such matters with you. But will you use my first name? Please?"

Sarah disliked informality but knew that some people insisted upon it. "Very well—Lydia." She shifted her gaze to the floor.

"The missing person is my secretary, Anna Gilbert," said Lydia. "She and Lucinda traveled from Boston together. They got here yesterday, some hours ahead of Luther and me. Lucinda is staying in this house, but Anna is at a hotel closer to the convention site."

The separate accommodations struck Sarah as odd, but she remained quiet.

"All seemed well at first." Lydia wrung her hands. "I telephoned Anna at the hotel just after I arrived. She then met with Mrs. Lanvale and others shortly afterward but has not been heard from since."

"Perhaps she merely wishes to remain undisturbed," said Sarah.

"Anna values her privacy," said Lydia. "But it is unusual for her to remain out of contact for so long."

"You should know that dozens of unaccompanied women

arrive in Baltimore every day. Lotharios and criminals are known to prey upon them." Sarah's discomfort grew. Talking with prospective clients was not her strength. Jack, her detective partner, should be here.

"I did telephone the police," said Lydia. "But they were no help."

"The person of interest could be hospitalized," said Sarah.

"Oh, my." Lydia trembled. "I have a photograph of her—Mrs. Lanvale will pass it on to you. And if Anna is in a hospital and unable to communicate, the name tags sewn into her clothing should identify her."

"A woman's clothing may be removed during a crime. As I mentioned previously, young women, newly arrived and unaccustomed to the city, are prime targets for sexual violence and murder."

Mrs. Lanvale sputtered into her teacup. "What ghastly words! Show some discretion. This is my parlor, not some tawdry police station."

Sarah looked at Mrs. Lanvale and noticed a pronounced ghosting of cream-laden tea on her upper lip. The rules of etiquette stated that one should discretely notify someone with food or drink accidentally lingering on the face. She ran through all the possible ways to perform the required task while continuing to look at the woman's bedaubed *labium superius oris*.

"What are you staring at?" Mrs. Lanvale quickly put a napkin to her mouth and then threw it forcefully on a side table.

"My statement regarding unclothed deceased females is based on evidence," said Sarah, looking at a far wall. "I have conducted autopsies on such victims—"

Lydia moaned and began shaking, eyes rolled back in her head. "There is danger in love, for the precious worry us deeply," she said in a soft, girlish voice. Another person seemed to have taken over the woman's body. "We prepare for a great sorrow, a pain that almost resents love, it is so inflamed." The words tumbled out in a breathy murmur.

"My—what a stunning demonstration!" Mrs. Lanvale clapped excitedly. "Are there spirits about? Speak, oh you phantasmal visitors from the beyond!"

Mr. Fuller and Miss Pike grabbed hold of their employer's arms and imparted a vigorous shaking. Lydia's head lolled as she continued to speak quickly in a whispery voice: "An awful tempest mashed the air / The clouds were gaunt and few . . . "

More shaking caused a sudden retransformation. "I do hope no evil has befallen Anna," said Lydia as if as nothing unusual had occurred. Her two attendants resumed sipping tea.

"Sarah," said Mrs. Lanvale. "You can see that Lydia is much too delicate even to consider what might have befallen Miss Gilbert. Your help is required."

"Please, my dear." Lydia leaned forward, reaching for Sarah's arm. "I am so worried."

Sarah moved away quickly.

"I'm sorry." Lydia pulled back her hand. "I so need your assistance. I can pay you."

"You and your Mr. Harden currently have no clients," said Mrs. Lanvale. "Tell Lydia you will help her."

"Our policy is to discuss a potential case before accepting." Sarah clenched and unclenched her fingers, eager to leave this place.

"I understand," said Lydia. "Perhaps Mr. Harden could visit with us here?"

"Is that necessary?" Mrs. Lanvale held her chin high. "Mr. Harden would not feel welcome among the cultured class."

That was true enough. Sarah's detective partner despised sitting in parlors, referring to himself as "a man of the streets." She thought it an odd sobriquet, as he spent more time in saloons, pool rooms, and police stations than on pavement.

"I can meet at a place of your choosing on Monday morning," said Lydia. "I'm not picky. Just tell me where and when."

"Let us not forget your appointments, Lydia," said Mrs.

Lanvale. "You have consultations and séances. My friends are terribly excited to speak with their dearly departed."

Lydia's serene smile returned. "I am perfectly able to split my attention between the living and the dead."

"Well, then." Their hostess stood, followed by everyone else. "I'll see you out, dearie."

"Sarah. I take such pleasure in meeting you." Lydia clasped her hands over her heart.

"I offer my regards—Lydia. My regards to you, Mr. Luther Fuller. And my regards to you, Miss Lucinda Pike." The two assistants nodded in unison.

Mrs. Lanvale strutted to the marbled foyer where Niblett stood ready to open the enormous oak doors. The woman wheeled unexpectedly and backed Sarah against the wall. "Listen, you peculiar slip of a girl. You will help Lydia. Don't force me to be unpleasant."

"I believe your behavior towards me already conforms with the definition of unpleasant."

"Such impudence." The woman stepped closer. "And to think all that money your father left you includes funds stolen from my husband."

"That is incorrect." Sarah's claustrophobia spiked along with her anxiety. "My father, from what I understand, loaned your husband a considerable sum to cover his financial losses. Your husband never repaid the loan."

"No. When we lived in London those many years ago, your father swindled us. My husband told me so just yesterday."

Sarah shrank against the wall like a scolded child. "I know nothing of that claim. In any event, your husband died fifteen years ago and therefore is incapable of telling you anything from that time forward."

"He talks to me from the beyond." Mrs. Lanvale threw out her fleshy arms, hemming Sarah in even more. "If you don't help Lydia, I'll sue for damages."

"Am I to believe you would undertake legal action based on spoken testimony from a person after their death?"

"Don't underestimate my son." Mrs. Lanvale tossed her head. "Barnabas is a judge with considerable influence, and he is devoted to me."

Sarah stared silently at the marble floor.

"Help Lydia, or I will also destroy your reputation by telling everyone Mr. Harden has deflowered you." Mrs. Lanvale produced a photograph. "This is Anna Gilbert. Go on, take it. You need to find her."

The object was inches from Sarah's face, and she grabbed it as an act of self-defense. She glanced at the photo and could hardly believe her eyes—it was the same young woman Grace had presented as murdered in that peculiar dream.

"Are you going to stare at that all day? Those silent spells of yours are quite strange."

"Good day, madam." Sarah slipped past the woman and charged out the door while clutching the eerie photograph.

THE ENOCH PRATT FREE LIBRARY READING ROOM WAS mercifully quiet. Earlier it had been full of students and their incessant whispering and paper crinkling. The librarian shushed the offenders far too infrequently for Sarah's liking.

Despite the quiet, distress still gnawed at her. How was it possible that a dream had forecast the murder of Anna Gilbert, personal secretary to a supposed spirit medium?

Anxious and unsettled, she turned to a favorite remedy: reading. She sat with a stack of books in her usual place. The volumes related to purported communication with the deceased.

The first book noted that conspiracies, superstition, and other ideas not rooted in fact naturally attracted some people. Such individuals also were skeptical of expertise, preferring to place their trust in charlatans. Doing so channeled their personal grievances into a larger worldview. The practice also gave people a sense of mastery: they claimed to see through the supposed manipulation of forces pitted against them.

Sarah closed the book and thought of Jack. While he was in no way a follower of crazed conspiracies, he did believe in ghosts. He also sometimes mocked her expertise, calling her ridiculous names such as "Miss Smarty" and "Doctor Do-Good." Here was an explanation—Jack represented a wider population resentful of her professional authority. It was as if her achievements came at the cost of conferring failure and shame upon those less successful.

If only Jack could understand how little she knew about life, that she felt superior to no one. Quite the opposite was true. Her social awkwardness left her feeling excluded and isolated.

A second book told the remarkable story of how the Fox sisters launched the spiritualist movement in 1848. While living with their family near Rochester, New York, Maggie, then fourteen, and Kate, nine, claimed an ability to communicate with spirits of the dead. With the girls present, spirits would answer questions via raps or knocks. This demonstration astounded observers, as neither girl appeared to make the sounds. Word spread, and soon the sisters were traveling the nation, drawing crowds and collecting hefty fees.

In an era of high child mortality and short adult lifespans, the notion of communicating with the dead was a powerful comfort. The departed were not really gone at all—they were merely lurking beyond the thin curtain of living reality. All one needed was a person with the ability to serve as a conduit—a medium—between the living and the dead.

The fame of the "Rochester Knockers" grew over the years, despite denunciation from skeptics. The downfall of the Fox sisters came, ironically, not from expert debunking but from love and alcohol. Maggie Fox began a relationship with a wealthy adventurer who ordered her to quit spiritualism. She obeyed but felt stifled and fell into alcoholism. Distraught after the man's tragic early death, Maggie confessed that the sisters were frauds from the start. They had cracked different joints in their toes and ankles to make disembodied sounds and fool observers. Maggie died penniless and alcoholic in 1893. Her sister Kate died a year earlier after a drinking binge, forgotten.

Following the lead of the Fox sisters, most of the innumerable psychics and mediums who came forth were women. Mediumship was, to be sure, one of the few lucrative professions open to females, as the practice was linked to traits popularly associated with the so-called "weaker sex"—nervousness, heightened sensitivity, and flighty behavior.

As Sarah mulled the story of spiritualism, she marveled at how popular perceptions change. If some years earlier the Fox sisters had claimed to communicate with spirits, they would have been dragged to the stake and burned as witches.

"Are you reading for business or pleasure?" Sarah jerked her head up to see a red-bearded, middle-aged fellow smiling at her. A gangly young man in a worn suit stood behind him.

"Why do you wish to know, sir?"

"I am a seeker of knowledge." He sat at the table and rebuked the young man when he started to do the same. "Go get started with the research, boy."

"As you wish, professor." The young man bowed and left.

"My name is Professor William Jaworski, most recently employed by the American Institute for Psychic Studies. And I know quite a bit about you, Dr. Sarah Kennecott."

She noticed the awful smell of artificial mint, perhaps from cologne or hair pomade, wafting from the man. "How may I assist you, sir?"

"A girl is so much more appealing when she smiles." He drew an exaggerated arc with his finger in front of her face.

"That is your personal opinion." Sarah disliked few things more than a man presuming to explain something to her. What they said was frequently foolish, simplistic, or wrong, and not infrequently, all three. "Once again, sir, what do you want from me?"

"Just a bit of your time." He pulled a meerschaum pipe and a tobacco pouch from his jacket. "I'm writing a book about the life and exploits of Lydia Nightingale. You, of course, will be in it."

"I do not understand." She leaned further away from the odiferous man while staring at the table.

"Oh, come now. Don't be coy." He loaded the pipe, carefully tamping the tobacco. "Let's do an interview. It's a chance to tell your side of the story. Give me some rich material, and I promise to portray you in a good light."

"I fail to comprehend your line of reasoning."

"Okay, play that game. I've already got lots of gossipy details about you. Readers eat up that personal stuff almost as much as they do ghost stories." He leaned in close and spoke with a quiet urgency. "Speaking of which, have you ever experienced anything supernatural?"

Sarah would bolt but for the fact that he blocked her in with his bulk.

"I saw an evil spirit two years ago in England," said Jaworski. "I was walking during a moonless night in the countryside. Suddenly, a hideous flying creature swooped down and flexed its sharp, bloody talons. I stared into its blazing red eyes, ready for my doom. Then the creature spoke. 'Remember me,' it croaked. 'And tell the world anyone may encounter us, anyone can die at our hands.' It then flew off."

"Hands? You said the creature had talons."

"You are so literal," Jaworski said with a laugh.

"I believe your account is untrue."

"It's the story that matters, not the truth." He lifted his pipe and pointed to the bust of a bearded man carved on the bowl. "This is the Greek Herodotus, known as the father of history. I prefer his other nickname: the father of lies." He lit the pipe while sucking loudly on the stem. "I can write anything I like about you, and people will believe it."

Sarah gagged on the foul smoke wafting from the pipe. She stood, causing her chair to scrape loudly as it moved across the wooden floor. "I remain baffled by your entreaties and offended by your pointed rudeness. Good day, sir." She gathered two unread volumes in one hand and placed the other hand over her nose and mouth. Jaworski waited for a long moment before moving to let her pass.

The librarian jumped, startled at Sarah's sudden approach.

"I request to check these out." Sarah handed over the volumes.

"I saw you chatting with Professor Jaworski," said the librarian as she stamped the books. "Isn't he charming? He and his student will be here all this week researching spiritualism. The subject fascinates me. A psychic—Madame Polyhymnia—said I would marry my Henry before I even met him."

"You married because an alleged psychic told you to do so?"

The woman looked up, eyes squinched. "She said I would marry a tall man with light hair who was two years older. Four months later, I met someone who matched that description. I knew right away we were fated to marry. And look." She held up her left hand to show off a small gold band.

"Madam Polyhymnia's characterization was general enough to fit a multitude of men. Surely you do not assume any causation between what she said and your romantic relationship?"

The librarian lowered her hand with a frown.

It dawned on Sarah that she had mishandled the interaction. When a female reveals she has married, she expects words of approval, particularly from other females. "I withdraw my question and offer felicitations on your acquisition of a husband."

"Thank you," said the librarian with a sigh. "But marriage isn't for everyone."

CHAPTER 4

JACK—SATURDAY, APRIL 16, 1910, 5:00 P.M.

"*H*ey, mister." The voice came from far away. "You okay?"

Jack looked up to see the grimy face of a ten-year-old boy. "Yeah. Yeah, I'm fine." He looked around, relieved to neither see nor hear any ghosts.

"Need me to get you some whiskey?"

"I don't have the jimjams. I don't even drink." People often attributed his ghost episodes to booze—or the lack of it. "It's just nerves."

"Sure," said the kid, who wore a torn shirt, ragged pants, and no shoes. "Whatever you say." The boy, with his gaunt face and twig-like arms and legs, clearly wasn't getting enough to eat.

"Your ma and pa live nearby, buddy?"

"They're both dead. I hang out here and there, selling newspapers."

"Tough life." Jack knew swarms of children lived on the streets. The clever ones avoided the hell-holes known as orphan asylums. But the price of freedom meant poverty and, more often than not, exploitation at the hand of abusive adults.

"Ain't so bad. I got friends." The boy turned to leave.

"Hang on, half-pint." Jack reached into his pocket and found a quarter. "This is for you."

"I ain't letting you do nothing to me, mister. And I ain't doing nothing to you."

"No strings." Jack tossed the coin, which the kid caught.

"Gee, thanks. Don't often run across a nice drunk." The boy grinned and ambled off.

Despite the feel-good glow, the day was lost. He needed to earn, not dole out the little cash he had left. An unemployed nutcase couldn't afford random acts of charity.

He was still jittery from encountering the ghosts and needed to burn off energy. Just as well he had to move double-time across town to keep a dinner appointment.

Striding west along the waterfront, he noticed a procession of multi-decked sidewheel steamships coming from the long piers on Light Street. The ships looked like big white birthday cakes with smokestacks for candles. Some went north, but most of them traveled to points south. That made sense. Baltimore sat just below the Mason-Dixon line, and tradition linked the city to the former confederacy.

Jack had no nostalgia for the Old South, but he liked the clashing human currents that gave the city its edgy atmosphere. The population mainly consisted of southern whites, but it also had a higher proportion of blacks than any other American city. Plus, hundreds of Eastern European immigrants arrived at Locust Point—Baltimore's equivalent of Ellis Island—every day. Add in a booming economy propelled by the city's seaport and the Baltimore and Ohio Railroad, and you got rigid tradition splintering against relentless change. That, in turn, led to conflict, greed, vice, and corruption—mother's milk for a private detective. One who could think straight, anyway.

He was meeting Sarah for dinner. Although he hadn't seen her in a week, she was the one person keeping him anchored. Jack had only been able to handle a couple of cases since Christmas, but she was still committed as his detective partner. Not that Sarah had any trouble keeping herself occupied otherwise. She worked at some loony bin and was forever giving lectures at local medical schools about cutting up dead bodies. The places loved her because she was so darn brainy. Not to mention she never charged them a cent.

Sarah was a natural-born detective with a keen analytical mind and a determination that just wouldn't quit. She could appear cold and unfeeling, but her stiff demeanor hid powerful emotions, including a deep passion for helping people.

He'd never cared for any woman more than Sarah, and he had to fight the urge to romance her. But, at her insistence, they had agreed to avoid that from the start. He suspected that she liked him as much as he liked her, but she had never wavered from her expressed opposition to a love relationship.

It was a head-scratcher why a woman so smart, classy, and humane wanted to hang around with somebody like him in the first place. She was going to dump his crazy ass sooner rather than later. How could she not? He wasn't worth caring about.

This was it. Jack was near the end of the line. The mental pain was unbearable—it was like standing near an open window on the twelfth floor of a burning skyscraper with the exits blocked. The fire was now getting so hot that jumping out the window seemed better than getting burned alive.

CHAPTER 5

SARAH—SATURDAY, APRIL 16, 1910, 6:00 P.M.

*T*he floorboards of the library lobby creaked as she paced, stomach rumbling. She was accustomed to eating at an earlier hour, but Jack was picking her up for dinner.

She wished to be already seated with a menu in hand, but women were not permitted in restaurants without an escort. A female out alone during the evening was regarded as a prostitute, and no respectable restaurant wanted association with such a person.

What foolishness, she thought. No one could ever mistake her for a prostitute. She lacked the beauty, charm, approachability, or whatever quality it was that drew men to a woman.

Sarah turned her thoughts to Jack and his cyclical mental distress. He had been unable to undertake any of the detective cases offered to them over the last number of weeks. She might have handled some of them alone—if she had the confidence.

Despite her multiple requests, Jack stubbornly refused to talk about his torment. As with most males, he kept problems to himself—even when that approach clearly was not practical. All she knew was his condition stemmed from witnessing a massacre of civilians while overseas in the army. The trauma manifested for him in the form of hallucinations: imagined ghosts representing the people killed.

Drastic measures were required, as he was deteriorating rapidly and was at risk of harming himself and others. He needed to enter the Sheppard Pratt Hospital. It was one of the most advanced mental health facilities in the country, known to treat patients kindly in a curative environment.

But Jack would not admit he suffered from emotional illness. And he would fiercely resist placement in what he would crudely term "the nut farm." Sarah had to convince him that unless he dealt with his problem, the authorities would eventually commit him to the Bayview Asylum, a horrible place where the city sent the destitute insane. If Jack ended up in there, he was as good as dead.

Even if he managed to avoid Bayview, it was clear their relationship was fraying. His pain turned him rude and contemptuous, a far cry from the man who used to treat her with understanding and respect.

Sarah was accustomed to aloof, formal dealings with people. Six months ago, she met Jack and found him a remarkably good companion. Despite their agreement to avoid romance, she had observed within herself a growing attachment—and perhaps even an attraction—to the man. And now, after months of growing to trust him, he was receding from her.

SHE ANALYZED MULTIPLE QUESTIONS IN PARALLEL while walking with Jack to the restaurant. How to broach the subject of Sheppard Hospital? How should they proceed to investigate Anna Gilbert's murder? Why had Lydia Nightingale sought her out? Who was Professor William Jaworski, and why was he so insistent on interviewing her?

"Hey, hold your horses," said Jack.

"I own no horses—"

"Slow down. You're walking too fast."

A quick backward glance revealed a man in distress. Jack's hair was long and unkempt, his face sickly pale. Brown gravy spots splattered his wrinkled white shirt. Even his shoes—normally shined to a mirror finish—were dull and scuffed.

"What hifalutin books did you read today?" He jerked his thumb behind at the receding library building with a dour expression as they walked.

"I read several books on the subject of spiritualism."

"Why bother? You've already made up your mind—everyone who sees ghosts is a superstitious idiot. Like me."

She stopped. "That is an inaccurate and derisive description of my position. I have never used such offensive terms regarding yourself. Why do you taunt me so?"

"Why are you so sensitive?"

Sarah swayed on her feet for a few seconds and then resumed walking. Jack said nothing. His sharp comment followed by lingering silence indicated melancholia, which reduced the already limited possibility that he would entertain the idea of entering Sheppard Asylum. Perhaps a conversational gambit would encourage him to be more communicative. She waited until they were seated in the restaurant. "The weather is warmer than the seasonable average. I noticed partial cloud cover during the mid-afternoon."

"That's the first time I've ever heard you talk about the weather." He gave her a glassy-eyed grin. "You hate small talk. Am I such a mess that I've forced you into it? How horrible for you."

She blinked at him, unable to think of a reply.

"Let me tell you about my day," he said. "A guy offered me a job, but I turned it down. Then I got in a fight. After that, I gave away some of what little money I have left."

"Why did you not consult with me about the potential case?" Sarah abruptly shifted a leg, which hit the table, causing their water glasses to wobble. "That is contrary to our agreement. We are to discuss all offerings and then jointly decide if we wish to accept them."

Jack stared at the ceiling while scratching his stubbly chin. "You wouldn't have liked the job. Too crooked."

"You have no right to summarily preempt my participation or to make judgments about what does or does not meet my ethical standards."

"All right, then—the job was too low-class for a rich, fancy type like you."

"That is a cruel remark," she said. The lower Jack's mood, the more he dwelled on their different backgrounds in terms of money and class. The difference did not matter to her—all she cared about was his decency and intelligence.

"Sorry," he said. "I'm terrible company tonight."

"Perhaps you wish me to depart." She chopped the air with a hand, narrowly missing a water glass before clasping both hands tightly in her lap.

"Don't," he answered dully, staring at the tabletop.

Silence hung over them as the waiter served dinner. Jack launched into his food immediately, gobbling forkfuls without looking up. At least his appetite was fine.

Sarah considered strategy. Admonishing him for breaking their agreement or speaking rudely would yield no benefit. But if he was going to be contrary anyway, perhaps the best course was to plunge right into the prospect of Sheppard Pratt Hospital. She drew in a breath. "Jack. I am concerned about your state of mind. Your wartime experience is clearly causing you terrible mental pain. As I care for you, your distress is causing me anxiety and discomfort." She lifted her eyes from the table and met his gaze before looking away. "Substantial anxiety and discomfort."

Jack wiped his mouth with a napkin and then crushed the cloth into a tight ball. "Look, I'm in one of my bad states. I know something's got to be done. That's why I looked into that shady job. I need money to go to Hot Springs, Arkansas, for the radioactive water cure."

"There is no evidence that water of any kind—including that with radioactivity—helps nervous disorders." Her hands flopped in her lap. "Advertisements that promise relief are bogus. You need intensive psychotherapy."

"I forgot you know everything." He tossed the crumpled cloth napkin on the table and watched as it slowly expanded. "And yet the only thing you can suggest is for me to blather at some quack. How do you know that psycho-talk works any better than hot baths?"

He had a point. Psychotherapy—known as the "talking cure" or, more colorfully, as "chimney sweeping," was a new approach and unproven. Supposedly, trauma blocked in the subconscious finds expression, either through physical ailments or mental disorders. When sufferers spoke to trained therapists about repressed thoughts and feelings, trauma was exposed to consciousness and defused. That was the theory.

"I can recommend an excellent clinical environment," Sarah said as she clutched bunches of the tablecloth in her fingers.

He dropped his palm on the table. "Now you want the men in the white coats to cart me off to the funny farm. Not interested. It's my problem, and I need to solve it. By myself."

She glanced at him and noticed classic signs of extreme tension: sweat and contraction of jaw and neck muscles. If she pressed the matter, he could escalate to shouting. That might draw the restaurant manager over, which in turn could provoke Jack to physical aggression. "Very well." A change in the subject of discussion was in order. "I wish to discuss a proposed case involving a missing person. The requestor is Miss Lydia Nightingale, a visitor to our city."

Jack jerked his head up, eyes bulging. "Lydia Nightingale, the psychic medium? She's in Baltimore?"

"I met with her this morning." Sarah jammed her hands under the table and began rocking in her chair.

"And she wants to hire us?"

"Correct. She has a missing associate, who I believe has been murdered."

He appeared not to have heard her. "I know about Lydia Nightingale—she talks to dead people—spirits." He threw his hands into the air. "I was thinking about going to Boston to see her but figured she wouldn't give a guy like me the time of day. And now I can work with her."

"To solve a murder."

Again, he ignored her. "I need a good medium to get in touch with my ghosts. They want something from me. They won't leave me alone."

"What you describe is a manifestation—"

"No!" He hit the table, harder this time. "Don't give me that smart stuff. I know what I see. I know what I hear. These ghosts are real. I've seen them ever since . . ." His voice trailed off as he sank in his chair.

"Since the deaths you witnessed in the Philippines." She knew only the bare outline of the horror.

He glared at her. "You're so damn helpful this evening."

She chewed her lip, trying to decide if he was communicating appreciation or disdain. People often said things not meant to be interpreted by the literal meaning of their words, such as with irony and sarcasm. If only language included some sort of indicator to clarify intent.

"I don't need a quack. I need somebody who can talk to ghosts."

"At the risk of further incurring your contempt, I must observe there is no assurance that Lydia will address your concerns. Her secretary is missing—"

"I want to meet with her."

"Very well. I will arrange for a meeting on Monday morning so that we may undertake the case."

"Wonderful." For the first time that evening, he seemed to relax. "You're the best."

RIDING HOME IN A HANSOM CAB, SHE CHOMPED ON A
thumbnail, deeply displeased with Jack. She had never experienced him so selfish and dismissive. He had breached their
agreement to discuss potential cases. He had raised a foolhardy
"water cure" for his severe nervous problem and would not
consider her well-founded idea for treatment. Worst of all, he
had shown more interest in the putative powers of a psychic
than he did about catching a murderer.

She kept her expectations of others low because most
people, regardless of how they initially presented themselves,
eventually proved untrustworthy. In Jack, she thought she had
finally found someone who could see past the quirks to the core
of her being, including the vulnerability and neediness no one
had ever fathomed.

She must now reconsider that premise.

CHAPTER 6

JACK—JOLO ISLAND, PHILIPPINES, WEDNESDAY, MARCH 6, 1906, 12:00 P.M.

*L*unch was the same as always: tinned meat so bad everyone called it "embalmed beef," powdery vegetables, and coffee that tasted like dirt mixed with kerosene. Jack ate everything and was glad for seconds. Unlike many of his fellow troopers, dysentery hadn't twisted his gut into a wretched disaster.

His cavalry regiment had come to this tiny island at the far southern tip of the Philippines the previous year with orders to put down a native rebellion. The Moro people didn't care that Spain had surrendered their lands to America as part of the Spanish-American War. But they fought back fiercely when the Americans interfered with their customs and demanded unconditional obedience.

Jack had charged their cottas—forts constructed of logs, rocks, and earth—and knew the Moro warriors were ferociously brave. They fought with ancient muskets, spears, and finally, wavy kris swords and knives. The weapons were no match for the American cannon and Krag-Jorgensen rifles, and the natives took terrible casualties. But they were always ready to fight again the next day.

He had no fondness for the Moro. They were followers of the

Muslim religion, about which Jack knew nothing. Odd customs abounded, including men "running amok" to stab random people in a crazed frenzy. Yet Jack stopped short of believing, like nearly all his fellow soldiers, that the Moro were subhuman savages. He'd seen too many supposedly civilized white people behave far worse.

"Here he comes." Private Pete Nelson poked Jack. "Our great leader is going to give us a peppy speech."

The captain swaggered to an overturned crate, stepped up, lost his balance, and stumbled back down. He gave the box a kick and stepped on it again. A delicate man, the captain was short and thin with a narrow chest. He wore his hair in long blond locks, just like his hero, General George Armstrong Custer.

"Listen up now, men," the captain said in his reedy voice. "We're mounting up for a fight. A bully of a fight. There will be blood. Who's ready for the splendor of battle?"

A trooper in the rear belched.

The captain stood on his toes, looking for the offender. "You damn well better take this serious. Remember, we're here to bring law, order, and civilization to this savage land."

"And this savage land is here to bring misery to our stomachs," whispered Nelson near Jack's ear.

"Men, we're bound for fame and glory!" The captain raised his fist in the air and paused as if expecting a cheer. None came.

"Prepare to move out in thirty minutes." The captain pointed toward the horizon, causing the crate to wobble. After flapping his arms to keep upright, he stepped down and strode off, saber scabbard dragging on the ground.

Jack tossed his tin plate into a bin and rushed to the barracks. He put on his full uniform—thick cotton khaki pants and blouse, ill-fitting and much too heavy for the sweltering heat. His suspenders had shrunk so much in the tropical climate they cut into his shoulders; the metal fitting in the rear had rubbed his back raw, forming an oozing sore that felt like a red-hot branding iron. His boots collected sweat and cheered on fungus. A pointed felt campaign hat completed the costume.

"I'm praying our leader's a bullet catcher," said Nelson. "Let him lead his own one-man charge."

"He's hungry for promotion. Blasting with cannon at a distance won't cut it. He wants hand-to-hand fighting—maximum blood and guts."

"Our blood. Our guts. Not his. I'm not playing that game."

"Doesn't your father expect a hero? You said he charged up San Juan Hill with Teddy Roosevelt and his Rough Riders."

"Dad will just have to take me as I am." Nelson grinned as he buckled on his cartridge belt. "By the way, I've asked him to find you a job after we get out of the army. He runs some sweet crime rackets in the Bowery, my home turf. That's New York City, man."

"Crooked work doesn't much appeal to me."

"Suit yourself. But he knows you're my buddy and expects you to keep me safe. That's worth a lot to him—and to you."

Jack shrugged as he holstered his Colt revolver.

"The downside is that my father doesn't like people disappointing him. Doesn't like it at all."

"Stay off the front lines, then. Better for both of us."

They rode their horses a couple of miles to the homestead of a white farmer at the foot of the towering mount Bud Dajo. Some Moros had stolen livestock from the farmer and gone to the top of the mountain. Supposedly, there were lots of them hunkered down in a fortified volcanic crater, waiting for the reprisal.

As Jack tied up his horse, Nelson poked him in the ribs. "This is crazy, even for this man's army. All because of some stolen chickens, we got to climb a mountain two thousand feet tall, covered in jungle, and steeper than a mule's ass. And then we have the privilege of fighting those wicked devils."

"Men, I'll give it to you straight," said the captain. "I've volunteered for us to take the toughest trail to the summit on foot. It's a hard climb but worth it for triumph and glory. Let's show them we can fight just as hard off a horse as on."

"The only thing I want to show them is that guy with a dagger in his chest," muttered Nelson.

Starting out was easy, the slope gentle. Halfway up the mountain, the trail turned into a narrow hogback ridge with stomach-churning ravines on either side. Jungle growth choked the path forward.

Jack gasped in the brutal heat and humidity. His rifle and rucksack chaffed at his aching flesh. Finally, they got the order to make camp—if a rocky, overgrown, pitched slope can be called that. Wedged against a tree was the only way to sleep without tumbling down the mountain. The night was terrible, with the bugs, heat, and chatter of nearby Moro warriors.

Early the next day, they climbed within five hundred steeply sloping feet of the crater lip. Random shots and taunts came down from the Moro defenders.

Moving uphill required grabbing onto tree roots and pulling up the slope, hand over hand. Moro warriors sent boulders crashing down, one of which took a man down a ravine to his doom. Other troopers suffered broken legs and fractured feet. After a torturous hour of crawling, Jack and his squad came to a dense thicket of punji—sharpened bamboo stakes—blocking the way. The Moro had a clear line of fire at the stakes.

The captain came up and stood behind a tree. "Hell, a bunch of sticks isn't going to stop us. Find a path on your bellies. Forward!"

Nobody moved. "That's an order—get going."

"Captain," said Jack. "Shouldn't we wait for more men so we can have covering fire?"

"I'm in charge here, trooper." He pointed to Jack and Pete Nelson. "You two lead the charge."

Jack headed for the stakes, but Nelson beat him to it. "Guess I'll have my Rough Rider moment after all," he said with a grin. "If anything happens, tell my dad it wasn't your fault."

Nelson made it twenty feet before a musket ball hit him in the head, causing a gushing wound. Jack tried pulling him back to safety, but the man's trousers got caught on a punji. Shots pinged off the stakes as Jack got to his knees, freed the fabric, and brought Nelson back to the rest of the squad. The man wasn't quite dead but was clearly a goner.

"You were ordered to advance, soldier." The captain's thin shout from behind his tree was barely heard over the musket fire.

"I wasn't going to leave him there." Jack took off his hat to wipe away sweat and noticed two bullet holes in the pointy crown.

"It's 'sir' to you, trooper."

Jack was six inches taller, thirty pounds heavier, and by this point indifferent to rank. "I once knew an ass named 'Sir.' Sir."

The officer stepped back. "I'm writing you up for insubordination when we get back." He turned to the others. "All right, the second squad's here now—spread out and provide covering fire. I want the first squad to move through the spikes and engage the enemy. You go first, Harden."

Jack led the way through the maze of sharp sticks as musket balls whizzed past. A low wall on the crater rim marked the summit. Warriors popped up from behind to fire muskets and throw rocks. Reaching the wall, he grabbed his rifle by the barrel, pulled himself over, and clubbed the nearest Moro. Another lunged with a wicked curved knife, but the tip hit a cartridge pouch on his belt and glanced off. Jack pulled his Colt revolver and shot the attacker dead. Other troopers came over the wall and, after a brutal fight at close quarters, all the defenders were killed.

Jack looked west and saw another troop column had used a wheel-mounted machine gun to exterminate a long trench filled with Moro warriors. The crew had rolled the weapon past the trench and were setting it up on a knoll overlooking a cluster of huts about thirty yards away. Noise to the south revealed a third column positioning a second machine gun pointed in the same direction.

"Let's go kill more savages before those gunner boys get them all," called the captain, saber in hand. "Men, fix bayonets."

Many hundreds of Moro—elderly, women, and children—crowded around the huts. A few white surrender flags fluttered.

"Captain, it's just civilians down there," said Jack. "They're no threat."

"You too yellow to finish this fight, soldier?"

"Killing unarmed women and children isn't a fight. It's criminal slaughter."

"Charge!" The captain raised his saber.

Jack grabbed his belt from behind. "You've got to stop this."

The man wheeled and slammed Jack's chin with the saber handle before taking off, whooping and hollering as he ran at the terrified people.

Jack watched as the machine guns cut down hundreds of people. Others were shot at close range with rifles or bayoneted. A group of screaming women and children fled east to relative safety, only to have the captain charge in their direction. The man got to them quickly, slashing wildly with his saber while troops lunged with bayonets.

A solitary woman carrying a baby came stumbling in Jack's direction. She held her wailing kid close, wrapped in a cloth bundle. The woman got to within feet of him, pleading in a foreign tongue. Their eyes met just before the captain cut her down and continued hacking at her body, his saber casting off strings of blood.

That was the last thing Jack remembered until waking in leg irons back in the barracks.

"You're in big trouble." A middle-aged major stood nearby.

"How can I be the one in trouble?"

"You went after an officer like a crazy man, yelling and cussing. Lucky your friends held you back before you could hurt him too bad. You're getting court-martialed."

"Me court-martialed? After what happened?"

The major shook his head. "Look, there's a way out for you, boy. Army's worried about bad press, so if you promise to sign a statement saying everything went fine up on that mountain, we can let you go with an honorable discharge. Here, take a look."

The statement claimed a glorious victory at Bud Dajo and commended the captain for magnificent leadership in subduing a vast Moro army. "Regretfully," read one line, "a handful of women and children were accidentally killed in the crossfire."

"This is crap."

"So what?" The major frowned. "You get to save your skin."

"And he gets a shiny medal and a big promotion."

"He's getting that anyway, no matter what you do or don't do."

"Forget it. I'm not signing. The captain's a criminal. And he's got lots of company."

JACK WAS BOOTED OUT OF THE ARMY WITH A dishonorable discharge citing "cowardice before the enemy." Then a ship dumped him off in San Francisco. A recent earthquake had nearly destroyed the place, and the devastation matched his mood.

His first night back, weaving drunk down a dark, rubble-strewn street, he ran into Pete Nelson. "You should've protected me," Nelson said, shaking a bloody fist. "Instead, you got me killed. There's hell to pay for you, Harden." Jack yelled back, but the figure vanished.

Two nights later, in his fleabag boarding house, Jack saw the shrieking ghost of the Moro woman with her baby, as real as the sweat-soaked sheets twisted around his legs. He swatted at her, but his hand went straight through and did nothing to quiet the cries. She and other Moro ghosts kept coming back, night after night. Nothing kept them away—not whiskey, not women, not backbreaking work on the docks.

Jack caught a break when a fellow stevedore offered him a bottle of rotgut liquor to find a guy who owed him ten dollars. He tracked the man down, roughed him up a bit, and returned the cash. Word spread, and soon others wanted Jack to take care of their business. He would have made lots of money if not for his reputation as a violent drunk who screamed at shadows.

He also discovered a natural talent for reading people— knowing what they wanted and what they feared. He took to calling himself a private dick, and nobody argued, not even the slick Pinkerton detectives he encountered from time to time. They treated him like a pal, someone just as capable and morally bent as they were.

One morning Jack woke up dirty and hungover in a China-town alley with hands bruised from a fight. Thoroughly disgusted with himself, he swore off the booze. But that wasn't enough. He needed another big change if he had any shot at crawling out of his dark hole.

A train schedule lay nearby on the trash heap. He opened it and saw the rail line went all the way east. Somehow he'd kept his bankroll and had enough money to go as far as he liked.

He chose Baltimore, the seventh-largest city in the country and growing like mad from its proximity to Washington, DC, and its seaport on the Chesapeake Bay. The town was awash in cash from its steel mills and whiskey distilleries. Baltimore was also busy rebuilding hundreds of downtown structures lost in a catastrophic 1904 fire. All that meant people stumbling around with money in their pockets, which in turn meant a super-charged urban underbelly of crime and corruption.

Jack laughed, thinking about how he would seek a better life by profiting off human weakness and immorality. All he had to do was find a moral code somewhere deep in his sick soul and stick to it.

CHAPTER 7

"*J* got some fancy tea for you, Miss Sarah."

She had just entered the Monumental Lunchroom, and the waitress was already at her side. "Thank you, madam. But I can tolerate what you typically serve."

"Oh no, no." The woman waggled a finger. "A proper lady needs the right tea—not the swill my other customers gulp down. Come on, I've saved your favorite table in the back."

The woman moved swiftly across the room despite her crooked alignment from a humped back. She pulled out a grey rag, swiped at the table, and gestured for Sarah to sit. "I'm counting on you to help Jack, Miss Sarah. That boy ain't right up in his head. He needs settling." She leaned in close. "We know a man's got to have a wife to straighten him out. Stop him from being selfish and stupid."

She was so close Sarah could not help but notice the abundance of long hairs sprouting from the woman's chin.

"Now, some might say it's wrong for a high-class girl to marry down. But if two people like each other—say they meet all the time at the same lunchroom—I say let love take its course." She rapped the table quickly with a knuckle and left.

Marriage. Completely ridiculous. Sarah had vowed long ago

over the graves of her murdered sister and father to devote herself to forensic pathology. Her single goal in life was to bring killers to justice. That was more important than any husband could ever be.

True, no man had moved her as had Jack. But the feeling had to be suppressed—it was alarming and distracting. Thankfully, he had kept to their agreement to avoid romance. If he had sent subtle amorous messages verbally or nonverbally, as some people apparently did to conduct the practice known as flirting, she had not received them.

Perhaps his recent effort to establish emotional distance was a good thing. Distance was appropriate in a professional relationship.

"Good morning." Jack took his seat. "Thanks for setting up the meeting with Lydia."

She observed his freshly cut hair, neat shave, and clean clothes. His shoes once again gleamed. Dark circles still hung below his eyes, but altogether he looked better than he had in weeks.

"Greetings. Your appearance makes me hope that your mental state has improved since Saturday evening."

"I feel pretty good. Hey—I like your new look."

"To what are you referring?"

"Your hat. So stylish and smart." Jack reached for his coffee. "You look swell."

All morning Sarah had tried to ignore the enormous "cartwheel" hat brim that hung at the top of her vision like a claustrophobically low ceiling. From edge to edge, the diameter was well over two feet. She moved the hat back and felt the weighty mounds of tulle, lace, and silk flowers resettle on her head. Whoever decided that women should have such excessive millinery surely never had to wear it.

"My friend Margaret Bonifant insisted I acquire new clothing and accessories." Sarah's tea arrived in a mismatched china cup and saucer. "As a rule, I dislike novelty and resist change. But

Margaret informed me that my old clothing was so out of style as to appear odd. Given our original interest in acquiring clients, I decided to refurbish my wardrobe to reduce the impression of eccentricity." Margaret was Sarah's friend, a loving surrogate mother who had done her best to fill the void when Sarah's actual mother abandoned the family many years ago.

"Practical, as always," said Jack with a smile that faded. "Look, I'm sorry that we haven't netted any clients lately. I've been a mess. But I feel good about the future—right this minute, anyway."

"I am pleased to hear that statement." She noted how a sense of optimism appeared to help his nervous condition. Reaching for her tea, she noticed the cup had a hairline crack running from lip to base.

"When is Lydia coming?" Jack slurped his coffee.

"She agreed to meet us," Sarah checked her watch, "exactly three minutes from now."

"Let's hope she's as punctual as you are." He drained the coffee and motioned to the waitress for another. "I can't wait to meet her."

"Please do not mention that her missing associate has been killed. Lydia is not yet aware of that fact."

"What?"

"I told you previously that the missing woman was a victim of murder."

"How do you know that?"

"I prefer not to discuss the matter at this time."

"Is the tea okay, Miss Sarah?" The waitress hovered near, eyes fixed on the full cup.

"The fracture in the cup could harbor mold and bacteria, which could contaminate the beverage."

"The cup?" The woman's eyes widened.

"Everything's fine," said Jack with a smile. "She loves it."

Sarah's hands flopped in her lap as she wondered whether to

correct him. No. His misrepresentation of her statement likely had an altruistic intent.

"Hello again, Sarah. I do hope I'm not late."

Lydia stood before them in a white jacket and matching dress with a hat even bigger than Sarah's. Jack leaped to his feet and grabbed her hand.

"Miss Nightingale, I'm Jack Harden. I'm pleased as all get out to meet you."

Sarah gasped at his faux pas. Propriety demanded that she introduce Lydia before Jack said anything. He would never, ever learn correct manners.

"I'm pleased to meet you, Jack. Please call me Lydia." She smiled back at him as he continued to pump her gloved hand. "Perhaps we should sit?"

"Yes, sorry," said Jack as he offered her a chair. "I'm a social oaf, as Sarah can tell you."

"Etiquette is a silly business," said Lydia as she glided into the seat. "You should have seen the consternation I caused during my recent visit to San Francisco. I showed up late to a dinner party, kept my napkin on the table while dining, and sipped champagne before acknowledging a toast in my honor. I shudder to imagine what people out there think of me. But there are more terrible things to occupy one's mind than memories of misbehaving in public."

"Frisco. Hmm." Jack was back in his chair, slurping coffee.

Sarah drummed fingers on her thigh, eager to get useful information about the missing murder victim.

"Do you know the city?" Lydia kept her eyes on Jack and leaned in towards him.

"Yeah." He slumped and gazed at the tabletop. "I lived out there for a while after—after the army."

"You had a difficult time there. And before then, too. I can tell."

"How?" Jack focused every bit of his attention on the woman.

"I sense your aura—the waves of psychic energy flowing from you. The energy is horrendously powerful." She gave a sharp gasp. "You've seen terrible things."

"What else do you sense about me?"

Lydia trembled. "I shouldn't tune into your aura because it is so intensely painful—" Abruptly, her eyes rolled back into her head. Her whole body quaked as if she were a marionette with jerked strings.

"Jack! She is having a seizure," said Sarah. "Help me lay her on the floor."

"Do not worry about her. She is like the bird caught in a spring gust, swept unknowing aloft." Lydia was now still, her voice a girlish whisper. Her head lolled to one side, and her face was rounder and softer. She extended a gloved hand toward Jack and spoke:

I measure every grief I meet
With analytic eyes;
I wonder if it weighs like mine,
Or has an easier size.

I wonder if they bore it long,
Or did it just begin?
I could not tell the date of mine,
It feels so old a pain.

I wonder if it hurts to live,
And if they have to try,
And whether, could they choose between,
They would not rather die.

Jack took her hand in both of his and spoke, voice cracking. "It really does hurt to live."

Sarah wondered, amazed, if he would weep. She stared at Lydia. The woman who quoted the hauntingly beautiful Emily

Dickinson poem appeared transformed, just as she had at their first meeting. Medical journals mentioned cases of multiple personalities. It was a rare condition, and its actual existence was debated. Many doctors and even some psychologists believed people exhibiting such symptoms were either outright frauds or merely highly neurotic.

"I see specters all around you," said Lydia in the same altered manner. "They clamor and make you ill. You cannot rule yourself. When things cannot pass from our minds, we observe them, again and again, like a fly buzzing round our head. We meditate upon oblivion."

Jack was deathly pale and gasping for breath. "What do I do? Tell me."

"The aggrieved dead are like bees circling a destroyed hive. Anger, torment, suffering. Ghostly vengeance. Jack . . . I have more for you . . ."

"Tell me!" Jack's voice was a quavery shout.

Lydia's head straightened, and she withdrew her hand. "Sorry—I lost my train of thought. Where were we?" Gone was the transformed voice and appearance.

"Lydia," said Sarah. "You just displayed behavior consistent with a dissociative experience."

"What was that all about?" Jack was on his feet, pointing at Lydia. "Who was that person talking about wrecked beehives? How did they know about my ghosts?"

"Everything's okay, hon." The waitress spoke in a slow, calm voice, her hand on his arm. "Jack, have a seat, and I'll freshen up that coffee for you." He sat with his head down.

Lydia put her hands on either side of her face. "Oh, dear. She was here. This should not have happened."

Jack looked up. "She who?"

"I am truly sorry." Lydia looked at Sarah. "I didn't want to displease you, dear. Really, I didn't."

Jack leaned in close to Lydia. "She who? Tell me!"

"My spirit guide." Lydia drew in a breath. "A deceased soul

who is my guide between the living and the dead. Mr. Fuller and Miss Pike help contain her, but I thought it best to meet with you alone. I pleaded with her to stay away but—well, Jack, your torment drew her out."

"Your spirit guide. Okay, I get it." Jack nodded and leaned back in his chair. "She said she has more to tell me. I've got to hear it. You have no idea how much."

Lydia nodded. "I can read so much about your troubles just sitting here."

"This is absurd." Sarah was on her feet. "I refuse to believe a spirit took possession of you and spoke those words."

"Sarah, have a seat." Jack spoke calmly. "We agreed to talk with Lydia about her case. Please."

Sarah swayed, torn about what to do. But Jack was more engaged with a potential client than he had been in a long time. She sat.

"If she called your name, Jack, she wants you to attend a séance," said Lydia. "I have one scheduled for this Wednesday evening. You must attend. And you, too, Sarah. If you wish."

Sarah sat and focused her gaze at an irregular patch of plaster on the wall beyond Jack's left ear. Her jaw ached from clenching. If only she could exit this ridiculous situation, go off by herself with some favorite books, and dwell on more rational topics. Her legs twitched with the desire to run away. No. She had to solve Anna Gilbert's murder.

"You bet I'll be there," said Jack, sitting tall in his chair. "Sarah says you're worried about a missing person. You're talking to the right detective."

"My secretary Anna—Anna Gilbert—arrived at her hotel in Baltimore on Friday to make arrangements for my appearance before the—" Lydia looked at Sarah. "Can I say the name of the convention?"

"It is a factual matter."

"My appearance before the Death as Transformation and

Opportunity Spiritualism Convention. Anna was to inspect the lecture hall and book appointments for séances."

"How do you know she got here? What hotel did she use?"

Jack was interested in details. Sarah flapped her hands, remembering all the prospective cases he had walked away from without asking a single question.

"The Belvedere Hotel," said Lydia. "I telephoned and spoke with her the day she arrived. We have not talked since. I called the hotel, but they have no record of her registration. No one seems to know anything about her."

"What does she look like?"

"Sarah has a recent photograph, don't you, dear?"

"Yes." Sarah pulled the photo from her bag and placed it on the table. She felt another weird chill looking at the face she had seen in a dream.

"Pretty girl," said Jack.

"Will you try to find her?" Lydia put both hands over her heart.

"Yes," said Jack, nodding. "I'll take the case myself."

"Jack," Sarah said, jerking her hand and sending the teacup crashing to the floor. "We work on cases together."

"I'll do it if you help me with my ghosts." Jack pounded the table. "Sarah doesn't believe ghosts are real."

"I'll do what I can to help with your haunting, Jack. But I insist on paying as well. Here, take these thirty dollars. Sarah, I want you to help, too," said Lydia as she counted out the money.

Sarah crossed her arms and stared at the table.

Jack pocketed the cash. "I'll get on your case faster than you can say *scat*."

Lydia laughed softly as she put her hand on his arm. "I like you very much. You're so informal—it's such a welcome change." Lydia stood, as did Jack. "I had best get back to the convention."

"Yeah," he said. "You've got to be the star of the show. I'm sure they're paying you plenty."

"Thank you, but I charged no fee. Spending time among the faithful is payment enough."

"Must be nice to afford that."

"I'll make some money through séances and private consultations. Enough to meet expenses."

"What kind of consultations?"

"I meet with a person and invite their spirits to join us. Sometimes I use mesmerism to lower a client's inhibition, so they are more receptive to visitors from the other side."

"Mesmerism?"

"Hypnosis. I'm pretty good at it, I must confess." Lydia touched his arm again. "Please find Anna."

"I'll let you know as soon as I learn something."

"You lighten my heart, Jack. Goodbye for now." She turned to Sarah and began extending a hand to touch her shoulder before pulling it back. "I so very much hope to see you again, my dear." Lydia gazed at Sarah for a few seconds longer before gliding away.

"I guess we need to talk," said Jack.

"We have nothing further to discuss." Sarah got to her feet and placed three dollars on the table. "That is for the teacup I knocked to the floor."

"Sarah. Please. Where are you going?"

"The Enoch Pratt Free Library."

She turned and marched out the door, furious with Jack's brazen disregard in taking the case for himself. He was acting like a typical male bully—arrogant and dismissive. She would not tolerate it. Jack must treat her as an equal partner or their relationship was finished.

CHAPTER 8

JACK—MONDAY, APRIL 18, 1910, 10:00 A.M.

*B*altimore Street was jammed with streetcars, horse-drawn wagons, motor cars, pushcarts, and pedestrians. The mix of shouts, honking horns, and clanging bells signaled that, as usual, everyone was in everyone else's way.

What a screwup I am, thought Jack. He was near broke and half-cracked, and now he'd angered Sarah, the only true friend he had.

Still, he couldn't help but feel buoyant about the prospect of Lydia Nightingale's help. He'd seen newspaper stories about how mediums brought the living and the dead together to share messages. Maybe a séance with Lydia would resolve his trouble with the Moro ghosts. One way or the other, he had to get them to go away before he went to the crazy house—or jumped off a bridge.

He stepped around rotting garbage spilling from the overfull trash cans in front of a saloon. The saloon-keeper must be late with his graft payment to the city sanitation department. The joint's plate-glass window was busted, which probably meant the beat cop was feeling shortchanged, too. New ownership was inevitable unless the owner coughed up the required cash—and soon.

He turned his thoughts back to Sarah, about how she was brainy but narrow-minded. She only believed in things she could mix in a test tube, see under a microscope, or cut open with a knife. But smart people like her didn't have all the answers. Human experience was too big, too complicated. And seeing is believing, right? He'd seen ghosts, heard them, felt their torment. They were as real as anything he'd experienced.

Jack was headed to the Belvedere Hotel to find Anna Gilbert. That shouldn't be hard. Her picture showed a pretty young woman with a sassy, knowing look; she was more than likely spending time with someone special and was in no hurry to stop having fun.

He jumped on a streetcar rattling up Charles Street and packed with school kids on an outing. They shrieked with unfettered joy while racing up and down the aisle. A harried teacher yelled at them to no effect. Two rowdy boys dangled off the running boards inches above the pavement while passing a covert cigarette.

Jack watched the boys, wondering what it must be like to have the freedom to act like a perfect fool. He'd been born on a remote farm to sickly parents and an older sister who was a sadistic religious fanatic. Things got so bad he ran away young and lived by his wits. He never had the chance to kick up his heels and act like a kid.

It was for the best. He learned the most important life lessons early: assume that most people are out to screw you, don't let your guard down, and never think anyone owes you a thing. Those boys on the running board were having fun yucking it up, but hard lessons awaited.

He got off at the Chase Street intersection and approached the massive brass and glass revolving door of the Belvedere Hotel. The place catered to the well-heeled, and a guy like Jack wouldn't get ten feet across the lobby before a lackey was on him. Private detectives were judged a notch below prostitutes.

A side alley took him to the kitchen loading dock, where a

grunting crew unloaded crate after crate of vegetables. It was a sure bet the upper-crust guests didn't spend a second thinking about the backbreaking work needed to keep them in fancy eats. Then again, if he had lots of dough, he wouldn't think about it either.

Nobody said a thing as he walked into the kitchen. Lunch was being served, and the place was swarming like a kicked anthill. Waiters crowded around the chefs, clamoring for their orders of smoked pork shoulder with cabbage or roast saddle of mutton with snap peas.

"Who wants to make a quick five bucks?" called Jack. A couple of waiters looked, but he got no takers. "How about ten? Get yourself a sawbuck for five minute's work."

Two men stepped over, but one was quicker. Jack yanked the cash away before the guy could grab it. "I got a good memory for faces, buddy. Remember that."

"Time's wasting, mister," said the waiter, a swarthy young man with thick wavy hair. "Five minutes late gets me yelled at. Six gets me fired." He rubbed his fingers together for the money.

Jack handed it over. "Go find the hotel dick, Chance McCall. Say that Jack Harden wants to see him." The guy shot out the swinging doors to the dining room. Jack eyed the brimming platters loaded onto serving trays and envied the swanky types waiting for the food.

The kitchen doors slammed open as a portly guy in a sharp blue suit with a rose pinned to his lapel entered. "Damn, boy, heard it on good authority that you were either dead or in the booby hatch." He grinned, highlighting the wad of tobacco in his cheek.

"Yeah, I wrote a letter to the editor denying both stories, but they printed it in the funny pages. How are you doing, McCall?"

"Dandy. I'm on a big winning streak at the track." He clapped Jack on the back. "How can I help you?"

Back when Jack was flush with long green after cracking the

Lizzie Sullivan murder last fall, McCall was deep in debt to a loan shark. Jack covered his payments until the man was back in the graces of Lady Luck. It was the decent thing to do—and one good turn certainly deserves another.

"Need to check on a guest. Name's Anna Gilbert." Jack gave him the photograph. "Checked in two days ago, probably under a false name. Hasn't been heard from since."

"Got it. Let me go check with reception." McCall slammed the doors on his way out.

Jack moved to a spot against the wall and thought about what Lydia—well, Lydia's spirit guide—had said about the ghosts around him, how he couldn't rule himself. Something about a fly you couldn't get rid of; stuff about oblivion.

Was it a bunco game, maybe? It was common knowledge around town that he was a nervous wreck with ghost problems. A halfway decent private eye could dig all that up and more before breakfast. Why, though, would Lydia want to con him? He had nothing worth stealing.

Strange also that she seemed so fond of Sarah, whose blunt manner usually put others off. And why would Lydia, of all people, plead with a spiritualism skeptic to take her case?

Bang. McCall was back. "Hope you ain't getting paid by the hour, boy." He grinned and held up a large brass key. "She checked into a room under the name Kate Turner. Still there."

"Let's go." Jack followed the man through the busy dining room to the elevator. "I prefer the stairs."

"That's right—you can't ride in an elevator without going batcrap." McCall leaned over and sent a brown stream of tobacco juice at a nearby cuspidor. "You're in luck, nervous Nellie. She's on the third floor."

When they got to room 306, McCall chuckled. "This room's supposed to have a hoodoo curse with a ghost and all. Scares the maids out of their boots. The dim broads call it the haunted chamber."

"Right now, I'm worried about walking in on a person who doesn't want to be disturbed. Knock first."

McCall pounded his fist on the door. "Miss Turner or whatever your name is. We know you're in there, so open up." He knocked again, louder. "Last chance, honey." He turned the key with a smooth, well-oiled sound and pushed the door open.

Jack felt a chill, unnatural presence from above as he walked into the room—it was as if something evil hovered in the air. He looked at the ceiling but saw nothing.

"Excuse me, miss," McCall shouted at a woman lying on the bed in a dressing gown. "Wake up now." He switched on the overhead electric light.

Jack recognized Anna Gilbert, Lydia's secretary. The sense of eerie coldness spiked as he noticed her face had a waxy pallor with greenish streaks. She was clearly dead, but he touched her neck for a pulse anyway and found none. "She's gone."

"Why you shaking, boy? Ain't you seen a dead dame before?"

Jack tried to ignore the sinister presence and forced himself still. Looking at the bedside table, he saw an opened bottle of champagne and a jar labeled *Veronal—Soothes Nerves and Comforts Neurasthenia.*

"Cripes, just what I need, another broad croaking herself with pills and booze," said McCall. "Cops. Paperwork. Newspapermen. Why couldn't she have checked herself out in some other guy's joint?"

"Let me make a call before you report it." Using a handkerchief to keep fingerprints off the device, he telephoned the Enoch Pratt Library and dictated a message for Sarah: "Found a body. Belvedere Hotel, room 306. Come immediately."

He wasn't going to breathe a word about the haunted chamber business. She had heard too much about ghosts from him already.

CHAPTER 9

SARAH—MONDAY, APRIL 18, 12:30 P.M.

*S*he usually felt nothing but curiosity before viewing a corpse. But that was not the case as she walked down the third-floor corridor in the Belvedere Hotel. Her stomach was tight with unease, and her back was stiff and achy. A word floated into her mind: *foreboding.*

Jack and another man were standing in the hallway in front of an open door.

"Dr. Sarah Kennecott, this is Chance McCall, hotel detective," said Jack.

"Doc," said McCall, tipping his hat.

"I assume the deceased young woman lying on the bed in the yellow dressing gown is Anna Gilbert."

The men looked at each other. "Good guess about the name," said Jack. "But how did you know she's laying on the bed in a dressing gown?"

"I do not wish to discuss the matter at this time."

Jack shrugged. "She registered under the name Kate Turner."

The body lay in a natural position exactly as it had in Sarah's dream. The yellow dressing gown was undisturbed, as were the bedclothes. The woman's face and neck had greenish-black streaks—early indications of decomposition—but there were no signs of violence.

"Jack. Help me turn the body."

"Are you sure we should touch her?" He rubbed the back of his neck.

"I need to examine the body now to obtain the most accurate approximation of the time of death."

"Whatever you say." He put both hands under the corpse's back and carefully lifted one side.

Sarah raised the dressing gown and nightdress to reveal purple-black blotches on the back of the thighs. Next, she grabbed an ankle and flexed the leg. After pulling the clothing back into place, she motioned for Jack to lay the body back down.

"Lividity is fixed. Rigor mortis has departed. The blood vessels near the surface of the skin have marbled. The abdominal cavity is bloated. She has been dead for roughly seventy-two hours."

"That means she died the day she arrived." Jack turned to McCall. "That's a heck of a long time to lie here dead. Why didn't a maid or somebody find her?"

"Like I told you." McCall yawned. "The maids are scared of this room. They say it's cold and creepy."

Sarah looked at the bedside table. She noted the nearly full bottle of champagne sitting in a metal chiller next to a single glass and the bottle of Veronal—a barbiturate used to calm nerves. Barbiturates were relatively new but already heavily abused and an increasingly common choice for suicide. The drug was particularly fatal when mixed with alcohol.

Sarah walked around the room. Two large, unpacked trunks of clothes. A few dresses hung up, all labeled as belonging to Anna Gilbert. The dresser held neatly folded underclothes. One sign of disorder was a lady's handbag with its contents dumped on a table. Hairbrush, hairpins, train ticket stub, a small tin of flavored candies—and an empty money purse.

"Travelers usually carry cash," said Jack. "She didn't report a theft. Maybe someone helped themselves after she self-croaked."

"This is not a suicide." Sarah chopped the air swiftly with her hand. "This is murder."

"You, the one who's always telling people not to jump to conclusions until examining all the evidence—now you take one look at a body and yell murder?"

Sarah knew he was right to question her declaration. She had no tangible evidence to support a claim of homicide. And after all the times she had disputed Jack's claim of seeing ghosts, she was in no hurry to tell him that her sister Grace was serving as a murder informant from beyond the grave.

"Everybody out." She turned to see Baltimore City Detective O'Toole and a uniformed policeman enter the room.

"Detective, the deceased is Anna Gilbert. This is her photograph." Sarah held up Anna's photo.

O'Toole looked briefly at the photo before blowing cigarette smoke in her face, causing her to cough.

"Didn't expect to see you, Snake Eyes," said Jack. "Thought you'd be out raking in the graft. Either that or catching *Mama's Boy*, that new moving picture playing at the Hippodrome. Supposed to be a real tearjerker."

O'Toole flicked his cigarette and hit Jack's trouser leg with a shower of orange sparks. "Clubber," he said to the uniformed officer. "Clear the room. Use your nightstick."

Jack calmly brushed his trousers. "Keep your grubby mitt off the hickory, Clubber. We're leaving." He went out the door, and Sarah followed.

"Remember that poke in the eye I gave you a few months back, Harden?" O'Toole lit another cigarette. "Same thing can happen to your smart-guy mouth."

Sarah whirled to face the detective. In addition to tobacco smoke, he smelled disgustingly of onions, whiskey, and stale grease. "Detective Terrance O'Toole. You are fortunate that your blow to Jack's eye last year with a brass apparatus attached to your fist was nonfatal. Nevertheless, I filed an official report of police misconduct against you and will not hesitate to do so again."

O'Toole lowered his pitted, purplish face close to hers. "Get along now, little freak. Circus wants you back in the sideshow."

Jack spoke over Sarah's shoulder. "She's a fine lady. You better treat her like one."

"Do not debate the point, Jack," she said. "Let us depart."

"You going to make me treat this weirdo skirt like a lady, snooper?" A slow grin crossed the detective's thin lips, showing his snaggly yellow teeth. "Fat chance."

"Do not respond." She pushed back against Jack in the direction of the hallway.

"Tell your ignorant goon to stand down, and I'll make you!"

"Who you calling a goon?" The officer known as Clubber pointed his nightstick at Jack. "I'm going to bash your thick head in."

Sarah sighed, recalling the many times she had witnessed males talking loudly at each other, refusing to listen to reason, absorbed in their primitive masculine posturing. It was much like great apes beating their chests or rams butting heads. She pushed at Jack again, harder. "Good day, detective. Good day, officer. Jack—we have work requiring our immediate attention." He resisted her push for a moment, then moved into the hallway.

"Perfect pair of spastic lovebirds," said O'Toole.

Jack tried to maneuver back into the room, but she blocked him. "We have no time to waste on foolishness. I must examine the body when it arrives at the city morgue."

He continued to stare over her head at the detective before slowly moving down the hall. "I can't stand that guy insulting you."

"There is no time for you to defend your concept of my honor. We have a death to investigate."

He turned to her with a smile. "I just knew a dead body would warm you up to Lydia's case. Even if it's just a suicide."

"I told you earlier. She was murdered."

"You keep making that claim. What's your evidence?"

She knew dreams were incapable of providing reliable information about anything beyond the dreamer's own psyche. And yet, she was relying on a dream rather than scientific observation and analysis. She could not make sense of it. "I do not wish to discuss the matter at this time."

"You can't keep saying that. We're partners, remember?"

She marched ahead a few more steps before facing him. "Earlier, you did not treat me as an equal, and now you dare to assert partnership when it suits you? I am highly vexed and demand you relate to me as a coequal associate from this point forward without interruption."

"Can you say that in English?"

She began flapping her hands. "You must have a basic understanding of what I said."

"Look, I can see you're upset—"

"I am not upset!" she said, hearing the echo of her voice in the corridor.

"Sarah, I apologize. We're equal partners from now on, one-hundred percent."

"Very well." She tried to release some of the terrible tension in her shoulders and neck. "I, in turn, admit to a personal bias against spiritualism. And while there is no verifiable scientific evidence of communication with the dead, I have a new openness to the possibility. At the very least, I admit some overlap with ideas about the subconscious and different perceptions of reality."

"If all that fancy talk means you won't have a fit every time the subject of ghosts comes up, that's great."

"I must go to the morgue and wait for arrival of the body."

"Wait—shouldn't we tell Lydia what happened to Anna?"

"Collecting evidence from the corpse is more important from

my perspective. Lydia is staying with Mrs. Lanvale. You could telephone to arrange a visit."

"I'll do that. I'll also telephone Mayor Lipp to make sure everything goes smoothly for you at the morgue."

"Must you?" Sarah was less than happy that Jack was extorting Mayor Lipp to ensure cooperation. She did not like leveraging the secret fact about the mayor they had uncovered during the investigation the previous October into the murders of Lizzie Sullivan and Nick Monkton.

"Trust me when it comes to playing crooked. It's the only way to make things work in this town. Bye now—I'm meeting up with Chance McCall in the hotel bar." He turned and walked off.

"Let me again state my opposition to any action that is illegal, unethical, or dishonest." Sarah spoke to Jack's retreating back, her words drowned out by his tuneless whistling.

THE CITY MORGUE'S DISSECTION ROOM WAS different from the last time she had visited. A modern refrigeration system replaced the crude ice chests for body storage, and an extra row of electric lights hung over the autopsy table where the unclothed body of Anna Gilbert lay.

"Dr. Kennecott, thank you for adding a woman's touch to this autopsy," said the coroner. Jack must have indeed communicated with the mayor, who in turn had ordered the coroner to cooperate. This was the same man who, six months earlier, had shown her nothing but crude disrespect in this very space. What hadn't changed was his capillary-exploded face and whiskey reek.

"Hello, doctor," said the medical examiner. He was a younger man, hired on her recommendation—another benefit flowing from Jack's ethically questionable sway over the mayor. "What do we know about the decedent?"

"The body is that of a twenty-six-year-old personal secretary. She was found in a hotel room under an assumed name." Sarah pulled on rubber gloves, eager to commence with the examination. "I inspected the scene and observed a partially empty bottle of champagne and a bottle of barbiturate tablets."

"Croaked herself with pills—clear cut," said the coroner, rubbing his thick hands.

The medical examiner turned to the clerk. "Put in the notes that Dr. Kennecott is leading the postmortem examination."

Sarah saw no injuries or marks of interest after examining the front and back of the body. She opened the abdomen and then the stomach, which yielded a sample of thin, whitish liquid smelling faintly of alcohol.

"A final barbiturate cocktail?" The medical examiner peered at the sample flask.

She used a pair of cutters to snip the ribs and open the chest cavity. The heart and lungs were normal. After opening the skull, the brain likewise showed no abnormality.

Sarah again looked at the stomach content, which was limited—only about three ounces. If the whitish material was residue from the barbiturates, the number of tablets ingested appeared below a lethal dose.

"Confirm for me, doctor," said Sarah, "that the heart and arteries show no sign of embolism, thrombosis, aneurism, or myocardial infarction."

The medical examiner checked the chest cavity. "Correct. The heart has no structural abnormality, and the arteries are unobstructed. Do you suspect sudden cardiac death?"

Sarah stared at the floor, thinking. A healthy 26-year-old dying from a sudden heart attack was unusual but not unheard of. Laboratory tests would determine if barbiturates or some other substance was the cause of death.

"Okay." The coroner stretched his arms. "We're done here."

"No." Sarah picked up a large magnifying glass and began

inspecting the corpse's left arm, then the right, then the legs and feet.

The coroner gave an exasperated sigh. "This is a waste of time, sweetness—I'm mean doctor."

"Tell me what this looks like." She handed the magnifying glass to the medical examiner and pointed to a spot on the ball of the corpse's right foot.

"It is a puncture wound, like what you get from stepping on a thumbtack. Ouch."

"Or the wound could be from a hypodermic syringe injection. I believe this is a case of homicide."

"Come on." The coroner crossed his arms. "A prick on the foot isn't proof of murder. I supposed you're using your giddy female intuition. This is no time for hysterical leaps of imagination, *doctor*."

Sarah said nothing. While washing up, she thought how the coroner, like most men, viewed women as unstable, emotional, and given to capricious ideas. She had battled this assumption all her life. It did not matter that she had consistently demonstrated a meticulously analytical approach to everything, especially her work as a physician.

Until now, that is. In this instance, she was assuming murder because of an uncanny dream. If that were known, no male doctor would ever treat her seriously again. Obtaining solid evidence for the cause of death was essential for maintaining her professional reputation, and more importantly, for bringing a killer to justice.

CHAPTER 10

JACK—MONDAY, APRIL 18, 1910, 1:30 P.M.

*E*verything about the Belvedere Hotel's Owl Bar whispered wealth and privilege. Even the barman looked classy with his perfect haircut, clipped mustache, and natty bowtie.

"What is your pleasure, sir?" he asked in a genteel English accent.

If the guy wasn't wearing a short white jacket with "Edward" stitched above the heart, Jack could easily believe he was an aristocrat standing behind the gleaming mahogany as some kind of rich man's joke.

"Branch water."

"Of course, sir. Do you want cubed or crushed ice?"

"No ice, thanks." Jack smiled, thinking of all the low-rent barhops who had given him grief for ordering water and not rotgut. Sipping from the glass, he looked around at the dark wood paneling, oil paintings, and stained-glass windows. A gilt mirror ran behind liquor bottles set on two long shelves. A pair of large wooden owls, painted in lifelike colors, kept an eye on things from a central ledge high over the bar.

"Eddie—two shots of Pikesville Rye here." McCall dropped heavily onto the next stool.

"Nothing for me," said Jack. "I'm fine with water."

"Hell, they're both for me." McCall threw back a shot and slammed the glass on the bar. "Snake Eyes O'Toole is a mean cuss. Treated me like dirt. I hate dealing with that cop." The second shot glass rose and fell. Jack pointed to McCall's empty glasses, and Edward refilled them in one smooth motion.

"Yeah, he's a prince." Jack felt the scar below his left eye from where the detective had clobbered—and nearly killed—him with brass knuckle-dusters last fall. "What did he get on the dead gal?"

"Not much. Clothing tags identified her as Anna Gilbert. The only evidence tied to her death was the bottle of bubbly and the nerve tablets. She cashed herself out, no doubt about it."

"Any visitors?"

"None checked in at the desk, but plenty of people skip that rule and go straight up to the guests."

"O'Toole question anyone?"

"Naw." McCall snorted and drank down another shot. "He was in a hurry—kept looking at his watch."

"So much graft, so little time." Jack chuckled. "I assume he didn't bother to collect fingerprints."

"That old dog ain't doing any new tricks." McCall laughed and downed his remaining whiskey.

"Suspected as much." O'Toole wasn't the most diligent detective, and was especially lax when investigating apparent suicides. No murder suspect meant no fun smacking someone around in the interrogation room.

"Tell me—what's the story with you and that lady doctor?" McCall lifted an empty shot glass and let the remaining drops dribble into his mouth. "She's not your type."

"What's my type?" Jack braced himself for booze-fueled blather.

"A good-time girl. You know, friendly, easy laugh. And way, way better looking than that Kennecott broad."

"Keep your ignorant opinions to yourself."

"I mean, she's colder than a brass toilet seat in an Alaskan outhouse. And such a prissy schoolmarm—"

Jack jabbed a finger in the man's chest. "One more word about her, and I'll punch you in the face."

"Okay." McCall lowered his head and spat into a spittoon. "Whiskey makes me run my mouth. A man's taste in women is his own business. You know, it reminds me of the time when I was with this opera-singer gal who was taller than me, but—"

"Sorry, but I've got to run. Point me to a telephone."

McCall grumbled until Jack smacked enough cash on the bar to cover another round. "Sure thing, old friend. Use the horn in my office."

MRS. LANVALE WAS HAUGHTY ON THE LINE. NO, MISS Nightingale was not available. No, she could not take a message. She was about to end the call when Jack told her Anna Gilbert was dead, and gosh, shouldn't Miss Nightingale be informed? After a lengthy pause, Mrs. Lanvale said Lydia would return at 3:30 p.m. and hung up.

The Lanvale house was in Sarah's neighborhood, which meant it had to be fancy. Jack got a shoeshine and checked his look in a mirror outside a barbershop. The morning shave was holding up, but his necktie had a food stain just under the knot. He tried to rub the spot off with a thumb but only managed to smear it.

When he arrived at the Lanvale address, the mansion was even ritzier than Sarah's place. It was five stories of fancy red brick with a massive round turret on one side. A series of small round windows ran under the ornate roof eaves. One window was broken, and he smiled, knowing that plenty of bats also called the place home.

Next to the front steps was a sign that read: "All Tradesmen MUST Use the Rear Entrance." He brushed his lapels and trousers, adjusted his hat, and eyed his uneasy smirk reflected in the colossal brass knocker. It dropped with a hollow thump that sounded like a shovelful of dirt hitting a coffin lid.

The ten-foot-high door opened, and a well-groomed butler looked at Jack with haughty disdain. The man was about thirty-five and wore a black suit, gray vest with brass buttons, starched white shirt with a wing collar, and black silk necktie.

"I'm here to see Mrs. Lanvale. Name's Jack Harden."

The butler looked him up and down slowly. "Is she expecting you?" The question was posed as if the answer couldn't possibly be yes.

"Yeah, and it's important. I haven't got all day here."

After a pause, the butler gave a slight nod and began closing the door, but Jack stuck his foot against the jamb. "You're getting on my bad side, limey."

"I indicated that madam shall be notified . . . sir. Please allow me to do so."

Jack pulled his foot back, and the door closed.

After a long wait, the butler returned. "Please wipe your feet thoroughly before entering."

"Why? It's dry out, and I haven't stepped in anything."

The butler looked even more disapproving as it dawned on Jack what this was about—the rich regarded working people as dirty. Dirty smell, dirty clothes, and, of course, dirty shoes. He could have shown up in spanking new footwear with a receipt certifying a bath an hour ago and still have gotten the same treatment. High-class people always had to make a regular guy feel small.

"This is crap, pal." Jack made a show of brushing his shoes on the mat, and the butler stepped aside.

"Your hat, sir."

"What about it?"

"May I take it?"

"No."

The butler shrugged. "This way, Mr. Harden."

After a stroll on plush carpets past big china vases, portraits in showy gold frames, and enough furniture to fill a hotel lobby, they came to a thick-waisted older woman standing in a fancy dress. "Mr. Harden," she said, nose in the air. "I am Mrs. Lanvale." She did not extend her hand. "Thank you, Niblett."

"Yeah, Nibs, thanks a lot." Jack grinned as the butler kept his stony face while padding away.

The woman flashed a tight, phony smile. "I was so hoping Miss Kennecott would accompany you."

"She's engaged elsewhere."

A frown replaced the smile. "Miss Nightingale was close to Miss Gilbert. Lydia has a most sensitive temperament and has agreed to live with me as a refuge from the world. I see myself as her guardian and will intervene if you are crude and manage to distress her."

"Lady, I'm all you got."

She lifted her chin even higher. "Be quick, then."

They walked into a vast, well-appointed parlor. Jack spotted Lydia sitting on a sofa with a young mortician-looking guy on one side and an older woman on the other.

"Jack, how wonderful to see you." Lydia stood and extended her hand. "Jack Harden, may I introduce my assistants, Miss Lucinda Pike and Mr. Luther Fuller." Each nodded.

"Hello, Lydia. Miss Pike, Mr. Fuller."

"We know each other, Harden."

Jack turned and recognized Judge Barnabas Lanvale standing by the fireplace. Lanvale was well-known around town for his massive gambling debts, which explained why he was easy to bribe. On top of that, he killed a guy during a poker game a while back and got off on a dubious claim of self-defense. An all-around swell guy. "Judge. First time I've seen you without my hands cuffed."

The man gave a curt nod and looked away.

"I am Reverend Jared Smartwell, sir." A large gent with brown eyes popping out of a round, pudding face approached and offered a hand. "Of the First Baltimore Church of Spiritualism. I am pleased to make your acquaintance. I do hope the dawn broke brightly upon you this morning, if I may say so, sir."

"Any morning I'm still drawing breath is a good one, padre." Jack took his hand, which was soft as a woman's.

"Just so, sir." Smartwell's jowls bounced as he chuckled dryly. "I like a man who is frank about the challenges of life in this vale of tears."

"Are you a pal of Lydia's?"

"I am here to minister with love and compassion." Smartwell clasped Jack's hand with both of his. "I suffer with all who suffer, sir."

"Good for you. I guess." Jack pulled his hand away.

"We are all here because we care for Lydia," said Mrs. Lanvale in a soulful voice that was as fake as a wooden nickel. "Now, Mr. Harden, please get on with conveying your report."

"Lydia, please sit down." Jack looked for a place to sit close to her, and seeing none, went to the wall and dragged a heavy hardback chair over the floor to the sofa. Mrs. Lanvale gasped, but he paid her no mind.

"All of this is making me terrified about Anna," said Lydia tensely. "Do you have bad news?" She was again seated, each assistant gripping one of her hands.

"I'm sorry, but she's dead."

Lydia's eyes rolled back and she began shaking, just as she had in the lunchroom. "The stillness round my form / Was like the stillness in the air / Between the heaves of storm." There again was the high, girlish whisper that seemed to come from a different person.

Jack watched as Luther Fuller shook her by the arm. Lydia continued to speak rapidly in an eerie voice:

"She argued with the birds, she leaned on clover walls and they fell, dropping her. With jargon sweeter than a bell, she grappled buttercups, and they sank together, the buttercups the heaviest."

"What the devil—" said Barnabas Lanvale as he stepped closer.

Fuller shook Lydia again, rougher this time. Her head snapped forward, her body rigid as a board, as she spoke:

My life closed twice before its close;
It yet remains to see
If Immortality unveil
A third event to me,

So huge so hopeless to conceive,
As these that twice befell.
Parting is all we know of heaven,
And all we need of hell.

Miss Pike slapped Lydia twice, first on the left, then the right cheek.

"Oh, Jack. Poor Anna." Lydia acted as if her spell—or spirit guide appearance—hadn't taken place. She began wailing and ignored Fuller's offered handkerchief for a long moment before finally pressing it to her face. After more sobbing, she lowered the cloth. "How did she die?"

"My dear." Mrs. Lanvale hovered over Lydia. "Please don't listen to the awful details from this man."

"Mother is right," said Judge Lanvale glaring at Jack. "Harden shouldn't be the one to elaborate on this dreadful news."

"No." Lydia spoke with a quaver. "I must know. Let him speak."

"Sarah—Dr. Kennecott—is checking on the cause of death." Jack preferred giving it straight to clients. "Right now, it looks like suicide from mixing sleeping pills with champagne."

"Suicide!" More tears spilled down Lydia's cheeks. "I don't believe that. Anna was so full of life." She dabbed forcefully at the tears.

"Did Anna make a habit of mixing pills with booze?" Questioning Lydia now was awkward, but Jack didn't know when he'd get another chance. "And does the name Kate Turner mean anything to you?"

"You've got no right to question her in this manner." Judge Lanvale had the perfect courtroom voice—loud and menacing. "Madam, you do not need to answer."

"Sir." Lydia drew herself up and glared at the man. "I will decide that for myself." She looked back at Jack. "Anna enjoyed a glass of wine with dinner. And she did take a tablet occasionally for her insomnia. As for the name Kate Turner, it is unfamiliar to me."

"We found her in a hotel room registered as Miss Turner."

Lydia looked away.

"You said earlier that you telephoned Anna at the hotel after she arrived," said Jack. "All calls go through a switchboard, and callers must ask for guests by name. How could you reach Anna if you didn't know the name she registered under?"

"Why—I just asked the operator and was put through."

"But you also told me that when you called the hotel later, they had no record of her."

"I don't understand." Lydia began trembling again, but a firm shake from her bookend assistants stopped it.

"That's enough, Harden," said the judge with a frown.

"One more question. Do you know anyone who had a disagreement with Anna? Anyone who might have wanted to hurt her?"

"Good heavens, everyone loved Anna. She was the sweetest person." Lydia held her handkerchief tightly wadded in trembling hands.

"You must rest now, dear." Mrs. Lanvale rested a hand on the woman's shoulder. "Please."

"Very well. I suppose you are right. I'll retire to my room." Lydia stood. "Thank you, Jack, for coming here to tell me. It was kind."

"I'm sorry it was such sad news."

"I refuse to believe Anna killed herself. Can you please find out what really happened?"

"Sure thing."

"I will pay. Lucinda, how much money do you have on your person?"

Miss Pike opened a small purse and removed a few bills. "About twenty dollars."

"Give it to Jack."

He pocketed the cash.

"Can you return for a larger payment tomorrow—with Sarah? I would so love to have her help." Lydia gave him a teary, imploring look.

"Madam, you are a wealthy woman," said the judge, arms crossed. "It is not wise to have financial transactions with this man. Or have him in this house again, for that matter."

"I will decide how to spend my money, Barnabas," said Lydia sharply. "Jack, I know Sarah lives nearby. I'll call and arrange for a visit with her tomorrow to provide payment."

"Sarah's not used to hosting social visits."

"I hope she'll see me. Good afternoon."

As Lydia left, Jack thought he saw something familiar in her profile, but it was just his flaky mind playing tricks. "I'll keep Lydia posted about the case," he said to Mrs. Lanvale.

"The hell you will," said the judge as he stepped close, face flushing red.

"Pal, Lydia's the client. Not you."

The judge pulled out a fat bankroll, the kind high-rolling gamblers carried to impress suckers. He peeled off some bills and thrust them inches from Jack's face. The cash smelled like grubby fingers and cheap cigars. "Now I'm paying you, lowlife. Get lost and stay that way."

"Your money stinks." Jack brushed the hand aside, and the bills fluttered to the floor.

"You piece of garbage—" The judge cocked a fist and was

ready to throw a punch, but his mother anticipated the move and stepped between them.

"Barnabas, remember that we use Niblett to take care of troublesome people." She turned to Jack with a deadly glare. "Do not return to this house under any circumstances. If you do, the butler will turn you away."

"Yeah? I can handle the nastiest sneer Nibs can deliver." Jack smiled broadly. "And judge, if you swing at me, know that I'll knock you down. This isn't a courtroom—there's no bailiff to protect you."

"You're a dead man, buster. Count on it." The color of the judge's face was moving toward purple.

"Niblett—remove this man," said Mrs. Lanvale. "Immediately."

"Padre, I hope the dawn breaks right for you, too." Jack waved at Reverend Smartwell, who stood across the room behind a large armchair, safely away from the confrontation.

"Thank you, Mr. Harden," said the reverend. "And bless your efforts to help Lydia. May earthly and celestial forces align to assist you, sir." He nodded his large head solemnly.

Niblett approached, still supremely formal but with a hard set to his mouth that telegraphed experience with such situations.

"Keep cool, Nibs. I'm leaving." Jack strode to the foyer and left the front door open as he went down the marble steps. The door slammed shut behind him with a thump like a body plummeting from the gallows.

CHAPTER 11

SARAH—MONDAY, APRIL 18, 1910, 5:00 P.M.

*T*he jarring drop shook the motor taxi mightily. Sarah's big hat slipped to the side, barely held in place by the nest of pins running through her hair. Somehow, the vehicle kept moving up Monument Street.

"Sir," she said to the driver. "I do not appreciate rough transport. Please steer around the potholes."

"What's the matter, honey—corset too tight?" The driver snickered. "I'll pull over so's you can loosen it. I'll help."

"I see that your permit number is 68. If you make any additional offensive statements, I shall report you to municipal authorities. License revocation will swiftly follow."

Silence reigned the rest of the way home.

After changing into her nightclothes, Sarah studied toxicology textbooks in her library late into the night. A barely touched plate of cheese and fruit sat on the table next to an empty teapot. Pages of yellow foolscap paper covered in her cramped handwriting were scattered about.

She had reviewed details about how barbiturates worked in the body. Depending on the dose, the effect ranged from mild sedation, through the loss of consciousness, to death. Did someone use the drug to incapacitate Anna Gilbert before injecting her with some lethal substance? Presumably, the killer intended to make the death appear as a suicide. But there was no known suspect and no known motive.

She jiggled a leg, thinking hard. Was Anna Gilbert's death tied to her association with Lydia Nightingale? Perhaps, but Sarah needed more information before forming the wildest of conjectures. She had little evidence and suspected the police had not uncovered much more from the hotel room.

Apart from Anna Gilbert's autopsy, she could think of no avenue to pursue hard forensic facts. That meant the case now rested in Jack's area of expertise—gathering subjective details from various people, at least some of whom were unreliable to the extreme.

Jack. His behavior at the hotel was as engaged—and stable —as it had been for a while. Her heart fluttered with the memory of him defending her against Detective O'Toole. Jack referred to her as *a fine lady*. Strictly speaking, she was a person with the conferred social status of *lady*. Is that all he meant? Or was the qualifier *fine* meant to express a sentimental attachment?

Emotional connection was, for the most part, terra incognita for her. She had dearly loved her father and Grace, and had been driven to distraction when they were murdered eight years ago. Other than her long-term friend Margaret Bonifant, Sarah had felt close to no one since. Except for Jack. To a degree. A large degree. He understood her quirks and appreciated her investigative talent more than anyone. She thought of his touches to her hand and the one time they had embraced some months ago. His lips had brushed her cheek . . .

Such musings amounted to nothing but silly thoughts clouding her orderly mind. She had no room for romance in her life. Never had, never would. She must appreciate Jack's friendship and leave it at that.

Sarah began pacing in a tight circle, thinking again about how her dream had forecast a murder. Surely there was a psychological explanation, likely tied to the workings of her subconscious.

She charged up the stairs to her bedroom, eager to talk to the porcelain dolls that Grace had given her many years ago. Her sister knew Sarah had trouble communicating with people, which in turn led others to treat her with exasperation and intolerance.

The dolls, however, listened patiently to whatever Sarah said without comment or judgment. That gave her rare freedom to release her unspoken feelings. She laughed until her sides hurt and cried until exhaustion while articulating her hopes and fears to them. It was nonsensical, stream-of-consciousness blather, but she always felt so much better afterward.

"I dreamed of Grace recently," she said, looking first at one doll and then the other. "She was kind and loving, and it cheered me. I have been so lonely lately." Sarah hugged both dolls tightly. "Grace revealed something terrible to me in the dream and asked me to resolve the matter. It makes no sense, I know—but I feel that I must do as Grace requested."

CHAPTER 12

*F*ells Point was more treacherous than usual. The Jones Falls waterway had overrun its banks, and when the flood receded, it left corrupt, shoe-sucking mud a foot deep on the neighborhood's streets nearest the stream.

This was no ordinary muck. It was a black gumbo of rotted aquatic life, animal carcasses, human waste, and industrial pollution. The overwhelming stink pressed in from all sides like a bogeyman bent on harm.

Jack skirted the mess as best he could while thinking about Lydia's insistence that Anna Gilbert could not have committed suicide. People always reacted that way because they couldn't believe their cherished friend or relative would do such a thing. And, more often than not, people were wrong. The scene in the hotel room sure looked like a suicide. He'd seen more than one just like it—booze, pills, a body stretched out as if in dreamland. But Sarah said it was murder, and she was rarely wrong on that score.

He heard a cow's fearful call ringing down an alley, followed by a wet thump and then silence. Some family was butchering the animal, looking forward to steak tonight. This was the heart of Baltimore's immigrant neighborhood, with tenements packed with new arrivals from Southern and Eastern Europe. Conditions were primitive, with no sewer lines, spotty water service, and inadequate ventilation. The remains of slaughtered animals —such as that unfortunate cow—were left to rot where they were dumped.

The booming voice of Enrico Caruso greeted him in the next block. Someone had a Victrola going behind an open window, blasting "O Sole Mio." Jack didn't care for the song—the tune was slow and gummy with sentiment. Ragtime piano music, with its bumpy, propulsive rhythm, was his cup of tea.

Crossing Albemarle Street, he thought about the ragtime music composers Scott Joplin and James Scott. Funny—two Scotts. He almost didn't see the motor truck wagon but jumped aside just as the contraption roared by, with a rush of air knocking the derby off his head. The rear of the vehicle read: "Oriole Whiskey—Fastest Delivery in Baltimore."

He snatched his hat from the pavement and made a beeline for the sidewalk. Close calls happened all the time in the city, especially with automobiles multiplying left and right. But this was more than careless driving, speedy delivery or not. It sure seemed like somebody had tried to run him over.

His next stop was the Silverstrike Hotel, a favorite spot for Baltimore's underworld. It was the best place to get dope on a murder case—and to hear excellent ragtime piano. The joint was just ahead, with the usual cluster of dope fiends hanging around out front. Twitchy and desperate, they were waiting for the lowest of the low hop peddlers to show. The drug of choice was cocaine, but opium, morphine, and marijuana were also in demand. A bottle of rotgut passed from trembling hand to trembling hand.

Stepping into the Silverstrike, Jack marveled at its timeless quality. No matter the time of day, certain things were always the same: the smell of cigarette smoke, stale beer, and greasy boiled meat; sawdust an inch deep on the floor to soak up beer, tobacco juice, and blood from the occasional fight; and continuous piano music. The patrons included smiling politicians, slack-jawed drunks, wide-eyed average citizens slumming for a thrill, and hustlers looking for marks.

It was also a rare black-and-tan ginmill, with blacks and whites congregating in the same space. Most saloons in town were segregated, but nobody seemed to mind the races mixing at the Silverstrike. Maybe it was because Baltimore's own Bob Foster, middleweight boxing champion of the world, owned the place. Bob was black but was adored by almost every white guy in the city, no matter how bigoted.

Jack asked for branch water, drawing a glare from the barkeep. "You're a private dick, right?"

"The genuine article."

"Thought there was a rule that all you guys had to be hard-boiled boozehounds. Doesn't the teetotalling hurt your image?"

"Easier to throw a punch sober than drunk. Simpler to duck one, too."

The booze clerk shook his head and served up the water. Jack took a sip and then winced at the start of a shaky rendition of "The Palm Leaf Rag." The piano player was either hungover or had some busted fingers. Looking around, he saw nobody else seemed to care about the music—they were either too stoned or too busy conducting shady business.

A slick cocaine hustler dressed in a sharp orange suit sidled up and causally flashed enough snow to send someone flying to the North Pole without Santa's sled. Jack waved the guy off. Hop peddlers were always mistaking his bad nerves for a twitchy coke hankering.

A new piano player took over and began pounding out a great melody. The lyrics made him smile:

Oh, you are my Sarah dear,
The sunlight of my soul.
All of my love you stole.
You are sweetness to my lips,

Your tender voice I love to hear.
And when I am near, you've nothing to fear.
Believe me, Sarah dear.

The words hit home—even though he could never describe his Sarah's voice as "tender." She was forever using big words he didn't understand. Still, there was the "sunlight of my soul" part.

"Hey, now, here's Happy Jack, all grinning and jollified. What's the good word, buddy boy?"

Jimmy "Knuckles" Vogel was ready to kill him six months ago over an insane gambling debt. But after Jack had finally managed to pay up, the guy was again as friendly as a big, good-natured dog.

"Everything's jake, Knucks. I've got my wits about me right now, so don't try to draw me into any more sucker bets on the horses."

Vogel gave him a mock hurt look. "Why so grumpy, man? Let me buy you a drink. Barman, give this fine gent another. What're you drinking there—gin?"

Jack grinned as another glass of water appeared. "Thanks. You're a real pal."

"Maybe you can help me out." Vogel sipped from a glass of beer. "You were fronting Chance McCall's payments for a while last fall. Care to do it again?"

"Couldn't if I wanted to. Besides, McCall just told me he's winning big. Let him handle his own marker."

"McCall's a liar. He's into me for two G's and late with a payment. He claims to have a line on a wad of cash and keeps putting me off. Man's about to get hurt." Vogel produced a pack of Sweet Caporal cigarettes. He tapped the box expertly and popped out a single smoke, which he offered up.

"No thanks, but I'll take the Honus Wagner baseball card that comes on some of those packs."

Vogel flipped the pack over to show a Ty Cobb card. "You want this one?"

"Cobb's a rough mope. No, thanks."

"That so?" Vogel sparked a match with a quick thumb scrape and lit up. "I got a soft spot for rowdies. Just hired on a couple as collection agents."

"The loan-sharking biz must be good if you're acquiring new leg-breakers."

"Lots of people need money these days. You'd be surprised, some of the muck-a-mucks I do business with."

"No, I probably wouldn't."

"I got some big shots on the hook. Go on, take a guess who needs my services."

"How about Judge Barnabas Lanvale?"

Vogel nodded with a smile. "His mama's loaded but cut him off. The guy needs my money but still thinks I'm scum. It ain't fair."

"It's the way of the world, Knucks," said Jack. "Those characters think they're way better than guys like you and me."

"Yeah, ain't it the truth." The man slammed his glass on the bar. "My little girl's turning sixteen. Has her heart set on being one of those deluxe girls trotted out at the Lord Baltimore Debutante Ball. Tried to talk her out of it, but she's stubborn. Offered up a pony, a motorcar, even a trip to gay Paree, but no dice. She wants a big party with lots of fancy people looking at her swirling around in some pricy dress and gloves up to her elbows."

"Forget breaking into that la-di-da world unless you have a society type willing to help you out."

"All the ones I've asked turned me down. Ingrates."

"Wait until one of them comes up short, then insist."

"Thought of that." Vogel drained the rest of his beer. "But my baby's going to ask me if I twisted arms, and I can't lie to her. Somebody's got to offer so's I can tell her she's a twenty-four-carat legit deb."

"Your daughter's a hard ticket—a chip off the old block."

"True, true." Vogel clapped Jack on the back and tossed a couple of silver dollars on the mahogany. "You ain't half bad, you know? Have a third one on me." He flashed a row of gold teeth and moseyed off.

Anna Gilbert's handbag had been pilfered in the hotel room. If McCall were over his head with a guy like Vogel, he'd have a motive to steal—and maybe do even worse. Jack waved a five-dollar bill and drew the barkeep's tepid interest.

"I'd like to see Bob."

"Yeah? I'd like to see Mary Pickford standing there instead of you."

"Tough. She's not the one offering you a fiver."

The man snatched the money. "I'll check."

After a wait, the man ambled back. "He can spare five minutes. That's it."

"You charge more per minute than the priciest mouthpiece in town."

The guy shrugged and went back to polishing glasses. Jack found Bob Foster tacking a poster to his office wall. It read: "July Fourth, Bob Foster vs. Jack Johnson, Boxing Match of the Century!"

"Now, that's a fight I want to see."

"Best tickets go for fifty bucks a pair," said Foster. He stood back and looked at the poster. "Funny, don't you think, that whites will pay that much to watch two colored guys? Most of the time, your people would prefer black folk didn't even exist."

"I don't care about color. I—"

"Stop. I don't want to hear crap about how you don't have a racist bone in your body, blah blah. Fact is, you want to ignore the entire subject of race, not even think for a second about the bad treatment blacks get every single day in this city. There's more prejudice in Baltimore than in Chicago, Atlanta, New York, you name it. It's easy for you to be color-blind. It ain't for a guy who looks like me."

"I was going to say—"

"Saw a front-page headline in the paper today: 'Local White Man Almost Lynched.' The actual lynching of a black man might make the back pages after stories about cotton prices and mint-julep cotillions." He snorted. "Baltimore."

Jack held up a hand. "I was going to say that you and Johnson are the best fighters around, period. And even though he's got twenty pounds on you, you're better because you can move and pick the right time to throw that left-right combination."

"That's more like it. Care to use up the rest of your time sweet-talking me?" Foster smoothed the front of his crisp white shirt and adjusted his green silk cravat. A big emerald stickpin glinted in the gaslight.

"Chance McCall. I hear he's in bad with a loan shark."

"Yeah. Guy thought he knew about a fixed race a couple of weeks ago and bet the ranch. He was right about the fix, but wrong about the horse."

"What's Chance willing to do?"

Bob gave him a look before sitting behind his big desk. "Isn't he a dick, just like you? A snoop. A busybody. Ready to cash in on other people's trouble. What won't a gumshoe do for a buck?"

"Guess I'm in big trouble if the cops ever ask you about me."

"Oh, no, no." Bob shook a finger. "All the Baltimore cops want from me are autographs and free tickets. They'd never question me about a white man, even someone like you."

"You know anything about a girl who died at the Belvedere? McCall and I found her today."

Foster laughed. "What, you think I got a crystal ball? Or that maybe I'm clairvoyant, and the Marquess of Queensbury's spirit jabbers in my ear about every crime in town right after it happens?" His serious look returned. "All I know is that McCall's putting out feelers far and wide. Guy like that usually doesn't have a problem finding a taker."

"What about Judge Barnabas Lanvale? Heard he has a loan-shark problem, too."

"All I'll say on that score is that Mrs. Lanvale is more crooked than her son, the judge."

"Okay. I'll see you later, then."

"Wait. I got something else that I'll pass on because you've helped me in the past. Somebody's mad at you."

"What else is new?"

"You're not going to laugh when you hear the details. Ever hear of the Black Cat Creeper?"

"As in 'Here kitty, kitty'?"

"This man's a contract killer, one of the best around. He works out of New York City and makes big money. Specializes in killing bosses, crooked politicians, police informants, and the like. Now word is that the Creeper's in Baltimore, looking for you."

"Makes no sense to pay lots of money to croak a little fish like me." Jack yawned and stretched his neck from side to side. "But I'll keep some milk handy, just in case a cat shows up at my door."

"The Creeper plays with his victims like a cat does with a mouse. Likes to dish out close calls, get people good and scared before applying the coup de grace."

Jack remembered the careening motor truck that almost ran him over earlier that evening. "Who sicced this killer on me? And why?"

"No idea. But it's like you just got a sudden allergy to cats. A fatal one."

"I'll avoid rolling around in catnip."

"Listen up now." Bob's face went stone serious. "You stay out of my club and away from me. I don't want any association with a guy the Creeper's after."

"Scared, huh?"

"You're damn right."

82

CHAPTER 13

SARAH—TUESDAY, APRIL 19, 1910, 8:15 A.M.

*T*he replacement teacup had a chip missing from the rim. A mismatched saucer sat underneath, broken, and poorly glued together. A hideous yellow teapot squatted nearby.

"I sure hope you like this cup better than the last one, Miss Sarah." The waitress beamed.

Sarah could not help but wonder how well everything had been washed, as the items likely had been purchased from a sidewalk dealer in secondhand goods. Still, the waitress was remarkably benevolent and doing her best to please—a kindness Sarah rarely encountered.

"Thank you very much, madam. I sincerely appreciate your thoughtfulness."

"Oh, it's nothing. If you need anything else, just whistle." She looked up. "Oh, look, a handsome man is headed this way. Better go fetch his java."

"Morning, Sarah." Jack sat down. "Another new hat. You look pretty as a painting."

Why was he lying? She was not pretty, and no hat would ever change that. He compounded the falsehood with his incorrect assumption that she prized compliments about her appearance. Looks were hardly the most essential quality for a female. Intelligence, skill, determination—why didn't people praise those attributes? Instead, Jack, like nearly all men, lauded women in the most superficial manner possible. "I accept that your comment is meant to please me."

"You okay?" Jack began slurping his coffee before she answered.

"Rather than engage in aimless chatter, I would prefer to discuss our case and determine a plan." She poured a tiny bit of tea but could not bear to sip from the cup. "I determined during autopsy that Anna may have been injected with a substance that killed her. I will obtain further information from laboratory tests."

"Injected? Like with a needle? I thought only doctors and hopheads used those things."

"I observed an injection mark on the ball of the foot." She said nothing about the possibility that the mark also matched the profile of a thumbtack wound.

"Saw your friend Mrs. Lanvale yesterday," said Jack. "You must feel right at home in that hoity-toity mansion." He grinned at her over his coffee cup.

"I do not." Sarah flapped her hands on the table, causing it to wobble.

"The place had a stuck-up butler," said Jack as he steadied the table. "You know the type, right?"

"Again, I do not." She clenched her jaw, teeth gnashing. Jack was expressing passive hostility toward her. He knew very well that she despised the trappings of high society but still could not resist taunting her under the guise of humor. Sigmund Freud had written in *Jokes and Their Relation to the Unconscious* that humor often masked suppressed sentiments that could not be raised comfortably in a serious discussion.

"Come on. You've been around snooty butlers your whole life."

Sarah glared directly at him. Why were Jack's jibes so bothersome? She was no stranger to ridicule from people and was adept at ignoring it. She dropped her gaze to the grimy floorboards.

"Anyway, that Lanvale woman's meaner than a snake," said Jack. "I don't know how, but she's convinced Lydia to move in. And get this—she sees herself as Lydia's guardian."

"That is curious." Sarah began scribbling notes.

"I relayed the bad news about Anna Gilbert. Lydia immediately went into another one of those trances like we saw here."

"Describe that—trance."

"She did that strange thing with her head, and then her spirit guide started blabbing about stuff like birds, buttercups, and immortality. No idea what she was talking about, but it was spooky as heck. Those two helpers treated her like an organ-grinder's monkey—Miss Pike slapped her a couple of times. That brought Lydia back to herself."

"Did you encounter anyone else at the residence? Other than the butler, whom you reduced to a stereotype to taunt me in accordance with your unresolved antipathy."

"My auntie who?"

She wrote in silence.

"I saw this funny Reverend Smartwell guy. And Judge Barnabas Lanvale, who was in his usual foul mood." Jack gulped coffee and then belched.

"What information did you obtain from Lydia?"

"Not much. Lydia claimed everyone loved Anna and that she would never kill herself." Jack smiled up at the waitress as she plunked down a steaming plate of greasy eggs and hash brown potatoes. "Now, this is what I call first-class eats. Just what I need."

"What you need is a wife to cook for you, hon." The waitress winked at Sarah and left.

"Did Lydia telephone to set up a meeting at your house?" Jack shoveled a forkful of potatoes into his mouth.

"Yes. I am meeting with her later this morning."

"If Lydia knew I wasn't coming, you could've met her at your friend Mrs. Lanvale's place. Seems I'm not good enough to be there."

"Beatrice Lanvale is not my friend." Sarah saw people look over but did not care. "I find it vexing for you to refer to her as such." She slashed her hand over the table, barely missing the squat teapot.

"Calm down." Jack put a finger to his lips. "I'm just joking."

"I must return home and prepare for Lydia's visit." Abruptly, she reached into her handbag and put one hundred dollars on the table.

"The waitress is going to love that tip," said Jack.

"The funds are for your investigative expenses."

He drummed his fingers. "Lydia's already given me fifty bucks. Give your servants a raise instead."

"Stop this childish mockery immediately. I am weary of it." She stamped her foot and pushed the bills at him. "You require money to do your work. Consider this an advance against our fee, which Lydia has agreed to pay while the investigation into Anna Gilbert's death remains ongoing."

"I need to earn my money." He took the cash reluctantly. "A guy's got his pride. Try to remember that."

"I could hardly forget, given the constant stream of what you call jokes."

"Okay, so I'm a jerk sometimes. Maybe more than sometimes. I'm sorry." Jack sighed. "I'm going to try and see Judge Lanvale. And Chance McCall, the Belvedere Hotel dick. I hear he's in trouble with a gambling debt."

"Is he involved with Anna's murder?"

"Maybe." Jack's fork landed on his clean plate with a clatter. "When are we meeting up next?"

"I must categorize my research notes this evening." As she lifted the teacup to inspect it, the flimsy handle snapped off. She held onto the curl of china, flummoxed. "Let us meet at my residence tomorrow morning to debrief."

"Sure thing." He got up. "You can leave that broken piece on the table."

She set the handle down carefully and looked up at Jack. His grooming was good, and his clothing was clean. "Let me see your hands."

Jack hesitated for a moment before extending his hands over the table, revealing a tremor. He quickly pulled them back.

"Your mental state appears to have stabilized," said Sarah. "But you remain emotionally attenuated and could easily relapse. I advise caution."

"And I thought Lydia was spouting gibberish." He offered a weak smile before walking off.

EIGHT YEARS AGO. THAT WAS THE LAST TIME SARAH had guests in her parlor. The visitors had been her friend Margaret Bonifant and her husband, assorted leading citizens, and a couple of Grace's friends. The gathering—which Margaret had insisted upon—had been to celebrate the conviction of Sarah's stepmother for murdering her father and Grace.

Sarah's notification about Lydia's impending visit did not faze the housekeeper. The woman was practiced at coping with the occasional odd request from her employer and had the sheets off the furniture quickly. After a vigorous dusting and plumping of cushions, the parlor was ready for company.

Sarah sat on the edge of a chair, chewing her nails. She hated having strangers in her house. It was an unwelcome intrusion that distracted from routine and made her even more anxious than usual. She managed to endure interactions with others by telling herself she could, if necessary, withdraw to the solitary safety of home. That escape was blocked when she was forced to entertain guests.

The knock at the door made her flinch and bite into the flesh of her right index finger. She quickly pulled on white gloves and opened the door.

"It is lovely to see you again, dear." Lydia looked at Sarah with red-rimmed eyes. Despite the woman's apparent grief, she wore no black—her dress was an elegant drape of ivory luxe silk with an oversized lace collar and three-quarter-length sleeves. Miss Pike and Mr. Fuller stood on either side.

"I offer greetings." Sarah extended a hand.

Lydia looked down at Sarah's rigid hand for a moment without clasping it. "Have you injured your finger?"

Sarah glanced at the red splotch on the snowy tip of her glove and quickly withdrew her hand. "A minor accident." *How could I be so stupid?* she thought. *As if these people did not believe me peculiar enough.*

"May we come in?" asked Lydia in a calm voice.

"Yes." Sarah stepped aside, stumbled, and had to grab the doorknob to steady herself. The encounter had barely begun but was already a disaster.

Lydia stepped inside, eyes wide. "It is just as I remember it. Remarkable."

Sarah closed the door behind Miss Pike and Mr. Fuller. "You were previously in this house?"

"Yes, many years ago. But we're not here to discuss the past."

"Did you know my father? Did you meet my sister Grace?"

"I am so weary. Do you think we could sit down, dear?"

Sarah looked up from the floor. "Certainly." She marched into the parlor, struggling with an urge to flap her hands. The guests followed. Lydia went straight to the big chesterfield sofa and turned to look at Sarah, who remained standing in the middle of the room. Mortified, Sarah realized that everyone was waiting for her. She scurried to an armchair and sat.

The housekeeper appeared with tea and cakes. The woman also took it upon herself to pour each cup. Sarah was relieved— she was too nervous for a task requiring a steady hand.

"I am fond of Beatrice Lanvale but must confess to some relief that we are meeting without her today," said Lydia as she sipped daintily. "She is a domineering force of nature, and sometimes one has trouble discussing certain matters."

"I find her a difficult, unpleasant person." Sarah accidentally slopped a bit of liquid from her cup onto her dress.

"You are so refreshingly blunt." Lydia laughed softly, covering her mouth. "I would not blame Jack for feeling as you do about Mrs. Lanvale. She treated him quite badly yesterday."

"I understand Jack posed some inquiries to you concerning Anna Gilbert. I would also like to do so."

"My, you have your notebook at the ready. You really are quite the detective." Lydia carefully set her teacup and saucer on a table. "I've got payment for another few days of your services. Lucinda, please hand me the envelope."

"I will accept payment after our meeting," said Sarah. "I wish to know more about matters that may assist in probing the demise of Anna Gilbert."

"This is not a good time," said Miss Pike. "Lydia is grieving and exhausted. We don't want to encourage any unplanned visits from the spirit guide."

"Thank you, Lucinda, but Sarah must determine what happened to our dear Anna." Lydia gave a wan smile.

"It is my understanding that Anna Gilbert traveled from Boston to Baltimore with Lucinda Pike."

"Yes. Anna usually travels with me, but I was thrilled when she volunteered to help Lucinda with advance arrangements for the convention."

"Why did Anna register at a hotel while Miss Pike stayed with Mrs. Lanvale? It would have saved money and been more efficient for them both to reside at the Lanvale residence." As Sarah began writing, she noticed the spot of dried blood on her glove's fingertip. It seemed far less important now that her mind was fully engaged.

"Anna and Mrs. Lanvale did not get along," said Lydia. "You said Mrs. Lanvale was unpleasant—Anna felt the same way."

"Did they have a specific disagreement?"

"Not that I know of. They simply did not mix well together. I hoped to mend the rift, as Mrs. Lanvale has kindly offered to let us stay with her for an extended period. Boston had become a bit boring, so I accepted."

Sarah chewed on her pencil. There was something off about Lydia's answer, some bit of illogic lurking. "Why did Anna register under an assumed name at the hotel?"

"She might have wanted to avoid the enthusiasts," said Miss Pike.

"Enthusiasts?"

"People who want something from Lydia." Miss Pike blinked and looked away from Sarah's unwavering gaze. "Fanatics. Some of them are harmless, others not."

"Do you think such a person may have hurt Anna?" Sarah scribbled furiously.

"It's possible. Disturbed individuals turn up around us frequently."

"That is a very dark view of my followers, Lucinda," said Lydia softly.

"Sadly, I agree with Miss Pike," said Mr. Fuller. "The number of maniacs demanding Lydia's attention is growing by the day. We have discussed hiring bodyguards."

"If Anna had a practical reason for registering under a false name, why would she not inform you?"

"Anna was sweet but could be impetuous." Lydia sighed. "She also treasured her privacy. Perhaps she just wanted a day or two of anonymity."

Mr. Fuller gave an annoyed sigh and crossed his arms. Sarah was not sure what to make of these nonverbal cues. Perhaps they related to her own sense that Lydia's explanation for Anna's behavior bordered on the absurd. "What exactly was her role as personal secretary?"

"She assisted me in so many ways, large and small," said Lydia.

"Did Anna have a fiancé or suitor?"

"The job required her complete devotion to me." Lydia's eyes misted with tears.

"Are you quite sure? From her photograph, it appears Anna was the variety of female that men pursue—youthful and physically attractive."

Nobody said anything. Sarah rocked back in forth in her chair, aware that her line of inquiry had caused discomfort but unsure as to why.

"Sarah, I will gladly sit here as long as you have questions, but I'm afraid that there really isn't much more to say about Anna," said Lydia. "I don't have a clue about what could have happened to her. As I told Jack, there's not a chance she killed herself. She loved life."

Sarah wrote in silence.

Lydia pulled a handkerchief from her sleeve and pressed it first to one eye, then the other. "You're a doctor. Do you think Anna simply died in her sleep?"

"I autopsied her corpse and found no clear cause of death. The heart, for example, was normal in terms of structure, appearance, and weight."

"You removed her heart—and placed it on a scale?" Lydia pressed the handkerchief to her lips as her tears flowed.

"Of course. I also removed and weighed the liver, spleen, pancreas, lungs, and kidneys. And brain. That is standard procedure."

Lydia sobbed and began tremoring. Her assistants each took an arm and shook vigorously. They stopped, peered at their employer, and shook her again.

"That is enough for now," said Miss Pike. "She must return home and rest."

"Before we go, I have a request," said Lydia, her voice thick.

"Please remind Jack about the séance dinner tomorrow night. He must come. I'll manage Mrs. Lanvale."

Sarah stared at her shoes. Jack was desperate for Lydia's help with his purported ghosts. Nothing would please him more than attending the séance. But the high society setting would confound and perhaps anger him to the point where he would be ejected. Jack needed someone to keep him focused. He needed her. "Jack and I will both attend."

"How lovely." Lydia's tear-stained face broke into a smile. "You can meet Professor Jaworski. He's also very smart."

"We have already met." Sarah stood, as did her guests. "Thank you for coming."

When Lydia reached the open door, she lightly touched Sarah's hand. "Until later, dear." Mr. Fuller nodded and left with her.

"I have your payment. And—may we talk?" Miss Pike remained inside.

"We may." Sarah closed the door and accepted the proffered envelope.

"There's more you need to know about Anna. And the void she has left in Lydia's life."

"Very well."

"Anna was in love with Barnabas Lanvale. He asked her to marry him, and I helped them make plans to elope."

"Lydia was unaware of the plan?"

"Neither of us had the nerve to tell her." Miss Pike twisted her hands. "Lydia was very dependent on Anna and could not bear to have her leave. In the end, though, Mrs. Lanvale destroyed the marriage plans. After Reverend Smartwell's blunder."

"How so?" Sarah was amazed at this sudden torrent of new information.

"The evening of our arrival, Anna and I met with the reverend to plan the convention. She mentioned something in passing about our travel costs, and he wanted to settle the matter immediately. Anna asked for cash, but the man doggedly insisted on getting Lydia's bank account number to wire funds officially.

"This put Anna in a difficult position. She and I manage Lydia's banking. We both knew very well to keep the bank details secret. But Reverend Smartwell kept wheedling, and Anna, exhausted and on the brink of tears, finally gave him the account number at the First Chemical Bank of Boston. The reverend said Mrs. Lanvale would wire the money, as she managed all church finances through her personal bank account."

"How does this relate to Anna's intended marriage to Barnabas Lanvale?"

"Shortly afterward, Mrs. Lanvale arrived at the meeting. Like a dog with a bone, the reverend mentioned the reimbursement again and asked for Mrs. Lanvale's bank account number. She scolded him, saying no one but herself was to know that information. The reverend claimed he only wanted to lessen Mrs. Lanvale's workload since she was no doubt busy planning for her son's marriage to Anna. Reverend Smartwell is such a foolish man."

"Mrs. Lanvale was surprised to hear of the wedding plans?"

"I'll say. The woman flew into a terrible rage and swore the marriage would never take place. She even threatened to kill Anna. The poor girl left, crying. I never saw her again."

"Does Lydia know about this altercation?"

"No. It would only add to her suffering." Miss Pike wiped away a tear. "Lydia is in a bad way. She needs support and protection."

"Protection?"

"From those who would exploit her, such as that Lanvale woman. And Professor Jaworski—he claims to be a serious writer, but Anna knew he was a scandalmonger. She kept him away from Lydia."

"Both individuals now appear to have gained Lydia's trust."

"I'm afraid Lydia isn't the best judge of people. That's why she needs your help."

"I am working to investigate Anna's death, as requested."

"She's looking to you for more than that, don't you see? It's only natural."

"What are you inferring?"

Miss Pike buried her face in her hands again before looking back at Sarah. "For heaven's sake, she is your mother."

"That is incorrect. I have not seen my mother for twenty years."

"Oh—please pardon my mistake." The woman wrung her hands. "I wasn't supposed to say anything."

Sarah closed the door behind the departed guest as an uncomfortable twinge shot through her stomach. Most unwelcome, as the pain might signal a bout of intestinal distress.

What a preposterous notion—that the mother who abandoned her as a small child would appear after all this time and present herself as a complete stranger. Sarah pulled off her gloves and chewed her nails as the pang in her stomach intensified.

She rarely thought of her mother because the matter was deeply traumatic. It was said her mother had left to become a full-time medium, convinced she could talk to the dead. Spiritualism meant more to the woman than her family, including three-year-old Sarah. Her mother's betrayal lay at the root of Sarah's fierce denial of ghosts, communication with the dead, and all things supernatural.

Sarah nearly doubled over as her gut twisted in agony. Clearly, she was coming down with influenza or possibly something worse. She went upstairs to rest. Once in her bedroom, she stood on tiptoe to pull down a dusty object from the wardrobe's top shelf. Father had given her the box on her sixteenth birthday, saying it contained keepsakes from her mother. She had left it unopened, but now seemed the right time to peek inside.

The first item in the box was a letter from Boston, dated soon after her mother left. "My dear husband, I am awash in sadness and guilt. To spare you and my dear Grace and my dear Sarah from shameful association with me, I am granting a divorce and changing my name to something new." Sarah dropped the letter, unable to read more. She next examined a photograph depicting a family of four: a man, a woman, and two small girls.

Sarah fell to the floor, numb from head to foot. The photograph showed six-year-old Grace sitting in her father's lap and little Sarah with a woman who, while twenty years younger, was obviously Lydia Nightingale.

CHAPTER 14

JACK—TUESDAY, APRIL 19, 1910, 9:30 A.M.

The Baltimore City Courthouse was a grim pile of granite blocks dressed up with a bunch of Greek columns. The public went in through polished brass doors, walked on slick tiled floors, and gawked at gloomy oil portraits of judges. Do-gooders liked to call the place a temple of justice. Those on the wrong side of the law called it the palace of doom.

Justice sure didn't mean much to the dozen or more small children hustling for pennies at the foot of the courthouse steps. Newsboys, bootblacks, pushcart peddlers, and plain old beggars, none older than twelve—two years younger than the law supposedly permitted kids to work legally. Each child gave his or her earnings to an adult boss. If a kid didn't earn, they got the back of the hand.

Jack walked past the bored guards and into the lobby with its murals claiming to "illustrate Maryland's glorious history." One painting showed Leonard Calvert, the first governor of Maryland, making peace with Indian leaders in 1634. Jack shook his head, having heard that white Maryland settlers killed or drove away nearly all the Indians before Baltimore's founding in 1729. Apparently, the neighboring colonies of Virginia and Pennsylvania were a bit more hospitable.

Just goes to show people need a rosy recollection of the past to keep their consciences clear in the present.

He went to the main courtroom, with its domed ceiling and fancy Italian marble. A white-haired judge leaned back in his chair, half-asleep, while a defense attorney pleaded before a jury, claiming his client was shocked when cops broke through a steel door in his saloon and found slot machines, roulette wheels, and blackjack tables. The defendant had no idea what was going on in that back room. After all, announced the lawyer somberly, his client was president of the Society of Christian Men Opposed to Games of Chance.

Jack snorted, recognizing the defendant as the boss of Baltimore's biggest gambling ring.

A bailiff told him to check next door about visiting Judge Barnabas Lanvale. "Saw him earlier. You be careful—the judge was in a bad mood, even for him."

Jack walked into the court administration office and caught the attention of a man sitting at the front desk. A nameplate identified him as "George Funston, Clerk." The guy was rail thin and wore small round spectacles perched on the end of his pointy nose.

"I'm here to see Judge Lanvale."

"Do you have any funny business in mind?" asked Funston, who had the faint shadow of a greasepaint mustache smeared on his upper lip.

"I'm here to discuss a spirit medium."

"Hear the one about the psychic run over by the streetcar?" The guy's face remained utterly deadpan. "She never saw it coming."

"You've got a vaudeville act."

"What I got is robbed, pal. Somebody stole my spotlight."

"I'm sure you got a million of them. How about if—"

"Got into showbiz late. I was going to be a doctor but figured I wouldn't have the patients for it."

"I'll just go knock on the judge's door."

"Knock knock," said the clerk as he did an exaggerated pantomime of pounding on a door.

Jack sighed. "Who's there?"

"Justice."

"Justice who?"

"Justice I thought, you don't recognize me," he said, rubbing his eyes with a fake sob.

"I suppose you're going to pull a rubber chicken out of your pants next." As Jack walked past, the guy jumped up and did a few soft-shoe dance steps next to his desk. The clerk had to be both new on the job and destined for unemployment—no judge would put up with those antics for long.

Jack rapped on Lanvale's door and walked in. "Hello again, judge. Got a minute?"

Lanvale gave him a black look. "Get the hell out, Harden."

"It's got to do with your money troubles."

"Always the wise guy." He lifted the telephone earpiece and spoke into the microphone. "Get me the guard station."

"Thought you might like to know that I'm on good terms with Knucks Vogel and can maybe help you out." Jack knew this was a risky move—Lanvale was a hothead and could blow up. But if the guy was in hock deep enough, he just might be open to a discussion.

Lanvale hung up the telephone. "Figures you know Vogel. Birds of a crooked feather." He pointed wearily at a chair in front of his desk.

Jack took a seat. "Knucks is a reasonable guy, for a loan shark. I think he's open to negotiation. Maybe you could offer a certain favor instead of repayment."

"If you think I'm getting into the gutter with you and do something corrupt—" Lanvale slammed a palm on the desk and put on a dramatic look of indignation.

"Oh no, judge. Not at all." Jack gave him a knowing wave of the hand. "What I've got in mind is perfectly legal. It's a fun thing, actually. I'll lay it out if you answer a couple of questions about Lydia Nightingale."

"I barely know the woman. She's my mother's responsibility."

"What's your mom's plan for Lydia?"

"How should I know?"

Jack leaned forward and stared the guy in the eye. "If you want to hear my suggestion, you need to do a whole lot better than that."

"Mother's taken an interest in Miss Nightingale and thinks her talent needs better management." Lanvale toyed with a stray paper clip. "The people around the woman are incompetent."

"Seems like Lydia's done all right so far. Supposed to have some money."

"It's mismanaged. With proper investment, it could grow faster. Mother helped my father manage his money and knows about finance."

Jack chuckled. "Pity the money skills didn't get passed down to you."

"Miserable scum." Lanvale stood, hair spilling down over his reddening forehead. "You really need your ass kicked."

"We can't talk about Knucks and fight at the same time, can we?" Jack smiled up at the man, who exhaled sharply and crashed back into his chair. "Just one more question. How well did you know Anna Gilbert?"

Lanvale got up again and stomped to a side table. He tore the cork off a bottle and slopped a big pour of whiskey into a crystal glass. Jack took the opportunity to look at the papers on his desk. He was good at reading upside down—a handy skill for a snooper—and scanned the first sentence of a document: "I, Luther Fuller, assistant to Lydia Nightingale, do solemnly swear that my employer is unstable and requires close supervision—"

The crash of shattering glass made Jack look up. Lanvale had hurled his tumbler across the room into the dark walnut paneling. He charged forward and stood over Jack, breathing heavily.

"You're having a swell time tormenting me, aren't you, Harden?"

"I'm just a dick grubbing for dope. And look, judge, the sooner we finish our chat, the sooner I'll be out of your hair."

Lanvale went behind his chair, fingers digging into the fine leather. "I loved Anna, okay?" The man was now sad and deflated. "I didn't expect that to happen, but it did. We were going to get married."

Jack scratched an ear, pondering this unexpected information. "How did your mother feel about that?"

"Next question."

"Any idea how Anna died?"

"The police say it was suicide."

"You believe that?"

He looked down. "There's no proof otherwise." His voice was soft, unsure.

"Know anyone who had it in for her?"

"No. She was a lovely girl." Lanvale sat. "That's it for the questions. Give me your suggestion about that sleazy leg-breaker and be on your way."

"It's a simple thing, really. Surprised you didn't think of it yourself."

"Get on with it."

"Vogel has a kid who wants to be a debutante. Sadly, his social status isn't quite up to snuff. You could offer up your mother's sponsorship for the girl at the Lord Baltimore Debutante Ball. Knucks just might be grateful enough to cut you some slack with your debt."

Lanvale's mouth hung open for a good five seconds before snapping shut. "You can't be serious. Mother would have to introduce the graceless daughter of a low criminal to the cream of high society. She'd be humiliated. A laughing stock."

"Just a suggestion." Jack stood up. "You can forget it if you've got your marker covered, of course."

"Get out of here." Lanvale spoke dully while pointing to the door.

"Hey," Jack called to the skinny clerk on his way out. "Did you hear the one about the guy whose friends all laughed when he told them he was going on stage with a comedy act? Nobody's laughing now."

"Nice." The guy nodded as he scribbled on a scrap of paper. "I'm stealing that."

EDWARD, THE OWL BAR BARTENDER, RECOGNIZED HIM immediately. "Hello, sir. Are you having a pleasant afternoon?" He served up an immaculately clean glass of water. The place was nearly deserted, but Jack got the sense this guy would have treated him the same if the joint was packed.

"I suppose you know how rare it is for me to get good service in a classy place like this." Jack drank down most of the glass, and a fresh one appeared.

"I received my training in a London gentlemen's club. Members included rough men who served with General "Chinese" Gordon in the Sudan and frightful snobs who sat in the House of Lords. Obnoxious, drunken behavior was common. Yet everyone was to receive the same high quality of service at all times."

"Amen to that. If only all Brits were like you. I ran into this puffed-up butler yesterday who acted like he was miles better than me."

"You should know that most English butlers come from poor families. They're trained from a young age to assume the formality and prejudices of their masters. Unfair, really, because no butler can ever dream of rising to the upper class. All they can do is serve them."

"That must make a guy plenty twisted."

Edward looked behind Jack. "Hello to you, sir."

"What's the good news, Eddie?" Chance McCall sat and downed a shot of whiskey the instant after it was poured. "Hey, Harden, I ever tell you the one about how I caught the guy who robbed banks dressed up as a nun? He was a short fella with this sweet-looking face—"

"The ponies are running good for you, that right?" Jack eyed the man carefully.

"Oh, yeah. Real good." McCall spun his empty glass on the bar. Edward stood with the bottle ready. "I left my bankroll at home. Could you cover me, Harden?"

"Sure," Jack nodded, and the whiskey poured. "Funny that Knucks Vogel thinks you owe him two grand."

McCall sputtered whiskey down his chin. "It's a temporary thing." He pulled out a dingy handkerchief and mopped his mouth while Edward quietly wiped the mahogany clean.

"How's about we go to your office for a private chat, Chance?" Jack tossed cash on the bar and stood.

"Fine by me." McCall drained what was left of his drink and left the glass tilted to his lips to catch the final drops. Then he stood and swaggered out of the bar to a nearby office. McCall tried a door behind his desk, and satisfied that it was locked, sat down.

Jack felt the same weird chill in the office as he had in Anna Gilbert's hotel room. "You got a wicked draft coming in under that door, Chance."

"Naw, there's no draft from my private staircase. It's sealed up tight." McCall rooted through his desk drawers. "Damn. I'm out of liquor. I'd settle for the nastiest glass of bug juice in the city right now."

"You're stealing from guests." Jack couldn't shake the weird sense that something evil was with them in the room. His eyes darted about but saw nothing unusual.

"Don't know what you're talking about." McCall went through the desk drawers a second time.

"Cut the crap. I know you're in deep with Vogel and have

been swiping cash from guests. Easy pickings for a hotel detective with a key to every room."

"Yeah, you're no saint, see." McCall gave up on his search for a bottle and looked up with a tense smile. "And you ain't turning me in, boy."

"Don't be so sure."

The smile disappeared. "You're off your box again, Harden. Explains why you look like you've seen a ghost."

"You went to Anna Gilbert's room with champagne and then stole her money."

"Yeah, right. Classy girl lets a guy like me into her room to sip bubbly." He tipped back in his chair. "Maybe I did go into the room, saw she was dead, and borrowed some cash. Somebody else killed her."

Jack grabbed the man by his lapels and brought his chair crashing forward. "How'd you know she was murdered? Somebody paid you off."

McCall grinned as Jack shook him. "You going to beat it out of me right here? Not bloody likely." Tobacco juice ran down from a corner of the man's mouth.

Jack pulled him closer. "Tell me who killed her before the same guy puts you in a pine overcoat. I got a spooky hunch you're in danger."

"Yeah, and you're a well-known lunatic, too. I ain't talking, except to say I got all the angles covered. Got a sweet piece of evidence that's keeping me safe as a mouse in a cheese. It's also going to make me big money."

"Let him go immediately. I'm calling the police."

Jack turned to see the hotel manager glaring at him through the open doorway. "Be my guest. Old Chance needs to get something off his chest."

"Naw, don't bother calling the cops, sir. Harden's leaving now and ain't coming back."

"Your funeral, pal." Jack walked out, glad to ditch the sinister chill but steamed that he didn't get five more minutes to make

McCall spill who killed Anna Gilbert. He had to catch him alone again as quickly as possible. The lobby clock said the time was just after 3:00 p.m. Jack would have to wait for McCall outside.

He stood on the sidewalk near the front entrance, glad for the warm, dry weather. McCall's favorite watering hole was just across the street—the place let him run up a hefty tab, unlike the Owl Bar. The guy was desperate for a drink, so he would surely toddle over to the joint or another nearby saloon in short order.

As the minutes ticked by, Jack remembered that the Black Cat Creeper was supposedly gunning for him. A careful look around revealed nothing out of the ordinary. He patted the Colt revolver in his waistband for whatever assurance it offered, which wasn't much. A professional killer would take care of business before the victim could even think of defending himself. Well, okay. If the hammer was going to fall, let it. No point getting tied up in knots.

A sharp poke hit his arm. "Move along, sonny." A cop gestured with his nightstick.

"Officer, I'm just waiting for someone."

"You're a two-bit, good-for-nothing piece of trash waiting to give honest citizens trouble." The cop raised his club. "Beat it, or I'll beat you."

Jack sauntered away. He'd have to keep an eye on the Belvedere entrance from around the corner of the building for the next fifteen minutes or so until the cop mooched whatever he could in the area and moved on.

He thought about Sarah. She'd been whip-smart, as usual, in pegging Anna Gilbert's death as murder. And if it were possible to catch the killer, Sarah would figure out how to do that, too. Wonderful—she was nothing less than that.

JACK STOOD IN THE SHADOWS WATCHING FOR McCALL into the night. He grew hungry as the temperature dropped and his feet got cold. He snorted, remembering the many women who'd cozied up to him because they thought private eye work was exciting and romantic. Not one of them ever imagined the many hours of his life he'd wasted on mind-numbing stakeouts.

He called it quits at midnight. McCall loved to strut through the lobby on his way in and out of the hotel, so it was unlikely he used the rear entrance. That meant the guy must have somehow gotten his hands on a bottle inside the place and drank himself into a stupor, feeling safe as a mouse in a cheese.

The guy was too thick to understand that an enterprising cat knew cheese was the perfect place to find a rodent.

CHAPTER 15

SARAH—TUESDAY, APRIL 19, 1910, 1:00 P.M.

*T*ime stopped as she lay on the floor, shattered. Her face was squished into a puddle of tears, stomach sore from contorted sobbing. *I could completely shut down*, she thought.

"No," she said aloud in a low croak. She would retain custody of her senses. Somehow.

Sarah used every bit of her willpower to stagger downstairs to the library. She said nothing when the housekeeper inquired about dinner and did not touch the bowl of soup that appeared on the table.

She rocked in her chair, flooded with an undammed torrent of memories. Her mother's disappearance, followed by a few short visits from a pale, dark-haired woman that upset Sarah terribly. Father saying it was not her fault that Mother had left.

That was the only time Father ever lied to her.

Sarah had been a strange, difficult child, unusually sensitive to sights and sounds and unable to stand anyone's touch. Even a slight change in schedule or routine caused a tantrum, often involving repeated head banging on the floor. She showed scant interest in people. By age three and a half, when Lydia left, Sarah lived in her own world, flipping through books in the library. She mainly spoke to herself, repeating the same memorized railway timetable over and over.

Mother obviously left because Sarah was defective—a child not right in the head and physically ugly. A child unworthy of love, even from her own mother. Hot tears streamed as she recognized a peculiar keening sound as her own wailing, long, low, and pitiful. She threw her hands over her ears to give the sound a dull, deadened quality.

Sarah knew she was close to falling into a catatonic state. She had done so once before, after her father and sister died from arsenic poisoning. Comatose for several days, she was sent to a horrible insane asylum by her murderous stepmother. She absolutely must keep a firm grip on her mental faculties. But how? She depended on keeping her emotions at a distance while managing life with logic-driven perfection. That coping strategy was now in tatters. She had nothing to hold onto, nothing to stop her rising fear.

Cold dread wrapped her in a suffocating embrace. She sprang up and began furiously pacing, heart pounding and feeling terrible pain in her chest and shoulders. Breaths came in short ragged gasps as sweat poured down. A feeling of impending doom mixed with an odd sense of unreality descended.

Something horrible was happening. She was losing control. She would go insane and then die.

Her medical bag. Morphine. A shot would stop this terrible panic. She fetched the bag and yanked it open. Everything was so neatly organized. She frantically dumped the contents and raked through the items until she found the morphine. She lifted the vial with a shaky hand.

Sarah had never tried any drug more potent than sherry. In medical school, professors told stories of doctors who used morphine for nerves and became hopelessly addicted. Several classmates dropped out after developing an opium or cocaine habit. During gross anatomy class, she had dissected corpses of addicts—malnourished, diseased, and covered with ghastly injection scars.

She tossed the vial back on the table.

Sarah had always strived to acquire knowledge and use it to solve problems. Often she focused on mastering some narrow branch of learning, working obsessively to keep unacceptable thoughts and feelings at bay. That approach had its limits—one never knew when random life events would be so extreme as to prove uncontrollable. How do people manage despair without drugs? She had little experience relying on support from others. Her friendship with Margaret Bonifant had been important to Sarah since childhood, but it was difficult to imagine asking Margaret for help at a moment such as this.

Jack. She closed her eyes and imagined being vulnerable with him. He would understand her awful, urgent terror. He would take her in his arms, hold her tight, and tell her everything would resolve satisfactorily. He would quietly tolerate her hysterical wails and addled behavior. She held the thought for a long while, taking slow, deep breaths and releasing tension from her body. Gradually, she felt a little better.

She went to the shelves and assembled a collection of favorite books, including *Middlemarch, Alice Through the Looking Glass,* and *On the Origin of the Species.* Over the next several hours, she read through them while savoring the feel of their pebbly covers and thick creamy pages. Every so often, she would jam her nose between pages to inhale the exquisite smell of ink on paper.

Happier memories came back. Father reading books aloud while she snuggled close. His regular professions of love and tremendous pride in her early intellectual ability. And, of course, Grace, whose comforting hugs Sarah treasured. How kind, loving, and patient Grace had been. She worked tirelessly to help Sarah relate to other people. Grace regularly told her that she was special, that she had something unique to offer others.

So what if Mother had left because Sarah was an unusual child? Her father and sister had truly loved her.

Still—anger. Anger toward Lydia. Sarah noted how curious it was that she had never been entirely in touch with the feeling about her mother previously. Rage flared as she thought how wrong it was for her mother to forsake her. But, despite the primacy and power of the emotion, she had to let it go. Lydia's abandonment was heartrending, but enduring resentment would only make the situation sadder and more painful.

Sarah reorganized her medical bag while thinking about Lydia calmly. Why had the woman suddenly appeared after all these years? Why had she requested Sarah's assistance without declaring her relationship? And what of Anna Gilbert's murder?

Anna Gilbert had been robbed of the opportunity to wrestle with life. Denied the chance to expand her perspective, deepen love, lessen and perhaps even resolve painful family conflicts. Her murder was the most terrible aspect of this entire business. Securing justice for that young woman—proving who killed her and ensuring they accounted for it—mattered most of all.

Sarah took solace in knowing that the murder investigation would draw fully on her talent. She would devote hours to assembling evidence and constructing hypotheses. Blissful distraction. But that approach would not necessarily sequester her destabilizing emotions. She was still at risk of becoming overwrought, of breaking down, of falling into catatonia.

Intimacy and support. They were alien concepts, but it would surely help her state of mind if she could rely—to some limited degree—on other people.

More specifically, on Jack.

CHAPTER 16

JACK—WEDNESDAY, APRIL 20, 1910,
7:30 A.M.

*N*o nightmares. No sweat-soaked sheets. No midnight pounding on the wall from the next room over complaining about the shouts and screams. Jack found himself humming a forgotten tune as he shaved. The warm, sunny morning seemed to call for his new shoes and one good suit, and he was happy to oblige. Plus, he wanted to look good for Lydia's séance later tonight.

He left his Fells Point boardinghouse and headed across town toward Sarah's place. Approaching President Street, he smelled the mud before it came into view. The stink galloped up his nose and blotted out everything else. Only a witch could brew such an evil mix of putrefaction, toxic chemicals, human waste, and who knows what else.

A ragged crew was at work shoveling the stuff back into the Jones Falls stream. Not one of the men was much older than about thirty-five, the age by which years of hard work—and hard living—began to reap its toll on the body. If older guys were lucky, they found easier work, maybe even doing something inside. The unlucky ones ended up dead. Or as good as, broken in the gutter.

He went west over the Baltimore Street bridge, thinking how

Sarah would ask a bunch of tough questions about what he'd learned from Judge Lanvale and Chance McCall. Her smarts forced him to make connections he usually wouldn't.

Sarah was brainy all right—but wrong to think spiritualism was bunk. Sure, there were plenty of fake mediums and clairvoyants out there duping suckers with rigged séances and sham messages from the dead. There were also plenty of swindlers hawking bogus get-rich-quick schemes and politicians peddling lies. The trick was to know who was a phony and who was the real deal.

Lydia was legit; he just knew it. She—rather, her spirit guide—saw his ghosts and knew how much they tormented him. Nobody else ever had. Beyond that, Lydia had practically promised to help him. After years of suffering, he finally had hope of ditching his terrifying spooks once and for all.

He needed to get back to doing steady work. Unlike Sarah, he didn't get satisfaction crusading for justice or righting wrongs. He was in the game to frustrate criminals—uncover their secrets, disrupt their ugly schemes, hurt their wallets and their pride. Doing so made him feel less crooked himself. Maybe doing it a lot would make him feel more like a worthy human being.

Steady work also meant spending more time with Sarah. Jack wasn't much for the lovey-dovey stuff, but Sarah had a quality that drew the best out of him and made him feel glad to still be alive and kicking.

Yeah, okay, it was foolish to imagine they'd ever be more than business partners. She claimed not to care about the yawning gulf between their class, wealth, and education, but that couldn't be true. A gal accustomed to caviar would never be happy settling for crackers.

A shiny new penny glinted on the sidewalk ahead. Just as he stopped to pick it up, a wooden crate came crashing down, missing him by less than a foot.

Oysters—the smell came from dribbling cans as they rolled

from the splintered crate. The can labels depicted the cartoonish figure of a big, buck-toothed man licking his chops before a plate piled with mollusks on the half shell.

No point running upstairs; the culprit who had tried to brain him was already on the run. But the message was clear. First, a motor wagon almost runs him over, now this. Bob Foster was right about the Black Cat Creeper: the assassin was playing around before going in for the kill, just like a cat torturing a mouse before sinking its teeth into the rodent's neck.

Jack had no idea who'd hired the killer. All the bad guys he knew were cheap and simple. Whoever hired this character was neither.

Tense and paranoid, he made it to Sarah's place without further incident. He rapped on the big front door, once, twice, with no answer. He knocked again, louder, and was about to start pounding when it finally opened.

She looked awful, with puffy red eyes and blotchy face, hair down and tangled. She still wore a long dressing gown and slippers and said nothing before turning and marching away.

The entry foyer was usually brilliantly lit from an array of overhead electric lights. Now, however, the only illumination came from distant, dimly lit gas jets. Closed drapes further darkened the place and muffled sound. The house was so gloomy that a bunch of grief-stricken mourners in black bombazine dresses would fit right in.

Sarah went into the library and sat at the table. "What's the matter?" Jack asked while fumbling for a chair in the semi-darkness. "I've never seen you so blue."

"I did not sleep."

Her voice, always a flat monotone, was today a thick murmur drained of energy. She lifted a teacup to her lips with a hand shakier than his own.

"You're upset. Tell me why."

Her chin trembled as tears gushed. He sat in shock for a second or two before thinking to hand over his handkerchief. He was even more astonished when she leaned over the table, body heaving with great wailing sobs.

After all they'd been through, she'd never once cried. She always appeared unflappable, unfailingly calm and logical. Despite how she presented herself, Jack knew Sarah felt things as strongly as any human being. But unlike others—especially other women—she rarely let her emotions show.

Not now. She was as upset and distraught as possible, suffering beyond the comfort of words. He stepped behind her chair and lightly put his hands on her shoulders. He staggered when she leaped up, knocked her chair to the floor, and flung herself into him. They embraced as she let loose guttural sobs that vibrated against his rib cage.

"Hey," he said as he stroked her back. "Everything's going to be okay." It was an unoriginal thing to say, and maybe even a lie, but so what. She pressed her face into his chest, arms clasping him tightly.

Jack held her, feeling her grief as plainly as he did the knobby bones of her spine. Gradually, her sobbing turned to sniffling. Abruptly, she broke away and blew her nose into the hand-kerchief.

"Dye apollogize pour dis dumseemly diplay."

"You've got nothing to apologize for. Or to feel embarrassed about."

She blew her nose again and took several deep breaths. "I owe you an explanation. Let us sit."

Jack picked up her chair and held it as she sat. "You don't have to say a thing if you don't want to."

Sarah switched on an electric table lamp with an elaborate stained-glass shade. "Please partake." She gestured at a mug of coffee and a plate covered by a silver dome. "My housekeeper knows what you favor."

After his eyes adjusted to the sudden light, he looked at her closely. Apart from the puffy blotchiness from weeping, her face was set in its usual impassive look. Her arms twitched from moving her hands under the table. "Sure you're okay?"

"I am fine," she said, her voice stronger.

He shrugged, unsure about how to probe a woman who never discussed her feelings. He took the silver dome off to reveal a plate packed with scrambled eggs, hash browns, and sausage. "Any chance your housekeeper could bring me break-fast every day?" He chuckled and went after the food, fork clat-tering on china.

"That would be difficult, given the distance she would have to travel between here and your rooming house. Perhaps if we arranged for a carriage—"

"Sorry—I was joking. I know she can't feed me every day." While chewing, Jack reminded himself that Sarah did not appre-ciate humor, however well-intentioned. Right now, she needed as much consideration as he could muster.

"I was told something unexpected yesterday," she said. "In retrospect, I should have made the discovery myself. But it appears I constructed a psychological barrier to the knowledge, thus allowing me to deny an evident reality."

"You heard something painful, maybe even heartbreaking—is that what you're getting at?" Jack put his fork down and gave her his full attention.

"Yes." The tabletop shook slightly as her hand flaps began bumping against its underside. "Miss Lucinda Pike informed me that—" Her voice cracked and chin quivered, but she recovered and pushed a photograph toward him. "This is my family. I am the infant."

The photo showed a well-dressed man and woman seated together, each with a child on their lap. A beautiful golden-haired girl of about six sat with the man. A toddler with dark hair and a blank look sat with the woman—who, while much younger, was clearly Lydia Nightingale.

"She's your mother?" Jack dropped the photograph and looked at Sarah, whose eyes were fixed on the tablecloth. "Why the heck didn't she say so? What a damned cruel thing to show up and act like a stranger. It's not right."

"She apparently hoped to pass unrecognized. I was about five years of age the last time I saw her."

Jack shook his head, angry at the depth of human cruelty. How could Lydia abandon a small child and then come back years later and pretend not to know her? Did the woman really expect to get away with that? "Let's drop this case."

"No." Sarah was up, pacing rapidly from one end of the room to the other. "Anna Gilbert deserves justice. We must find her killer, and doing so will require ongoing dealings with Lydia. Her status as my mother must not interfere. We must continue to interact with her as a client."

Jack stared at her flitting form, knowing that once Sarah started talking about justice, there was no use arguing—her mind was firmly set.

"There is also another consideration." She stopped in front of him and gazed down at her wiggling fingers. "Lydia has invited us to dinner and séance at the Lanvale residence this evening. I am aware of your desire to participate."

"Jeez, you hate that kind of stuff." His hand jerked and bumped the mug, sending a sloppy splash of coffee onto the pristine white tablecloth. "And you're torn up about Lydia to boot. No way can you go to that shindig." He threw a napkin over the coffee stain, knowing he should have said, "no way are *we* going."

"Again, I must disregard my personal views. You have made your interest clear regarding Lydia's—" she stopped short, searching for the right words, "exhibition of her alleged mediumship. Note that the séance will take place in conjunction with a formal dinner. Given your ignorance of social protocols and how easily you are provoked regarding class distinctions, there is a high probability you will be ejected from the residence before the séance. You require my assistance to avoid that outcome. I, therefore, must accompany you."

"So, I need a minder to make sure I don't eat with my hands and offend my betters—"

She held up a hand. "You have just proven my point."

As usual, she was right. He grumbled and finished what was left on his plate.

"We should also regard the event as an opportunity to gather further information."

"But you were so upset just now—"

"Jack," she cut him off. "Please do not reference that—thing. I do not wish to be reminded of it." She stood still, hands clenched tight before marching to the table and picking up a notebook. "We must now discuss what each of us has learned since we last met. I will begin." She began flipping pages.

How anyone, especially a woman, could turn their emotions on and off like an electric light switch was a complete mystery to him. Many a gal in her situation would weep buckets for hours. Jack was a bit ashamed for feeling grateful she wasn't acting that way.

"Miss Pike stated that she and Anna Gilbert met with Reverend Smartwell shortly after arriving in Baltimore."

Apart from some huskiness, Sarah's voice was back to normal. He listened as she described the meeting, including Mrs. Lanvale's threat to kill Anna to stop her from marrying Barnabas. "That whole business seems fishy. And why the heck would Smartwell spill the beans to Mrs. Lanvale—in front of Anna, no less?"

She glanced at him and then quickly turned back to the notebook. "I do not know the answer to your questions. Lucinda Pike characterized the reverend as foolish."

"The guy seems like a stooge, but appearances can be deceiving." He tapped a finger on the table. "One thing for sure is that Mrs. Lanvale is a nasty piece of work."

"I agree."

Jack downed the last bit of stone-cold coffee. "I also dug up some good stuff. Chance McCall let it slip that Anna was murdered—I'll bet the killer paid him off for something. I didn't get a chance to wring a name out of McCall, but I'll do it later this morning."

"You have uncovered an important clue. Who do you imagine enlisted him in the murder plot?"

"Maybe Barnabas Lanvale. I saw a document on this desk—some sort of statement from Lydia's assistant, Luther Fuller, claiming that Lydia was nuts and needs someone to look after her."

"That is yet another vital piece of evidence. Such statements are used to justify a court order when an individual cannot manage their own affairs due to physical or mental incapacity."

"Maybe Mrs. Lanvale wants Lydia's money to pay off to pay off her son's gambling debt."

Sarah flexed her fingers rapidly. "Perhaps Judge Lanvale has prepared a guardianship document. And perhaps that is why Mrs. Lanvale has invited Lydia to live with her."

"Yeah, maybe." Jack shook his head with a grin while considering the irony of the skeptical Sarah stuck in the middle of a case involving murder in a haunted hotel chamber, a psychic medium, and a séance. Not that there was anything funny about the medium turning out to be her long-lost mother. She had enough on her plate—no need to tell her that the Black Cat Creeper was out to kill him.

"Let us now outline our plan for the day." Sarah again referred to her notebook. "I will interview Reverend Jared Smartwell."

"Chance McCall is my priority," said Jack. "I don't care if the guy is sober, drunk, or hungover—I'll get him to talk. Then I'll drag him to the cop house to repeat it."

"Very well. In any event, return here at 6:00 p.m., and we shall depart for the Lanvale residence."

"I don't know." Sarah was very nearly herself. Much of the puffiness had left her face, and her eyes were red but showed no sign of tears. Everything seemed under control. Jack thought back to the distraught woman wailing in his arms on the verge of a total breakdown just a little while ago. That person now was hiding behind a wall of fierce composure. "Maybe I should hang around for a while longer."

"I have told you to go. Do not concern yourself."

"Yes, ma'am." He was sure Sarah had merely swept her distress under the rug, where it sat like a ticking time bomb.

CHAPTER 17

SARAH—WEDNESDAY, APRIL 20, 1910, 10:00 A.M.

*A*fter Jack left, she bathed and spent over an hour getting ready to go out. The process would go much faster if she employed a lady's maid, as her friend Margaret Bonifant had long urged. But she hated the thought of someone constantly hovering about and touching her. She would make do herself, even if it required more work and the results were less than perfect.

Sarah began by brushing her thick, tangled hair and then braiding, coiling, and pinning the stuff on the back of her head. A woman's hair was supposedly her most important asset. As such, it had to be kept long. The hair must also be neatly put up in a convoluted style for display under a hat outside the home. The guardians of fashion—all men, doubtlessly—insisted that no lady could do otherwise.

She longed to cut her hair and avoid all the bother. But short hair was unheard of for an upper-class lady, and if she dared take that route, it would convince people that she was even more bizarre than they suspected. That, in turn, would hinder her ability to find detecting clients. Finished at last, she checked the result in the mirror. A few unruly tendrils hung down, having escaped the pins and combs. She ignored them.

Next came another laborious process she despised: pulling on all the clothing a woman needed to venture out in public. The accouterments of her femininity consisted of drawers, chemise, long-line corset, silk stockings, camisole, petticoat, narrow-silhouette navy skirt, white shirtwaist with a high lace collar, and long navy jacket. Even after all that, she still was not finished, as there were the clunky shoes to pull on and button up.

She resisted the throbbing anger demanding her attention, as surrendering to it was not helpful. Children do not understand that people disappoint and cause pain because all people are imperfect, some more so than others. But an adult should know that holding on to resentment poisons the mind and keeps the anguish alive. With enough time, Sarah hoped to resolve her anger and—what was the word associated with various religious traditions?—*forgive*. Forgive her mother.

Enough. She could not resolve things through rumination posing as self-analysis. More practical matters demanded her attention. She telephoned for a taxi, and while waiting for it to arrive, used three long hairpins to attach a hat to her head. One could only hope for no wind—despite the sturdy pins, even a mild gust might send the enormous piece of millinery flying away.

Situated in a hansom taxi, Sarah tried turning her thoughts to Reverend Smartwell, the spiritualist minister she was off to meet. But her mind, battered from stress and lack of sleep, refrained from its usual practice of churning out a logical sequence of interview questions.

She idly watched the fine old rowhouses passing by the open carriage window. Past an intersection, she saw the hulking structure that was the Maryland Club. Four gentlemen in straw skimmer hats stood talking in front of the place. Jack, were he with her, would notice far more about them than she, such as what their individual dress and so-called "body language" indicated about their differences in status and temperament. He had such an extraordinary ability to under-stand people.

She should not ruminate on Jack, either. How mortifying it was to break down before him. Revealing her deepest emotions to another—something she had only previously done with Grace —left her feeling exposed and ashamed. Jack's ability to soothe her upset was, however, a considerable relief. He surely could be counted on again to render such a balm if so required.

She forced herself to stop these runaway thoughts. She was too exhausted to extrapolate from her recent experience with Jack accurately. He was not typical in all ways, but he was still just a man.

The carriage lurched to a halt next to a red brick church with a square bell tower and three arches facing the street. With a sharp click, the trapdoor in the hansom roof opened.

"Here we are, missy." The driver held his hand just inside the trap. Sarah gingerly presented the fare and a generous tip with her gloved hand. The driver threw the lever that popped open the passenger door. She carefully apprised the eighteen-inch drop to the street. A pile of horse manure was just below the step. With careful aim, she missed the excrement with only a moderate wobble to her step.

Two small girls came rushing at her, one carrying a basket of bruised, overripe apples, the other with a tin cup holding an assortment of stubby pencils.

"Miss, I got the freshest apples in town." The child was perhaps ten years old with snarled, dishwater blond hair, a grubby dress, and bare, dirt-encrusted feet.

"Hey, miss. I know you need to write stuff." The pencil seller was younger still, with a soot-smeared face and a torn dress much too big for her. Her feet were also bare and dirty.

Sarah stepped away and held up a hand as they advanced. "Stop. Come no closer."

"I'll get beat if I don't sell at least one apple. Only cost a nickel." The older girl stuck out her lower lip.

"Me, too. I need a nickel for a pencil to keep him off me."

Sarah hurriedly retrieved two dimes from her change purse. "Extend your wares, and I will place the payment in the respective containers."

The kids looked at her vacantly.

She reached her hand as far as she could toward the children with the dimes between gloved thumb and forefinger. The pencil seller grabbed the coins and ran off.

"It was bad for her to steal that money," said the apple peddler. "One of them dimes was for me, right?"

Sarah produced two more dimes and offered them, but the child stayed put. "If I get a dollar, I won't get beat for a week."

"Get lost, you disgusting varmint." An older man in a grey homburg hat shook his cane at the girl, who snatched the dimes and scampered away. He turned to Sarah. "Don't be giving them money. It only encourages the scoundrels to keep pestering well-bred people."

"I find it difficult to deny children a pittance to prevent their physical abuse."

"Your concern is wasted." The man sneered. "Those gutter-snipes all need a regular whipping." He slammed his cane against the sidewalk and strutted off.

Sarah let out her breath and approached the front door of the church. A placard sat nearby:

Proclaim and cherish the union of the material world and the SPIRITUAL REALM! Rejoice in the natural and supernatural instruments of social and moral PROGRESS! Glory be to those who abstain from drink and seek votes for women!

The promotion of women's rights made sense, as most spiritualism followers were female.

She opened the church door and stepped into the dark entry hall. A light drew her attention to the right, where an older woman sat with two disembodied faces suspended over either shoulder. The faint sound of an organ dirge floated in the still air.

Sarah tapped her foot, irritated by the theatrics. The figures were clearly from an enlarged photograph lit by a spotlight. The organ music was Bach, professionally played, and more than likely a phonograph record. "Hello," she called out, her voice echoing in the darkened space.

Light spilled into the hallway as a large man stepped out of a doorway. He wore a white suit with a glittering watch-chain that stretched a great distance over his protruding stomach. "Pray tell, is that you, Miss Kennecott?"

She marched down the hallway and reluctantly extended her hand. The practice of touching hands was distasteful but expected in such situations. "I am Sarah Kennecott."

He snatched her hand with both of his and pressed vigorously. "Miss Kennecott, I offer a most decidedly heartfelt welcome."

She jerked her hand away and stepped back.

"If I have offended you, I implore—I beg—your forgiveness." He flitted pink fingers near his mouth before clasping his hands. "I am so filled with joy that, ergo, I express joy, perhaps with less discretion than some prefer. I am Reverend Jared Smartwell. At your service, if I may say so, miss."

"I dislike excessive touching."

"I understand. I understand completely. All men—myself included—must refrain from unwanted touching, even if it comes from a place of love, per se. We must scrupulously monitor ourselves and use great care to demonstrate respect for woman, even if men such as I take to heart the scripture of Timothy: 'For God hath not given us the spirit of fear; but of power, and of love, and of a sound mind.'"

"You follow the Bible?"

"We take lessons from many sources as part of our loving acceptance of humankind. It behooves us to consider any teaching that may help in the quest for communion with the transcendent. We place special faith in spiritual healing, psychic energy channeling, and communicating with the departed."

"I am not here to discuss such matters."

"Certainly, Miss Kennecott, certainly. I know you are studying the sad—shall I say profoundly sad—demise of Miss Anna Gilbert." Smartwell lowered his head in silence for several seconds and then looked up. "Please enter so that we may formally converse."

She followed his bustling form into a large, unkempt office. Shelves held books sitting at strange angles; several volumes were splayed on the floor below. The desk was strewn with files and newspapers. A chair next to the desk held a colossal crystal ball and, tilted against it, a box labeled: "Ouija: The Talking Board."

Smartwell went to a pair of upholstered armchairs and accidentally knocked over a small framed photograph sitting on a nearby table. He reset the picture, which showed a younger version of Smartwell seated with a woman about his age. The translucent forms of an older couple hovered behind them.

Sarah pointed at the image. "You are aware that such images are false representations produced using photographic trickery?"

"It's a matter of faith, miss. Abiding faith." Smartwell gestured for her to sit before sinking deeply into his own chair. "All photographers—dare I say all artists—strive to present a fuller, more inclusive version of reality." He nodded at the picture. "I receive comfort from the spirits of my deceased parents, who remain at the family home in Illinois. My sister, who remains among the living, keeps them company. Alas, my duties keep me from spending as much time with the family as I wish. Yea and amen, I take great comfort in this photograph, as it shows us communing as a loving family."

"I see only a counterfeit photograph meant to deceive."

The reverend laughed, sending fleshy waves across his torso. "An intelligent woman such as yourself surely knows that many great artists, including Michelangelo, were accused of misrepresenting their subjects." He ran a pink hand over his forehead. "Oh, my, I fear I have spoken too freely. I meant no disrespect by forcing my views of art history upon you *con brio*. I apologize most sincerely."

"There is no need." She took out her notebook and forced herself to concentrate on the reason for her visit. "Mrs. Beatrice Lanvale is active in your organization?"

"Verily, verily." Smartwell steepled his fingers and smiled. "She is a blessing, dare I say. She has such energy, such tenacity. Some of us are perhaps a bit too cerebral, too timid, to engage forcefully in material matters. That is Mrs. Lanvale's great strength, miss. You must, however, also note my admiration for her metaphysical affinity. The spirits all sing her praises." He glanced heavenward and raised his arms.

"Spirits sing?"

Smartwell dropped his arms and chuckled dryly. "Very clever, miss. I see you are a droll young woman—a blithe spirit, one might say. Hah." He slapped a knee and peered at her as if expecting a reply. When none came, he cleared his throat and continued. "Of course, spirits don't often sing, but they do pass on messages. Just last week, Queen Victoria appeared at a séance and wrote a lovely note about Mrs. Lanvale on a slate. I have it here somewhere." He sprang up and began riffling through a stack of material on a bookshelf.

"Thank you, sir, but that is unnecessary." Sarah's leg was churning up and down with exasperation so great that her heel repeatedly thumped on the thin carpet.

"Where is it?" Objects fell to the floor as he moved from pile to pile. "I must find it. It's here someplace. Must find it. Simply must."

Her host was perseverating oddly. She thought of Lucinda Pike's account about how the reverend could not let the matter of Lydia's travel reimbursement go. The man perhaps suffered from an obsessive-compulsive disorder. She checked her watch.

Smartwell moved to his desk and rooted through one drawer then another, muttering "must find it" to himself over and over while frantically scattering papers. "Ah, hah!" he finally cried.

His shout made her jump, and she could not help but cringe when he came rushing at her.

"See for yourself what her majesty had to say." He thrust out what looked like an ordinary school slate.

The chalk writing was spidery and faint: "We commend Mrs. Beatrice Lanvale for her noble service on behalf of our spiritualist kingdom of the departed. Victoria, VRI."

"This is absurd. Queen Victoria died in 1901. How can you claim she wrote this last week?"

Smartwell sat in his chair, again knocking his family portrait over. He made no move to pick it up as he stared fixedly at the slate. "As I say, her spirit appeared at a séance. And note the use of 'VRI' in the signature—V for Victoria and RI for Regina Imperatrix, which means—"

"Empress of India." Sarah drew in a breath. "Please inform me as to Mrs. Lanvale's activities on behalf of you and your organization."

"Where to start." He casually placed the slate on the table and stroked his chin. "She planned our recent convention practically by herself. And she has done wonders for the church finances. After all, *Absque argento omnia vana.* Dear me, I beg pardon for lapsing classical. You must think me unbearably pompous. I meant to say—"

"'Without money, all efforts are useless.'" Sarah wrote the Latin phrase in her notebook.

"Well done, miss. You know the ancient tongue quite well, if I may say so." Smartwell mopped his shiny brow with a lace-trimmed handkerchief. "Mrs. Lanvale organized our books and brought in new revenue. For example, she got Miss Nightingale to speak at the conference, and that doubled—nay, trebled—our registrants. Lydia's fee was quite large but worth it."

"Did Mrs. Lanvale transmit the fee?"

"Yes. I expected her to wire the money to Lydia's Boston bank, but Mrs. Lanvale insisted on presenting the fee in cash. One hundred dollars in currency is more impressive than the same amount on a bank statement, I do suppose."

Sarah scribbled a note. Lydia had claimed she charged no fee for speaking at the convention, which possibly meant Mrs. Lanvale embezzled the supposed payment. "Does Mrs. Lanvale manage the church finances by herself?"

"She volunteered. None of the rest of us care much about such matters. Mrs. Lanvale has been kind enough to handle all our funds through her own account. She is utterly selfless, bless the dear soul."

"What do you know of her son, Judge Barnabas Lanvale?"

"I don't know him well. But Mrs. Lanvale is devoted to him. Her warm, caring nature makes her an ideal parent, I am sure. Dare I say, she is the sweetest of mothers."

Sarah glared at Smartwell, wondering if the man could possibly be as naïve and otherworldly as he seemed. He looked back, his broad face beaming serenity.

"How well were you acquainted with Anna Gilbert?"

"We were professional acquaintances." His smile faded. "I must confess to causing the poor young woman much pain during her final hours before she passed into spirit. I was exuberant regarding her upcoming marriage and foolishly exposed the plan to the groom's mother." He looked at the floor for a long moment, wringing his hands. "I am filled with mortification for my unpardonable verbal emission. Sadly, I can offer no excuse for the blunder other than to say that I was, in all sincerity, unaware that Mrs. Lanvale did not know of the planned nuptials."

"How did you learn of the intended marriage?"

"From Miss Gilbert herself. We spoke by telephone about conference planning before her arrival. She told me of her plans with Judge Lanvale, and I don't recall her swearing me to secrecy. I know that sounds self-serving, but—"

"How did Mrs. Lanvale react after learning of the intended wedding?"

"With firm maternal concern." Smartwell nodded slowly. "She was naturally upset that her son would take such a step without consulting her and discouraged Miss Gilbert from the match. Some without charity might say Mrs. Lanvale was violently angry, especially when she told Miss Gilbert, 'I will kill you.'" Smartwell waved a pink hand. "The words were uttered in the heat of the moment, mind you."

"What makes you so sure?"

"Tell me, Miss Kennecott—do you have children?"

Sarah hoped the warmth creeping up her neck was not a blush. "No. And I do not intend to. I fail to see—"

"Each and every mother loves her children beyond measure and wants to keep them under a veritable wing, even after they reach adulthood. However murderous Mrs. Lanvale may have sounded at the time, the woman merely expressed natural maternal devotion, not an actual threat of bodily harm."

Sarah clenched her jaw so tightly the joint popped. The man obviously knew nothing about motherhood. Still, his story corroborated Mrs. Lanvale's threat against Anna.

"I am so very sorry, Miss Kennecott, but I have another visitor coming shortly. Can I be of any further assistance?"

"How well do you know Lydia and her assistants, Miss Lucinda Pike and Mr. Luther Fuller?"

"I know Miss Nightingale by her marvelous reputation as a medium, of course. As for her two helpers—" He raised his palms limply. "There are whispers about them having too much predominance, particularly in connection with their employer's finances." He sighed. "It's distressingly common, I regret to say."

"How so?"

"True spiritualists are naturally open and trusting. We tend not to concern ourselves with money and the like. We are, sadly, easy targets for scoundrels." Smartwell's shoulders sagged, making his belly even more prominent. "Female confidence artists have played me for a victim more than once. I fall in love too easily, you see. Whilst in the grip of infatuation, I open everything wide—my heart, my soul, and alas, my wallet." He stifled a whimper and dabbed his eyes with a frilly handkerchief. "That is why I was so pleased to turn the church finances over to Mrs. Lanvale. You see, I do not have a head for money. More broadly speaking, I confess to needing assistance in navigating the base, often corrupt, domain of the living."

"As a matter of trust, perhaps you should arrange for an audit of your organizational finances—"

"Dearest me. Look at the time." With some effort and a series of grunts, Smartwell rose from his chair. "Do come visit again, Miss Kennecott." He picked up the framed family photograph and reset it on the table, but it promptly fell over again on the slate with Queen Victoria's purported message. The reverend did not seem to notice as he moved out the door. Sarah followed his form down the dark hallway when a burst of daylight from the front entrance made her shield her eyes.

"Damn it Smartwell, I told you I don't like doing business in the dark. Turn on the lights." It was Professor William Jaworski with his student lingering behind.

"My apologies, dear Professor. Pardon me whilst I attempt to locate the light switch." The reverend scurried off.

"Fate keeps throwing us together, Sarah," said Jaworski with a grin. "I say it's preordained that you must sit down with me for an interview. When's a good time?"

"There will be no interview, as I have reason to suspect you of scandalmongering, sir." She turned back to the dark interior. "Thank you for our meeting, reverend."

"Certainly, certainly," came Smartwell's disembodied reply. "I will see you at the séance this evening, miss. We should have an illuminating encounter, if I may say so. Ah, here it is." Bright electric light filled the hallway just as she left the place.

~

BACK HOME IN HER LIBRARY, SARAH WAS EAGER TO
learn more about Professor William Jaworski and the organization he had worked for, the American Institute for Psychic Studies. Fortunately, she had borrowed the institute's proceedings
from the public library.

The first volume outlined the institute's purpose. Pointing to
the existence of "an important body of evidence concerning the
supernatural that defies current rational understanding," the
institute proclaimed itself committed to the scientific examination of psychic experiences, ghost sightings, and communication
with the dead.

The most eminent scientist involved with the group was
William James, an original thinker with great insight into the
workings of the human mind. James remained interested in the
potential validity of spiritualism despite encountering a succes-
sion of fakes. He stated: "to upset the conclusion that all crows
are black, there is no need to seek demonstration that no crow
is black; it is sufficient to produce one white crow."

In other words, a single authentic medium would verify the
concept of spiritualism even in the face of a thousand frauds.

James eventually claimed to find his white crow: Mrs. Lenora
Piper, a Boston housewife. James spent years observing—and
participating in—her work as a medium, which involved having
clients speak to her palm, or as she termed it, "her spirit telephone." James waffled on his belief in spiritualism but did claim
that Mrs. Piper was "in possession of a power as yet unexplained."

Although Sarah had tremendous respect for James, she had
long assumed his interest in spiritualism was misguided. But
that was before her dead sister Grace appeared in a dream and
accurately forecast the murder of Anna Gilbert.

Sarah massaged her forehead, recalling Bayes's theorem.
Named after the eighteenth-century philosopher Thomas Bayes,

the rule called for rigorously revising one's assumptions based on additional evidence. That meant a rational observer must always be prepared to change her most deeply held beliefs if presented with new information. While remaining skeptical, Sarah had to try and maintain an objective mind regarding supernatural events.

She could only find two mentions of Professor William Jaworski in the proceedings. The first was his report of discovering a mute English farm girl who allegedly channeled the spirit of the Russian Empress Catherine the Great. In breathless prose, Jaworski related how he observed the girl slip into a trance and recount, in fluent Russian, her memories of King Louis XIV. Sarah tapped the page, annoyed the story did not bother to explain how Empress Catherine could have memories of a king who died fourteen years before she was born.

The institute retracted the article shortly afterward. Independent investigation revealed the girl was not mute and not English, but rather the daughter of a Moscow couple sent to live with an aunt in Manchester. "Professor Jaworski," concluded the retraction, "is no longer in our employ."

Other reports documented supernatural encounters deemed both plausible and unexplained. One such incident involved an English country squire who was out walking one night when he met his typically unsociable neighbor. On this evening, however, the neighbor was eager, even desperate, for company. The man implored the squire to accompany him home. The squire had a dinner engagement and declined, despite the neighbor's repeated and anxious requests. Around 10:00 p.m. that evening, the squire heard his front gate open and shut, followed by screams, wails, and agonized weeping.

The next morning the squire checked by his gate and found no footsteps in the frost. He also learned the same neighbor who had pleaded with him for company had committed suicide at home about 10:00 p.m. the previous evening by drinking a powerful acid, which caused a lingering, painful death. The squire never had such a supernatural experience previously and emphatically did not believe in ghosts. Many similar tales involved seemingly levelheaded people encountering a spirit conveying information that later proved true.

Sarah thought again of William James. She knew of his claim that people live in a "normal, waking consciousness," but that different forms of reality also existed, separated by "the filmiest of screens." Under certain circumstances, James said, anyone can cross into a separate existence that is as undeniable as it is inexplicable.

She shuddered. Until a few days ago, the idea of separate realities seemed pure fantasy. A startled cry caught in her throat. Perhaps she really had seen what, for lack of a better term, could be described as Grace's ghost.

CHAPTER 18

JACK—WEDNESDAY, APRIL 20, 1910,
10:45 A.M.

A gaggle of newspapermen clustered around the
Belvedere Hotel entrance. A hack in an ill-fitting green
suit recognized Jack and rushed over, pad and pencil at the
ready.

"Hey, Harden, what is it about this joint that makes people
cash in their chips?" he asked. "Do you think Holy Joe reverends
need to counsel guests? What about cops telling folks that
kicking one's own bucket is against the law? Come on, I need a
good quote."

"I'm not talking, least of all about the cops. They've already
got it in for me. Why are you still hounding around here,
anyway? Anna Gilbert's death is yesterday's news."

"Read the morning edition, you uninformed mug," said the
reporter. "Chance McCall chased pills with whiskey in his office
last night. First the Gilbert dame and now the hotel dick. Looks
like two suicides in two days."

Jack brushed past him and into the lobby where Snake Eyes
O'Toole and a uniformed cop stood with the hotel manager.

"That's the man I told you about, detective," said the
manager, pointing at Jack. "The one I saw assaulting Chance
yesterday afternoon."

O'Toole looked at Jack and grinned, his close-set, dark eyes cold and dead. "Thanks for saving us the trouble of hunting you down, snooper. Cuff this man and take him to the station."

"What's this about? I didn't hurt the guy," said Jack, presenting his wrists. The uniform snapped on the irons, good and tight.

The detective lit a cigarette and casually tossed the match on the plush rug. "Give the prisoner a ride on the midnight express." O'Toole's grin widened while watching the manager scurry to stomp on the flame.

Jack grimaced. The *midnight express* was a rough ride in the police wagon. It was a particular flavor of Baltimore cop curb-stone justice usually reserved for blacks. Any black man who wasn't totally submissive—and plenty who were—got thrown around in the back on the way to the lockup. Many guys wound up with broken bones. Or dead.

Jack was manhandled out the front door and thrown into the wagon, much to the appreciation of the gathered news hounds. After closing the wagon door, the cop punched Jack in the face, sending him to the floor. The nightstick was coming, and he turned to let his back take the blows. After laying down six good whacks, the guy was breathing hard—most likely from excitement rather than exercise.

The cop left and the wagon jerked forward, careened wildly from side to side. Jack managed to brace himself on the floor between the wagon benches, so the ride didn't mess him up too bad. And while the cop had laid into him, it wasn't the worst nightstick tapping he'd ever had.

He sat handcuffed in a chair in the station interrogation room for over an hour before O'Toole sauntered in. "How you feeling, Harden?"

"Fresh as a daisy. Look, there's no solid evidence connecting me to Chance's death, so there's no legit charge. You can get your jollies by knocking me around some more and even lock me up for a bit. But parading me in front of the press was a bad idea—Mayor Lipp's going to find out quick. You can bet the mayor doesn't want me unhappy with any part of the city government because then I'll be unhappy with him." Jack shook the cuffs. "You've had your fun. Now turn me loose."

"I know you and your little weirdo girlfriend got dirt on Lipp." O'Toole took out a hip flask and took a long pull. "But he ain't going to be mayor forever."

"He can complicate your life today."

The detective stowed the flask in his threadbare jacket. "That suit's just out of the store, ain't it?"

"Nah. I won it off a guy years ago playing chess."

O'Toole put two fingers in Jack's jacket breast pocket and pulled, ripping the cloth. "Fabric's second-rate. You got to get yourself better quality." He bent down and unlocked the cuffs.

"Louse," Jack muttered as he rubbed the welts on his wrists.

O'Toole gave the torn pocket flap another pull, tearing it halfway down the jacket. He stood back, hands on hips, a lead blackjack and .38 Police Special visible on his belt. "You man enough to come at me?"

"You dream about me, don't you Snake? Not about women, not about money. Me. Flattering, but strange."

The detective snorted. "You're just a two-bit peeper. City's full of them, just like cockroaches. I step on both whenever I get the chance."

"If I'm a roach, you've got nothing to lose telling me what McCall's death scene looked like."

"Had his head on the desk, a bottle at his elbow, and pills scattered everywhere. Manager says you were the last person seen with the guy before he turned up dead. Maybe you held a gun on him and made him do it."

"Is there any evidence of murder?"

"Just you assaulting the guy before he died. A smart prosecutor could make a manslaughter charge stick."

"All the smart prosecutors are now defense mouthpieces. What do you know about what happened to Anna Gilbert?"

"It's a suicide. Coroner wants to rule it that way, but a certain fruitcake skirt doctor won't let him do it just yet." O'Toole pulled out a set of brass knuckle-dusters and slipped them on his hand.

"Don't you think it's odd that two healthy people died two days in a row at the same place?"

"Happens." O'Toole dropped his fist with a bang, leaving four deep dents on the table. "People up and die all the time. I've seen two guys croak in this room within a week. Both somehow managed to grab my gun and shoot themselves in the head."

"You've got to strap that thing down better."

He called Sarah's house from the pay telephone in the lobby of the cop house. The line rang ten times before she answered.

"How are you doing?" he asked.

"Fine."

"You saw Reverend Smartwell? Did he have good information?"

"Yes."

"You've got the chance to cut open another body. Chance McCall is at the morgue. Supposedly killed himself, just like Anna. He was found dead in his office with pills and whiskey. The thing is, he was out of booze and broke when I saw him yesterday around 3:00 p.m."

"I will depart immediately." Click.

Jack hoped she would get helpful evidence from the autopsy. She would also have access to the police report. That information was important, as right now he knew next to nothing about how McCall died.

On second thought, scratch any hope of a helpful police report. Snake Eyes O'Toole was the investigating detective, and he was notorious for overlooking evidence and scrimping on paperwork. Whatever talent the guy had, it wasn't as a detective.

JACK WENT BACK TO THE BELVEDERE HOTEL AND stood outside, thinking. Lydia was the client, and she was paying them to investigate Anna Gilbert's death. Chance McCall let on that Anna was murdered just before he died in a manner similar to hers. The deaths had to be linked.

He needed to investigate McCall's death along with Anna's. The hotel manager would be a good source of dope, but the guy would call the cops if Jack showed his face inside. That left McCall's favorite watering hole across the street. The only thing the man liked more than drinking was talking, so it was definitely worth checking the place out.

"Yeah, I heard about Chance," said the barhop. He was an older man with an elaborate handlebar mustache complete with spit curls at each tip. "Shame. He left a twenty-dollar tab."

"He ever talk about shady, violent characters?" Jack sipped his water, annoyed that the glass was dirty. He needed to stay on the barman's good side and so didn't complain.

"You mean like a shifty guy with a fresh bruise on his cheek and a ripped suit coat?"

Jack tried tucking the torn flap into what was left of his suit jacket pocket, but the material flopped back out. "Not every guy the cops beat up is crooked. I'll bet most aren't."

The bartender shrugged. "Chance moaned about being behind on payments to a loan shark. He was scared out of his wits until a couple of days ago when his tune changed. Said he was coming into some big dough."

"Where was this cash coming from?"

"No idea." The man took a fresh wad of chewing tobacco from a Red Man pouch, stuck it in his mouth, and worked his jaws like a bellows for a few seconds before leaning down to spit a stream of juice. "But he kept saying 'nothing gets by Old Chance and his eagle eye.' Funny, because Old Chance was usually blind drunk."

"He hang around with anyone?"

"Whores and whatnot. Saw him the night before he died with a cute little floozie. Had this big white bow in her hair. Chance said she was a present from Lexie."

"Lexie Calhoun—she runs a cathouse over on Eden Street, right?"

"Yeah. Chance was a big customer, and Lexie can be very appreciative."

"Did you see him with any other men over the last week or so?"

The barkeep looked up and worked his tobacco chaw for a moment. "Come to think of it, yes. Couple of days ago, he came in with another big talker. Only this guy was cracking jokes nonstop. Even saw him do a bit of soft-shoe."

"Who was he?"

"Don't know his name, but he was a thin guy with glasses. Ordered something stupid like water. No, wait. Sarsaparilla."

Jack smiled and took a pull from his glass. "Water's a stupid drink?"

"I charge by the glass. You could've had a whiskey to take the edge off instead of your fifty-cent drink of nothing."

"It would take a whole lot more than whiskey to take my edge off. Trust me on that, pal."

THE BARTENDER DESCRIBED A GUY WHO SURE sounded like George Funston, the comedian clerk in Judge Lanvale's office. Why would Chance meet with Funston? Jack intended to find out.

But first up was learning about the gal with the bow who

was with Chance right before he died. It figured the guy would hang out with a prostitute in a bar. He needed a drinking buddy even more than he wanted sex.

But no matter how good a customer Chance had been, no way would Lexie Calhoun let him have a girl for nothing. Jack knew her reputation as a sharp grifter always on the make.

After a streetcar trip across town, he stood outside Lexie's address. He looked harum-scarum with his shredded suit and bruised face, but worse-looking guys probably showed up here regularly. He held his bankroll in plain view as he knocked.

A woman, well over fifty, opened the door. She had dabs of pink rouge on her cheeks and blood-red paint on her lips. Her tight, low-cut dress showed off curves that many a gal thirty years younger would kill for.

"Help you, honey?"

"Hope so. I'm lonely."

"Ooh," she said in a purry growl. "Lexie will be your friend. Come on in and stay awhile." She opened the door wide, eyeing his cash.

The place looked less like a dump than he expected. The two purple velvet sofas were new and had lace doilies on the arms. Quality wallpaper with red flocked lilies covered the walls, and a fancy Victrola played a ragtime tune. The sound was faint, meaning there were socks—or underwear—stuffed into the big enameled sound horn. Right above the Victrola was a photograph portrait of Mayor Adolph Lipp bearing his compliments and signature. Too funny—the rigidly moral, Bible-pounding Lipp staring down on a scene of continuous debauchery.

"Such a big, handsome fella like you would tempt a good girl to go bad." Lexie put a hand on an ample hip. "And a bad girl to go worse. What's your pleasure, sugar?"

He eyeballed the three young women sitting on the sofas, all wearing nothing but drawers and camisoles and flashing coy looks of varying sincerity. The oldest looked no more than twenty.

The madam rubbed against him with a husky growl. "Hey lover, just remember that an older gal is like a great cook. She gives you exactly what you want and serves it up just right."

"I want her." He pointed to a pretty girl with a floppy white bow on top of her head.

"Sure, play it safe with a rookie." Lexie gave a throaty laugh as she held out a hand. "Five-dollar house fee. You pay the kid separate."

He handed over the cash, and the girl headed for the stairs. "Come on down after for a chitchat," said Lexie. "I can keep a man up all day with my mouth." She winked and strolled back near the door, hips swaying like prairie grass before a thunderstorm.

The girl closed the bedroom door and peeled off her camisole.

"Tell me about Chance McCall. You took something from him, right?"

She smiled. "Talk or sex, take your pick, baby. Both cost the same."

Jack held up a five-dollar bill. "Talk."

"Lexie told me to lift a receipt from the guy. It had a picture of a champagne bottle on it. He kept it in a trouser pocket, so it was like stealing candy from a baby."

"What did the receipt say? Any names?"

She looked away. "Don't know. I can't read. Just gave the thing to Lexie like she asked."

"Thanks." He gave her the cash and went downstairs.

"She should've kept you up way longer than that, sugar," said Lexie with a sly grin.

"Who paid you to steal that receipt off Chance McCall?"

"Ten bucks." She held out a palm.

He handed over the money. She counted it and stashed it below her neckline. "I don't know who the guy was."

Jack grabbed an arm and pushed her against the wall. "You've got to do better."

"Ooh, tough guy, huh?" She smiled.

"Back off, mister." One of the underwear-clad young women pointed a pistol at him. "You wouldn't be the first bastard I shot."

He let go of the madam. "I'm not leaving until you tell me more."

"You didn't give me a chance to finish, babe." Lexie looked at the woman with the gun. "Plug him if he touches me again."

"I'm listening." Jack remained standing close.

"This guy calls and says Chance has something of his—a receipt. Offers me ten bucks upfront if one of my girls can get the thing and ten more if I send it to him at a post office box. I said okay, and the upfront dough arrived in an unmarked envelope. Got the rest after I mailed the receipt back."

"What did the guy sound like on the telephone? Young or old, what?"

"Just a man, sweetheart. He did crack a bad joke, though— 'the girl needs to take a chance with Chance and make him pant without his pants.'" She rolled her eyes.

"Okay." He turned to leave.

"Come on back soon, you hear?" Lexie planted a sticky kiss on his neck just before he made it out the door.

CHAPTER 19

SARAH—WEDNESDAY, APRIL 20, 1910,
2:00 P.M.

*H*orrible, stinking mud. The hansom wheels sunk almost a foot deep into the muck, and the unfortunate horse made a gruesome sucking sound each time it lifted a hoof. Running parallel to the Jones Falls, President Street was the first to collect flood sludge and the last to lose it.

Sarah did not recoil from the smell of formaldehyde, putrefying flesh, or any number of other odors associated with the dead. But this disgusting glop was worse than anything she had encountered in an autopsy chamber. She pressed a glove tightly to her nose and mouth and tried to inhale as little as possible.

The carriage stopped just beyond the morgue entrance. "This is as close as I can get, miss," said the driver through the roof trap. "Sorry." She paid him and looked down from the open carriage door. Four steps would be required through the shimmering mess before reaching the steps.

Bunching up her long skirts, she plunged one foot, then the other, into the gloppy ooze. Lifting the first foot took so much effort that she staggered and fell on one knee into the muck. She stood and managed the remaining distance to the steps, losing a shoe along the way.

The morgue foyer had dirty newspapers scattered on the

floor. Sarah sat on a nearby bench and pulled off the orphaned shoe. After scanning the room and seeing no one, she hiked her filthy skirts far up. Her silk stockings drooping with black foulness, one of them soiled well up the thigh. She undid the corset garters and peeled off the ruined hosiery. Legs spread wide, she worked with a dirty towel found on the floor to remove as much mud as possible from herself.

A sudden sense of discomfort caused her to look up. The coroner was leering at her, his red, fleshy face twisted into a perverted smile. She hurriedly pushed her skirts down. Stomach lurching and face burning, she barely noticed the heavy wetness against her bare legs under the muddy fabric.

"Well, hello there, sweetness." The smirking coroner strolled over and handed her a clean towel while ogling her bare feet.

She vomited on his shoes.

"What the—damn it!" He stepped back and shook a foot energetically. "You are the most disgusting broad I've ever run into."

Sarah dabbed her lips with the towel. "You are to address me as *doctor*. Is that sufficiently clear?"

"You minx—"

"At all times, under all circumstances." She stood and marched past him to the dressing room. Her skirts were an abomination beyond dirty, and she was sorely tempted to take them off and make do with just a floor-length white surgical gown, but that seemed immodest. A much too large pair of rubber boots did provide provisional footwear. After removing her hat, she washed her hands and donned a gown.

The man known as Chance McCall was laid out on the autopsy table in the body chamber. In the harsh electric light, the skin had a definite yellow tinge. Lifting an eyelid, she noticed a yellowing of the sclera—signs of liver disease, possibly cirrhosis.

"Hello, Dr. Kennecott," said the young medical examiner.

"Greetings to you, doctor. Will you permit me to conduct the postmortem?"

"Certainly. But before you begin, I have the lab test results from Anna Gilbert."

"What do they indicate?"

The attending clerk handed over a clipboard. "The stomach fluid was a mix of alcohol and barbiturates," said the medical examiner, looking at the report. "Blood tests reveal the drug dose was sufficient to seriously relax the central nervous system and perhaps cause the loss of consciousness."

"Not a bad thing for a gal," said the coroner with a breath freshly loaded with whiskey. "All relaxed and not jibber-jabbering."

Sarah ignored him. "The ingested drug was less than a fatal dose?"

"Yes. And there was no sign of any other toxin."

"Okay, so if it's not a suicide it's a sudden death." The coroner belched and then hiccupped. "Let's call it that and get the Gilbert broad off the books."

"No." Sarah stamped her big boot with a hollow thump. "Additional evidence may yet emerge to prove she was murdered."

"And pigs might fly," the coroner said with a grumble.

Sarah turned to the autopsy table. "I will now commence an examination of the body, which is that of a white male, approximately forty-five years of age." A look at the front and the rear of the corpse revealed no sign of trauma. She estimated the time of death as roughly twelve to eighteen hours earlier.

She used a magnifying glass to look at the ball of the right foot. "There is a fresh puncture wound on the ball of the right foot. It possibly is the site of a hypodermic injection. Note that a similar wound was found in the same location on the body of Anna Gilbert."

"Ridiculous." The coroner lumbered over to a table and rummaged in a box. "These were the stiff's." He thrust out a pair of men's shoes, soles up. One had a red thumbtack embedded in the heel, and the other had a white thumbtack in the sole. "That puncture mark on his foot is from a tack, not from a needle. Stop making things up."

Sarah remembered Jack saying the body was found with a bottle of liquor and scattered pills. Perhaps another piece of evidence would point to a hypodermic. "Let us review the police report documenting the scene."

Silence.

"Mr. Coroner?" Sarah continued to look at the body.

"What?"

"Where is the police report detailing what was found near the body?"

"Beats me."

Sarah turned and stepped so close to the man that his liquor reek was almost unbearable. "It is your job to liaise with the police and obtain reports before the postmortem. Why have you failed to carry out your responsibility?"

"I was busy."

Her shoulders shook as her throat tightened. "You are incompetent and unfit for the position you hold."

"Calm down, honey. Just because you flashed your skinny stems at me—"

"That's enough." The medical examiner took the coroner's arm. "You're drunk, and I won't hear any more of your insults directed at Dr. Kennecott."

"That so, sonny boy? Well, it so happens—" The coroner yanked his arm away with too much force. He stumbled and had the misfortune of slipping on a wet spot and falling hard on his rear end.

"Damn, that hurts," he said, getting to his feet slowly. "Give me a shot for the pain, doc."

"Clerk," said the medical examiner. "Call an ambulance."

"What? It'll take forever for them to get here. All you got to do is give me a little morphine—"

"Clerk, before you call, please escort the coroner to the front office."

After the man left, Sarah forced herself to make eye contact with the medical examiner. "Thank you for your assistance. It is appreciated."

The man threw up his hands. "That coroner's an ignorant fossil. I can't believe how he treats you—the most brilliant pathologist I ever expect to meet."

Sarah dropped her eyes and felt herself swaying. Until today, no man had seen any part of her leg above the lowest part of the calf. And until today, no man had ever called her brilliant.

She returned to autopsying McCall's body. The internal examination revealed cirrhosis of the liver and coronary arteries with substantial plaque, but neither condition was the cause of death. As with Anna Gilbert, there was no clear sign of anything fatal. She collected samples from the body and set them aside for laboratory analysis.

After changing out of the surgical gown, Sarah threw her single shoe into the trash and clumped into the lobby in the oversized boots and mud-caked skirts. The medical examiner had told the orderlies to shovel a path from the morgue steps to a cab. While she waited for them to finish, the coroner lay slumped on a bench while shouting angrily into a telephone microphone about "Kennecott's vulgar mistreatment" and "profound disrespect for a person of prominence."

Who could possibly take such a man seriously?

SHE TOOK A LONG BATH AT HOME AND CHANGED INTO a new evening dress for the dinner and séance at the Lanvale residence. Sarah had thought the dress far too revealing when she tried it on in the shop, but her friend Margaret had insisted on the purchase. The style was new and daring: translucent pink chiffon with scalloped short sleeves, deeply scooped neckline, high waist, and slim profile. The hem ended nearly a foot above the ankle. It was by far the shortest skirt she had ever worn.

The sales lady claimed the item did not need a petticoat. "The new look is Grecian goddess," she said. "Diaphanous and free-flowing. Simple and unconstrained." Looking at herself now in the mirror, Sarah could see the faint outline of her legs through the sheer fabric. She felt practically naked.

She was about to pull the dress off and replace it with something more familiar—and much less audacious—when a knock came at the door. Jack had arrived early. She put on the new white pumps Margaret claimed matched the dress and flew downstairs.

Jack stood speechless as he looked at her up and down. She fussed with the neckline, trying to pull it higher. "You may enter."

He stepped inside. "Sarah—gosh, do you look nice." His eyes lingered on her décolletage.

"I am pleased you approve of my appearance. I am, however, uncomfortable with your unabashed appraisal." She turned and marched into the library.

"Sorry about the googly eyes," he said while following. "But a guy's going to look at a pretty girl in a dress like that."

She spun around to face him. "You regard me as—pretty?" She was used to overhearing talk about "poor, plain Sarah," how she was "far too thin—no hips, no bust," and that "no man is *ever* going to look at her twice." She was indifferent to such comments, having little interest in her appearance, and even less in drawing the male gaze.

"Well, yeah. You don't go all-out like some gals, but I like that about you. And when you *do* dress up—" He was looking away, turning hat in hands.

She noticed his suit was dirty, with a big flap of torn material hanging from the chest of his jacket. Buttons were missing from his shirt. She was about to comment when she saw a smear of red paint on his neck in the shape of two lips. "I see evidence on your person of a woman's kiss. Was she more attractive than myself?"

"What?" He wiped his neck, looked at the red paint, and laughed. "Oh, golly, don't worry. She was a madam—you know, the kind who runs a bordello."

"Did you engage in fornication with her or with one of her employees?"

"Sarah. There was no—you know." He looked up at the ceiling. "Look. You insisted from the start that romance was out of the question for us. If we're just business partners, why do you even care what I do with other women?"

She stared at the wall. Jack's logic was correct. "I apologize if my question was interpreted as intrusive."

"I got tangled up with the bordello madam because I think she's connected with the death of Chance McCall."

She drew a deep breath. "Your appearance is inappropriate for our social event. Fortunately, I have clothing of yours that you may change into."

"You kept that old suit of mine? The one I was wearing when you took care of me after Snake Eyes coldcocked me last year?"

"Yes." The suit was hanging in her bedroom closet, mended and cleaned. She regularly tended to it with a lint brush, which she never did for any of her own clothing. "I will retrieve the garment and place it in a bathroom upstairs. You may then prepare yourself for our visit to the Lanvale residence."

He took her bare arm and pulled her close. Flustered, she dropped her head, heart pounding furiously. What was he doing? With a jolt, she realized he was initiating an intimate encounter. How should she respond?

He let go of her arm, breathing heavily. "Sorry for that. I'm a fresh mug." They remained standing very close.

Sarah knew that if she raised her lips, he would kiss her. Time slowed in a peculiar manner as she considered the terrifying prospect. No, she would not do it. Well, maybe she would. But how does one kiss a man? Her ineptitude surely would turn a tender moment awkward and regrettable. She stepped away, hands flapping in a blur. "We should review what we have learned concerning our case. I will begin."

He cleared his throat. "Sure thing."

She began pacing, trying to relax. The strong physical pull in her groin was more disconcerting than the flood of emotion in her head. "Toxicology tests reveal that Anna Gilbert ingested a sublethal dose of barbiturate." Reciting concrete facts was calming. "From a medical standpoint, the evidence points to a natural cause of death: sudden cardiac arrest. I hope we may obtain additional evidence that proves homicide."

"What about Chance?"

"I autopsied the body this afternoon, and, pending laboratory tests, the death also appears to be sudden cardiac arrest." Now standing still, Sarah glanced at Jack and saw that he was looking at her legs. She turned away. "He had similar puncture wounds in the same location as did Anna Gilbert—the ball of the right foot. Again, we need further evidence to prove homicide."

"Yeah. McCall hinted about blackmailing Anna's killer with something he found, like a receipt. I think the killer arranged for a prostitute to steal the receipt back from McCall, then killed him, just to be sure he didn't cause any more problems."

Sarah returned to pacing furiously, filmy dress fluttering.

"Please stop trooping around the room. I'm getting tired just watching you."

She ignored him.

"Something bothers me about Lydia," said Jack. "She used the telephone to contact Anna at the hotel. Callers have to ask for guests by name so the switchboard can connect them. That means Lydia had to know about Anna's fake name. Why did she lie about that?" He clutched at his back. "Hey, you mind if I sit down? Got a couple of taps from a nightstick today."

She retrieved a hardback chair. "Remove your jacket and shirt. I will examine you."

"It's no big deal. The cop didn't have his heart in it."

She helped him undress and noted the half-dozen oblong contusions, all blue-black, striping his back. Some were swollen and oozing blood. "These are serious injuries."

"I'm fine."

She fetched ice along with her medical bag and applied a compress to his back. "You should remain in bed for the duration of the evening."

"Not on your life. We're going." A muscle spasm caused him again to flinch with a groan.

Sarah tapped her foot, weighing risks. The contusions were not life-threatening. Jack's episodic, hallucinatory anguish, on the other hand, was potentially deadly. He needed whatever kind of emotional placebo Lydia's séance might provide.

"It is a violation of medical ethics to use narcotics in place of proper treatment. As you know, I take ethics most seriously."

"Yeah, so?"

"I will make an exception in this instance." She pulled a bottle from her bag, poured a bit of its contents on a cotton swab, and dabbed his injuries.

He sat up. "I don't care what rule you broke because all the pain is gone."

"You must dress." She capped the bottle and returned the tincture of heroin to her medical bag. "It is time for us to attend the séance."

CHAPTER 20

*N*iblett gave Sarah a prim smile. "Miss Kennecott."
The smile faded as he looked at Jack. "Mr. Harden."
But unlike Jack's last visit, the butler allowed him inside
without instructions to wipe his feet.

"May I take your wrap, Miss Kennecott?"

"Yes."

"Your hat." Niblett extended a stiff hand. "Sir."

"Nah. I'll keep it."

"Jack. This is a formal event," said Sarah.

She had coached him about the hat business, along with
other dos and don'ts for this carnival, but he'd already forgotten
most of them. He took off his derby. Niblett handled it like a
dirty diaper before leading them into the parlor.

Jack was on cloud nine and didn't mind the butler's snooti-
ness. Arriving at Sarah's, he had been tense, close to a breaking
point from his worsening nerves. But whatever Sarah put on his
back took away every trace of his physical and mental pain.

The guests included Mrs. Lanvale and Barnabas, Reverend
Smartwell, and several other people Jack didn't know. Lydia,
wearing an airy, high-waisted white tunic with bare arms,

rushed over to them. Fuller and Miss Pike followed in her billowy wake.

"Sarah. How wonderful to see you—your dress is absolutely stunning. And hello, Jack. You're even more handsome than I remember." She offered a hand along with a warm smile.

He had the odd urge to kiss the back of her hand like he'd seen in moving picture shows. He gave it a gentle shake instead as Sarah went to look at books on a shelf. "You look good yourself, Lydia." She was taller with a longer face but had a definite resemblance to her daughter—the same delicate features, the same slim build. But unlike Sarah, Lydia knew how to flirt.

"I just adore you, Jack. You are so delightful." She laughed while adjusting a long white scarf around her swanlike neck. "I'm glad this dress appeals to a good-looking man. I'm used to only attracting spirits."

"I can't speak for the spirits, but I guarantee the men in this room will have their eyes on you tonight."

"I'm blushing." Lydia laughed while fanning her face with a hand. "You're sweet to flatter me. See that space?" She pointed to an enclosure of four curtains hanging from rods around a table. "That's where we will convene after dinner. It is already shimmering with spiritual potential."

A weird chill gripped Jack as he looked at the enclosure. The space was shimmering all right—with dangerous, unnatural energy. It was the same feeling he had in the rooms where Anna Gilbert and Chance McCall were murdered.

"Jack—are you well?" She moved close and touched his arm.

He turned quickly back to Lydia. "Yeah, fine." She smelled great—like lilac soap and a faint dusting of bath powder.

"I asked you if Sarah be all right during the séance. I don't want the spirits to make her distraught."

"I can think of only one thing that makes her distraught, and it's a person, not a spirit." Jack shrugged his shoulders, wondering what this woman's game was. Why didn't she own up to being Sarah's mother? And why did she seem fully recovered from the shock of Anna Gilbert's death?

"Lydia, you gorgeous doll. I'm so glad to see you in action, finally." A paunchy man with a trimmed red beard and wearing a tweed suit joined them. The suit had seen better days and had leather patches sewn over the jacket elbows.

"Hello, Professor," said Lydia as she stiffly accepted the man's embrace. "Where is your student?"

"Left him home. He's not much for social events."

"I see. Professor William Jaworski, let me introduce Jack Harden, a private investigator. The professor is an investigator himself—of supernatural phenomenon."

"Right now, finishing my book about the phenomenal Miss Nightingale is my only interest." The man grinned. "Amazing things happen around you, don't they, Lydia?"

"I am just a servant of the spirits, Professor."

"Oh, come now, darling." His grin grew larger. "Did the spirits encourage your Boston benefactor to change her will and leave you everything—just before she died?"

"The woman changed her will voluntarily, without interference from any entity, living or dead." Lydia gave a tight smile.

"The newspapers say you got a fortune," said Jaworski. "People have been known to do terrible things for less money."

"If you'll excuse me," said Lydia. "I must mingle."

Jack's dislike of Jaworski deepened as he shook the man's repellently damp, limp hand.

"That true about someone dying in Boston and leaving Lydia lots of dough?"

"You're a private dick, Harden. Dig up your own dirt."

Dropping the guy's hand, Jack wiped his palm against a trouser leg. "And you're a sleaze merchant looking to make a quick buck with a trashy book."

"That's a hundred percent true—about the money." Jaworski gave an openmouthed laugh, showing several missing molars. "I want lots of dollars to come running at me as quick as they possibly can."

"I thought you professor guys only cared about thinking deep thoughts in ivy-covered towers."

"I've done my penance teaching boneheaded rich kids—or as I like to say, casting imitation pearls before actual swine." He laughed. "It's time to embrace the free market, my friend. Offer up a product in demand at a good price and then just lay back and collect money."

"Just like a whore, huh?"

"Yep. Exactly like that." Jaworski chuckled and clapped Jack on the back. "I saw you come in with Sarah Kennecott. Now there's a study in contrasts: the coarse and the refined, the dick and the brain. You must favor, as Miss Austen says, 'obstinate, headstrong girls.'"

"I don't know any Miss Austen. And Sarah's a lady, not a girl."

"Come on, don't be a fuddy-duddy, man. That's a quote from *Pride and Prejudice*. You know, Jane Austen. Sarah's like Elizabeth Bennet in some ways."

"Elizabeth who?" This guy was getting on Jack's nerves big-time.

"Elizabeth and Sarah are both smart but also prone to making decisions they regret."

"Stop being cute, pal. Decisions about what?"

"Don't get all worked up. All I'm talking about is Sarah's stubborn refusal to chat with me about Lydia." Jaworski lit up a white pipe with some old bearded guy carved on the bowl. "She needs to tell her side of the story for my book. People are dying to know about the daughter."

Jack leaned down into the foul-smelling smoke wreathing the guy's face. "Leave Sarah alone. Or I promise to really get worked up."

Jaworski laughed. "You're a no-nonsense gumshoe, all right. A man who prowls the mean streets among the defeated, the dispossessed, the dangerous. Someone who dishes out his own brand of justice, someone who—"

Jack was ready to punch the guy in the nose but chose to walk away.

"Hello again, Mr. Harden, sir," said Reverend Smartwell, standing nearby with Mrs. Lanvale. "I trust you are having an entrancing—or shall I say *spirited*—evening?" He gave a lame chortle and then radiated a ridiculous grin.

"I hope the man can begin to appreciate his good fortune," said Mrs. Lanvale. She raised her chin and issued a loud sniff before walking off.

"And I hope she appreciates that I scrubbed under my toenails, just for her," said Jack.

"That is commendable of you, sir. I like a man who attends carefully to his grooming, indeed I do." Smartwell's eyes popped open wide as he wrung his hands. "Was your comment intended in jest, pray tell?"

"Don't worry about it."

"Please accept my humble apologies for missing the thrust of your bon mot." The reverend issued a forced laugh. "You are a droll one, sir. Quite waggish."

"Tell me, reverend, do you know anything about Mrs. Lanvale trying to get her mitts on Lydia's cash?"

"What?" Smartwell gave an uncertain chuckle.

"I'm dead serious."

"Sir. I have the utmost respect for Mrs. Lanvale." The man blinked rapidly, smiled, and then settled into a comical look of stricken embarrassment. "You are jesting with me again, are you not?"

A vibrating metallic sound caused Smartwell and the others to move off in the same direction all at once. Jack stood flat-footed until Niblett approached.

"Did you not hear the gong?" asked the butler.

"The only time I've heard anything like that was in a cabaret just before the hootchy-cootchy dancing girls came out."

The butler frowned as he spoke slowly and loudly, as if to someone who did not know the language. "Dinner. Is. Served."

Jack trotted to the dining room and found a long table crowded with gleaming crystal, silver, and china. He tapped the shoulder of an older gent sitting next to Sarah. "Excuse me, pops, but I'd like to sit next to my date."

"I beg your pardon?" The man looked as if a particularly obnoxious street beggar had cornered him.

"Jack. You are not seated here," said Sarah with a slash of her hand. "Look for your name on a card. That is your place setting."

Jack looked down and read the man's card: "Major General Augustus Tiberius Warfield IV, U.S. Army, Retired."

"Sorry to bother you, Augie." Walking around the table, he had to squint hard to make out the fussy curlicue script on the place cards. Those for the men had fancy titles such as Reverend, Professor, and Esquire except for one labeled: "Jock Harmon." Close enough. He sat down between two older ladies who both gave him identical scowls.

Jack looked over his place setting, which had enough silverware, plates, and glasses for six people. He had intended to watch the other guests for clues about the murder case. Looks like he had a more pressing need for clues about which fork to use.

Barnabas Lanvale stood up and made some curt welcoming remarks before introducing "my dear, dear mother." Mrs. Lanvale rose and began speaking in a fluttery, theatrical voice. A long story followed about how Lydia had, through hypnosis, sharpened Mrs. Lanvale's own psychic powers considerably. "I now converse with my dear departed husband more than when he was alive," she said.

"Lucky him," said Jack softly.

Mrs. Lanvale glared at the assembly for a moment before finishing her address with flowery praise for Lydia and her pull with the spirits.

As the food was served, Jack could hear Jaworski laying his obnoxious patter on Lydia. Reverend Smartwell sat on her other side and offered her flowery praise when Jaworski was busy eating. Lydia, for her part, mostly smiled.

Nobody else said much of anything. Barnabas's face grew slack as he drank glass after glass of wine, while Luther Fuller and Lucinda Pike kept eagle eyes on Lydia. General Warfield tried to interest Sarah in a story about the Panama Canal but gave up when she ignored him while staring at her plate.

"So, you see any ghosts lately?" Jack asked the lady on his right.

She turned to him with a sour look. "I assume you mean spirits, young man."

"There's a difference?"

She tut-tutted as if witnessing someone else's misbehaving child. "Most certainly. A ghost is someone who died a tragic death and has unfinished business with the living. They are menacing and dangerous. We do not seek them—they come to us unbidden, such as Banquo did to Macbeth."

"You mean Jay McBath—the guy who works in city hall?"

The woman tilted her head and gave him an odd look.

"Guess not." Jack shuffled his feet, realizing she had done the same thing as Jaworski—dropped some highbrow names to show off. And to demonstrate how stupid he was. "Anyway, how are spirits different from ghosts?"

The woman made a show of rolling her eyes before answering. "Spirits are shades of people who die a natural death. They visit because they love us, and we them. Spirits are interested in the affairs of the living and care about our hopes and worries. They want to help us. That is why the living seek to communicate with them. I'm hoping to talk with my dear departed sister this evening."

"Does that mean we're only going to see friendly ghosts?" Jack felt his heart drop.

"Spirits, young man, spirits. And yes, they are mostly

amiable. Although frightening, even dangerous apparitions may appear if a person among us has too much dark energy." The woman raised her eyebrows. "Are you troubled by ghosts?"

"I sure am."

She quickly looked away and said nothing more.

Jack wondered if this séance thing would be a boring family reunion rather than an opportunity to confront his ghosts. He slurped down a thin soup that tasted musty and woodsy and then turned his attention to the choice cut of meat on his plate with knife-scraping, lip-smacking gusto. More dirty looks came his way, but he paid them no mind.

After the last serving, Mrs. Lanvale tapped a glass. "Dear guests, it is time to move to the séance station. It is vital to keep the dinner seating arrangement, as the spirits receive exciting energy from participants sitting next to the opposite sex."

Jack failed to see how his placement between two matronly ladies would excite anything for anybody but sat as instructed at the round table in the parlor. The table's center held a fancy candelabra with six lit candles, a deck of odd-looking cards, and a steaming tureen of chicken soup. When everyone was seated, Niblett closed the curtains and withdrew.

"We already had dinner—what's the soup for?" he asked the lady on his left.

"The spirits," she said without looking at him. "The aroma reminds them of the living. Stop talking."

Jack squirmed in his seat, deeply uneasy. He'd come here hoping to confront his dead Moros. But that optimistic intent had melted, leaving him with an icy wad of ominous dread in his gut. The feeling was different than his usual ghost-related terror—it was as if some supernatural force threatened others besides himself.

"Let's get started," said Lydia. "I've held dozens of séances, and no two have been the same. I can't tell you what to expect. Sometimes hardly anything happens. Other times things can be a bit chaotic, with multiple spirits trying to communicate all at once."

"Do our spirits know we are here and wish to communicate with them?" asked a woman.

"Yes," said Lydia. "But the veil that separates our world from theirs waxes and wanes. They are also sensitive to our auras—the distinctive psychic energy field that surrounds each of us. That energy can either draw or repel spirits. We have some very powerful emanations here tonight." She shivered and sat still.

Jack drew in a breath, thinking her trance was starting. But there was more preliminary hoodoo.

"I will draw a tarot card to set the stage for our experience." Lydia flipped over a card showing an old guy walking on a dark road with a lantern. "Fascinating." Her voice was calm and silky smooth. "The hermit card means someone among us does not want to be here. But that person will get valuable information tonight."

Jack glanced at Sarah across the table. As usual, her expression was blank, but he knew all this talk of auras and spirits must be driving her batty. He was grateful that she was putting up with all of this for him.

"We will now join hands, and I will ask my spirit guide to join us. She will then invite other spirits. Often, they speak through me, although sometimes they will knock, move the table, or otherwise announce themselves."

"Will we see them?" asked Jaworski. "I'd love a good show. We all would."

"We most likely will not see them—although sometimes one can catch a glimpse of their form." Lydia drew in a deep breath. "No matter what happens, rest assured you are safe. The spirits wish us no harm. Let us begin."

Everyone held hands, and Lydia bowed her head. Within seconds she began murmuring, and then her body jerked, and her head flung back. She spoke, again in that whispery child's voice.

Admonished by her buckled lips
Let every babbler be.
The only secret people keep
Is Immortality.

Feet shuffled. A chair creaked. Jack's back twinged—Sarah's magic lotion was wearing off.

"Abigail. Abigail. I am here." The voice coming from Lydia was that of a woman with a broad southern accent.

"Lillian! Is that you?" asked the woman to his right. "It's Abigail."

"Abigail. Are you well? I miss you so."

"Oh, Lillian." The woman next to him trembled and gripped Jack's hand tightly. "How wonderful it is to hear your voice. I am well. How are you?"

"We long for the touch of our living loves, but we are content."

"We?" The woman gripped his hand even harder. "Who else is with you?"

"So many. We all watch over you. We know you are lonely and often fearful. You may rest easy, however, as we are always present to comfort you. And know that a person named Mary will soon have wonderful news. Goodbye, now."

"Wait—I have so many questions!"

"Who are you? What is your name?" Lydia's voice was almost too soft to make sense of the words. "Please . . . no . . ." She abruptly lurched forward and began speaking some foreign tongue in a high-pitched, sing-song voice. It was Jack's turn to shake—the language sounded like Moro or something like it.

The bloody Moro woman with her baby stood on the table staring at him—the same woman hacked to death before his eyes during the Bud Dajo massacre. It was the exact ghostly figure that had tormented him mercilessly over the last four years. "You again," he said. "What do you want? Tell me or leave me alone!"

"Shh!" whispered the woman on his left as she kicked his shin, hard.

The ghostly woman disappeared. He barely had time to react when Lydia started speaking again, this time in the gruff, deep voice of a man. "Jared, I am not happy."

Jack looked over at Reverend Smartwell. The man's eyes looked ready to pop out of his head.

"Jared. I expected more from you."

"Daddy?" asked Smartwell in a small voice.

"I do not laugh. I do not smile. I do not approve of your work."

"But Daddy, I'm not a bad person. And I'm still a Methodist at heart."

Lydia grunted and mumbled softly and then went quiet. The only sound was someone's labored breathing. The hair on Jack's neck still stood on end from having seen the Moro woman. His nerves were pulled as tight as a piano wire.

A breeze made the candles flicker. Jack felt a creepy panic in his gut along with a strong sense of evil. At first, the figure was hard to make out against the curtained walls. It was a white shape floating as if suspended by a string. The pale vision stopped behind Lucinda Pike, who cried out as if in pain. Abruptly, the figure disappeared with a gust of wind that blew out the candles and submerged everything into darkness.

"Lydia, why did you conjure that demon to harm me?" said Miss Pike vehemently. "You sent the very same creature to hurt Anna, didn't you? I had no idea you were such a wicked, wicked woman!"

Someone screamed.

"Turn on the lights," said Jack. "The lights—quick!"

The gaslights began glowing and revealed Miss Pike lying face-up on the table. Sarah started to rhythmically press on the fallen woman's chest, then feeling for a pulse, over and over, before eventually stopping.

"Alert the police," said Sarah. "She is deceased."

161

CHAPTER 21

SARAH—WEDNESDAY, APRIL 20, 1910, 9:00 P.M.

*L*ydia reclined on a divan, semiconscious and babbling softly. Sarah declared it a temporary state.

"Are you sure?" Luther Fuller asked while clutching Lydia's limp hand. "I've never seen her like this. And Miss Pike is the one—was the one—who knew how best to bring her back from a trance."

"She is suffering from emotional shock," said Sarah. "It should resolve within seventy-two hours."

"Okay, miss, tell me what you saw when the lady had her fit and died," said the responding police detective. The man wore a rumpled blue suit and had a damp cigar jammed into the corner of his mouth.

"I witnessed a white figure appear behind Lucinda Pike before the candles were extinguished," said Sarah. "I heard her loudly exclaim and then fall upon the table. I responded at once and applied repeated external chest compressions in a vain attempt at revival. After detecting no pulse, I declared her dead."

"You're that lady doctor. Harden's dame."

"I am nobody's *dame*, detective."

"Whatever you say, sweetie pie. How do you think she died?"

"I find the term 'sweetie pie' offensive. If you are requesting my opinion as a physician, you will address me as *doctor*."

"You're one of them nasty suffragettes, ain't you?" He squinted at her. "Okay, doc. What happened to this lady?"

"It appears she suffered volatile agitation with both somatic and emotional manifestations, followed by a sudden cardiac arrest."

The detective grunted. "In other words, she dropped dead."

"I cannot provide a definitive opinion without a forensic examination. But I will note the fresh puncture wound on the right side of the decedent's neck. The wound is consistent with injection from a hypodermic syringe."

"Yeah, yeah." The detective walked over to Mrs. Lanvale, who was holding a crystal tumbler nearly drained of whiskey, Barnabas at her side. "Evening, Judge. Mrs. Lanvale, ma'am. Real sorry this happened to you, in your fine home, of all places. I've called the morgue wagon. All this will be cleared up quick as a wink."

"Detective." Professor Jaworski approached. "I want it in your official report that a ghost appeared just before the woman went hysterical and died. I saw it with my own eyes. So did the others."

The detective rolled the cigar with his lips to the other side of his mouth. "You want me to report that a ghost killed her? Forget it, pal."

"It is unconditionally true," said Reverend Smartwell. "I distinctly saw a form behind Miss Pike just before she . . . expired. I would characterize the form as supernatural. A spectral visitor not of this world, dare I say."

"You were all playing a spooky game. It played a trick on your minds."

"Detective," Jack called from the open pantry door. "Come see this."

Sarah followed the detective and saw Jack pointing to a rubbish bin with a bedsheet, eyeholes cut in the middle, draped over the side.

"A ghost costume?" Jack asked.

"If so, the ghost has his name written on this tag," said the detective as he peered at a corner of the sheet. "Niles Niblett. Ring a bell?"

"The butler," said Jack. "Not sure why I know this but aren't butlers in charge of pantries?"

"The term *butler's pantry* refers to a space such as this where serving dishes are stored," said Sarah. "Typically, the house butler oversees the china and the silver in a cabinet such as that." She pointed to a small chest of drawers with a sturdy lock.

Jack gestured to Niblett, who stood nearby. "Hey, Nibs. Come open this up for us."

"I see no reason to do so," said Niblett, back ramrod straight.

The detective sighed. "Just do it, son. Don't make me drag Mrs. Lanvale in here and order you. The woman's a wreck, poor thing. And we sure don't want to rile up the judge, tell you what."

Niblett walked stiffly to the chest, inserted a key, and pulled open the first drawer. Laying in full view was a hypodermic syringe and a nearly empty vial of clear liquid. "I do not know where these objects came from," he said. "I have never seen them before."

"Looks like you dressed up in a sheet and killed the lady with a jab from that needle." The detective wiped his forehead with the back of his hand. "Now I got to run you into the station and do the damn paperwork. And I was really looking forward to a bucket of beer at the saloon."

"I didn't kill her." Niblett staggered against the shelves. "I swear I did not."

Sarah looked down at the objects. The syringe was an older

model with an unusually large-diameter needle and a complicated piston latch. The vial was of a type seen in chemistry laboratories. "Detective," she said. "For the butler to have killed Lucinda Pike with these objects, he would need experience with a specialty syringe and access to a laboratory. I recommend you determine if Mr. Niblett meets those requirements. After you check thoroughly for finger marks, of course."

"Think you know everything, don't you, cupcake?" The detective turned to Jack and shook his head. "There just ain't no accounting for taste."

SARAH, DRESSED IN HER FAVORITE NIGHTDRESS, dressing gown, and slippers, sat with Jack in her library. "Multiple persons observed a sheet-clad figure appear just before Lucinda Pike cried out and then collapsed. Let us assume for now the figure injected her with a substance that caused her death. The perpetrator then discarded the sheet and placed the syringe and vial in the silver cabinet."

"Okay, but—"

"The puncture wounds I observed on Anna Gilbert and Chance McCall matched the large bore of the syringe found in the cabinet. As did the wound on Lucinda Pike."

"Before we get too deep into that stuff, tell me how you're doing," said Jack. "You've had a tough couple of days."

"I am . . ." Why was he pursuing this topic? Sarah had barely managed to hold her emotions at bay since returning from the séance. She was teetering on the edge of another breakdown, and the last thing she wanted was to talk about her feelings. Her chin quivered, and she was horrified to hear a muffled sob rise from her throat.

Jack reached over the table and put his hand on hers. She could not bear to surrender to her sadness again and pulled her hand away. Holding off tears was a mighty struggle that she was losing. She grabbed a linen napkin and pressed it to her face.

"You can talk or not," said Jack softly. "I'll stay or go. Whatever you want."

"Stay. Please." She wiped the tears and blew her nose into the napkin, a terrible thing to do, but she did not care. "I am still coping with the fact that Lydia is my mother. The murder of Miss Pike during the exhibition has added to my sense of sorrow and outrage."

"I can see it's hard for you."

Sarah tossed the napkin on the table. "I do not wish to discuss my emotional state at this time."

"As long as you're okay."

She never in her life had uttered the vulgar phrase *shut up*, but she was now close to shouting it at the top of her voice. If Jack kept pressing, she would either do that or force a pathetically clumsy kiss on him. Perhaps both. She had to turn the conversation back to practical matters. "Tell me of your experience at the séance. I heard you call out at one point."

Jack leaned back in his chair. "Remember when Lydia was talking in that foreign language? It sounded like Moro. Anyway, one of my ghosts appeared on the table right in front of me. Suppose you didn't see it."

"No."

"She's my main ghost. She's got a baby. I tried to talk to her, but somebody kicked my shin, and the ghost vanished. Scared the dickens out of me."

Sarah sniffled while wiping away a final tear. "Did the event you describe provide any relief regarding your traumatic memories?" That was, after all, why they had attended the dreadful event.

"Don't know. But I'll tell you one thing—Lydia sure can communicate with dead people."

She rose from her chair. "Good night, Jack."

He stood and looked at her silently.

"Is there anything more?" She glanced at him and quickly dropped her eyes. She hungered for his embrace, his kiss, his loving touch. Her defenses were worn to a nub, and if he initiated intimacy at this moment, she would surrender to him completely—however much she might regret it later.

"Good night, Sarah. Sleep tight."

CHAPTER 22

JACK—THURSDAY, APRIL 21, 1910, 7:00 A.M.

*W*hile smaller than the show districts in New York and Chicago, the Baltimore Street entertainment strip was world-famous for its racy burlesque theaters. They pushed the limits of decency standards, with underdressed young women showing off their bodies in chorus kick lines or in wiggling dance numbers.

Preachers and other high-minded types decried what they termed depravity in halls of debauchery, but the scene was more about money than morals. Baltimore was a busy railroad transit hub, with a constant influx of traveling farmers, merchants, and salesmen. The seaport also drew a stream of sailors, flush with cash and ready for a good time. Other cities had "polite" entertainment that catered to settled families. Baltimore pandered to men far from home and with money to spend.

The strip was deserted at this early hour. All that was left after a typical raucous evening were broken bottles, nasty-looking puddles, and scattered handbills for shows like "The Frilly Frou-Frou High Kickers" and "Joe Legg and his Naughty Leggettes."

Jack knew one guy would still be awake, smoking and drinking like there was no tomorrow: the manager of the Gayety

Theater. He'd hired Jack a couple of times over the years to catch performers who had dipped into the till.

The theater lobby was dark as a tomb, but a bar of light showed from under the office door. He knocked and went inside.

"Harden! You came to ring in the dawn with me. Have a drink."

"It's past seven in the morning, man." Jack coughed in the fog of cigarette smoke. "And I'm still dry."

"That's right—you're a teetotaler for some nutso reason." The man tried to fill a glass and, finding the bottle empty, tore the cork off a new one. "That means you're here for business, not pleasure."

"Ever heard of a comedian named George Funston? He's a skinny guy with glasses."

The manager tipped back in his chair and sipped. "Yeah. 'Galloping' George Funston. He's a second-rate banana man."

"Banana man?"

"The guy in a comedy duo who plays off the straight man. Tells jokes, dances, does slapstick—whatever it takes to try and get a laugh. They've played here a time or two when another act canceled at the last minute."

"Funston's got a partner?"

"Yeah, a big guy with long hair and a beard. He stinks, too. Don't remember his name."

"Do you know where Funston lives?"

The manager opened a small file drawer and flipped through cards before pulling one out. "I got an address —110 Bond Street. Rooming house."

"You're solid gold. Thanks."

"I'd take care of myself better if I was made of gold." The manager took a pull from his glass and sparked up another cig.

~

Jack's agitation grew as he double-timed it to Funston's address. He'd hardly slept, and what little shuteye he'd managed was shot through with nightmares.

He couldn't get the ghostly Moro woman he saw at the séance out of his head and was worried she would show up again with all her spectral pals. Working the murder case had taken his mind off his troubles for a while, but he was slipping back into the haunted craziness that rendered him a useless wreck. And knowing that the Black Cat Creeper was out to kill him didn't make things any easier.

The Bond Street landlord took him to a room and knocked. "You got a visitor, George."

Funston yanked the door open. "Officer, I swear I'll pay my back rent later today. See, I got to get a new bank account. My old one's out of money."

"I'll have a real cop here next time if you don't pay up," said the landlord. "That ain't no joke." He stomped off.

"Look, Funston," said Jack, "I know you met with Chance McCall just before he was killed. And I've got reason to believe he had a certain receipt that you went to a lot of crooked trouble to get back."

"Why did the crook wear white gloves?"

Jack glared at the guy.

"Because he didn't want to get caught red-handed."

Funston started a little dance, but Jack pushed him into the room against a rickety wardrobe. "I once saw a one-legged guy do a soft-shoe routine. You're going to have to learn that trick after I break your leg."

"Rough guy, huh? I'll bet the onions cry when you slice them."

"Tell me about McCall."

Funston sighed. "McCall has a brother who manages the Mouse's Ear cabaret on East Fayette Street. I bought Chance drinks with the understanding he'd get me a gig at the Ear. But Chance is like the post office—he hasn't delivered."

"He's dead. I think maybe you killed him."

"That's rich. I kill a room, nobody cares. I don't kill a guy, suddenly I'm popular."

"You paid Lexie Calhoun twenty bucks to get that champagne receipt back. I'll bet it was for the bubbly in Anna Gilbert's room. You killed her, too."

Funston hooted and did a quick pirouette. "You got the makings of an act, pal. Not everyone can cram so much absurdity into three sentences."

"Cut the crap—"

"Take a look at how I live." Funston swept an arm around the dingy, sparsely furnished room. Spidery lines of black mold crept up the walls like blood vessels. "I'm about to be chucked out of this dump into the street because I can't make my rent. And you think I paid twenty bucks to get back a receipt—for *champagne*? That's a joke without a punchline."

Jack went over to a small table with an assortment of pens next to a stack of fancy paper inked with perfect handwriting. "Doing a little forgery?"

"Well, it ain't all legit, strictly speaking. Some of the material is, ahem, *borrowed*. And if you're sensitive, watch out—there're some blue sketches in there." Funston stroked the top of one index finger with the other while flashing a stern look.

Jack flipped through the written pages and found them covered in jokes and outlines for slapstick routines.

"Hey, I recognize you now, Mr. Dastardly Whiplash," said Funston. "You came to the office to see Judge Lanvale. That man draws more shady types than a virgin forest."

"A clerk's salary not enough to pay rent for this hole of a room?" Jack saw nothing else in the place worth examining.

"I just started that clerking gig. My first paycheck's like the right woman—I'm still waiting."

"Who's your comedy partner—the straight man?"

Funston grimaced. "He quit the biz. I'm strictly a solo act now."

"Maybe you should quit, too."

"No way. I love the spotlight so much that I do three minutes when a streetlamp comes on over me."

Striding away from the rooming house, Jack mulled over the guy's story. McCall was known to milk people for drinks, and Chance did have a brother who ran the Mouse's Ear cabaret. But Funston was a shifty character who was too slick for his own good.

Next up was a meet with Luther Fuller, Lydia's mortician-like assistant. Jack stepped into a telephone booth and called the Lanvale house. A woman answered, sounding terrified. "I hope you can hear me when I say that Mrs. Lanvale is unavailable. If you want to leave one, say so. I mean, give me your message. Are you ready to talk into this thing?"

She was probably a maid forced by Niblett's arrest to do the butler's job. Maybe she'd never even used a telephone before. In his most soothing voice, Jack asked for Fuller, who came on the line and agreed to meet at Mount Vernon Park at 11:00 a.m.

Jack went next door to the Monumental Lunchroom for a quick breakfast. Sitting right up front was a grinning Professor William Jaworski with newspapermen crowded around yelling questions.

"Boys, I'm more than happy to spill about the Séance of Death," said Jaworski. "But let me repeat: I'll give an exclusive to the paper that offers me the best deal. I want money upfront and the guarantee of a rave review for my book." When the shouting resumed, Jaworski held up his hands. "In the immortal words of the great Baltimore Orioles right fielder Wee Willie Keeler, 'I hit 'em for the man that pays me to hit 'em.'" Amid great laughter, he tilted back in his chair with a smile.

"Ain't you worried one of the others at the séance will blab for free?" asked a reporter. "You'll lose your leverage."

"Go on, try any of those snooty people. You'll get a door in the face. And even if someone did talk, they couldn't explain what they saw. I'm an expert. I've spent years studying this stuff scientifically. I'm the only one who can give you the full story about the killer ghost that your readers are dying for." The reporters kept shouting questions, but Jaworski ignored them while attending to a plate of scrambled eggs.

"Listen to them jackals. All eager to hear about how a ghost killed some poor woman. Disgusting." The waitress scowled.

"Séance of Death?" asked Jack as she served his coffee. "Who came up with that?"

"Him." She hooked a thumb at Jaworski. "He's quoted in all the early editions. Must have called the story in late last night but held back on the racy details. Hey, hon." She poked his arm. "Where's your special lady? You darn well better be treating her right, or I'll smack you like a braided rug hung out for spring cleaning."

"Sarah's busy at the—" If the waitress heard Sarah was cutting open Lucinda Pike's body at the morgue, there would be no end to the questions. "The hospital. You know, helping sick folks."

"She's such a good woman. Too good for the likes of you." She gave his arm a hard poke and ambled off.

Sarah was too good for him, all right. If by some chance they became lovers, she would certainly come to regret being ruined by a low guy like him.

And there was the matter of her mixed messages. Yesterday morning she'd been weeping in his arms, desperate for comfort. That crack in her shell revealed a powerful need and a desire that was sexy as hell—until she flipped back to the cool and distant woman who couldn't stand his touch. He wanted no part of a situation where he pushed for sex in the moment only to have her feel sullied and regretful afterward.

"How much do you want?" Jack looked up to see Jaworski glowering.

"For what?"

"For keeping your trap shut." The man sat and jabbed a finger. "You show up here when the press guys are hot for the séance story. It's obvious you want to horn in on my action."

Jack laughed. "For a professor, you sure talk like a streetwise hustler."

"I've got a doctorate in sociology and have taught at Cornell, Amherst, and Oxford. Got two scholarly books and a score of articles published. But I'll make more cash from this story than everything I've earned as an academic."

"Congrats. I won't get in your way if you answer a couple of questions. I'm investigating the death of Anna Gilbert. Two other deaths might be linked—including that of Lucinda Pike."

"Yeah, that's right—you're a private dick." Jaworski scoffed. "Who hired you? Can't be old lady Lanvale. She thinks you're common as dirt."

"She up to something shady?"

"You know it, pal. See, I've been keeping an eye on Lydia for months. She's got a gaggle of fans, lots of people who want to get close to her. Who kept that mob away? Anna Gilbert. She was an ace gatekeeper. But Barnabas Lanvale seduced the girl to get his mother access to Lydia. How convenient that Anna killed herself—Mrs. Lanvale now has all the access she could ever want without giving up her baby boy."

Jack looked at the man carefully, wondering why he was blabbing so freely. Was he naturally chatty or just feeding him a line of bull? "Barnabas Lanvale told me he wanted to marry Anna."

"Sure. I've got a bridge you can buy, too." Jaworski leaned in close. "The only woman Barnabas cares about is Mommy. And he'll do anything—repeat, anything—she tells him to."

"Who do you think killed Lucinda Philips?" Jack didn't trust the guy one bit, but there was no harm in listening to his patter.

"The cops collared the butler. The butler works for Mrs.

Lanvale. With Miss Pike out of the way, Lydia's truly ripe for the picking with only that boy Fuller left to help her."

"What was the relationship between Fuller and Anna?"

"She was rough on the kid. Bossed him around like nobody's business. He didn't like it."

The waitress put down a plate of eggs, and Jack gobbled down a mouthful. "You tell a good story, sport. But I can think of another one. You wanted to pump Lydia for your trashy book, only to have Anna, the ace gatekeeper, keep you away. But you're a smart guy. Smart enough to kill Anna and make it look like a suicide. Now you can quiz Lydia all you want."

Jaworski grinned. "Only a lousy dick would come up with a dime-novel plot like that. What kind of poison did I use, Sherlock? Curare, like *A Study in Scarlet*? Now that's an original idea."

"But you got greedy and decided to really spice things up—and we get the Séance of Death. You set up another big payday for yourself."

"Get a grip, man." Jaworski stood. "I've got a best seller in the can. The book is full of juicy details—including lots of dirt about the supposedly unworldly Lydia Nightingale. Turns out she's a grifter who doesn't mind sending the living over to the spirit world, if you know what I mean. First the bumped-off Boston benefactor, now the Baltimore séance of death. You heard what Lucinda Pike said about the conjured demon—only maybe it was Lydia's hireling under that sheet."

"First you say the Lanvales are behind your Séance of Death, now it's Lydia. Which is it?"

"Let's just say that maybe—just maybe—Niles Niblett works for the highest bidder. You'll have to buy my book for the full story."

"I wouldn't buy a ham sandwich from you if I was starving. What do you know about needles and poison?"

"Nothing. Except for what I read in cheap detective stories." He began walking away.

"You got the Wee Willie Keeler quote wrong," said Jack. "It's 'I hit 'em where they ain't.'"

"Yeah. I know," said Jaworski over his shoulder before greeting a seedy newspaperman waving a wad of cash.

TEN BUCKS SPREAD AMONG THREE COPS IN THE jailhouse got Jack into Niles Niblett's cell. The butler looked like a different man. Grubby jacket and trousers replaced his fancy duds, and his hair was sticking up in ragged tufts.

"You came to laugh at me," he said. "How the tables turned on the limey snob. Go ahead. I don't care."

"I don't kick down, bub. Just want to ask you some questions."

Niblett touched his side carefully. "The police have already asked me enough questions."

"They worked you over. Don't take it personal. Anybody brought in without a high-priced mouthpiece right behind them gets thumped. Cops say it speeds up questioning. Me, I just think they like beating on guys."

"I told them, over and over, that I had nothing to do with what happened to Lucinda Pike. I never saw that syringe before and have no idea who put it there. Have the police even confirmed the needle is related to what happened?"

"That'll be looked into this morning at the morgue. Look, Nibs, you're clever. Too clever to leave your ghost costume half-hanging out of a trash can right after killing someone. Say I believe you're innocent. Who'd want to frame you?"

"I have no idea who would want to stitch me up. I am on excellent terms with Mrs. Lanvale and her son. I have no doubt they value me and all I have done for them. There is the occasional friction with those I supervise on staff, but nothing serious."

"Got gambling debts? A drug or drinking habit? You spend time with whores—girls or boys?"

Niblett stood tall, back ramrod straight, face a mask of discrete disdain. "How dare you ask me such questions? My personal life is entirely above reproach. I am a man of absolute honor and dignity. Absolute, sir."

Jack knew he'd touched a nerve. Not only did Niblett protest too much, something about the guy's manner seemed forced, as if he was trying too hard to play the role of a proper prig. "Who else has a key to that silver cabinet?"

"Mrs. Lanvale, of course."

"There a back door to the outside near the pantry?"

"A private entrance connects the pantry to an alleyway."

"Was anyone new in the house over the last week or so? Like a plumber or other tradesman? Think carefully."

Niblett lowered his head. "Yes," he said, looking up. "An electrician came to the back door a few days ago. He claimed the city government had sent him to inspect the wiring. He presented official identification as well as an order from the director of public works. The man had the run of the house for an hour."

"What did the guy look like?"

"I don't pay attention to mere tradesmen."

"Too bad. There's a good chance that guy swiped a key to your silver chest and used it to plant evidence against you."

"For what purpose?"

"So you'll hang and not him. Tell me what you know about Lucinda Pike and Luther Fuller."

"Both are devoted to Miss Nightingale. Miss Pike had seniority and directed Mr. Fuller quite firmly. He resented the treatment. Once I overheard him muttering some shocking language after a heated exchange with Miss Pike."

"What about Lydia? Anything shady about her?"

"Absolutely not. She is a kind, lovely person."

"Did she pay you to do anything?"

The man stood tall again. "You acknowledged my innocence. Now you are asking if I am a killer for hire. I am deeply offended."

"I'm just checking all the angles—"

"The answer, sir, is no." Niblett's expression was one of quiet, classy outrage. "It is absurd to even consider that I could commit a murder."

The guy was overdoing it again. "You said the Lanvales are great pals of yours. If so, why hasn't the judge sprung you? Have they at least set you up with a lawyer?"

Niblett's shoulders sagged, his haughty act deflated. "I have not heard from the Lanvales as yet. But I expect their assistance at the proper time."

"You might want to consider a backup plan, just in case." Jack handed him a slip of paper and rapped on the bars for a guard. "That's the name and number of a decent lawyer who owes me a favor. Mention me, and he'll help you out."

Niblett looked from Jack to the paper and back again. "Thank you very much, Mr. Harden. Sir."

CHAPTER 23

SARAH—THURSDAY, APRIL 21, 1910, 9:00 A.M.

She sipped tea while nibbling on dry toast in her library, looking forward to a third trip to the morgue in as many days. Lucinda Pike's death was unfortunate, but if autopsies were necessary, she enjoyed the challenge of performing them.

Sleep had come in fits and starts during the night. Waves of emotion rose and fell with the regularity of the seaside. None of them had crested as high as yesterday's surge, and for that, she was grateful. Murders must be solved—time spent struggling with emotional turmoil was time wasted.

Sarah was eager to know if today's postmortem would again reveal no apparent cause of death. She also needed to learn more about the syringe and vial found in the butler's silver cabinet. The police found no fingerprints on the items and only those of Niles Niblett on the cabinet. Jack invoked the mayor's name and had the police turn over the syringe and vial. Both objects were now in the hands of a professor of toxicology at Johns Hopkins School of Medicine.

The telephone's harsh ring from the hallway made her flinch. She closed the door and ignored the pestering sound, hoping it would soon cease. When its metallic bleat persisted, she was forced to answer.

"Dr. Kennecott, I'm calling from the morgue," said the young medical examiner. "Something unfortunate has arisen."

"To what are you referring?"

The man cleared his throat. "Mr. Ralph Stack from the Maryland State Medical Licensing Board visited me. He's conducting an investigation. A sensitive investigation." The earpiece went silent except for a faint hiss of static.

"You may continue."

"Mr. Stack is looking into serious allegations made by the coroner. Against you."

Sarah tapped her foot with irritation. "That man can level no truthful allegation of wrongdoing against me. I will see you shortly. Goodbye."

"Wait, doctor. Please. The coroner requests that you stay away from the morgue until the investigation is complete. Given the gravity of the charges, I must concur."

"This is absurd. What are the charges?"

"I would rather not discuss them over the telephone. Mr. Stack said he would call at your residence this morning with further information."

Her fingers hurt from gripping the earpiece with force. "It is imperative to examine the body of Lucinda Pike as soon as possible to gather and compare evidence."

"I will perform the postmortem right away and will be sure to have samples analyzed as we did for Miss Gilbert and Mr. McCall. I will also check carefully for injection marks."

She began swaying on her feet.

"And Dr. Kennecott? I will contact you afterward with the postmortem findings. You are owed that, at a minimum."

"Are you prepared to rule out homicide for any of the deaths? That is what the coroner and the police desire."

"I will make no ruling until discussing all the evidence with you first. Your judgment—I mean, your forensic judgment—is impeccable."

Sarah placed the earpiece on its hook while considering use of the qualification about "your forensic judgment." Was he implying other aspects of her judgment were flawed?

She returned to the library and began pacing. What ridiculous charges could the coroner have lodged? That she refused a precipitous rush to dismiss a death as suicide? That she objected to his crude remarks and called him incompetent? Neither could justify a serious charge.

And yet. She was all too familiar with the double standard for female doctors. In medical school, professors scrutinized her work more carefully than they did for the men. Disagreement with a male student in class typically led to laughing speculation about her menstrual cycle. Most men—and most male doctors—believed a woman physician could never be steady, competent, and trustworthy. That meant a bogus charge that would not adhere to a man might well attach to her.

A booming knock at the door caused her to freeze in mid-step. *Go away*, she thought. *I wish to see no one.* When the pounding summons came again, she remembered the investigator was to visit with details of the allegations.

She pulled the door open just as the man raised his hand for a third round of knocking. The fist remained posed menacingly as she stared at the man on her stoop. He was in his thirties, clean-shaven, and wearing a stylish suit with a bright red bow tie. "Dr. Kennecott? I'm Ralph Stack from the Maryland State Medical Licensing Board." He presented a badge with great solemnity. "I need to convey some information. Please summon your husband."

"I am unmarried."

"My information concerns a salacious matter that, in my opinion, is unsuitable to present to a lady such as yourself. I would prefer relaying the details to your lawyer or another gentleman of your acquaintance."

"Let me be the judge as to the suitability of the information. Come in."

"Miss—doctor—I am reluctant to speak with you alone in your home."

Sarah threw up her hands. "Do you prefer discussing this so-called salacious matter on my doorstep?"

"Very well. I will enter."

She ushered the man into the library. Stack took out a note-book—much like the one she used—and jotted quickly. "The board has asked me to look into some serious complaints made against you by the Baltimore City Coroner."

"What charges?" She crossed her arms tightly and began rocking in her chair.

Stack flipped pages. "I don't want to shock or offend you. The language is quite blunt and—"

"Proceed. I want to hear everything."

"As you wish." Stack cleared his throat and pulled on his collar. "The coroner accuses you of immoral behavior. He states that you acted in a provocative and lewd manner by removing your clothing in front of him as part of—and I quote—'a bizarre striptease.' He also claims you invited him to engage in sexual contact with yourself."

"That is false. Ludicrously false." She rarely smiled but felt the urge to do so now. "I find the man utterly repulsive."

"I will note your denial. But please understand. The coroner is a senior municipal official. The board feels strongly that such gentlemen must have complete trust in the integrity and profes-sionalism of all licensed physicians. That goes double for physi-cians involved in criminal investigations."

"Are you saying my medical license is in jeopardy?"

"Not if my investigation determines your innocence. I'll need answers to some questions."

She sat quietly for a time, unable to speak or even properly form thoughts. The situation seemed unreal.

"Dr. Kennecott? We can meet another day."

"Ask your questions."

"As you wish." He patted his tie and flexed the arm holding his pencil. "Were you present on the morning of April 20 at approximately 2:00 p.m. at the Baltimore City Morgue?"

"Yes. I was there to conduct a postmortem."

"Upon your arrival at that location, did you lift your skirts, remove your stockings, and reveal intimate parts of your person in the presence of the coroner?"

"I walked through a foot of mud to get into the building, and my legs and skirts were foully soiled. I sat down to clean myself. While engaged in that activity, I observed the coroner leering at me."

"The answer to the question is yes?"

"I had no intention of revealing myself to anyone. I checked to ensure no one was present before I commenced cleaning. The coroner appeared without my awareness afterward. He is a voyeur, or as it is popularly expressed, a peering . . ." She could not recall the nonsensical term.

"A 'Peeping Tom'?"

"Indeed. A gentleman would have withdrawn immediately upon seeing what I was doing."

Stack wrote for a while before speaking. "After revealing intimate parts of your person, did you invite the coroner to—and I quote—'Come here and get dirty with me, you big stallion'?"

Sarah opened, then quickly closed her mouth. How could anyone imagine she could say such a thing? And to that despicable man?

"I'm sorry." The man squirmed in his chair. "But I need an answer."

"I made no such statement. I did reprimand the coroner for spying on me. I also vomited on his shoes."

"The coroner also alleges that you are holding up death findings for corrupt purposes."

"Preposterous."

"You autopsied two bodies recently at the morgue. The

evidence for both deaths points to suicide. Is it true that you insisted upon regarding both as homicides with no substantive proof whatsoever? Furthermore, is it true that you are receiving ongoing payment to investigate at least one of those deaths as a homicide?"

Her heart hammered against her ribs. The man had caught her in a trap she should have anticipated. Lydia was paying for an ongoing investigation into Anna Gilbert's death, and Sarah had used her influence to keep the case open as a potential homicide. That was a conflict of interest or at least the appearance of one.

"Doctor?"

"I admit to an unintentional conflict. My motivation was, however, securing justice rather than financial gain." How could she have been so stupid? It would have been easy enough to decline the payments from Lydia. Except for Jack. His foolish pride insisted on earning money.

"Thank you for your candor." Stack closed his notebook. "I will be interviewing others to ensure the board has a broadly sourced account."

"I can give you multiple names who will attest to my personal and professional character."

"That won't be necessary." Stack stood. "I plan to wrap this up quickly and provide a report with my recommendation to the board. I'll keep you apprised. In the meantime, here's my card if you have any questions."

Sarah saw him out and stood for a while with her forehead pressed against the inside of the closed door, balanced on the knife-edge of another fit of extreme emotion.

That would serve no useful purpose. Instead, she called for a motor taxi.

As the motor cab moved up Broadway past the line of people at the public comfort station, Sarah noticed a large poster declaring: "NO SPIT, NO CONSUMPTION."

Very good. Citizens were largely ignorant of how germs spread tuberculosis, and as a result, the city had a distressingly high number of "lung blocks"—clusters of disease that were difficult to abate. Education was necessary to improve public health.

She frowned, recalling an ugly aspect of Baltimore's efforts against tuberculosis. City officials had launched a nationally acclaimed campaign of infectious fear, depicting blacks as the prime source of the Mycobacterium tuberculosis bacterium. The city coerced many so-called "incorrigible black consumptives" into segregated institutions that were more akin to jails than hospitals. She attended a lecture given by the Baltimore City Health Commissioner, who stated that blacks were "the most difficult tuberculosis patients" due to "the natural insolence of their race." Sarah attempted to rebut the statement as prejudiced, noting that she had observed a great many discourteous white consumptives, but the man merely scoffed at her.

Sarah turned her thoughts back to Mr. Ralph Stack's unfathomable investigation. It was astounding that the State Medical Licensing Board believed the coroner, an incompetent alcoholic. And, while there was a slim basis in fact regarding some charges, surely a group of reasonable people would acquit her of any intentional wrongdoing.

The taxi dropped her at the Johns Hopkins Hospital Pathological Building entrance near Wolfe Street. In short order, she was sitting in the office of the toxicology professor to whom she had sent the syringe and bottle of liquid found after the death of Lucinda Pike.

"Fascinating, doctor," said the professor, a tall man with black hair and a bushy beard. "I've never seen anything like the concoction in that vial."

"You may elaborate."

"Our tests show the liquid is a mixture of adrenaline and potassium chloride. Traces of it were in the syringe, which also had fresh blood on the needle. The syringe was used recently to inject the mixture."

"I understand that adrenaline triggers the body's so-called fight-or-flight response," said Sarah. "It was synthesized recently and shows promise for alleviating asthma and raising blood pressure. Potassium chloride is not much used in medicine, but could help supplement low levels of potassium in the blood."

"You are very well-informed, Dr. Kennecott. Most physicians are ignorant about both substances."

"I read the literature. Continue."

"In large doses, adrenaline causes acute emotional overreaction and tachycardia. A big dose of potassium chloride interferes with the chemical balance that keeps the heart beating. A person injected with a mixture of both substances would first experience extreme agitation and then suffer sudden cardiac death."

"The foot would be as effective as any other injection location," said Sarah.

"An injection anywhere would reach the heart in seconds."

"And since both substances occur naturally in the body, an injected dose is impossible to detect during a postmortem, even with the most sophisticated laboratory test."

"Correct," said the professor. "It's the perfect method for murder without detection. As far as science can tell, the victim simply dropped dead."

"Except for the injection mark."

"Well, yes. But that's hardly conclusive of anything. If it's even found."

"What can you tell me about this device?" Sarah pointed at the syringe lying on his desk.

"It's an older model based on a French design with locking ring handles. The needle has an unusually large diameter."

"That is not the type of instrument most physicians would now use."

"No, it isn't. Nor would a drug addict."

"It might be the tool of a killer."

"If so," said the professor, "that person is experienced with a syringe and knows their chemistry. And also fiendishly clever."

CHAPTER 24

JACK—THURSDAY, APRIL 21, 1910, 10:30 A.M.

*L*uther Fuller sat stiffly on a park bench next to a statue of some bare-chested guy with his foot on a lion and his arm around a kid. A plaque read: "ORDER" in bold letters. A smashed whiskey bottle lay at the statue's feet, but a white-clad street cleaner was headed over with a broom and pan.

Order was expected here at Mount Vernon Square, the ritziest neighborhood in Baltimore. A millionaire out walking his pedigree dog shouldn't have to see a broken bottle, even if the same guy threw it there late last night after a drunken night at his club.

Jack strolled up to the bench and sat next to Fuller. "Nice spot, eh?"

"If you say so." In the bright sunlight, Fuller's pale face glowed against his black fedora and black suit jacket. His eyes were a bright cobalt blue, the same color as the bottles used for phony patent medicines.

"Must be hard for you now to mind Lydia all alone, what with the deaths of Anna Gilbert and Lucinda Pike."

Fuller nodded. "I am looking for replacement assistants."

"That's good for you, right? You'll be the head guy."

"I'd be lying if I didn't agree." Fuller looked down at the sidewalk. "Anna and Lucinda took turns bullying me. I don't mourn their loss."

"Things worked out well." Jack leaned in closer. "It's almost like you planned their deaths."

A person accused of a serious crime usually did one of two things: they laughed it off, or they got mad. Neither reaction meant anything—guilty or innocent, a person could respond either way. For Jack, it was the start of working on someone, not the endpoint.

Fuller was different. His eyes went hard, and his lips set in a humorless smile. "Yes, you could say it looks like that."

"Just looks like it?"

"Both women were leaving, one way or the other. Lydia told me to terminate them."

"Terminate?" Jack couldn't keep the surprise out of his voice.

"End their employment." Fuller let loose a strange chortle—dry and puffy like he was trying to inflate a balloon.

"Why?"

"Just before coming to Baltimore, Lydia found letters to Anna from Barnabas Lanvale discussing their plan to run off together. The letters also made it clear that Miss Pike was helping Anna. Lydia wanted them both gone."

"Fired—or dead?" Jack rubbed the back of his neck as he let the information sink in. Maybe Lydia really did have something to do with the deaths of her companions.

"Is there a difference when people leave one's life?"

"The law says so."

"The law doesn't control the dark corners of our minds."

Fuller's creepy smile grew larger, and Jack half expected him to throw his head back and give a melodramatic laugh. One thing was for sure—this guy wasn't the type to confess to murder. He was just having some sick fun. "What did you do before working for Lydia? Tell scary stories to kids around a campfire?"

"Lydia offered me a job right after I dropped out of Harvard College." Fuller stared back with his unsettling blue eyes wide open. "I was studying chemistry but lost interest. I wanted to do something more challenging. And more rewarding."

"Mixing chemicals sounds plenty hard."

He looked up at the sky. "Chemistry is easy. I mastered the basics early. See?" He held up his left hand, which was missing parts of its index and middle fingers. "I did this at age twelve; it was my third dangerous explosion. It takes most talented chemists until their early twenties to lose a finger."

"The psychic game was more exciting than blowing yourself up. And Lydia's cash was an even bigger thrill."

"I was only at Harvard because they gave me money to attend. I grew up poor, you see. So poor that a five-dollar tip to a psychic seemed wildly extravagant. At first." The guy again gave an odd little smile. "After working with Lydia for a while, I wanted money, too. And the only way to make money—lots of it —is to do things others won't."

Jack had had enough of this kid and his games. "Stop playing around with me, Fuller. Did Lydia pay you to kill Anna Gilbert and Lucinda Pike?"

"For a common man, you do have a vivid imagination."

"This common man knows about that legal document you witnessed for Judge Lanvale saying Lydia's crazy. I think it's about stealing her money. What's your cut?"

If Jack had managed to surprise the guy, he didn't show it. "My sole interest is getting Lydia the short-term medical help she needs."

"Suppose I go to the cops and report you for fraud and murder?"

Fuller laughed his dry breathy laugh. "Go right ahead. I already spoke with Detective O'Toole about Anna's death. He was satisfied with my answers. In fact, we got on rather famously."

Of course, thought Jack. Snake Eyes O'Toole would have

recognized Luther Fuller as a fellow creep. "Watch out for yourself, Fuller. O'Toole doesn't always play nice."

The man stood and pointed what was left of a blown-off
finger at Jack. "You had better watch yourself, too." He flashed
his baleful smile and then walked off stiffly like a statue—
almost, but not wholly—come to life.

Jack was on his feet, red-hot at the pasty-faced punk's threat
and ready to try and shake the truth out of him. But that was
pointless. Fuller was the kind of nut-job who'd smile through
the roughest treatment.

STRIDING DOWN CATHEDRAL STREET, JACK HAD A
brainstorm. Hotel bellboys were hungry for tips. That meant
they kept a close eye on guests as they came and went, eager to
swoop in with whatever help was needed. Maybe a bellboy at
the Belvedere Hotel could remember who'd last visited Anna
and McCall. All he had to do was find out which of the two-
dozen hops might have a lead.

He stood outside the Belvedere for over two hours, waiting
for some big shot to check out. So far, he'd only seen busi-
nessmen stroll in for lunch and stagger out later, three sheets to
the wind.

A crumpling thud followed by shouts and screams came
from the street intersection. A motor wagon going north on
Charles Street had crashed into a horse-drawn wagon making a
left-hand turn from Chase. The wagon got the worst of it—the
horse looked dead, and the wagon was flipped, with barrels scattered every which way. The smell of whiskey filled the air, and a
couple of men were cupping their hands to slurp from booze
gushing from a busted barrel.

Nobody had yet figured out how to deal with the new danger
of motor traffic. Horse-drawn wagons were slow enough that
drivers and pedestrians had time to get out of each other's way.

With their greater speed—and the indifferent arrogance of their operators—motorized vehicles were constantly running people over and crashing into things. All this led to calls for stop signs and traffic signals. But many opposed the idea, claiming fundamental freedom as Americans to do as they pleased on the streets. Crashes and deaths were a small price to pay for liberty.

Jack turned back in time to see a bellhop coming out of the hotel, pushing a cart piled high with trunks and cases, followed by an older couple. The man wore a shiny top hat, fur jacket, and striped trousers. His companion also wore fur, along with an enormous feathered hat. After waiting for the bellboy to hump the luggage into a big carriage, Mr. Top Hat presented a single coin. The hop made a face but took the offering and mouthed something in return.

After the wagon pulled away, Jack buttonholed the hop. "Hope you told that cheapskate to go screw himself."

"A working stiff can only think about saying that, brother. I thanked him." He frowned and held up a quarter.

"How'd you like to make an easy sawbuck?"

"Sorry. Already got an exclusive deal with Diamond Harry to refer his girls to guests."

"I'm not a pimp—I'm a private dick looking into the deaths of Anna Gilbert and Chance McCall. I'd like to talk with any of your guys who might have seen comings and goings."

"That so? McCall was all right. He tipped me to a winner at the track once." The hop scratched his ear. "Okay, two other guys besides me might have dope. Ten bucks for me now and five bucks for each of them later."

Jack pulled out a ten-dollar bill. "Where and when?"

"My name's Lefty. Meet me at Clark's Saloon. Noon tomorrow."

"How about sooner?"

The guy chuckled and reached for the cash.

"Promise you'll show?" Jack yanked the bill out of the guy's reach.

"Desperate, ain't you?"

"No. Just careful." Jack handed the sawbuck over. Of course, the guy wouldn't make any promises. But asking him to do so telegraphed just how important the information was. The hop might demand more money or, worse still, peddle his dope to someone else.

"Yeah, I'm careful, too." Lefty pocketed the cash. "Careful to give the best service to the best tipper."

CHAPTER 25

SARAH—THURSDAY, APRIL 21, 1910,
1:45 P.M.

From his business card, Sarah knew Ralph Stack had an office in the Continental Building. At twelve stories, the place was Baltimore's tallest skyscraper. It was also the same building where she had met Jack last year when she worked for the Pinkerton National Detective Agency.

She felt no sense of nostalgia glancing up at the two decorative falcons perched high above the building's Baltimore Street entrance. Rather, she admired their fine, lifelike craftsmanship. Most modern builders were content with crude approximations of living creatures.

Sarah had to convince Ralph Stack that the coroner's charges had no substantive merit. It was patently absurd for anyone to think she would engage in a "striptease" before him—or any man. As for the potential conflict of interest, she would return Lydia's money.

His office was on the fourth floor. A frosted glass door had "OFFICIAL INVESTIGATIONS" painted in black letters. She walked in, expecting to find a reception room. Instead, she saw the man sitting behind a desk in a small, dingy room.

"Mr. Ralph Stack. I would have knocked had I known the door opened to your private office."

"Dr. Kennecott." He stood and gestured to a chair next to his desk. "It's not a problem. I was hoping to see you again soon."

The office was stuffy and reeked of cigarette smoke. "Do you mind opening the window for some air?"

"Sure. Please have a seat." He got up and, after a struggle, opened the single window to the dark air well.

"I can supply witnesses to testify as to my proper conduct, as well as to my pronounced modesty. That should be more than sufficient to rebut the coroner's slanderous claim regarding the intimate presentation of my body."

Stack lifted a thick file folder. "As I mentioned, the coroner's complaint is serious in itself. But I also see a larger pattern of unprofessional behavior on your part."

Sarah began rocking in her seat. "Please elaborate upon that statement."

Stack opened the folder. "Let's start with your choice of reading material. According to the public library, you checked out *Progressive Health in America*, a book touting socialist medicine. It contains quotes such as 'Once all physicians are government workers, they will treat all citizens without the barrier of cost. This means doctors will earn less, but that matters less than improved public health.'"

"I read numerous medical texts. Politics do not concern me."

"You must know that the board strongly opposes socialized medicine. You also read *The Jungle* by Sinclair Lewis. The book has a pronounced socialist message."

"Again, I have no interest in politics. I read widely on many subjects."

"Including, so it seems, subjects of a sexual nature. Did you perhaps linger over the *Illustrated Atlas of Male Genitalia?*"

She dropped her arms, hands clenched into fists. "That is a medical textbook. I am a physician."

Stack flipped a page. "Maybe. But you also read *The Awakening*, by Kate Chopin, which discusses female physical desire and how it led a woman to abandon her family. The book has been ordered censored, but you read the uncensored version."

"Am I to be sanctioned for reading books commonly available in a public library?"

He dropped the folder on his desk. "Dr. Kennecott. The board is strongly committed to maintaining the untarnished image of the Maryland medical profession. As you no doubt are aware, most of our members are men. Fairly or not, the behavior of females licensed to practice comes under careful scrutiny. Their activities must be above reproach, lest the public thinks immoral women are drawn to the practice of medicine."

She stood, arms rigidly by her sides. "Male physicians of my acquaintance are alcoholics, adulterers, and sellers of narcotics. Many are demonstrably incompetent. And, because of my sex, I am held to account for scurrilous accusations and the books I read?"

"I also have many accounts of your rudeness and unsociability," said Stack as he jotted a note. "Please sit down, if you would."

Sarah swayed on her feet, wondering what to do. She wanted to leave immediately, but that would only add to the man's list of her supposed infractions. The best course was to remain and continue asserting her innocence. She sat.

"I have found additional evidence against you that the board will find most disturbing. I refer to your illicit sexual involvement with a Mr. Jack Harden. Would you care to comment?"

The ability to speak deserted her. All she could do was rock in her seat and struggle to maintain her composure.

"I have statements from two of your neighbors stating Mr. Harden comes and goes from your residence at all hours. The most recent account details how he arrived wearing one suit of clothing and departed at a late hour in another. You offer no rebuttal. Very well." Stack set his pen down. "Dr. Kennecott, I am sorry, but I must tell you that my report will recommend immediate suspension of your medical license."

"I will contest your findings." To her ears, her voice sounded very far away.

"That is your right, of course. But the process will be messy and drawn out. Regardless of the outcome, your personal and professional reputation will be destroyed." Stack leaned back in his chair. "There is another option. Do you want to hear it?"

She managed a slight nod.

"Fortunately, none of your transgressions are as yet widely known. And the coroner might be convinced to withdraw his charge—I suspect it will dawn on him that complaining about a young woman showing off her body makes him look foolish."

She stared at the desktop, saying nothing.

"You could leave Baltimore. Move to New York, or even better, Europe. If you would do that expeditiously—say, within the next week or so—I will recommend the board drop the matter. No action would be taken against you. Take some time to think. But I'll need to know your decision in the next twenty-four hours. Otherwise, I will submit my report, and you will be finished as a physician."

CHAPTER 26

JACK—THURSDAY, APRIL 21, 1910, 4:30 P.M.

*H*e strolled past the Lanvale mansion on the way to meet up with Sarah at her place. There ought to be some sign of the family's crookedness, like a pirate flag fluttering from the roof. But it was just a big house with lots of windows, all of them with curtains closed.

Seconds after he dropped the knocker on Sarah's door, something flew past his neck and left a gaping hole in the door. The angry crack of a rifle sounded from behind.

"Sarah—move away!" Jack forced the door open and rolled into the entry hallway.

"What is happening?" Sarah stood close by, blood running down her forehead.

"Move away from the door and get down!" he said with an urgent shout. "Somebody's shooting at us."

She joined him on the hallway carpet. "We must call the police."

"You're bleeding bad."

"The wound is minor. Lacerations to the scalp bleed freely."

He peered out a window, Colt revolver in hand. "Stay where you are." In a crouch, he went to the door and looked out with one eye.

"Do not go outside," said Sarah, cheek to the carpet. "Wait for the police."

"The guy's on the lam now. Maybe I can catch him." Jack looked across the street and saw blinds fluttering from a second-floor window. The shooter had probably gone out the back to the alley and taken off. But in which direction?

He sprinted to the north intersection and was almost to the alley entrance when an automobile came flying out with a screeching right turn onto the main street. He leveled the Colt and had a clear shot but didn't pull the trigger at the receding vehicle. There was no way to know for sure if the driver was the shooter.

He went back to the house just as Sarah finished calling the police. A thick line of blood ran from the part in her hair down her face. "We need to stop that bleeding."

"No." She waved off his advancing handkerchief. "That cloth is germ-laden and unsanitary. I will attend to the matter properly myself."

After she strode off, Jack checked the bullet hole in the door. The shot had missed his neck to the right by no more than two inches. With Sarah walking to open the door on the inside, the bullet had just grazed her head.

She returned with a bandage pressed to her scalp and hair damp with antiseptic. He checked the wound and saw the scrape on the top of her head. If the bullet had been a fraction of an inch lower, she would be dead. Without thinking, he pulled her close. Unlike the couple of other times they had embraced, her body was stiff and unyielding. He let her go and stepped back.

"Sorry. I'm just glad you aren't hurt worse."

She stood looking down at the floor, her face with its usual deadpan look. "I, too, am relieved. The incident is, however, indicative of how foolish I have been to invite you to my residence."

"What's that supposed to mean? This is the first time somebody tried to kill me—us—around here." She sagged and steadied herself against the wall. He reached out, but she stepped away.

"I must recline." She staggered into the parlor and dropped onto a sofa covered in a white dust cloth.

He grabbed a wool throw and put it over her. "What can I do to help you?"

"Nothing."

After getting shot, she had every right to be shaken. But Jack wondered why she didn't want comfort afterward when she had seemed so desperate for it a day earlier. She was sending him more mixed messages.

"Your visits here have caused a scandal." Her voice was unsteady, and her face white as chalk above the dark throw. "The fault lies not with you. I am solely to blame."

"You had better keep quiet." She was slipping into shock. He found another blanket and spread it on her. Then he tracked down the housekeeper, relayed what had happened, and asked her to bring Sarah hot tea.

The sound of a clanking motor indicated arrival of a police motor car. Snake Eyes O'Toole and a uniformed cop lounged in the vehicle, passing a flask back and forth.

Jack went outside and tapped on the automobile hood. "You boys here to investigate an attempted murder or to celebrate St. Patrick's Day late?"

The detective finished his drink and leisurely stepped out. "I was hoping you were cold meat, Harden."

"If I get bumped off, I hope you don't pull the case. I'd prefer somebody who cares more about catching killers than shaking down whorehouses."

"Nobody gives a rat's ass about you, gumshoe." O'Toole pushed by and went to examine the bullet hole.

"It's hard to miss a still target with a rifle at fifty feet," said Jack.

"Yeah. Maybe the shooter just wanted to scare you and your weirdo girlfriend."

He got in O'Toole's pitted face. "Lay off her. Got it?"

"Well, now," said the detective with a hard grin.

Jack knew he'd stepped over the line. Nobody threatened this guy and got away with it. "Want to croak me, Snake? Take a number."

O'Toole curled his lip, showing off teeth that looked like tombstones in a long-neglected cemetery. "I go to the head of the line whenever I want, chump." The guy's breath was terrible, and Jack stepped away just as Sarah joined them at the open door, the bandage still pressed to the top of her head.

"Looks like someone took a slice out of little miss fruitcake." O'Toole's ghastly grin widened.

"How can I assist your investigation into this crime, detective?" Sarah was still deathly pale and unsteady on her feet.

"Where do you entertain Harden, sweetheart? Bedroom mostly?"

"No. We spend most of our time in the library."

Jack tensed with fury, dangerously close to punching the dick's ugly mug. The uniformed cop chose that moment to come back from across the street.

"Owner ain't home, detective. Somebody broke in through the back door. Found this in the upstairs front bedroom." He held up a spent brass bullet casing.

"That's from a Winchester .30-30," said Jack. "Powerful rifle."

"Found this, too." The cop held up a detailed pencil sketch of a black cat batting at a terrified mouse. A message in block letters read: "Mr. Harden: The fun ends Saturday. R.I.P. –The Black Cat Creeper."

"The guy's a real artist," said O'Toole. "Looks like he plans to paint you out of the picture in a couple of days."

Jack glared at O'Toole. "What do you know about this Creeper business?"

"That somebody besides me hates your stinking guts."

The detective asked a couple of disinterested questions and then left.

"We have much to discuss," said Sarah. She closed the door and walked to the library.

Jack followed. "You've had a bad shock," he said. "Go rest."

"Tell me about the so-called Black Cat Creeper."

"You should lay down." He exhaled through his teeth. This willful woman would do exactly what she wanted, damn the consequences. "I don't know much other than what you heard. Some looney who likes to scare people is after me. I'm sorry—and plenty steamed—that you got hurt."

"I invited you here foolishly. Not just today." She sat at the table, pressing the bandage to her head.

"Sarah, no way is this your fault. I brought the trouble to you."

"There is malicious gossip regarding your visits."

"I'll leave."

"No."

Jack rubbed the back of his neck with a sigh. It had been clear as day from the start that his coming and going from this place would draw notice. Sarah was a proper lady with high social standing. Ironclad rules said she should avoid entertaining a man alone—and certainly never see a guy like him—but she had never seemed to care.

"Please sit." Her eyes met his and slid away.

He dropped into the chair. "Since when do you worry about gossip?"

"When it jeopardizes my eligibility to practice medicine."

He listened carefully as she related the story about Ralph Stack and his investigation. "What are you going to do?"

She started rocking. "I could contest the report and appeal directly to the board. Eminent doctors would vouch for my character. But the charges would become public. Damage would ensure, even if I prevailed."

"Surely nobody's going to take the word of that drunken lech of a coroner over yours?"

"The overall thrust of his story is, of course, false. But is true that he observed private parts of my body and dress."

"Come on. You're not to blame for getting muddy and then cleaning it off. And if the coroner had an ounce of decency, he wouldn't have gawked at you." Jack felt the blood pounding in his ears. He wanted nothing so much right now as to knock the guy down.

"Correct. But it prevents me from issuing a categorical denial of his charge. I also cannot deny reading those books or accepting payment from Lydia." Her eyes again met his, lingered for longer than usual, then looked away. "In addition, my entertaining you alone is now common knowledge."

"So what? Nothing's ever happened. I've never even kissed you on the lips!" He slapped his thigh.

"I am aware of that." She crossed her arms. "Very well aware. But in this case, the appearance of impropriety is all that is required."

He nodded. People always assumed the worst about others while reserving the benefit of the doubt for themselves—it was one of the least admirable aspects of human nature. "You should fight it. I'll help."

"I will review my options and make a decision in twenty-four hours." She held up a hand to stop his reply and then rang a bell to summon the housekeeper. "The matter is no longer under discussion. We will now dine and review the facts of our case."

"Sure. Of course." Jack threw his hands up with exasperation. Here she was, rocked with terrible things right and left, and she wanted to talk about dry facts. How about the not-so-dry fact that they both had almost been killed less than an hour ago?

"I will begin." Sarah opened her notebook. "The vial found in the butler's silver chest contained a mixture of adrenaline and potassium chloride. When an individual is injected with the mixture, they experience extreme agitation, and shortly afterward, their heart stops."

"Sounds like what happened to Lucinda Pike. What are the results of her autopsy?"

"I am not allowed in the morgue while Mr. Ralph Stack's investigation is ongoing." He heard a tinkle of glassware announcing the housekeeper's arrival with a dinner cart. Sarah kept on talking as the woman set the table and began serving.

"The medical examiner will inform me about the postmortem results. But an autopsy, even with the best laboratory tests of blood and tissue, cannot differentiate an injection of those chemicals from what occurs naturally in the body. If Lucinda Pike was so injected, her death would appear to be from sudden cardiac arrest, as were the deaths of Anna Gilbert and Chance McCall. The murderer either has considerable chemistry expertise or is working with such an individual."

"Luther Fuller," said Jack. He watched as the housekeeper finished her task and left, seemingly indifferent to the discussion of blood, guts, and murder. "Fuller says he studied chemistry before working for Lydia. And get this—he told me Lydia wanted to terminate—fire—Anna and Lucinda. She knew about the secret elopement plan and was not happy."

The tip of Sarah's pencil broke with a snap against a page. "If Lydia knew about Anna's romantic involvement with Judge Lanvale, I find it most odd that she did not convey that information to us." She picked up a new pencil from the table.

"Yeah." Jack began wolfing down steak, mashed potatoes, and boiled carrots. "I also spoke with Niblett in the lockup. Claims he's on great terms with the Lanvales, but they're not helping him. Could be that mother and son are happy to let the butler take the fall."

"Is Niles Niblett guilty of murdering Lucinda Pike?"

"I'm not sure. Something's off about the guy, but I don't

know exactly what. Still, he's not stupid. If he was the killer, why would he leave that ghost costume in full view? Anyway, I gave Niblett the name of a lawyer, so he owes me. I'll talk with him again—maybe he's hiding some dirt."

"Yes, perhaps."

"I ran into Professor Jaworski at the lunchroom this morning," Jack gave a scornful snort. "You're right—the guy's a jerk. He's looking to cash in on a newspaper exclusive about what he's calling 'the Séance of Death.' That's a motivation for murder in my book. But get this—he had the gall to hint around that Lydia was a killer. What a lying sleaze." He mopped up the last bit of food with a slice of bread, which he stuffed into his mouth.

She had her hands over her ears and was looking at the floor.

Jack knew that meant his manners—or lack of them—had offended her again. At this point, he understood she wasn't trying to make him feel like a slob. She was experiencing genuine discomfort with what she saw and heard. He'd been trying to keep her extreme sensitivity in mind, but obviously still had a long way to go. He finished chewing and waved to get her attention. "Sorry—I said I saw Jaworski this morning."

She leaned over to sniff her food, which by now was cold. "I heard what you said about the man and agree he is a suspect."

"Yeah. But, we're back to the bedsheet—the only one of our suspects who could have been under it is Niblett."

"Perhaps the killer is someone we have not yet considered. That individual might be collaborating with one or more suspects. I have a suggestion."

"Who?"

"I have twice encountered Professor Jaworski with a young man referred to as his student. That person did not attend the séance."

"You think the student was under the sheet?"

"Possibly." Sarah's leg began bouncing under the table. "You have mentioned another person with potential motivation for murder."

"I did?"

"Lydia Nightingale."

Jack tossed his fork on the plate with a clatter. "Come on, Sarah. I know you're upset with her—"

"My speculation has nothing to do with personal emotion." She ate a tiny forkful of mashed potatoes, chewed daintily, and dabbed her mouth with a napkin. "Consider what you just relayed. Anna Gilbert, her close confidant, was about to leave with Lucinda Pike's assistance. Lydia is reportedly angry with the perceived betrayal. From your account, Luther Fuller may have enough knowledge of chemistry to concoct the lethal mixture we found after the séance."

"Okay, but both Lydia and Fuller were also sitting at the table when the fake ghost appeared. So that would mean a third killer, which makes things much too complicated. And let's not forget that Fuller's working with the Lanvales on some shady legal business against Lydia."

"I acknowledge your points." Sarah carefully cut a boiled carrot into six identical pieces. "I will ask to meet with Lydia tomorrow for additional questioning." She ate two of the pieces before placing her silverware on the plate.

He shrugged. "Okay." Only Sarah could seem emotionless about the prospect of interviewing her long-lost mother as a murder suspect. No doubt she had a whirlpool of feelings churning away behind that barricade of blank fortitude.

"Jack." She fidgeted with her fork while staring past his right ear. "I need your assistance in reviewing books borrowed from the library. Please plan to spend all day Saturday here."

He slurped water while thinking about how to respond. No way Sarah needed any research help, least of all from him. And with that guy Stack sniffing around, she had to know having him here all day was a bad idea. Why was she fibbing—something she never did? "No thanks. I'm more useful working the streets."

She abruptly stood. "I rarely ask for your assistance. And now, when I do, you refuse!" She was shouting and waving her arms like someone trying to warn an onrushing train about a washed-out bridge on the tracks ahead. "You are selfish and inconsiderate!"

"Look, there's plenty more for me to do on my own. You don't need me to help you do research."

"How dare you presume to know what I need? You are assuming a patriarchal authority that is both unwarranted and offensive."

He stood. "Sarah, just relax. You've had a real tough day, including getting shot. You need to lay down and rest."

"Have you forgotten that I am a medical doctor with expertise in managing injury? And who are you? A man with no formal education whatsoever. I will tolerate your boorish behavior no longer. You will now leave this house!" She pointed to the door, her mouth set in a thin white line, bright pink spots on her cheeks.

Jack had never seen her like this. "Sure, whatever you say, your ladyship. Have fun with your books. They're dead, so you'll get along just fine." He stomped out of the house, slamming the big entrance door behind him. After walking less than a block, his anger cooled and turned to remorse.

Sarah was mad not because he refused to help with research or because he was an uneducated patriarch or something. She was upset that he wouldn't lay low on Saturday, the day the Black Cat Creeper was supposed to pounce. She was desperately concerned about his safety. If Jack had any sensitivity, he'd have tried to reassure her instead of getting mad.

But that raised another problem: what could he have said to her? A promise to avoid the attack would have been hollow bravado. He couldn't have agreed to hide like a scared rabbit. Certainly, he couldn't have revealed that he wasn't especially worried about the Creeper, that he half-wished the assassin would put him out of his misery.

Right now, Sarah didn't want to lean on him, didn't want whatever meager comfort he could offer. Maybe she'd finally had enough of his loutish, ignorant, and impolite ways.

Now that was something to worry about.

CHAPTER 27

SARAH—FRIDAY, APRIL 22, 1910, 8:00 A.M.

ountess Olenska's Tea Room was an oasis of quiet amid
the clamor and commotion of downtown. The shut-
tered windows blocked the street noise, and the smell of freshly
baked cakes was a reprieve from the stench of horse manure and
festering garbage pits. Sumptuous carpets and tapestries hushed
the occasional clink of china and tittering laughs of elegant
ladies seated at the damask-covered tables.

This was the sole outpost of Baltimore high society that
Sarah enjoyed. She came here often with a book to savor the
silence and relax. This morning, however, she had no book. And
she was far from relaxed.

Mr. Ralph Stack's investigation worried her deeply. Whenever she managed to push that concern away, immediately came
the anguish of knowing an assassin was after Jack.

The hostess, a full-figured woman wearing a flashing array of
jewels and an old-fashioned dress with an enormous bustle,
approached. "Mademoiselle, your guest has arrived." She
gestured to a chair, and Lydia appeared behind her and sat
down.

"Is she really a countess?" asked Lydia watching the hostess sail away, her orange silk dress trailing on the floor. "She has such a regal air. And that Russian accent is quite something."

"I do not know. I wish to discuss other matters with you."

"Sarah—your forehead is bleeding."

"Do you have a hand mirror?"

"Yes." After rooting in her handbag, Lydia handed over a small mirror.

Sarah saw a trickle of blood just below the crown of her enormous hat. She reached under the millinery and pulled the bandage forward over the seepage. The wad of gauze remained visible as she returned the mirror.

"I don't suppose you care to tell me what happened."

"No." Sarah's leg was bouncing up and down.

Lydia lifted the pot lid. "Such lovely tea. Orange Pekoe, do you think?"

"Why did you not immediately identify yourself as my mother? And why are you here again after all these years?"

Lydia dropped the lid back with a rattle. "I've tried to prepare myself for this conversation for twenty years. I still can't find the right words."

"I request you make an attempt."

The hostess appeared again. "Mademoiselle." She held up a finger to her lips.

"Acknowledged." Sarah shot a thumbnail to her mouth, only to remember she was wearing gloves. She dropped the hand to the table and forced herself to take a deep breath. The hostess nodded and left.

"I've felt such guilt for leaving you. And what makes it worse is I can't offer an explanation you will understand, much less accept. Yet I must try."

"I know why you left." Sarah looked steadily at the sugar bowl, heaped with glistening white squares. "I was too strange for you to mother. Too bizarre for you to love."

"That is not true." Lydia tilted her head back, and for an awful moment, Sarah was afraid the woman's alternate personality—her "spirit guide"—would emerge. "You mustn't ever think I don't love you."

"You rejected me as a small child. And then you returned and chose not to tell me who you were. I can only assume you never wanted a maternal relationship because you judged me too eccentric. Perhaps you are here now to fulfill some morbid curiosity, to compile a list of my shortcomings to justify your original decision to abandon me."

"I can't blame you for saying that." Lydia cried softly, gloved hands covering her face.

Sarah's shoulders relaxed, and the knot in her abdomen lessened. What was the point of venting harsh sentiments if the target meekly agreed? This weeping woman was not the powerful agent of harm that lived in Sarah's imagination.

"If I can convey one thing to you, it is this: I never stopped loving you from the moment you were born. Yes, you were different from Grace—so sensitive, so solitary—but that only made me care for you more. I never once had a regret, never once felt disappointed. The opposite, actually. You were a special child who drew even more of my attention."

Sarah was horrified to feel her own tears flowing. She hurriedly swiped at her cheeks. "That statement is inconsistent with the facts. That is, unless you have a perverse definition of *attention* that includes maternal abandonment. I demand a clear explanation for your action."

"I'll get to that shortly." After a sip of tea, Lydia continued. "But let me first say that I could not be prouder of you. You are a strong, independent woman who has achieved remarkable things. Graduated with honors from top schools. A doctor—an exceptionally good one, from all accounts. I am honored to be your mother."

More tears fell despite Sarah's efforts to quell them. "But I am obviously eccentric. I am awkward and uncomfortable with others. I do not understand people, and they do not understand me."

"I regard your difference from others as a gift to the world. Some people are too narrow-minded to see it, of course. But others know of your ability and appreciate you dearly for it. Such as Jack."

"I do not wish to discuss Jack. Do not mention his name again." That was a whole other compressed ball of emotion that she absolutely did not want to spring loose at this moment.

"Let me tell you why I left the family," said Lydia softly. "I'll do my best to explain, even though I don't fully understand myself—and even though you may still regard me as cruel, insane, or both.

"I, too, was an unusual child. From a young age, I communicated with spirits—they were my best friends. My parents urged me to become more normal. They wanted a traditional life for me—marriage and children. I wanted to please them, and that seemed possible when I met your father. He was a wonderful man, and I gladly married him. We were overjoyed when Grace was born and equally so upon your arrival. I still spoke with spirits, but they didn't interfere overly with my life as a wife and mother."

Lydia offered more tea, which Sarah declined. "About three years after your birth, I had a life-altering experience. I was in bed with a bout of fever, reading Henry Wadsworth Longfellow's *The Song of Hiawatha*. I felt an unusual presence, looked up, and Longfellow's spirit was standing before me. Using the most fantastic language I'd ever heard, he told me I had a unique talent, that I must help the living communicate with the dead.

"He said this was the most important work I could ever do—that I would ease the suffering of many and narrow the barrier that separates the living from the spirit world. I asked how best to do this while caring for my family, and he—" She pressed the handkerchief to her eyes. "He commanded me to leave you behind and travel to Boston.

"I did not want to go. But—and this is completely beyond my understanding—his spirit entered my being. After that, my will was not my own. I left. And Longfellow was correct—I have connected countless people with departed loved ones: husbands grieving for wives; mothers grieving for children. The comfort they receive—the joy—is remarkable."

"You blame a dead man for compelling your actions." Sarah's hands were flapping in her lap.

"I don't blame the man's spirit for providing me irresistible encouragement."

"Yet you now recite the poetry of a woman—Emily Dickinson—during your dissociative states."

Lydia looked around and then spoke in a whisper. "It is true that Longfellow's spirit is no longer with me and that another poet has taken his place. But she insists that she is nobody.'"

"As in 'I'm Nobody! Who are you? / Are you nobody too?'" Sarah dropped her palm on the table. "The poet is clearly Emily Dickinson—who died over twenty years ago."

Lydia trembled. "Please, dear, I beg you, no more of that. It upsets her greatly."

Sarah had observed insane patients suffering from flamboyant delusions. In addition to their fantastical beliefs, they also typically presented with illogical thinking, incoherent speech, and bizarre behavior. Lydia had none of these symptoms and appeared sane. That meant her "spirit guide" could be a projection of her subconscious mind—or a willful fraud. In any case, Sarah wanted to move the conversation to another topic. "Please now discuss your reasons for involving me during your visit to Baltimore."

"I must add *coward* to my list of shortcomings." Lydia sighed. "I did visit you and Grace after I left, but the meetings were painful. You would get so upset, screaming and banging your head on the floor. I finally had to stop coming. I was afraid that seeing me again, even all these years later, would upset you. I didn't identify myself because I feared you would reject me."

"I would have preferred to have had that choice."

"I know, dear. I'm sorry. Anna Gilbert knew how much I

wanted to see you and concocted a scheme. She would travel to Baltimore beforehand and check into the hotel under an assumed name. That way, I could claim she was missing and enlist your services to find her. I could see you at least once—anonymously—before you found her."

"Anna traveled here unaware that you knew of her plan to elope with Barnabas Lanvale, correct?"

Lydia flinched. "People we love can disappoint us. We both know that all too well."

"You were angry with Anna. And with Lucinda Pike, because she was helping Anna with her plan to leave you."

"Yes." Lydia took a long sip from her cup. "I was heartbroken and planned to fire them both after the convention."

"That information is highly relevant to our investigation into Anna's death. You failed to mention it."

"I didn't feel it was relevant. And, gracious, I'm the one who's paying you to find out what happened to Anna. It's not like you work for the police."

"You are the nominal client. But my ultimate intention is to serve justice. Therefore, I must ask: are you complicit in the murder of Anna Gilbert? In addition, are you complicit in the murders of Chance McCall and Lucinda Pike?"

Lydia sat back in her chair, stunned. "How . . . how can you ask such vicious questions after I have shared so much with you? I dearly loved Anna. And Lucinda was a fine woman with a good heart. I could never wish them harm—or anyone else, for that matter."

Sarah regarded the woman with a fixed stare.

Lydia flushed from the neck upward, as Sarah herself sometimes did. "I knew this conversation would be difficult, but I did not expect my own daughter to interrogate me as a murder suspect. You must hate me so."

"I feel no hatred toward you." Sarah switched her gaze to the large feathered hat that adorned the head of a woman sitting at a nearby table. "But you have withheld evidence that implicates you as a suspect."

"*Suspect*? I am your mother!"

"That fact has no bearing on my analysis."

"You are so terribly self-righteous, so smugly moral. I can't say I find that aspect of your personality appealing. Where is your compassion? Can't you even give me a chance?"

"Did you conspire with Luther Fuller to formulate and use a chemical mixture that is undetectable at postmortem?"

"That is enough." Lydia's words were clipped, her manner hard. "I will not listen to any more of your cold-blooded accusations."

"I need truthful answers from you to solve this case."

"And I need you to show me some respect. I've been a terrible mother, but I spoke to you today with an open heart hoping for a glimmer of empathy. My reward is unbearable cruelty." Lydia took the napkin from her lap, threw it on the table, and stood.

"Before you depart, you must take back your payments." Sarah extended an envelope.

"Gladly." Lydia snatched the envelope. "Seeing you was a mistake." She turned and left.

Sarah assessed the meeting while watching her tears splash the tablecloth. She had resolved the technical conflict of interest, and Mr. Ralph Stack no longer could truthfully claim that she had compromised her professional judgment. But that did little to lessen the anguish of suspecting her mother was a killer.

CHAPTER 28

JACK—FRIDAY, APRIL 22, 1910, 7:30 A.M.

*H*e'd spent the night staring at the ceiling, thinking about how to help Sarah. From her perspective, the best thing he could do was hide from the Black Cat Creeper. Second best would be to dig up more dope on their murder case. Number one wasn't going to happen, and number two was a given.

Something didn't seem right about Ralph Stack and his intrusive investigation. Jack washed, shaved, and dressed quickly for a trip downtown.

It was nice and early—he had time to find out more about Stack and then swing by for a visit with Reverend Jared Smartwell. Tough questions could make the reverend drop the bumbling fool act. Or, if he really was a bumbling fool, maybe he'd let loose something useful about Mrs. Lanvale. Or perhaps even Lydia. After seeing the reverend, he had a 2:00 p.m. appointment with the Belvedere bellboys. They might just want money and free beer, but it was worth looking into.

A newsboy drew his attention, waving the morning edition with a shout of "Little children slaving away packing Baltimore oysters, read all about it." Jack bought a copy and saw a photograph of a six-year-old kid, filthy and in rags, hard at work shucking. The headline screamed "Baltimore Oyster Packers Worst in the Nation in Exploiting Kids." Maybe this would prompt a crackdown on child labor. But he sure wasn't holding his breath.

"Mr. Harden! Got a message for you!"

He turned to see a boy, maybe fourteen, running toward him.

"What is it, kid?"

"I'm supposed to tell you that Little Miss White Bow's hurt real bad and needs you. She's at Lexie Calhoun's place."

"Who sent you—hey!" The kid ran away as fast as he appeared.

Jack hot-footed the three blocks to Eden Street, wondering what nasty business was waiting.

Lexie met him at the door with a grin. "I always can make a fella come again. It's one of my many talents."

"Cut the crap. Where's the girl?"

"Up the stairs, first door on the right. I need her gone toots sweet, sweetie. She ain't got no family, but seeing as you and her had such a nice time the other day, I figured you're the next best thing. Plus, I got you pegged as soft under that tough guy act."

The girl lay on her back, naked. Her face was a bloody mess, both eyes swollen nearly shut, nose slanted brokenly to the side. Blood ran from a wicked blow to the head. Her breaths came in short, pained gasps.

"Peddy bah . . ." she whispered through broken teeth.

"Don't talk. Just rest easy." He draped a sheet over her and lightly pressed his handkerchief to her head wound.

He went to the top of the stairs and yelled down to Lexie with Sarah's telephone number. "Call her and get me a couple pans of hot water and something for bandages up here." There was nothing else to do but hold the girl's hand, and lie, saying everything would be fine.

Sarah arrived over an hour later in a fancy dress. "I was beginning to think you wouldn't show," he said.

"I had a social engagement." She pulled out a hypodermic and gave the girl a shot of morphine before examining her. "She has serious injuries and needs immediate transport to the hospital."

"Will she be okay?"

"I must call for an ambulance. Direct me to the telephone."

They went downstairs, and Lexie pointed to the telephone.

"Honey, I don't care how hard you squeeze, you won't get any juice out of that one." The madam jerked her thumb at Sarah's retreating form. "You're wasting your time—she ain't got the first clue how to love a man."

"Figures you wouldn't know a proper lady when she shows up in your patch of hell."

"A guy like you has got no use for a proper lady. You need an improper woman." She gave a throaty laugh.

"Who beat the girl?"

"Look, pal, I ain't diming on a customer. Even one who gets a bit carried away. But don't worry—I banned him for a month."

"Tell it to the cops. She's beat so bad they'll come talk to you."

"Yeah? Maybe my good friend Snake Eyes O'Toole will stop by." She laughed again.

Sarah joined them. "An ambulance will arrive shortly."

"Hey, sweet pea," said Lexie with a poke at Sarah's arm. "You and me got the same taste in men: tall, crude, and stupid. The best kind."

Sarah cringed and stepped away. "If the man in question is Jack, I disagree about your characterization of his intelligence."

The madam hooted as if she'd heard the funniest joke ever.

After the ambulance porters carried the girl away, Jack turned to Lexie. "I'm not forgetting this."

"I'm the kind of gal a man doesn't ever forget," she said with a wink.

Jack followed Sarah outside. Lexie rushed from behind and planted a kiss on his cheek just as a camera on the sidewalk flashed with a puff of white smoke. Two men stood next to the photographer. One was a barrel-chested guy with a darkly handsome face and a lead pipe dangling from his hand. The other man wore a sharp suit and a big smile.

"What's going on here?" Jack rushed down the steps, but the big guy blocked his advance.

"I'm Ralph Stack, an investigator for the Maryland State Medical Licensing Board." The man in the suit held up a badge. "This is the icing on the cake, isn't it, Dr. Kennecott? Hard proof of you and your paramour visiting a bawdy house together. Sad. Shocking. Lucky for you, my offer still stands."

Sarah flapped her hands and hung her head.

"How about I offer to belt you one, pal?" Jack pushed against the beefy guy but got shoved back, hard.

"More detail for my report. 'Subject's companion threatened physical harm to this investigator and had to be forcibly restrained.' Things just keep getting worse for you, doctor."

"Crawl back into the sewer, Stack. And take your numbskull slab of muscle with you."

Stack chuckled. "I'll have you know Pretty Boy here is quite sensitive. And you truly don't want to hurt his feelings."

Pretty Boy. Jack stared hard at the goon with his lead pipe smeared with fresh blood. This was the guy who'd beaten the girl. Jack reached for his revolver, but Sarah knocked his hand away.

"We are leaving," she said.

"There's something not right about Stack," said Jack as they walked off. "What kind of official investigator works with a gorilla?"

"Mr. Ralph Stack has a badge of authority."

Jack knew that Sarah often took what people said at face value, that she had trouble seeing through misleading human behavior. She also had great faith in authority. If someone flashed a badge, she would naturally assume he was who he said he was. Smart as she was about many things, she was vulnerable to simple human deception. "You said you visited Stack in his office? Where is it?"

"The Continental Building." She stopped walking. "My vexation with you has increased since last evening. You are more interested in pursuing mayhem and consorting with prostitutes than helping me solve murders."

"That mayhem wasn't about me. Your Mr. Stack had that girl beaten up."

"Use of the possessive for myself concerning Mr. Ralph Stack is unfair." The toe of one shoe began moving up and down on the sidewalk. "If you are inferring that I am to blame for this outrage—" Her foot was now tapping like a woodpecker on a tree. "I note you were the one first summoned to assist the naked young woman. Your sexual relationship with her lies at the root of this misfortune."

Jack blew out a breath. "This isn't worth fighting over. I'm off to talk with some Belvedere Hotel bellboys. It's possible one of them saw somebody going to or coming from Anna Gilbert's room. Getting good dope is a long shot, but it could crack our case."

"Why have you delayed interviewing those individuals?" Sarah pointed a finger at him before balling her hand into a fist. "You should have met with them long before this. But instead, you were wasting time philandering."

"Look, you don't understand detective work as well as you think." Jack felt his temper rise. "I can't just walk into the hotel and chat with those bellhops. It's taken time to set up the meeting. And don't forget I've been busy finding dead bodies, dealing with cops, and talking to people about your darn mother."

"How dare you refer to my—my—"

"Mother."

Her arms began to shake, causing items in her medical bag to rattle. "You ignorant, contemptible man." Her chest was heaving.

"I might be ignorant, but you're more interested in my sex

life than solving this case. A good detective would never do that."

Sarah's breath was coming in rapid and shallow gulps, her face bright red.

"Why are you so jealous? You won't even let me kiss you. And you sure as hell don't want to sleep with me. Tell me I'm wrong."

Sarah dropped her head and spun away. As Jack took in her trembling form, he knew he'd hurt her terribly. What was he thinking? "Hey, I'm sorry." He touched her arm, and she instantly recoiled.

"Do not touch me!" Her voice was shrill. "Stay away. You must stay far away from me, permanently." She raised a hand to hail a passing hansom cab.

"Wait. Let's talk."

She moved swiftly into the cab and hid her face in her hands. The driver closed the door, and the carriage promptly wheeled away.

CHAPTER 29

SARAH—FRIDAY, APRIL 22, 1910, 1:00 P.M.

*T*he librarian smiled and swept her hand toward a tidy stack of materials. "I found information for every name you provided, Miss Kennecott. It took me hours and hours."

Sarah sat at the table without a word.

"You're welcome," said the librarian before returning to her desk.

Jaws clenched, Sarah tried to quell the turmoil unleashed from the hurtful exchange with Jack. His taunts about her mother and her detective skills stung, eclipsed only by his charge that she cared more about fornication than bringing a killer to justice. And his claim that despite her supposed sexual fixation with him, she personally did not want . . . *that*. She uttered a strangled noise that made the librarian look up and frown.

Never had she behaved so emotionally—or been so humiliated—during a disagreement. She had many experiences debating overbearing men, and even when discussions turned unpleasantly personal, she had always maintained her equilibrium. The men might explode with anger and call her terrible names, but their attacks felt groundless and inconsequential.

How terrible it was to have Jack, the person she trusted the most, attack her most tender susceptibilities. He had no right to use the knowledge gained in trust as a weapon against her. And the gall of the man to try and instruct her about her own desire. He knew nothing about her yearning, her passion. In any event, he should never have even broached the topic of physical love. She was a lady, not some common trollop. His rudeness was appalling and unforgivable. She must never put herself in such a vulnerable position again—not with Jack, not with anyone.

She bit her lip and tasted blood.

The pain helped her refocus. She was here to research the backgrounds of persons suspected of murder and must devote all her attention to that activity. She opened the first volume and read a biographical sketch about the Lanvale family. It gave no indication that either Mrs. Lanvale or her son had any training in chemistry or medicine.

The information for Professor William Jaworski noted a doctorate in sociology from Princeton and a series of temporary faculty positions. She read details about his boyhood experience assisting his father, a country doctor in upstate New York. Jaworski was quoted saying: "I did everything a regular physician would do, including compounding medications and using a fearsomely huge needle to inject patients."

The professor had exaggerated the status of his book about Lydia. A recent trade journal stated that the book had yet to find a publisher. One house had, however, asked for a revised manuscript with more personal details, including a firsthand account of "something shocking and sensational." Sarah imagined Lucinda Pike's death at the hands of a ghostly figure during a séance would qualify on both counts.

Luther Fuller's material included a description of him as "a brilliant young chemist." He spent two semesters at Harvard, where he took classes in biological chemistry and advanced toxicology. A yearbook entry attributed a quote to him: "Success comes not to those who wish, plan, or try, but only to those who seize it with single-minded boldness—and do whatever it takes."

Lydia's background information revealed nothing about her education. An article in a popular magazine praised her medium skills, complete with glowing testimonials from people who claimed she had put them in touch with departed loved ones. There was no mention of Lydia's marriage, children, or subsequent abandonment of her family.

A newspaper clipping from a few months ago drew Sarah's special attention. It told the story of a wealthy Boston woman enthralled with Lydia's ability to communicate with the woman's dead parents. The woman had Lydia, along with her three assistants, move into her house. A month later, she died suddenly and left her entire estate to Lydia.

With no details about the benefactor's death, Sarah could not fully assess its significance. People passed away abruptly from many things, including stroke, embolism, and heart disease. They choked on pieces of steak, slipped in the bathtub, and overdosed on drugs. Sarah had no way of knowing if the death of Lydia's unfortunate Boston client was similar to the three recent murders in Baltimore.

One book and an envelope of newspaper clippings related to Reverend Smartwell. The book was a church biography noting his graduation from theological college. Curiously, the biography stated that he had received a medical degree some years earlier. She was mulling this new information when a loud, familiar voice assaulted her ears.

"I worked with Melvil Dewey, you know." Professor William Jaworski was speaking before the librarian as if he were lecturing to a packed auditorium. His student stood by silently.

"The man would bend my ear obsessively for hours about his Dewey Decimal System. 'You realize, Will,' he would say, 'that my decimals are the most important innovation in human history!' I'd have to bring him back to Earth. I said 'Mel'—only I can get away with calling him that—'Mel, don't forget about a tiny thing called fire.'"

"I so admire Mr. Dewey's genius," said the librarian with a rapturous smile.

"He'd like you, too." Jaworski chuckled. "Mel takes a hands-on approach when instructing young women about librarianship. But they must be pretty enough to justify his attention. 'Will, you can't polish a pumpkin,' he would say." Jaworski leaned over the librarian's desk and stroked her arm. "You, my dear, are no pumpkin. He'd want to teach you all kinds of things."

"Oh, professor. Please." She waved a hand, her smile even larger.

"Sarah, how lovely to see you again," he called out. "I do so hope you're reading up on feminine charm." Jaworski winked at the librarian, who used a hand to cover a grin unsuccessfully. The professor muttered something to his student, who headed for a table stacked with books.

Sarah tried to return to her reading, but Jaworski intruded. "May I join you?" He sat uncomfortably close.

"It is customary to wait for an affirmative reply, sir."

"Why stand on parlor manners when we're such old friends?" He reached for her arm, but she pulled away. "That's right—you object to a friendly little touch. Mel Dewey better stay clear of you."

"I do not wish to discuss anything concerning Mr. Melvil Dewey."

"But you're all about cold logic, right?" Jaworski spread his legs wide and snaked an arm over the back of her chair. "I'd think you'd support his brutally efficient spelling reform movement. You know, *have* spelled as *h-a-v* and—"

Sarah edged away and held up a hand. "Please stop. Your talk vexes me."

"My, you get right to the point." Jaworski scratched his beard with a smile. "I hope you're just as blunt when I interview you for my book." He pulled out a pad and pencil.

"I wish to interview you, sir."

"Me?" His eyebrows shot up. "Whatever for?"

"I regard you as a suspect in the deaths of Anna Gilbert, Chance McCall, and Lucinda Pike." She shuffled her feet, knowing that her direct approach would put the man on guard, but could think of no other way to broach the subject.

Jaworski threw his head back, convulsed with a barking laugh. "My darling Sarah, you are truly one of a kind. I'll be happy to answer your questions but will take notes of my own. Your queries will spice up my chapter on you considerably."

"I assume you know how to use a hypodermic syringe from assisting your physician father. What is your knowledge of chemistry?"

"You're quite the little researcher, I see. Yes, my father taught me how to use a needle. Most of the time, we injected morphine. Maybe some other stuff, but I don't remember. It was thirty years ago."

"Are you familiar with adrenaline and potassium chloride?"

"No."

"What of barbiturates, commonly sold under the name Veronal?"

"Those are nerve pills, right? Had a lady friend who was a lot more amenable when she took a couple."

"Do you have a supply of the drug?"

"My nerves are like steel. But have you tried it? Might loosen you up."

"What was your relationship with Lydia Nightingale's assistants? You may start with Anna Gilbert."

"You're sweet on that private dick, Jack Harden, right? I already talked to him about Anna. Let's just say she and I weren't friends. She wanted Lydia all to herself. Same with Lucinda Pike, although she wasn't as close to Lydia, if you know what I mean." He gave her a lascivious smile. "As for Fuller, I don't know the kid. He seems like you—smart, but a real cold fish."

"I see that to obtain a book publisher, you have been told to depict a sensational event in your manuscript. For that purpose, did you conspire to have Lucinda Pike killed during the séance by a putative supernatural being?"

"Sure. I asked the ghost of Vlad the Impaler to kill her."

"You then do admit a role in the murder?"

"Come on now, dear. I was being sarcastic." He drummed fingers on the table while watching her write. "I had no involvement in Miss Pike's demise."

"What about Mrs. Lanvale and her son Barnabas? How well do you know them?"

"They're vultures." Jaworski sat up straight, pencil in hand. "My turn to ask some questions. What did you think, Sarah, of seeing your mother again after all these years?"

"I have no comment."

"You must have mixed feelings, including jealously. Anna Gilbert was about your age—and so close to Mommy. Lucinda Pike was also attached to her. Did you decide to kill the competition, Sarah? Maybe Chance McCall, too, because he was on to you?"

"Your questions are absurd. I can only assume you are mocking me. I wish to resume with my questions."

"Fire away, sweetness."

"What is your relationship with Reverend Jared Smartwell?"

"Who's that?"

"You forget, sir, that I saw you arrive at the church for a meeting with the man."

Jaworski's jaunty manner stiffened. "Oh yeah, forgot that. He's a source for my book." He touched his face quickly. "That's it."

"Will he confirm that statement?"

"You're talking with him again? When?"

"Shortly. I also plan to interview Judge Barnabas Lanvale."

"Look. You haven't been hurt yet. But that can change." He stuffed his pad and pencil in a pocket and stood. "Stay away from the judge. I know what he's capable of. You should have a taste of that yourself."

"A taste of what substance?"

"Don't try to be clever. I know Judge Lanvale's derailing your medical career."

She stood and stepped close to the man. "Tell me what you know of that matter."

Jaworski bumped her with his belly. "I'll just leave you with another Dewey reform spelling to ponder: *d-a-n-j-e-r*." He walked out with a scowl, ignoring the librarian's friendly wave.

Sarah was now too agitated to finish reading the rest of the background material. She approached the librarian, who was marking a catalog card. "I wish to have material sent to my home," she said.

"Do you, now?" The woman continued to look at the card.

Sarah began swaying, unsure how to proceed. Perhaps the woman needed to reach a suitable stopping point in her work before attending to the request. But the hour was growing late, and Sarah had matters that required her attention. "I wish to have material sent to my home," she said again.

"I heard you the first time." The librarian glared up. "People don't like rude and brusque treatment, you know."

Sarah stopped swaying. "It appears you are exhibiting the same behavior you criticize. Is your hypocrisy meant to inflict your interpretation of that behavior on myself, a practice referred to in a nonsensical colloquial manner as 'giving me a dose of my own medicine'? Or is your hypocrisy an attempt to appear virtuous without actually adhering to the virtue in question?"

The woman threw her hands up. "Fine, fine. I'll have the material sent to your house." She sighed and shook her head. "I can't believe anyone actually talks the way you do."

CHAPTER 30

JACK—FRIDAY, APRIL 22, 1910, 1:00 P.M.

"Sign the pledge, brothers! Do it for your mother. Do it for your wife and your babies!"

The man was shouting and waving a clipboard ahead on the sidewalk. He wore a wooden sandwich sign proclaiming: "ABSTAIN from Spirits & Beer" on the front. People ignored him as they streamed past.

Jack was about to do the same when the board stiff stepped directly in his path. "Mister, isn't it about time to foreswear liquor?" he asked, thrusting the clipboard aggressively. "You know it's the right thing to do in your heart."

Jack pushed the clipboard away with so much force that it bounced off the signboard and knocked the petitioner down. The guy flailed his arms and legs like a beetle on its back. "I don't blame you, brother," he cried. "It's the booze that makes you a beast!"

"Can't blame liquor, bub." Jack took the man's hands and pulled him to his feet. "You'll have better luck with your pledge if you don't poke people in the chest with it."

"By any means necessary, brother. Mark my words, we'll make alcohol illegal from coast to coast." He reached for the clipboard on the sidewalk, but his signboard stopped his hand well short.

"You're dreaming." Jack picked up the clipboard and handed it back. "Working men will never give the stuff up, law or no law. It's a question of liberty. And thirst." He took a few steps before turning around with a final warning. "Try to keep your distance, hear? It'll be safer for everyone."

Anti-booze cranks were pests, but Jack regretted knocking the man over. He was still riled something fierce from all the crap that had happened earlier. A girl beat half to death by that Pretty Boy mug, no doubt with the involvement of the slippery Ralph Stack. And then Sarah had to nag him about working a case and get huffy about all the women he was supposedly sleeping with.

He shouldn't have said those mean things to her. Sure, she could be annoying, sitting on her high horse and making pronouncements. But he knew Sarah well enough to understand that she saw the world in black-and-white terms. She also had to be wildly anxious about what the Black Cat Creeper had in store for him. And since she had trouble expressing anxiety—or any emotion—directly, her feelings slipped out sideways.

He was also powerfully frustrated with her mixed signals about the nature of their relationship. Were they partners, buddies, companions, lovers-to-be? She couldn't make up her mind, so he couldn't make up his. But if they were kaput, it didn't matter. Sarah had been so hurt and angry when they parted that any type of relationship—heck, any association at all —could well be over.

Good move, Jack, he thought. *Real good move.*

Clark's saloon was a dirty dive on Greene Street a couple of blocks from Edgar Allan Poe's final resting place. Walking by the grave, Jack looked at the bird carved on the tombstone and bunches of dead flowers piled everywhere. Fans came from all over to gawk and earnestly recite "The Raven." Lately, bohemian types were turning up at the grave, drunk and ranting about suffering for art and other nonsense. Some nighttime visitors swore to have seen Poe's ghost, groaning about his death sixty years earlier after a wild night on the town.

Poe had plenty of company—lots of guys ended up dead after a night out in Baltimore.

A gal with circles of bright pink paint on her cheeks and a cigarette in her mouth was on his arm seconds after he'd pushed through Clark's swinging doors. She smelled of eau de whiskey along with some other powerful odor he couldn't quite peg.

"You look overdue for a good time, honeybunch." She gave him a snaggletoothed smile that was cut short by a wheezy cough.

Camphor—that was the other smell. Tuberculosis sufferers liked to smear camphor on their chests to help them draw breath. "Smoking makes lung trouble worse, you know," Jack said.

She let go of his arm. "This ain't no place for a health crank."

"You got that right." He looked around for the Belvedere bellhop, but the dim gaslight made it hard to see anything. Clouds of tobacco smoke complicated things even more.

The gal wasn't finished with him yet. "Hey. You got to at least give me some nickels for the automatic piano. Big trouble if you don't." The woman pointed to a large man standing by the bar and drilling Jack with a menacing stare.

He gave her a handful of change. "I better hear at least one song come out of that contraption. Ragtime number preferred."

Her smile returned as she pawed through the coins. "You got it." She sauntered over to the piano and dropped a coin into the slot. Jack nodded approvingly at the opening notes of Scott Joplin's "Maple Leaf Rag."

"Hey, buddy. Over here." He turned to see Lefty the Belvedere Hotel bellhop at a table by the wall with a pimply, red-haired kid and a guy in his mid-twenties with slicked-back hair and a thin filament of perfectly groomed pencil mustache.

Jack joined them. "I'm looking for dope on who visited Anna Gilbert and Chance McCall just before they died."

The man with the pencil mustache leisurely extended a palm, rubbing thumb against index finger. "The Don kept a sharp eye on that gal Anna," he said.

"You always talk about yourself in the third person, Don?" Jack gave him a five-spot and another to the red-haired kid.

"The Don don't hide his light under no bushel basket," the man said with a roguish grin that some women no doubt loved.

"Skip the part about peeping into the keyhole while Anna undressed," said Jack. "Just tell me who visited her."

"The Don don't bother with keyhole peeping." The man gave a smarmy laugh. "He has a lot more fun on the other side of the door."

Jack felt his temper rise and tried to put a lid on it.

Don smirked and took a swig of beer. "Listen, Anna's a type. She gets a room to have some fun. The Don was working his charm, and she was about to give in. Then she had to go and die without knowing what she missed."

"Get to the point, or the Don is going to get a black eye."

"I saw two guys. The first was that judge, Barnabas Lanvale. He showed up right after she checked in. Stayed for over an hour. Later, this young mortician-looking guy goes to her room carrying a leather bag. He stays for a few minutes and leaves in a big hurry." He flashed his grin again. "The Don would've stayed in the saddle a *whole* lot longer."

"What time did the young guy show?"

"Early evening, when she came back from somewhere all upset."

"Do guests always have to unlock the door to let visitors in?"

"Yeah. But the Don has plenty of experience getting gals to open up."

Jack turned to the red-headed kid. "What did you see?"

"I saw three guys go into Chance McCall's office from about

noon to three p.m.," he said. "The manager was in and out a time or two. Then some guy with a red beard showed up."

"Was he smoking a pipe and wearing a ratty tweed jacket with leather patches on the elbows?"

"Don't remember no jacket, but he did have a white pipe and was smoking something awful."

"Who was the third guy?"

"You, mister. I saw the manager shouting, and then you left. Later I noticed Chance's office door was closed, which it usually ain't. Door stayed closed until the manager found him dead at his desk early the next morning." The kid looked like he might cry.

Jack pictured Chance's office layout in his head. "There's a second door in that office, right?"

All three bellboys nodded.

"So, somebody could've used it to drop in on Chance without anyone seeing them?"

"Yeah, but unlikely." Lefty waved for another beer bucket. "Not many people know about that door. It leads to a private staircase that lets the house dick get to floors quick in an emergency. Each staircase door on every floor is locked, and Chance had the only key."

"But if Chance was expecting someone, he could have left doors unlocked," said Jack. "That someone could have taken the elevator upstairs and gone down the secret staircase to the office, killed McCall, and retraced their steps out. If they stayed clear of the rooms, none of you would have any reason to notice them."

Lefty snorted. "Maybe—but that's a real twisty story. Me, I always prefer a simple explanation. Such as Chance ended it all with a fistful of pills and a bottle of coffin varnish. End of story."

Jack also preferred simple explanations because that's the way the world worked. When water runs down a hill, it follows the least complicated path to the bottom. And most crooks were about as simple: they thought more about what to have for lunch than planning their dirty work.

But Sarah had cast doubt on the simple explanation for McCall's death. If she was right, someone went unseen into his office and gave him a lethal shot. McCall said he was out of whiskey—but was found with a bottle at his elbow. Somebody provided the booze, which was probably spiked with enough barbiturates to knock the guy out before getting injected.

"I think something spooky happened to Chance," said the red-headed kid in a creaky, quavery voice. "And to that lady."

"Don't start with that ghost stuff again," said Don with a cocky wave of his hand. "This guy'll laugh in your face. So will I."

"I'm not in the mood to laugh," said Jack.

"The room where Anna Gilbert died is haunted," said the kid. "A husband poisoned his wife there a while back, and the wife's ghost haunts the room, ready to punish anyone who does bad things. Anna Gilbert must have done something terrible, and the ghost made her pay."

Jack shivered, remembering the cold, creepy presence in Anna's room. "What's that ghost got to do with Chance?" asked Jack.

The kid gulped down beer. "I liked Chance and would never rat him out. But seeing he's dead, I guess there's no harm in letting on that he stole Anna Gilbert's money after she was dead. He was drunk when he told me."

"You think the ghost killed them both."

"Mister, I *know* it. Why do you think fate put Anna Gilbert in the haunted chamber? It was so the ghost could kill her. Poor Chance got crosswise with the evil spirit, too."

Walking out of the place, Jack was about ready to believe almost anything about this odd case. Still, he was reasonably sure the killer was from the land of the living, not the dead.

CHAPTER 31

SARAH—FRIDAY, APRIL 22, 1910, 5:45 P.M.

*T*he tap-tap of her footsteps resounded from the tiled floor of the deserted courthouse hallway. When she got to the judicial administrative office, it was dark behind the frosted glass door.

A slow turn of the polished brass knob opened the door with a squeaky groan fit for a haunted house. She stood still, heart thumping. Nobody challenged her from the shadowy interior, and she grimaced as the door creaked closed behind her.

Waiting for her eyes to adjust to the gloom, she listened to the ticking clocks and muffled street sounds. Anxiety forced a grab at a nearby desk for support. Never in her life had she entered a private space without an invitation. Never had she been so reckless.

But circumstances called for boldness. Judge Lanvale and his mother were prime murder suspects. Professor Jaworski also implied that Barnabas Lanvale was behind Ralph Stack's investigation. She needed information—and quickly.

After some hesitation, she rapped lightly on the door to Judge Lanvale's chambers. What to do if he answered? She considered stating a falsehood, perhaps that she was collecting money for some charitable cause. No, that was hopeless. She could not bring herself to lie. Here was a paradox—she could enter an office without permission but could not say something untrue. Thankfully, no one answered her knock.

Sarah turned the handle to no effect—the door was locked. After all this, thwarted by an insubstantial door. She briefly considered finding an object to hurl through the frosted glass before seeing a newspaper in a trash can. After pushing a paper sheet under the door, she inserted her pencil in the keyhole. One quick jab forced the key on the other side to fall. She pulled back the newspaper and used the key to open the lock.

The judge's chamber was dimly lit from a streetlight-facing window. She closed the door, which automatically locked. Feeling positively giddy, she replaced the key. Next, she sat at Lanvale's desk and turned on the electric lamp, revealing three orderly piles of paper and a framed portrait of his mother. A double pen stand sat in a marble block with an engraved plate: "To My Dear Son Upon His Entry-Level Judicial Appointment. Greatness Awaits Us. Regards, Mother."

She looked through the first two piles of papers and found nothing but routine court papers and letters from Judge Lanvale's creditors demanding immediate payment of sums, large and small. Many were stamped "Final Notice" and threatened legal action.

A pending court order titled "Nightingale Guardianship" in the third pile was much more interesting. "The court declares that Miss Lydia Nightingale shall be placed under the guardianship of Mrs. Beatrice Lanvale in accordance with the supporting documents. Mrs. Beatrice Lanvale is to be given absolute control over the person and any specifically identified financials of Miss Lydia Nightingale."

The remainder of the pile held the order's supporting documents, including Luther Fuller's signed witness statement. The certifying physician's report was from a man Sarah knew as an ethically challenged incompetent. The report contained a thicket of meaningless jargon that concluded with a diagnosis of "severe female hysteria with psychoneurotic flourishes, along with pronounced symptoms of menopausal psychosis, e.g., claims of communicating with spirits of the dead." Utter claptrap, but it was a sad fact that most courts accepted whatever a physician said, no matter how ridiculous.

Why had the Lanvales not executed the guardianship order and moved to obtain Lydia's money? Sarah could only think of two possible reasons for the inaction. One was the absence of the account number and other details needed to access Lydia's bank funds. Lucinda Pike had said that only she and Anna Gilbert knew the number apart from Lydia. That is, before Anna revealed it to Reverend Smartwell.

Another reason for delaying implementation of the court order was Sarah herself. The Lanvales may have assumed that, as Lydia's daughter, Sarah would object to the order upon its execution. That could freeze the action and spoil the plan. The Lanvales needed her out of town—just the step Mr. Ralph Stack was forcing upon her.

The anteroom door slammed, making her jump and scatter papers. A set of judicial robes hanging near the door was the only viable hiding place. She switched off the lamp and dashed behind the robes just as the chamber door opened and the over-head gas lights came up with an ominous hiss.

Heavy footsteps approached the desk. "That idiot clerk's going to catch it for messing with my files again," muttered Barnabas Lanvale as he sat heavily into the chair.

Sarah heard the telephone receiver come off the hook, and Judge Lanvale curtly issue a number to the operator.

"Fuller. This is Lanvale. I've got cash. Come to my office with Lydia's bank information." He paused while the other man spoke in a faint squawk. "No, but it's a considerable down payment." Another pause. "Hold on, son. I told you it would take some time to raise the entire amount. Why don't you—" The squawk grew louder. "That's a real bad idea. I'll make you regret it, I swear. Give us another day or two, damn you. Hello?

Hello?" The judge slammed the earpiece back on the hook with a curse.

Sarah looked down and saw that her feet, clad in high-top shoes, were clearly visible under the robes. The gaslights were now glowing brightly. The man could not help but discover her.

Lanvale spat out another number at the telephone operator. "Mother. He wants the whole amount. No, he can't be reasoned with. I tried—" Mrs. Lanvale's tinny voice sounded like an angry wasp. "That's a risky strategy, Mother. We should—" More of the waspish sound. "All right, all right. I'll see what I can do. Good night, Mother." The earpiece went back on the hook with a gentle click.

Sarah held her breath for so long while listening that she became lightheaded and started to swoon. She clutched the hanger post and found it wobbly—the robes swayed as if caught in a stiff breeze. How could he fail to see that? She forced herself to breathe slowly and deeply.

The judge muttered a string of vile curses that stopped with the sound of liquid poured and then promptly guzzled. His footsteps came closer. Any second now, the man surely would pull her out, shake her violently, and demand to know why she had broken into his office. Then he would call the police. Or maybe he would exact his own brutal punishment. The footsteps stopped. She could smell the alcohol on his breath. She gnawed a thumbnail to head off a scream.

The gaslights went down, and the door slammed shut. Footsteps receded into silence.

Sarah waited and waited, not daring to move. Beads of sweat ran down her flanks and spine. After a time, the musty, unwashed smell of the robes grew increasingly intolerable. She left the office and began walking, slowly at first but with increasing urgency, until she was out of the courthouse and standing safely on the sidewalk. Night had fallen, and the streetlights cast a flickering golden glow.

Heading for the safety of home in a hansom cab, she finally

had a chance to assess her adventure. A curious, tingling sense of pleasure radiated from her solar plexus. All her life, she had behaved, been as good a girl as there ever was. How thrilling it was to break the rules! More significantly, how remarkable it was to discover she had a broader, more flexible range of choices at her disposal—all in the service of truth and justice, of course.

Justice needed to shine its purifying light into the dark scheme swirling around Lydia. The conspirators—Mrs. Lanvale, her son, and Luther Fuller—were conniving swindlers.

They were also likely murderers.

CHAPTER 32

JACK—FRIDAY, APRIL 22, 1910, 4:30 P.M.

$\mathcal{T}$he swollen, dirty water of the Jones Falls swept by just under the Fayette Street bridge. Jack looked down from above while imagining the pleasure of holding Ralph Stack by his ankles and dipping his head into the brown current until the guy confessed to running a fake investigation.

Stack would also cough up the location of his helper, the beater of girls known as Pretty Boy. Maybe the guy would spill dope about the murders of Anna Gilbert, Chance McCall, and Lucinda Pike. And why not imagine Stack ratting out the Black Cat Creeper?

Jack shook his head, wondering why he was wasting time launching foolish hopes into the putrid vapors rising from the stream.

Strolling east over the bridge and into the Fells Point neighborhood, he saw that the last of the flood muck had been shoveled off the streets. All that remained was a thin layer of sludge dried into a crazy quilt of cracked shapes. The next rain would wash it away—and maybe cause another flood, starting the whole nasty business all over again.

It was late in the day, and he had only one realistic option to get information about Ralph Stack: go to the Silverstrike Hotel and revisit Bob Foster. Bob, fearing the Black Cat Creeper, had told him to stay away. But the guy loved to trade gossip and, as a result, had the best dope on almost every crook in Baltimore. Jack was desperate enough for leads to risk a beatdown.

He could almost hear Sarah demanding to know why he wasn't checking up on Judge Lanvale, Luther Fuller, or Professor Jaworski. The Belvedere bellboys had, after all, seen the three of them coming and going from two murder scenes. He had a hunch that going after Stack was more important. Sarah didn't understand a detective's intuition, but he knew it was as valuable a tool as her scalpel or microscope.

A lively crowd inside the Silverstrike clustered around the bar. Bob himself laughed and joked from behind the mahogany as three bottle jockeys worked like demons to serve up shots and beers.

It was beyond rare in Baltimore for a crowd of white men to gather joyfully around a black man. But Bob's boxing championship and his resulting celebrity cast a magical spell capable of turning racial hatred into starstruck love.

"Bob, what round will you kayo Jack Johnson?" called a seedy guy in a misshapen derby. "I'm looking for that sweet left hook of yours to do the job by round six."

"What's the matter with my right hand, friend?" answered Bob as the throng roared. "All I know is that Johnson's just upped his life insurance, so he's sure worried about something." More laughter. "All right, everybody. Time for me to go plan how to spend my winnings. Because you're the best fight fans anywhere, drinks are half-price for the next fifteen minutes." Cheers followed Bob as he left through the door to his private office.

The mass surged even closer to the bar, eager to get a cheap drink. Jack knew coming in that the chance of seeing Bob was small, but getting through the mob to even ask for an audience was impossible. He turned and headed for the exit.

"Get outta the way. Move it." Two huge guys were shoving

people to make a path for Knucks Vogel and a fleshy bottle blonde in a low-cut dress. Vogel spotted Jack and waved.

"Hey there, Happy Jack. I owe you, brother. But first, I got to introduce my lady friend to Bob."

"Can I cash in on your gratitude by going with you to see the man?"

"Sure. Come stand next to me while my boys clear the way. Lola, this is Jack."

"Hi ya, baby." Lola gave Jack the kind of vacant, wide-eyed smile that comes from taking lots of cocaine in a short time.

"Hello." He gave her a wave and smiled back.

Bob was less than thrilled to have Knucks barge into his office but shook Lola's hand with a toothy smile. "I'm charmed to meet you, Lola. Your beauty's enough, I'm sure, to tame the beast in Knucks."

Lola giggled and asked for an autograph, which Bob promptly provided. "What's Harden doing with you, Knucks? Didn't think he still had a soul left to sell." Bob gave Jack an unfriendly stare.

"Hey, it looks like old Happy Jack has got Judge Barnabas Lanvale practically begging to get my baby girl into the debutante ball. We got one hell of a guy here." Knucks slapped Jack's back hard enough to leave a bruise.

"Congrats, Knucks," said Bob. "Harden, I had no idea you flew in such high social circles."

"Neither did I." Jack smiled, knowing Bob's interest was piqued.

"Gents, excuse us, but Lola and me are going to catch the early show at the Gayety. Got front-row seats for Sophie Tucker. What pipes on that dame. She sings loud enough to reach ships at sea."

Bob sat at his desk and eyed Jack as the couple left. "I told you to stay away. I knew you were thick, but it seems you're a fool, too. Or wait—maybe you're a ghost. The Creeper killed you, and now your lily-white self is haunting me."

"You want to know how I swung Judge Lanvale over to help Knucks?"

"Maybe."

"The judge is getting his mama to sponsor the daughter in exchange for debt relief."

Bob gave a booming laugh and pounded his desk with a palm. "The judge's mother is the biggest snob in town. Now she has to show off the gum-snapping kid of a loan shark to the cream of society." He laughed again. "Man, I love it."

Jack plopped into a chair opposite the desk. "Let me just mention a name. You decide whether you want to say anything."

"Ralph Stack, right?" Bob grinned at Jack's reaction. "See, I know what you're going to ask before you say it."

"You're a wizard in and out of the ring."

"I hear Stack's giving your lady friend a real hard time." Bob put his feet on the desk, showing off two-tone shoes that cost at least seventy-five dollars. "Say now—what's the deal with you and her? I usually can figure people, predict their taste, and all that. But you and that lady doctor? You're crude, ignorant, and broke. She's cultured, smart, and loaded. Don't make sense."

Jack sank in his chair. Bob wanted something juicy before spilling on Stack. Sarah was none of Bob's damn business, but that only made the guy more interested. "We're business partners. That's it."

"Uh-huh." Bob nodded with a smile.

"No hand-holding. No spooning. No romance."

Bob's smile got even bigger. "Come on. She must have been a virgin. Now you're teaching her how to love a man from head to toe, right?"

Jack was up and over the desk, nose to nose with the guy. "Shut your damn mouth."

Bob's feet crashed to the floor. He stood, fists at the ready, violence in his eyes. Jack jumped back. *What an idiot I am*, he thought. *I'm going to get my butt kicked from now until Wednesday.*

Bob didn't throw a punch. He smiled instead and playfully

poked Jack in the chest. "Your reaction told me everything, hoss." He sat back down. "What you want to know about Stack?"

"What's the guy's story?" Jack fell into his chair, feeling an odd sense of warmth on his cheeks. Good heavens, was he blushing? "Claims to be a government investigator. I've got my doubts."

"Man's as phony as a dime-store engagement ring." Bob pulled an expensive cigar from his suit jacket. "Ralph Stack used to be a lawyer—until he went to jail for defrauding a client out of some big-time cash. Got disbarred and went west for a while. Figured people forgot about his trouble and moved back to town a couple of months ago. He's working some small-time cons."

"How did Stack know about the coroner's complaint to the state medical board against Sarah—Dr. Kennecott?"

Bob lit up his stogie. "The coroner complained about your woman in a saloon while Stack was buying him drinks."

"Why's Stack doing this? Who's paying him?"

"Unclear, but the coroner sure does hate the lady."

"What about Judge Lanvale? He have anything to do with it?"

"You got the judge on the brain, son." Bob moved the cigar over to the other side of his mouth.

"Stack has this henchman—big guy, carries a lead pipe."

"Pretty Boy." Bob looked grim. "Man's as low as they come. His passion is beating up whores. Word has it he's killed more than one."

"Where's he hang out?"

"The gutter, mostly. If he's not there, check Buck's Saloon. Low dive on the corner of Exeter and Lexington."

"Got it." Jack stood.

"Don't dare show your face here again, Harden." Bob tapped cigar ash on the floor. "Unless you can tell me the winning horses in all nine races at Pimlico racetrack. Or something just as good."

JACK HEARD THE RUMBLE AS HE APPROACHED THE railroad tracks slashing across the street. Despite the black night, the locomotive was unlighted. It rolled past like a lumbering dragon, spewing flames and cinders. Trains killed at least one or two people a week in Baltimore. Public safety bleeding hearts wanted lights and gates at crossings, but nobody wanted to pay for the improvements. Getting run over by a train was just one of the city's dangers, and not necessarily the worst.

Streetlights were also iffy in this part of town. Pimps and hop peddlers solicited from the shadows, and strong-arm stick-up types lounged on front steps looking for well-dressed marks. Cops rarely showed up after dark.

Howls—joy, pain, or some combination—echoed down from Buck's Saloon on the corner ahead. The joint was as rough as they come, offering a cheap glass of whiskey along with a fight, whether you wanted one or not. Sure enough, two bloody-faced guys were going at it in front of the place. An audience shouted drunken encouragement as the fighters flailed and staggered.

The fug inside would gag a garbage man: mildew, urine, vomit, and unwashed bodies. Every guy—and plenty of the women—looked like they belonged on a wanted poster. This was the kind of place that didn't like strangers, and he felt the hostility right away.

Pretty Boy stood with his back to the bar, eyes glued on Jack. An even bigger guy, bald with a skull and bones tattooed on his neck, stood near, also flashing the evil eye.

"Listen up, chump," said Jack to Pretty Boy. "You're going to pay for beating on a girl. And when I say pay, I mean with every-thing you got. Start by handing over all your cash."

"Ain't this a good one?" Pretty Boy nudged the big man. "This mope's going to die standing up for a whore." He tossed his drink at Jack's feet, splattering his shoes.

"I'll use what I take off you for a shoeshine, too."

"This is gonna be fun." The goon lifted a pipe from the bar and stepped forward in a crouch.

"Wait." Jack held up a hand. "Let's talk about the rules first."

"What?" Pretty Boy stood up, eyebrows arched in bafflement. "There ain't no rules in a bar fight."

Jack delivered a kick to the man's crotch, and the guy went down like a sack of cornmeal falling off a wagon. "Okay. Whatever you say."

The bald guy pulled a knife and stepped forward.

"Drop the blade," said Jack leveling the Colt revolver. "Then give me his cash. If it's not enough, I'll take yours."

The man spit. "You ain't got the balls to use that, you yellow-bellied—"

The Colt boomed, and the man stared at the foul brown stream gushing down his trouser leg from the bullet hole in a nearby spittoon. He quickly bent down and went through the groaning man's pockets before tossing a bankroll that Jack caught.

"Hey, everyone," said Jack in a shout. "Pretty Boy here's been telling a great joke around town about Baltimore City Detective Snake Eyes O'Toole. But, gosh, he tells it so much better than me. Just ask Pretty Boy to tell you the one about how O'Toole is a sissy cream puff who's scared of his own shadow. It's a scream."

CHAPTER 33

SARAH—SATURDAY, APRIL 23, 1910, 8:00 A.M.

*S*he spent the night thrashing about in bed, thinking about the next day.

Jack had left a message with the housekeeper requesting to meet in the morning. She did not want to do so. Perhaps if his message had included an apology or even a hint of remorse for his rude behavior, she would feel differently. But as the clock ticked through the small hours, she concluded they had to meet. Catching a killer was more important than protecting her wounded sensitivity.

The Black Cat Creeper had also pledged to strike today. Upset as she was with Jack, she was unbearably anxious about his safety. She had to prevail upon him to take suitable precautions. That likely would be an exercise in futility, as his male pride and attendant bravado would outweigh any rational argument. Still, she had to try.

Grimly determined, she managed to slip into the Monumental Lunchroom and approach Jack at a table without drawing the waitress's attention.

"You look lovely this morning, Sarah," said Jack as he held her chair.

"Dispense with comments about my appearance." She sat

prim, irritation rising. He needed to apologize, not try to placate her with false flattery. "What of the assassin who is stalking you? Are the police having success in locating the individual? As you recall, today is the day inscribed on the drawing attributed to the so-called Black Cat Creeper."

"I'm going about my business as usual. If a cat crosses my path, I'll deal with it." Jack sat down and munched on a piece of toast, scattering crumbs on the table. "And let's just say I'm not looking for any help from the cops."

"You project indifference when you should exhibit levels of vigilance and apprehension that are at least equal to my own." The bullet graze on her scalp throbbed, seemingly determined to remind her how close to death both she and Jack had come at the hands of the assassin.

"I'm not indifferent. I'm mad as hell and worried a lot more about you than I am about me." He reached for his coffee cup. "I meant what I said about your looks, by the way. Nice outfit."

The table shook as she dropped both hands on it with force. She cared not at all how she looked. How could she, with her trust in Jack wavering, three unsolved murders on her hands, and a professional killer prepared to strike? Nice outfit—bah.

"Miss Sarah, where'd you come from?" The waitress smiled at her while refilling Jack's cup. "Your tea will be right up."

"I want no tea."

The waitress put a hand on her hip. "You don't like my tea?"

"She's just feeling poorly," said Jack.

"I am in perfect health—"

"How about some more toast?" Jack spoke quickly.

"Sure, hon. Right away." She gave Sarah a sideways glance before moving away.

He leaned over the table towards her. "Look, I'm sorry for what I said to you yesterday. Honestly, the last thing I want is to hurt you."

Her eyes remained glued to the table. She knew he was

looking into her face, conveying unsettling messages. "I accept your apology."

"Here's something that will cheer you up—Ralph Stack is a con man without the authority to investigate a bowl of succotash. The guy served time in jail for defrauding clients."

She looked up at him, blinking rapidly. "But he has a badge of authority."

"You can buy one for twenty-five cents at any novelty store."

"I was misled." *No, I was terribly stupid*, she thought to herself. She should have suspected the investigation was false, as the supposed charges were nonsense. But she was so concrete, so rule-bound, she naturally assumed the man was legitimate. "How did Mr. Ralph Stack know of the coroner's complaint?" She tore into her thumbnail, barely noticing the pain from her throbbing cuticle.

"Stack and the coroner discussed you between shots of whiskey."

"This means no complaint against me is pending before the Maryland State Medical Licensing Board." How wonderful it was to make that statement. A terrible weight vanished, leaving her awash in a wonderful sense of relief.

"Yep. Stack lied to you about everything."

Sarah shook her head vigorously from side to side and flopped her hands on the table. She wanted to say "thank you," "what a bad man," and "I am so relieved" simultaneously.

"Knew you'd be happy—and look at that, you're smiling. Gosh."

She became aware of a slight muscle tension around the left side of her mouth, which indeed meant a rare show of facial expression. A smile. How pleasurable—if only she could do it more frequently. "I will personally report Mr. Ralph Stack to the police."

"If Judge Lanvale's paying Stack, the cops won't do anything."

"That is an outrage." Sarah swept her hand across the table, knocking over the sugar bowl, spilling white crystals everywhere. She was beyond frustrated with the laxity of the Baltimore police. "Very well. I will confront Mr. Ralph Stack myself."

"Forget it." Jack wiped at the spill but gave up. He craned his neck, looking for the waitress. "He's a shady character who might get rough. I'll handle him. Your time is better spent elsewhere."

"It is not for you to dictate how I allocate my time." She was tired of Jack's high-handedness, tired in general of men ordering her about. "I am perfectly capable—"

"No, you aren't." He cut her off sharply. "Stay away from the guy. I mean it."

Sarah's neck and shoulders tensed with fury. She should get up and leave. But there was information to discuss, murders to solve. "Tell me what you have learned," she said through clenched teeth.

"Typical man." The waitress tut-tutted as she cleaned up the spilled sugar. "Expecting a woman to clean up his mess."

"I'm a natural-born slob, sorry," said Jack.

"Better make it worth a gal's while, then." She winked at Sarah and left.

He shook his head with a grin and then relayed what the Belvedere Hotel bellboys reported.

She said nothing while jotting notes. When finished, she tapped the pencil rapidly on the table, mentally repeating an old Baltimore and Ohio Railroad train timetable to calm herself.

Jack broke the silence. "Did you get the morgue report for Miss Pike? Sarah, are you with me?"

Sarah jounced in her seat, startled. "The medical examiner confirmed that Lucinda Pike received an injection in the upper right neck." She paused and took a deep breath. "But the autopsy and subsequent lab results indicate no clear cause of death."

"That report matches up with results for Anna Gilbert and Chance McCall, right?"

"There is a high probability that all three deaths are attributable to a murderer, or perhaps a team of murderers." She tapped a foot while gathering her thoughts.

"Jaworski hinted around that Lydia murdered a Boston woman for her money." Jack leaned over the table. "Don't you think it's strange that people keep dropping dead around her?"

She glanced at him and then back at the table. "I questioned Lydia yesterday. When identified as suspect in the murders, she issued an agitated denial and left."

"Agitation plus denial equals increased suspicion. I'll drop by the Lanvale place and have a chat with Lydia later this morning." Jack downed the rest of his coffee with a dribbly slurp.

The sound caused Sarah to clap her hands over her ears. He tapped her arm, and she pulled back in her chair. It took her some seconds to fight off another impulse to storm away. She uncovered her ears. "I confirmed that Mrs. Lanvale and Judge Lanvale are planning to place Lydia under legal guardianship. After Lydia's bank details are obtained, Mrs. Lanvale can access her finances."

"How did you—"

She cut him off. "I also overheard a telephone conversation during which Judge Lanvale told Luther Fuller, quote 'I've got the cash. Come to my office with Lydia's bank information.' But when Judge Lanvale admitted to having less money than requested, Luther Fuller refused to provide the information."

Jack sat up in his chair. "Looks like the only thing the Lanvales need to complete their con is to meet Fuller's asking price. This is big." He cocked his head. "I'm dying to know how you listened in on that telephone call. You must have used some brainy science trick."

"I hid in Barnabas Lanvale's chambers and eavesdropped while he spoke on the telephone. Prior to his arrival, I examined papers on his desk."

Jack leaned forward, eyebrows raised. "I'd say you're fibbing, but you never do that. And until this minute, I'd have said you'd never have the nerve to break into an office."

"I am capable of surprising you, then. Good."

"You got some dynamite dope." He frowned. "But you shouldn't take risks like that. It's not safe."

She ground her teeth and then drew in a deep breath. "We need more information on Reverend Smartwell. I have a noon appointment at his church."

"Great."

"Tell me your plan for thwarting the Black Cat Creeper."

"I've got it covered, don't worry."

"When considering personal danger, you are nonchalant. Yet you are paternalistic and overbearing regarding my own safety. I find this inequitable treatment annoying."

"Care to say that again without all the fifty-cent words?"

She stood. "Let us meet at my residence at 2:00 p.m. to continue our discussion."

Jack rubbed his chin. "What about your nosy neighbors? Now you know for sure they notice when I come and go."

"As my medical license is not in jeopardy, what my neighbors make of your visits is of no consequence."

"I like how you snap your fingers at people and tell them to mind their own business."

"I have never done such a movement with my fingers." She looked at her gloved hands. "I do not even know how to attempt the action."

He laughed. "It's a figure of speech. Sorry, I know you don't like those. What I mean is that you don't give a hoot—you don't care what other people think about you. And you're also one hundred percent authentic. It's a fine quality."

On her way out, Sarah asked the waitress to keep Jack in the lunchroom for the next thirty minutes. When asked why she muttered something about surprising him with something special. The waitress gasped. "I knew it!" She moved in for a hug, but Sarah evaded her and escaped outside.

The statement about her supposed indifference to others lingered on her mind. Yes, she did have difficulty understanding individuals and often felt uncomfortable around them. But that was more a matter of eccentricity than indifference.

She was not disinterested in people. She wanted to help them, both as a physician and as a detective. And she wanted others to respect her ability. Most of all, she wanted Jack to treat her as an equal partner. She wanted him to appreciate her, enjoy her company, and view her as attractive, alluring, and desirable.

Enough. She would consider the full depth of her wants at a later time.

WOMEN HOLDING SIGNS PROCLAIMING: "BAN DEMON Rum," "Saloons are EVIL," and "Lips That Touch Wine Will NOT Touch Mine" clustered around the Continental Building entrance.

An older woman dressed in white stood on a box addressing a small crowd of smirking men. "We of the Women's Christian Temperance Union propose a simple remedy for the war on drunkenness," she said.

"Surrender the fight! That's the best remedy!" called a man, which caused others in the crowd to cheer.

The speaker pointed at the heckler. "The remedy, sir, is total abstinence from intoxicating liquor. The only way to achieve that is to ban the manufacture and sale of alcohol. When that is accomplished, all the evils that plague society will vanish. You, my fine sir, will spend more time with your family, not with saloon barflies. Your wife will have more opportunity to cherish you, to love you."

"Sister, the only thing my wife wants is more opportunity to nag me—the saloon keeps me sane!" Laughter drowned out the speaker's reply.

Sarah threaded her way through the crowd and into the

lobby. Riding in the elevator, she realized fury raged within her. Strangely enough, she was acting out of emotion rather than reason. How interesting.

Stack opened the door immediately after she rapped. "Dr. Kennecott, excellent."

She stepped inside and refused the offer of a chair. Stack ambled around his desk and slouched into his seat. "You're here to say you're leaving town. Wise move. After all, I have the makings of a very compelling report, which now includes a most damning photograph backed up by the scandalous testimony of a bawdy house madam." He lifted a thick file folder and plopped it onto his desk.

"You, sir, are a fraud. There is no official investigation." She picked up the file folder and flung it at him, scattering pages in his lap. "There is no complaint before the Maryland State Medical Licensing Board."

He stood, papers fluttering to the floor. "You are making a grave mistake, doctor. I tried to reason with you, but it's clear that won't work. I have no choice but to report you to the board."

"You have no legal authority. You are, in fact, a criminal."

Stack approached to within inches of her, towering a head taller. "You assault a government agent and attempt to destroy evidence. I'm within my rights to restrain you." He reached out, but she moved away.

"If you touch me, I shall scream and draw the police. As a convicted felon, I doubt you wish that."

Stack scratched the back of his head. "You're the one in trouble. I've got evidence that you aren't fit to practice medicine—"

"Enough of your contemptible drivel." She stepped close and jabbed a finger into his chest with force. "You will cease and desist your investigative charade immediately. Is that clear?"

Stack grinned, eyebrows raised. "You're a tough little mutt, aren't you?"

"If you are referring to the level of my determination and fortitude in this matter, the answer is yes."

"Okay, doc. I may not be official, but all this is still useful." He gestured at the scattered papers. "I could still send my evidence to the board. Maybe it's not enough to yank your license. But it would sure dent your reputation."

"You still have the gall to threaten me?" She shot her finger at him again, but he stepped back.

"Look, just leave town for the next two or three weeks. Take a slow boat to Europe or something. Do that, and I'll destroy everything, including the photographic negative."

"I will remain in the city. Send your tawdry reportage to whomever you like. Recipients will disregard the information when they consider its illegitimate source."

"Come on. Be reasonable."

"I am being far more reasonable than you deserve. Good day, sir."

Flying down the stairs, Sarah was determined to contact the police, despite Jack's admonition against the action. Mr. Ralph Stack must be held accountable for his extortion and misrepresentation. Her momentum slowed once outside the building as the crowd drawn by the picketing temperance women had grown larger and more unruly.

Someone pinched her behind, and when she spun around, three well-dressed men—no doubt all considered respectable citizens—grinned at her. With a fair bit of pushing and shoving, she broke free of the gathering and hurried along until stopping by an alleyway to catch her breath. Just then, a large black cat darted from behind an overflowing trash bin and disappeared into the shadowy depths.

The sighting reminded her of something. She closed her eyes and thought hard. Riding in the taxicab to the lunchroom that morning, she had passed a storefront on Eutaw Place with a sign in its window: "Le Café du Chat Noir. Coming Soon. Watch Your Step!"

Jack had spoken of plans to visit Lydia at the Lanvale residence later this morning. He would pass the storefront on his way. On this, the day the Black Cat Creeper had threatened a lethal strike.

She had to thwart the assassin's plan. Doing so required one quick stop on the way to the purported café that celebrated ebony-hued felines.

CHAPTER 34

JACK—SATURDAY, APRIL 23, 1910, 10:00 A.M.

The waitress outdid herself, holding him up at the lunchroom for at least a half-hour after Sarah left. She kept him trapped in his seat with constant coffee refills and nonstop talk about what a happy man her husband was and how it was nature's way for people to pair off and settle down. Every time a customer called for something, she shot them a dagger stare without a break in the monologue.

Jack had no doubt that her husband was fussed over morning, noon, and night. The guy also surely agreed with her about everything. He didn't dare do otherwise.

When he finally got away, it felt great to stretch his legs during the short walk down Calvert Street to the Continental Building. A bunch of temperance gals was clustered around the entrance listening to the head crank deliver a speech to a heckling crowd of men. The temperance crusaders wouldn't give up until booze was outlawed across the country. But if those righteous women had any sense, they'd know their plan was doomed to fail. And, if by some miracle liquor was banned, it would be a disaster. Criminalizing that particular pleasure would only make the cops more corrupt and the crooks even richer.

He pushed through the crowd and into the lobby, with its

fancy marble, plush Turkish carpets, big potted palms, and heavy furniture. The double elevator doors, covered with curlicue brass work, loomed at the far end.

Jack smiled as he remembered meeting Sarah in this very place six months ago. She had struck him as odd, brainy, and stuck-up. He was wrong about the stuck-up part.

A directory listed Stack's office, and he took the stairs to what was obviously the low-rent section of the building. The walls needed paint, and the carpet runners were dirty and worn. Many of the doors had signs on paper pasted over the names of former tenants lettered on the frosted glass.

Jack threw open the office door. "Get lost, pal," said Stack while standing at a window open to a dark air well. "I'm closed for business." He dumped coffee from a mug out into the murky void.

"This is a meeting you've just got to take." Jack grabbed the man by the neck, causing him to drop his cup out the window. It landed a couple of seconds later with a faint splash.

"I'm a government agent," said Stack, gagging.

"You're a penny-ante bunco artist." Jack pushed him closer to the window. "There's garbage and a foot or two of disgusting water down there. Probably not enough to break your fall much."

"Okay, let's talk."

Jack let him go. "I know all about your con involving Dr. Kennecott. It ends now."

"You think you're the smart guy." Stack rubbed his reddened neck. "Well, she's smarter. Already marched in here and gave it to me hot. Spunky broad you got there."

Jack saw the papers on the floor. What the heck had happened to Sarah's cautious nature, her reliance on brains over passion? Something had changed in her. "Judge Lanvale's paying you. Give me the particulars."

Stack sighed. "I knew Lanvale from my lawyer days. He asked me to find a way to get Kennecott out of town, and the coroner gave it to me, gift wrapped. I about had her convinced to move away."

"You had Pretty Boy beat that girl to turn up the heat."

"Things got out of hand." He gave a nervous laugh. "He wasn't supposed to hurt her that bad."

"You and Lexie both have got spots reserved in hell. Give me all your cash."

"Now you're robbing me?"

"I'm taking up a collection for the girl." Jack stepped close to the man. "I expect you to give until it hurts."

Stack handed over a pile of bills. "That's all I got. How am I supposed to leave town?"

"Catch a freight train and hope the hobos don't kill you in your sleep. Okay, now where's that ambush photograph?"

Stack went to his desk. "It's right here." He pulled open a drawer and quickly reached in, only to howl when Jack slammed it closed on his fingers.

"Stupid move." Jack pulled a .32 revolver from the drawer. "Bud, I'm out of patience."

"Negative's in the second drawer." Stack whimpered while holding his bruised fingers. "Didn't have a chance to get prints."

"Throw it outside."

Stack found the glass negative plate, went to the window, and heaved it out.

"Toss all these papers, too. Move it."

When the office was clear of paperwork, Jack dropped the pistol out the window. "Now get lost."

"How about some dope you don't know?"

"You're done, slick Willie."

"I guarantee you'll want to hear this. It's about how Lydia Nightingale knew you were crazy before she met you."

"What?"

Stack held out a palm. "Give me my money back."

Jack peeled off ten bucks and stuffed it into the guy's breast pocket. "That's all you get. And I'll take it back if you're blowing smoke."

"Judge Lanvale paid me to check you out. Seems you saw some civilians get massacred overseas, went off your nut, and got kicked out of the army. Ever since then, you've gone around half-cracked seeing ghosts everywhere. Lanvale told me to write a report for Lydia Nightingale. She knew all about you before hitting town."

Jack wanted to smash something—Stack, the desk, the window, anything. He made do with a savage kick to a metal wastepaper basket, which flew across the room spewing crumpled pages. He stomped out of the office, feeling equal parts angry and stupid. So much for Lydia's validation of the ghosts tormenting him. She was just another con artist.

It was one more reason to pay her a visit. If necessary, he'd push right past the high-and-mighty Mrs. Lanvale and make Lydia talk about why she was playing him for a sap—and what role she had in three murders.

Stepping into the lobby from the stairwell, he spotted danger brewing: twin boys, three years old, both dolled up in silly sailor suit outfits. One child held up a wooden train, taunting the other kid, who loudly whined that it was his. A governess pleaded with them to behave, with no success.

Jack jogged toward the front door, suspecting what was about to happen.

"Percival! Lancelot!" The governess spoke in a high, panicky voice that signaled desperation to reestablish authority. "Since neither of you will behave, I am taking the toy away." She pried the train from the possessor's grasping fingers and held it out of reach.

Both kids began jumping up and down, screaming at the top of their lungs. Jack, well short of the exit, staggered to the wall. He pressed his hands tightly over his ears, but that did nothing to reduce the wailing from the dozen or more Moro ghosts around him, more than he had ever seen. Leading the charge was the gory woman with the baby who appeared during the séance. Unlike the others, the woman made no sound. Her smoldering black eyes bored into him as she pointed a bloody finger. Jack screamed curses in a random stream. She moved closer as the whole unearthly crowd of torn and grisly apparitions crowded around in a smothering swarm.

At first, his blows sailed right through the figures, but suddenly he made contact. He turned his full fury on it, fighting for his life. The ghosts faded, and he saw that his opponent was a potted palm, now a mess of torn fronds, broken stalks, and spilled dirt. People stood gawking—frozen with the odd combination of fear and fascination that comes from witnessing a grown man go bughouse crazy. Even the two bratty kids were silent, mouths hanging open.

Jack snatched his derby from the debris and ran out of the building, shoving temperance ladies and drawing salty curses in return. After a block, he slowed to a fast walk while brushing shredded foliage from his coat sleeves.

Thank God this insanity would stop if the Creeper did manage to kill him later today. He laughed, big and crazy, and kept on laughing when two men approaching on the sidewalk crossed the street to avoid the maniac.

"Hey guys," he shouted. "Every silver lining has a cloud, don't you know!"

CHAPTER 35

SARAH—SATURDAY, APRIL 23, 1910, 10:00 A.M.

"*L*e Café du Chat Noir. Coming Soon. Watch Your Step!" The sign propped inside the window was neatly lettered and included an artistic image of a black cat staring back with menacing golden eyes. A heavy shade pulled nearly all the way down behind the sign blocked a view of the interior.

The front door had a plate glass window with a "Closed" sign dangling from the doorknob. A round convex mirror hung above the entrance to give the proprietor a view of pedestrian traffic.

Sarah had taken a motor taxi and arrived here quickly. Assuming that Jack was walking from downtown, he would pass this spot later this morning on his way to visit Lydia at the Lanvale residence.

She rapped on the door. Nothing. Peering through the glass, she saw only darkness. More rapping brought no answer. A flurry of conflicting ideas rushed through her mind. The name of the place might simply be a coincidence, and she should cease this fool's errand. Perhaps there was a rear entrance. Should she look for a policeman? She turned the knob and stumbled as the door unexpectedly opened.

The place was cold and musty. She closed the door and stepped forward carefully, giving her eyes time to adjust. "Hello?" she called out. "I intend to search these premises, and so if anyone is here, I request that you make yourself known."

"The girlfriend."

Hearing the voice from the darkness, Sarah startled with a full-body flinch.

"You've hit the daily double with your bet on Brave in the first race and Foolish in the second." The rasp and sudden glow of a match showed a man standing against the far wall. He lit a dim oil lamp and gestured for her to approach.

She took several small steps toward him. "Why are you here, sir?"

"I could ask the same, but why waste time?" He raised a long knife. "I'll just kill you instead." The man was not old and not young. His clean-shaven face was bland, with no distinguishing features.

"You are the so-called Black Cat Creeper." Sarah was terrified but also strangely relieved to have found the assassin.

"I used to hate that name," he said with a sigh. "It sounds so theatrical, so amateurish. But it's had a real impact on my marketability. People are willing to pay so much more for the services of a celebrity."

"How much were you paid to kill Jack Harden, Mr. Creeper?"

The man stepped closer. "You're seconds from dying a horrible death. You should be screaming, pleading for mercy, not asking about my fee schedule." He smiled. "But it's nice to have someone interested in my work. So, maybe I won't kill you—I'll take you to a basement and keep you chained up for my ongoing amusement."

"I will pay you handsomely to call off your assignment."

"What makes you think I care about money? Maybe I'm a lunatic." He jabbed the air in front of her playfully with his knife. "You know, like Jack the Ripper."

"I have observed the violently insane in asylums and am

reasonably confident that you are not among their rank. You likely have a narcissistic, anti-social personality with a profound lack of empathy but are sane. Killing for you is primarily a business with a secondary interest in satisfying a sadistic compulsion."

"And Mother said I'd never find a woman who would understand me," he said with a laugh.

"Will you permit me to reach into my handbag? I wish to show you something."

"If it's a weapon, rest assured I'll cut you—not to kill, but to cause unimaginable pain."

"It is not a weapon." Slowly, she opened her bag and pulled out a thick stack of cash. "I offer you one thousand dollars, freshly withdrawn from my bank account, to call off your assignment."

"For a gal who's not much to look at, you still manage to arouse me." He checked a watch. "Stand against the wall over there while I attend to business. Don't give me a reason to slash you."

They moved to the door with him positioned to look up at the mirror outside and observe oncoming foot traffic. His left hand rested on a lever rising from the floor. Whatever blend of nerve and desperation that had brought her this far was faltering. This man had something terrible planned for Jack, and she had no power to stop it.

Power. She knew some adults remain locked in the infantile emotional phase of struggling with their environment. A baby is thrilled to shake a rattle but also deeply frustrated to have so much else literally beyond their grasp. An infant facing this dilemma cries. An adult trapped within the same childish outlook has a constant need to prove their power, often through inflicting pain, misery, and even death.

"It is clear to me that you are highly intelligent and remarkably resourceful," said Sarah. "Once you undertake a task, you assume masterful command."

"If I didn't hate all of humanity, I might come to like you."
He gave a quick, high-pitched chuckle while watching the
mirror. "I do plan everything carefully. People are so thick I
could get away with a lot less effort. But that wouldn't be sport-
ing, now would it?"

"I would very much like to know of your expert plan." With
the right words, it might be possible to exploit his personality
flaw and disrupt his plot. The only other option was to grapple
with him physically, which was hopeless.

"I've outdone myself this time." He laughed. "I sat right
behind you at the lunchroom this morning while you and
Harden gabbed. What a gas it was to hear you ask about his
plan for thwarting me. That guy never had a chance. I'm way,
way smarter."

"You learned he will pass by here this morning."

"Yes, on his way to the Lanvale place. He's in for a surprise.
See those metal doors on the sidewalk in front? You know, the
kind that open to permit deliveries and then fold flat? A pedestrian considers the closed metal doors part of the sidewalk and
steps on them without a care."

"You installed that lever to make the doors open inward and
cause Jack to fall into the space below."

"Clever, right?" The man ignored the mirror and gazed
steadily at her. "He'll plunge eight feet and come to rest on a
bed of two-inch sharpened metal stakes coated with rat poison.
If he's lucky, a spike will pierce his heart or brain. If not, he
will die a lingering, painful death. Either way, the newspapers
will have a field day with my diabolical murder in front of the
Black Cat Café. The legend of my brilliance will grow still
larger!"

A policeman appeared at the door and pounded. "Open up. I
can hear you hollering in there, buddy."

"If you expose me, I'll kill you both. Understand?" The
Creeper hid the knife behind his back. "Talk to him."

Sarah opened the door. "Greetings, officer."

"Hello, little lady." He tipped his tall leather helmet. "Welcome to the neighborhood, folks."

"Thank you," said the Creeper. "If you will excuse us, my wife and I are dealing with an urgent matter."

The policeman stepped into the doorway. "What's urgent is that you need me to watch over this place. Watch it very carefully. There's been vandalism in this area. Arson, even."

"How much cash to get rid of you?" asked the Creeper in a strained voice. The arm holding the hidden knife twitched.

"I don't like your attitude, Charlie. What do you have behind your back?"

"Will ten dollars suffice, officer?" Sarah held out a crisp new bill.

The policeman's eyes got wide. "Indeed, it will." He snatched the bill. "When do you plan to open?"

"Get lost, you—"

"Very soon," Sarah offered another bill. "Please excuse the gentleman, officer. He is eager to conduct business."

The policeman glared at the Creeper while taking the additional money. "Count your blessings for the wife, Charlie. Otherwise, I'd have to teach you some manners." As he stepped away, Jack walked past at a quick pace, head down.

"Damn—missed him." The Creeper pressed against her. "Close the door, girly."

Sarah hesitated, knowing if she dashed outside, Jack would come to her assistance, as would the policeman. But the Creeper might attack anyone who tried to intervene and injure them terribly. She closed the door.

"Just so you know—if you'd run away, I would have let you go and dashed out the back to my waiting automobile." He laughed. "You'd be all safe and sound."

"You are a cruel man."

"You're about to find out just how cruel." He grinned. "Now that we've got the time, I'm going to have some fun with you. Take off your clothes."

"No."

With a flick, his knife cut a button off her suit jacket, opening it to expose the lower part of her shirtwaist.

"I'll cut the clothing off if you don't play along. Drop the purse and take off that jacket. Now."

Despite her terror, Sarah logically assessed options. The man was a sadist. If she resisted, he would not hesitate to inflict harm before forcing himself upon her. He might even derive more perverse pleasure from torture than from the sexual act. "Very well." She let go of her handbag, removed her jacket, and dropped it to the floor.

"There's not much to you, is there, girly?" He looked her up and down. "But you'll do. Unbutton that blouse."

She pulled the hem of the shirtwaist up from her skirt and undid some buttons from the bottom. "I wish to remove my hat." She reached to the back of her head.

"No. Leave the hat on." He stepped close and reached inside her open shirtwaist to stroke her corseted waist. "Take everything else off." His voice was husky.

Sarah pulled a three-inch hatpin from her hair and plunged it into the Creeper's right arm. He screamed as the knife clattered to the floor. She dashed to escape, but the man blocked her way, his back against the glass door.

"So, you want to play rough." With a lewd smile, he leaned back on his heels, pulled the pin from his arm, and let it drop. "Now it's my turn to ram something long and hard into you."

She pushed the man with all her might, causing him to lose his balance and crash through the glass onto the sidewalk. She opened the shattered door, but the Creeper got to his feet and blocked her way once again.

"What's going on here?" The policeman came running back, nightstick at the ready.

"Just a little marital spat, officer," said the Creeper as he brushed glass shards from his clothing. "You know how excitable women can be."

"This man is a hired assassin who was in the process of sexually assaulting me," said Sarah.

The cop looked at her unbuttoned shirtwaist. "Step aside, Charlie, and let the lady out."

"I assure you this is strictly a matter between man and wife." The Creeper moved away from the door.

"I am unmarried," said Sarah as she moved outside. "Officer, this man is highly dangerous."

The Creeper punched the policeman in the stomach, knocking him to the ground, gasping for breath. Then he turned to her. "I have some unfinished pleasure left with you, girly. I'm leaving town but will be back soon." He dashed inside and disappeared into the darkness.

She knelt and tended to the fallen man. "Sir, your diaphragm is spasming. Draw your knees to your abdomen to ease the injury." She helped push his legs into position, and he soon recovered.

"You've got one hell of a husband, lady."

"I have no husband."

"Wait here while I call for more men." He got to his feet and jogged toward the police call box down the block.

Sarah stood by the smashed door, wondering what to do. She usually would, of course, follow the policeman's instructions. But if she was caught up in this affair officially, there would be much unwanted attention, including from the newspapers. Her friend Margaret Bonifant would be horrified and would absolutely insist that Sarah cease detecting. And what of Jack? He would mollycoddle her even more, perhaps to the point where he might demand that she stop working immediately.

She was resolved to conclude this case and bring the murderer—or murderers—to justice. Beyond that, she had worked too hard to let other people dictate her choice of career.

Logic prescribed that the Creeper had fled the building before more policemen arrived. Sarah went back inside the storefront, looking and listening carefully. Confident that her attacker was not present, she hurriedly fixed her clothing and retrieved her handbag before stepping back onto the sidewalk, glass crunching under her shoes. She hailed a hansom cab and directed the driver to the First Baltimore Church of Spiritualism to keep her appointment with Reverend Smartwell.

CHAPTER 36

JACK—SATURDAY, APRIL 23, 1910, 10:30 A.M.

*T*he city has many ways to maim and kill. Streetcars, wagons, motor vehicles. Runaway barrels, rabid dogs, yawning construction pits. Sidewalks jagged with broken glass and slick with foul liquids. Violence, both targeted and random.

Pay attention or pay the undertaker.

"Get yourself straight. Watch out, damn it," Jack muttered to himself while loping away from his cuckoo bout with a potted plant.

His heart was smashing against his ribs, with everything still feeling hazy and unreal. Luckily, he had more time to settle down during the hike to visit Lydia. He could only hope to stay ahead of the ghosts that were, as always, close behind.

Nothing of much interest happened on the way to the Lanvale place. He stopped for a shoeshine—it wouldn't make a speck of difference to whoever answered the door, but it made him feel better. On Eutaw Place, a big cop leaned into a café doorway, no doubt shaking down the proprietors. The place wasn't up and running yet, so the blue boy probably had to settle for a bit of cash instead of free food.

Further up the street, Jack saw Niblett, the butler, coming

down the Lanvale's front steps, carpetbag in hand. The man nodded curtly in response to a wave.

"Looks like my lawyer friend was able to help you," said Jack.

Niblett smiled wanly. "He was, thanks, mate." His accent had slipped from plummy to something rougher and much less formal. "I'm out on bail while the bobbies investigate. They won't find anything because we both know they aren't that keen, yeah?"

"Yeah." Jack eyed the guy, who was now way looser—and shiftier—than he had been before. "What's with the bag? You going somewhere?"

"Aye. I've been sacked."

"The Lanvales cut you loose. Bad break."

"Bastards." He spit on the sidewalk. "They think I'll take it laying down. No bloody way that's happening."

"Let's talk."

"Nah, sorry, mate. Best thing for me to do is leg it. Cheers." He brushed past and walked away fast.

A young woman in a maid's outfit answered his knock. "Mrs. Lanvale is not at home. Sir." She twisted a feather duster in both hands while staring at Jack's feet.

"I'm here to see Miss Nightingale."

The duster fell, and the maid stooped to retrieve it. "Miss Nightingale isn't receiving visitors. Sir."

Jack was about ready to push by when Lydia appeared over the maid's shoulder. "It's all right, Mary. You can let him in."

Lydia looked tense and worn, with dark circles hanging under bloodshot eyes. Her ruffled white dress contrasted with the sickly grey-green color of her face. "Hello, Jack. You should know that Sarah has returned my money, so you're under no obligation to brief me."

Jack stepped inside. "Let's sit down."

"Lydia is quite fatigued from the terrible events of the past couple of days." Fuller loomed behind her. "You must leave."

"We need to talk." Jack glared at Lydia. "About a certain report you got before we met."

Lydia smiled faintly. "Let's use the sewing room. It's more private." She began walking.

Jack followed, wondering why there was a sewing room in this place. Mrs. Lanvale sure didn't seem like the type to work on a backstitch. After going down a long hallway, they entered a small room with no sewing materials in sight. Lydia and Fuller sat on the sofa, and he took the armchair opposite.

"I'd like to ask Fuller some questions before I start with you." He kept his gaze on Lydia.

"If you must." A hand flitted to her neck.

"Fuller, you're a boy genius when it comes to chemistry. I suppose you know all about potassium chloride and adrenaline."

"Regarding the first, yes, of course—it's a basic compound," said Fuller with a smirk. "As for the second, I've never heard of it."

"Know how to handle a syringe?"

"No, but I imagine it's a simple device." Fuller's hypnotic blue eyes were wide open in his pasty face, making him look like a figure in a cheap wax museum. "Are you referring specifically to the hypodermic needle found in the butler's silver chest?"

"The liquid found with the needle was a mix of those two chemicals."

"Only a man with especially low intelligence would think I could inject Lucinda Pike while seated in full view the whole time during the séance." Fuller gave his odd breathy laugh.

"Tell me why you visited Anna at the Belvedere Hotel around the time of her murder. And what was in that leather satchel you were carrying?"

Fuller blinked as his smirk faded. "You have sharp-eyed informants." He looked down. "I sorry you have to hear this, Lydia, but Anna was addicted to Veronal—barbiturates. She couldn't get enough of the stuff. It fell to me to ration it. That's why I visited her at the hotel. I had to hand over her evening's supply of pills—three, to be exact."

Lydia gasped. "I don't believe it—she never showed any sign of drug abuse."

"Lots of drug fiends can hide their problem," said Jack. "For a while, anyway."

"Anna was getting worse," said Fuller with a sigh. "She struggled with me that evening, demanding more pills. Said she was upset—heartbroken."

"Care to offer an answer for peddling Lydia's bank information to Judge Lanvale?"

"I—I merely—" Fuller stammered, his aloof composure finally cracked. He slumped forward in his seat, looking like a schoolboy about to get a tongue lashing from the headmaster.

"Anytime you're ready, sonny."

Fuller looked at Lydia. "I meant to tell you. Judge Lanvale had some investment ideas and asked for my help. I lied and told him I knew your financial details."

Jack scoffed. "You were going sell the judge phony information and skip town with his money."

The man squirmed, his eyes darting around the room.

"Luther, you are despicable," said Lydia.

"You haven't heard the worst of it," said Jack. "Fuller's working with the Lanvales to have you declared mentally unfit. They've got a guardianship document that gives Mrs. Lanvale total control over you and your money. Fuller signed it as a witness."

Lydia's face went from sallow to dead white.

"I can explain," said Fuller. "Please."

"Anna Gilbert and Lucinda Pike weren't in on your scheme to defraud Lydia, but they found out," said Jack. "You killed them to keep your secret. Fraud and murder. They go together like pork and beans."

"No!" Fuller was on his feet, sputtering. "I did not kill them. I swear."

"If not you, then who?"

"I have no idea." Fuller swiveled his head to look at Lydia, who would not meet his gaze. "Please—after all we've been through together. You know I'm loyal, that I only have your best interests at heart."

Lydia stood and slapped him. "Luther, you're fired. Get out."

"You can't cast me aside." Fuller touched the radish-red handprint on his pallid cheek. "You need me for that spirit guide business."

"Just go," she said.

Jack stood. "Son, you look good for the murder of three people. You can either wait for the cops to pick you up or take off. Your choice."

Fuller pointed at Jack. "You imbecile. There is no evidence tying me to any murder." He turned to Lydia and stammered for a moment before stalking out of the room.

With a low moan, Lydia fell onto the sofa, her body tremoring. She began speaking in her whispery alternative voice:

The Whole of it came not at once —
'Twas Murder by degrees —
A Thrust — and then for Life a chance —
The Bliss to cauterize —

The Cat reprieves the Mouse
She eases from her teeth
Just long enough for Hope to teaze —
Then mashes it to death —

Jack took Lydia by the shoulders. "I know this is an act, lady, so stop playing around with the cat and mouse stuff. Why did you hire the Black Cat Creeper?"

The tremors stopped and she smiled tensely. "It's not entirely an act. My spirit guide exists and does speak through me. I just find it convenient to mimic her from time to time."

He tightened his grip. "The Creeper almost killed Sarah. Was that part of your sick plan?"

"Is Sarah all right?" She gave him a genuine look of horror.

"Tell me why you set an assassin on me. On us."

"Jack, I swear I don't know what you're talking about. Was it the poem? We were in the thick of a discussion about murder, and those lines came to mind." She cried what looked like real tears. "How is Sarah?"

"You're a con artist and a killer."

"You're hurting me." She sobbed pitifully. "Sarah!"

He let her go. "Sarah's fine."

Lydia bawled into a handkerchief for a long moment. When she looked up with her puffy, blotchy face, she looked strikingly like her daughter after a good cry.

"I would die if anything happened to Sarah." She drew a shaky breath. "I don't care if you believe me, but it's true. And I only ever wanted to help you, Jack."

"Of course I believe you. I'm a fool and a nutcase, right?"

"I'm the fool. Luther and the Lanvales have more than proven that." She fell back against the sofa. "I had better leave this house. Can we meet again later?"

"I'm not letting you out of my sight until I get the truth. But not here. Pack your luggage, and I'll take you to Sarah's."

"I'm the last person she wants to see. She hates me."

"Yeah, she's unhappy with you all right. But the three of us need to talk."

He grabbed a bell sitting on a table and, feeling like an idiot, rang. The nervous maid appeared and agreed to help pack and then call for transportation.

Lydia stood and touched his arm. "Jack, your auric field is intense—many angry spirits are hovering. They appeared to you today in force, led by that woman with the baby, right? Resolution may be at hand."

"You're good." He looked her straight in the eye. "Too good to be true."

CHAPTER 37

SARAH—SATURDAY, APRIL 23, 1910, 12:00 P.M.

ells from the Baltimore Cathedral sounded twelve times, consigning one of her more difficult mornings to the past. Stepping from the cab outside Reverend Jared Smartwell's church, Sarah expected an uneventful meeting. Unlike the last two encounters, she had no confrontational intent. All she wanted was information.

The placard near the entrance had a new message: "Have faith in the radiant and glorious future! The SPIRITS will empower the living to reject LUST—for flesh, money, and deceit!"

Such a future seemed quite far away, she thought, as all the varieties of lust specified were well-represented during this investigation.

She entered the dark, silent foyer. Faint light spilled into the hallway from the reverend's office. Instead of calling out as before, she walked directly to the door, rapped once, and pushed it open.

Smartwell stumbled to his feet from an armchair, brochures tumbling to the carpet. "I'll knock you to the moon, you infernal scallywag!" He stared at her bug-eyed for a second before working to kick the fallen reading material under his chair.

Sarah saw the lurid cover of something entitled: "House of Pleasure, Boulevard de la Chapelle, Paris," featuring a nude woman frolicking in a boudoir. Another item depicted an ocean liner with the caption: "Take the White Star Line to Europe in Total Luxury!"

"I am sorry to disturb you, Reverend." Her new habit of barging in was unquestionably rude, but surprise had its advantages. "Do you wish to reschedule our appointment?"

"I beg pardon for my ejaculation, Miss Kennecott." He wrung his chubby hands furiously. "I meant no disrespect. Hah. Yes." Smartwell nudged the last brochure under his chair with a toe.

"I wish to talk if you are willing."

"Of course, miss, of course. I am always at the service of anyone seeking counsel about our moral duty to impart celestial wisdom upon our wicked world." He licked his lips as his gaze shifted around the room. "Oh, dear. I did not intend to allude to any spiritual deficiency on your part. Please accept my apology."

"I do not care about your view of my spirituality, Reverend, but I do have some additional questions about the deaths of Lucinda Pike and two other individuals."

"I like a woman who gets right to the point. Indeed, I do." Smartwell smiled while smoothing his maroon silk cravat with an odd repetitiveness. "Although I do fail to see what I can add to what is known about Miss Pike's tragic death. But, yea, please do sit."

Sarah sat stiffly and readied her notebook and pencil. "I have recently learned that you graduated from medical school."

"That was long, long ago." The reverend chuckled as he sat. "I found that spirits can offer people far more succor than any paltry medical ministration." He extended his pink hands to her in a gesture of supplication. "I apologize, nay apologize profusely, if I have offended you as a physician. I am sure you have succor aplenty to offer—"

"Sir, let us return to the subject of your medical education."

"Certainly. But what, pray tell, does my checkered past have to do with anything? You appear to be researching my humble, dare I say boring, history with great avidity."

"As you recall, a hypodermic syringe along with a vial of liquid were found after the death of Miss Pike. The liquid in the vial was a mixture of adrenaline and potassium chloride. The vial and syringe suggest medical training on the part of whoever used them to kill her."

He shifted in his chair with a nervous laugh. "Are you perchance venturing to suggest that I have some involvement in the tragic death of our dear Miss Pike?"

"I am merely seeking to clarify evidence and formulate one or more logical hypotheses. Hence my interest in your medical training."

"Logic, you say." He ran a twitchy hand over his forehead. "Tell me, Miss Kennecott, are you familiar with phonograph records?"

"Yes, but—"

"Those narrowly interested in logic care only about examining the grooves of the record and working out how they convey sound. But those with a broader view—those who seek to live fully and robustly—they listen to the music."

"Reverend, I fail to understand your point."

Smartwell looked at his watch and jumped to his feet. "Miss, I must further beg your forgiveness, but I am pressed for time. And time waits for no man. Or woman. Hah. Yes." He went quickly behind his desk and began shuffling papers.

Sarah stood across the desk from him. "I need answers to certain questions, Reverend Smartwell. I am quite determined."

"Indeed, you are. Hah. Indubitably." He began fidgeting with a letter opener.

Her gaze went first to the opener and then to a nearby box on the desk labeled "OUT." A familiar document bearing official seals lay facing her: a copy of the guardianship document declaring Lydia Nightingale mentally unfit. But the bold-faced name of Lydia's designated guardian wasn't Mrs. Lanvale—it was Reverend Jared Smartwell.

"Thank you for seeing me, sir. I will depart."

"Yes, yes. Good day, miss." His eyes shifted to something behind her. "What are you doing here? It's too early—"

A terrible blow. Bright flash. Falling, falling. Blackness.

CHAPTER 38

JACK—SATURDAY, APRIL 23, 1910, 2:05 P.M.

*T*he housekeeper brought a tea tray to the library and looked to set it on the table, but a pile of books was in the way. Jack pushed them to the side.

"Thank you, sir," said the housekeeper. "The public library just delivered those materials for Miss Kennecott."

"Any word from Sarah?" he asked. "She's supposed to be here by 2:00 p.m. It's a few minutes past."

"She telephoned and reminded me to serve you coffee, sir. She also anticipated returning from her meeting with Reverend Smartwell to meet you at the appointed time."

"Please let me know right away if you hear anything."

"Yes, sir." The woman left.

"Sarah got held up," said Lydia. "I'm sure it's nothing to worry about. How do you like your beverage?"

"I love it." He gulped from the steaming mug.

"Coffee served instead of tea?" Lydia arched an eyebrow. "You must spend quite a bit of time here. Are you courting my daughter?"

"Drop the games, lady. You couldn't play the concerned mother to save your life." Jack knew Lydia was a terrible parent, but only that for sure. He had grilled her about the Black Cat

Creeper and the deaths of Anna Gilbert, Chance McCall, and Lucinda Pike to no avail. She claimed to know nothing, and he was about ready to believe her.

"You know, I never did like this room," she said with a sweep of her hand. "Silverfish—those crawly bugs that live in books? I sense them all around. It's most unpleasant."

"Just like you sense my ghosts, right? I'd be a big casino spirit medium, too, if I got written reports in advance. Makes the job so much easier."

"Barnabas Lanvale sent me that report about you. I didn't ask for it. And I didn't need it."

"You know how to tap dance your way around a con, I'll give you that. Just like you dodged a murder rap when your Boston benefactor dropped dead."

"Jack, you give me far too much credit as a schemer." Lydia sighed. "I had to live with that woman in Boston, even though I did not like her. I was in desperate financial circumstances."

"That her death cleared up nicely."

"I was as shocked as everyone else, both when she died and when she put me in her will. As for the money—the newspapers reported the estate was large, and it was. But after paying the woman's debts, there was almost nothing left."

"What about your big Boston bank account?"

"I personally closed that pitifully small account before I came to Baltimore."

"To con Mrs. Lanvale. Too bad she had the same idea."

"Don't you understand?" Lydia gave a quick laugh. "I'm a leech, not a confidence artist. Mediums like me can't make enough money from séances to pay assistants, to live well. We need rich believers to take us in, to support our lifestyle. But eventually, they get tired of us, and we have to find someone else."

"How's that different from working a con?"

"I communicate with spirits. That's real."

He snorted.

281

"Doubt me if you wish, but I know about the native woman with the baby that appeared to you during the séance." Lydia looked him in the eye and stepped very close. "No one else but you saw her, did they? But I channeled her spirit. I know what she wants from you."

"Right." Jack looked down at the pile of books and noticed some newspaper clippings on top. One was from a 1901 Chicago paper and bore the headline "Doctor of Death Number One Walks Free." The story related how Dr. Jared Smartwell was indicted for the death of a wealthy man during a minor surgical procedure. Also charged was the man's young wife, who allegedly paid the doctor to become a widow. The trial ended with a hung jury.

"Jack? The native woman spirit wants two things from you. First, to apologize for the deaths of innocent people on that mountain. Second, she wants you to throw your pistol away. She says you used it to kill her husband during the battle before the massacre."

He barely heard, so strong was his sense of dread about Sarah's meeting with Smartwell.

"If you follow her wishes, your haunting will stop."

A clock chimed, reporting that Sarah was now fifteen minutes late. The bad feeling in his gut grew steadily worse. But the odds were that everything was fine. If he dashed out on a rescue mission, he'd get another lecture from Sarah about how she could look after herself, thank you very much.

He flipped to the next clipping, which was headlined "Doctor of Death Number Two Gets Off." A separate trial acquitted Smartwell's surgical partner, Dr. George Funston. Funston— "Galloping" George Funston, the comedian clerk in Judge Lanvale's office. He and Smartwell must be hatching another murderous plot. "Lydia, call the cops. Get them over to Smartwell's church. Sarah's in danger."

Her reply faded as he ran out the door into the early evening chill.

CHAPTER 39

SARAH—SATURDAY, APRIL 23, 1910,
2:15 P.M.

*H*er sister Grace stood near as a huge mechanical pile driver crashed down on a steel post with a resounding CLANG. Despite the mud, her sister wore pristine white shoes and a spotless yellow dress that fluttered in the breeze.

"A remarkable machine," said Sarah. "I am assuming it operates using high-pressure steam in conjunction with a positive valve gear. What is your estimate of the total foot-pounds of force exerted upon the target?"

CLANG.

"You know I have no mind for such things," said Grace. "Ask me about relationships. Better yet, about love."

"I prefer to consider aspects of experience defined by logic and the laws of physics." Sarah noticed filthy splatters on her white shirtwaist. Her legs were sunk above the ankles in vile muck.

CLANG.

"Yes, but you have feelings, too." Grace stepped closer. "Deep feelings, even though they make you uncomfortable."

"I am aware of my discomfort regarding emotion. That is no revelation, as you are a dream—a projection of my own mind."

CLANG.

"Accept your emotions, Sarah. And accept my advice that you try to express the love you feel."

"Love for what? Or who?" Sarah noticed her body was fast sinking into the mud, past her knees, past her belt, past her bodice. It was eating her up, as wholly as the tide rushing in over the sands.

CLANG.

Her eyes flitted about, unfocused. She was aware of shapes and murmurs, but an awful, pulsing pain dominated everything. Slowly, she recalled the church office and the exchange with Reverend Smartwell—that someone had interrupted with a blow to her head.

The reverend was speaking. "There is only one solution to this fine mess of yours. A four-year-old surely would know what to do."

"Okay, I'll just run out and find little Shirley, then," said an unknown man. "She'll fix things in a jiffy."

Sarah was lying on the floor where she fell. A pair of men's shoes stood close by while another pair paced back and forth. Standing seemed impossible. Just focusing her eyes took effort.

"Sir, you try my patience."

"Don't mind if I do. You can try mine, too."

"You infernal scallywag," said Smartwell. "Those puns are as empty as your wallet."

"I'll have you know I'm quite well-off as a comedian."

"Is that so?"

"Yeah. I'm better off stage than on."

"May I remind you, sir, that you put us in this most uncomical situation. I've tried in the past, with limited success, to emphasize the need for seriousness on your part. But since I've been away from you a long time—"

The other man fell to one knee and began singing:

I've been away from you a long time,
I never thought I'd miss you so.
Swanee, how I love ya! How I love ya!
My dear old Swanee.

"Stop that accursed caterwauling!" said Smartwell in a near
shout. "You are at fault, sir."

"People do tell me I have faults."

"Now we're getting somewhere."

"Supposedly I don't listen, and blah, blah, blah."

"You are a hopeless fool, sir."

"Oh, yeah? If you're so smart, why did you leave that paper
on your desk face-up? Now she's got the lowdown. She knows
what we're up to. We're about to be sold down the river. Up the
creek—"

"She did not uncover our grand plan. But now that you have
struck her, you must finish the job."

"Finnish? Yeah, but without Russian. Still, I need to make
sure nobody can Czech into my deed. People would Haiti me.
But if Iran—"

"Confound it, I entreat you just to give her a shot. Then I
will alert the police and state she burst into my office in a
hysterical state, collapsed, and struck her head on the desk. That
will account for the blow to the skull and her death."

"Call the police before you kill again," said Sarah in a
croaking voice, cheek resting on the carpet. "Turn yourselves in,
and you may avoid the hangman."

"A noose around my neck," said the other man, "is a knotty
proposition that I refuse to get roped into, lady."

"You can't even knock her out properly, you nincompoop,"
said Smartwell. "Here's yet another nice barrel of beets you've
pickled me in."

She managed to sit up, her back against the desk. A loose
lock of hair was stuck to the dried blood on her neck and pulled

her head into an odd tilt. "Reverend Smartwell. You have performed acts of murder."

"Wait just a parsnip-picking second," said the other man, who wore spectacles perched on the end of his nose and was as thin as Smartwell was portly. "George Funston here gets equal billing for those performances." He twirled an imaginary cane and tipped his derby.

"Encore, Galloping George, encore," said Smartwell. "Use your trusty hypodermic to kill again. I'll then take a chance with the Carabinieri."

"Good luck with that. I took a chance with Miss Cara Binieri and got my face slapped." Funston reached into his jacket and produced a syringe, which he filled with clear liquid from a vial. He then winked at Sarah. "I'm thrilled. I usually only get called for an encore after paying the rent."

"The police will trace my death to you both."

"Good gracious me, you have considerably more confidence in the local authorities than I, Miss Kennecott," said Smartwell. "They are ineffectual. As a man who firmly believes in law and order, that is no laughing matter."

"*No Laughing Matter*—how did you know the title of my memoir?" Funston stood with a hand on his hip. "It's either that or *We Killed the Room and A Few Others Besides*."

"Is that what all your scribbling was about lately? I thought you were stealing jokes to improve your pathetic comedic stylings. Or doing bad forgeries of good reviews."

"I'll have you know I am a master forger. I have certificates to prove it. And don't forget my skill will make us hilariously rich."

"Money is not funny, sir," said Smartwell.

"Now, that's also a good title for my autobiography, which can be summarized thus: 'A two-man team mixes slapstick comedy with uproarious murder antics.' Too bad it can only be published posthumously. Or should I say post-humorously."

"You, sir, have no literary talent."

"Maybe you're right. Then again, if my book makes the best-seller list, people will buy the thing no matter how bad it is."

"Perform the correct action and call the police." Her vision had gone blurry, and she was having difficulty concentrating.

"The correct action, sir, is to jab, not gab," said Smartwell." Get to it, man."

Funston kneeled and pulled off Sarah's right shoe. After tearing her stocking to expose a bare foot, he lifted the hypodermic. "Hey—do you think glass coffins will ever come into fashion?" He looked at her as he removed an imaginary cigar and tapped imaginary ashes to the floor. "Remains to be seen."

The office door banged open, and Jack walked in, revolver drawn. Marshaling all her strength, Sarah kicked at Funston's hand, knocking the syringe across the carpet. Funston stood, hands up.

"Well done, sir," said Smartwell. "I like a man who knows how to time his entrance. I suppose you want money."

"I want you to pay for three murders," said Jack. "Sarah—are you all right?"

"No, doctor, the patient is not well," said Sarah woozily. "We have a twenty-five-year-old female with a probable concussion. She requires immediate transportation to the Johns Hopkins Hospital severe trauma ward."

CHAPTER 40

JACK—SATURDAY, APRIL 23, 2:45 P.M.

*S*arah was hurt bad. Blood, some dried and the rest sticky, matted the hair on one side of her head. The high lace collar of her shirtwaist had gone from white to dark red. Her head was pitched at a strange angle, and the pupil of one eye was bigger than the other.

After phoning for the ambulance, Jack knelt by her while keeping the pistol leveled at Funston and Smartwell.

"Document," she said in a halting and slurred voice while weakly pointing up.

"Yeah, I saw it on the desk." While using the telephone, he glanced at the paper and saw that it gave Reverend Smartwell control over Lydia's affairs. Although surely bogus, it looked legit, with fancy seals, stamps, and the signature of Judge Barnabas Lanvale. He took Sarah's hand. "You shouldn't talk."

"Your question is elementary, doctor," she said. "Bones of the skull include the occipital, parietal, temporal . . ." She stared vacantly.

He made a shushing sound and lightly touched her unbloodied cheek.

"Romantic attraction is necessary to promote fornication and propagate the human species." She looked right at him with an unwavering gaze. "Thus, my attraction to Jack arouses physical desire. I have no sexual experience whatsoever and am extremely nervous about coitus." Her lips formed a loopy smile. "But the prospect of sexual intercourse with him is *very* appealing."

He squeezed her hand. "Quiet, now."

"Sir, you should take consolation in knowing the value of living flesh is exaggerated," said Smartwell.

"Shut up," said Jack. "The cops are coming for you soon. I know you killed Anna Gilbert and Lucinda Pike as part of your scam to get Lydia's money. Why did you murder Chance McCall, too?"

"I paid to use his hidden staircase to visit the distraught Miss Gilbert," said Smartwell. "But Mr. McCall proved to be unacceptably greedy."

"You purposely spilled the beans about the elopement to Mrs. Lanvale knowing she'd blow up at Anna," said Jack. "Then you went to the hotel to offer her comfort in the form of drugged champagne. She passed out, and you jabbed her. Later, Chance found a receipt for the bubbly in the room and tried blackmail."

"The receipt was, stunningly enough, in his actual name." Smartwell pointed to Funston. "As usual, I had to save the show from my partner's miscue."

"No, you overacted, as usual," said Funston while rhythmically tapping first one foot and then the other. "I used sexy Lexie to get the receipt back, slick and dandy. But you had to chew the scenery and kill the man anyway. Such cheap melodrama."

Jack scoffed. "Wearing that sheet to kill Lucinda Pike at the séance was an over-the-top performance, Funston."

"Sometimes one has to exaggerate, play it big, if the script calls for it." Funston crossed his arms and tossed his head. "Donning that sheet was yet another example of my heroic artistic effort to advance our boffo act: 'Fun and Smart: We Operate on Your Funny Bone.'"

"'Nit and Wit Kill for Fun and Profit' is more like it," said Jack. "You guys need to prepare for a farewell performance. On the gallows."

"Harden, seems like you show up at every crime in Baltimore," said Detective O'Toole as he strolled in. "A regular Johnny-at-the-rathole." He nodded at Sarah. "What, did you try to knock the weird out of her?"

"I've done your work for you, Snake," said Jack. "This pair killed Chance McCall and two others. They admitted it to me."

"I must say that claim is far too broad, detective," said Smartwell. "I personally am as innocent as a veritable babe in arms. As for this fellow—" Smartwell shook a fist at Funston, "you will find his fingerprints on that lethal syringe and chemical vial. He is, dare I say, the one guilty of murder."

"Professor," said Sarah in a mushy voice, "it is said policemen and criminals share a similar deviant mentality."

"Shut that oddball up, Harden, or you'll end up looking worse than her."

"Jack . . ." Sarah gave a strange gurgle and passed out.

Funston used the diversion to grab the syringe from the floor and then take hold of Smartwell's arm. "No way the straight man is going to steal this show!"

O'Toole drew his .38 Special. "I was hoping to shoot somebody today."

"The fat man killed Anna Gilbert and Chance McCall without finesse, with no theatrical style," said Funston. "I killed Lucinda Pike as part of my brilliant staging, and then moving portrayal, of a tormented spirit."

"Drop it." O'Toole cocked the hammer of his pistol. "I'm taking both you clowns in on suspicion of murder."

"George, you are indeed a fine dramaturgist, sir," said Smartwell in a high, strained voice. "And, I must say, a far superior comedic talent than my lowly self. Please—do not harm me, I beseech you."

"At last! He admits I'm the one with real talent. But count

me out for a gig with the hangman, detective. There's no chance of a repeat engagement." Funston jabbed the syringe into his own thigh and immediately launched into a brief, dazzling dance that ended with a spinning flurry of flick-kicks. Finished, he stood with arms spread wide. "I keep seeing ads for burial plots," he shouted. "Man, that's the last thing I need!" With a big smile, he pitched over face first.

The sound of hurrying feet came from the hallway. "We got a stretcher here," called an ambulance attendant. "Is that the brained broad for the meat wagon?"

Jack held Sarah's limp hand, willing her to hang on. "She's a lady, bud, and don't you forget it. Handle her gently, or you'll need a trip to the hospital, too."

The attendants worked carefully to put her on the stretcher and left. With Sarah's shoe and bloody hat in hand, Jack tried to follow, but a uniformed cop blocked his way. "Snooper, you're staying," said O'Toole. "Tell me your version of what went on here, reverend."

"Miss Kennecott," Smartwell pointed at Sarah's bloody hat, "appeared here making fantastical accusations. I tried to calm her, sir, but she grew steadily more hysterical and incoherent."

"She's a strange one, all right." O'Toole lit a cigarette and flicked the spent matchstick away. "Go on."

"Then, with no warning, that man," he gestured at Funston's spread-eagle body, "appeared and hit Miss Kennecott from behind. He, too, started ranting and raving, much as he did before killing himself just now."

"You know the guy?" The detective dragged on his cig and poked at Funston's body with a toe.

"He is an associate from my past, someone I haven't seen for years. I have no idea why he showed up and inflicted violence on poor Miss Kennecott. I imagine it was a sad call for help that went awry. Then, shortly after Miss Kennecott fell, that man," he pointed at Jack, "burst in and brandished a gun."

"This place is a regular Grand Central Station for lunatics."

O'Toole linked the fingers of both hands and pressed his palms out, causing knuckles to crack like a hammer hitting a bag of bones.

"He's lying, Snake," said Jack. "I got here just as they were about to inject Sarah. That guy," Jack jerked at thumb at Funston's body, "jabbed himself to avoid a murder rap, but he and Smartwell are equally guilty—"

Smartwell interrupted. "Thank heavens you saved me from this deluded fellow, detective. Let me say, sir, that I am a supporter of the police. A very generous supporter, if I may say so."

O'Toole flashed his hideous crooked teeth with a dead-eyed smile, and then dropped his cig butt into a teacup on the desk with a hiss. "I appreciate that, reverend, but you're going to the cooler. Something ain't right here." He glanced at Jack. "It's your lucky day, Harden. Get lost before I decide to whale on you for the hell of it."

Jack trotted out of the church and got a cab headed for Johns Hopkins Hospital. He didn't want to lose a minute getting to Sarah in case she—

She could not die. The world wasn't that evil.

Was it?

CHAPTER 41

SARAH—SATURDAY, APRIL 23, 1910,
6:00 P.M.

*I*ndistinct shapes, throbbing head, parched mouth. Hazy memory of what had happened. Her nose detected the sharp tang of hospital disinfectant. She moved a hand and felt a crisp bedsheet, then spongy gauze on her head. Apparently, she was lying in a hospital ward with an injury to her skull.

"What." The word came out as a raspy wheeze. Her tongue was leaden, lips dry and cracked.

"Welcome back. How about some water?"

Jack. She nodded at his blurry form sitting next to her and gulped from the glass at her lips, not caring about the cold dribbles falling on her neck and chest.

"You're at Hopkins Hospital," he said. "The docs looked you over and said you'll be fine after a long rest. You got a concussion but no fracture. Could have been a lot worse—apparently, your hat and hair cushioned the blow."

Amazing. She never imagined a silly hat and the tedious work needed to pin up her hair would serve any practical purpose beyond expected social conformity.

"You got whacked by a guy named George Funston. He's a buddy of Reverend Smartwell. Looks like they were the ones who injected and killed Anna Gilbert and the other two. Funston's dead."

"Document," she said. "On desk." She had more to say, but uttering just those words was almost impossibly hard.

"The guardianship order giving Smartwell control over Lydia's money? Yeah, saw it. Funston must have used his job at the courthouse to forge the document. He had access to every-thing—the originals, plus all the stamps and seals."

"Clever."

"There's more. Niblett, the butler, told me someone claiming to be a city inspector showed up at the Lanvale place a few days before the séance. I'll bet a dollar to a donut the guy was Funston, who took the opportunity to swipe a sheet and a key to the silver chest. He admitted to killing Lucinda Pike."

She nodded slightly as more facts behind the case fell into place.

"The cops arrested Smartwell, but I can't be sure they'll hold him," said Jack. "Or collect the right evidence from his office."

"Warn Lydia."

"She's left town." Jack exhaled sharply. "Lydia said she closed her bank account before coming to Baltimore. She claims to be near broke."

Sarah squeezed a handful of bedsheets with all her might, trying to push away the pain in her head. "First Chemical Bank. Boston. Telephone to confirm."

"Okay."

While he was away, Sarah was able to take in her surround-ings with more clarity. Her iron bed was painted white, one of the dozens lined up with precision in the ward. She knew the setting well—but only as a physician, not as a patient. The place was quiet, with only the muted talk of nurses ministering to patients some distance away.

She bore some responsibility for her placement here. Fair enough; she was investigating murders, and she willingly accepted the liability that came with the work. But had she put herself in too much danger?

Not by visiting Reverend Smartwell, a man who had given no prior indication of violence. Neither Jack nor anyone else could reasonably say she had taken an undue risk in going to the church.

The encounter with the Black Cat Creeper was a different matter. She knew going to Le Café du Chat Noir alone was perilous. It was also the best option. The police would not, in all probability, have taken her speculation about the Creeper seriously. If she alerted Jack ahead of time, he would likely have tried to confront the assassin and been killed. Given the stakes, the risk she undertook was acceptable.

Her impetuous and incautious behavior of late was unusual —and revelatory. Until now, her dealings with people had operated under a thick blanket of awkward restraint. She had always governed herself carefully according to rules and expectations. How liberating it was to know that she had the power to step around those barriers and take decisive action.

Her work as a detective required this kind of flexibility. It was as simple as that. Jack was gallant in his desire to shield her from risk, but she would continue to rely on her own judgment —and to relish the freedom that came with it.

Jack's footsteps echoed on the ward's linoleum floor. "Lydia closed the account, just like she said. The final balance was less than five hundred dollars."

She flinched. Was it possible that all the crimes committed in this case—fraud, forgery, murder—had been for nothing?

"It's tough luck for Smartwell. Even if the cops let him go, he'll end up empty-handed."

"Must hold him accountable." That was the heart of the matter: justice for three murdered people. Sarah thrashed her legs, frustrated that she couldn't emphasize that critical need.

"Hey, take it easy." Jack gently touched a sheeted calf,

calming the jerking limb. "That can still happen. The cops took my statement."

Sarah raised a finger but Jack kept talking.

"The problem is that Smartwell will deny what I said. And since he's an upstanding citizen, the cops will take his word for things, especially since there's nothing tying him to a syringe or poison. Funston, on the other hand, is conveniently tied to both."

Her hand dropped to the bed. He was correct. The only way to bring Reverend Smartwell to justice was to catch him in the act of committing a crime. But how was that possible? She thought hard as Jack's form faded behind a dark mist of pain and exhaustion.

"If Smartwell's turned loose, I'd like to think we could have set a trap for him at that Boston bank. He'd be in trouble if he tried to get money with a forged guardianship document. But I'm sure he's clever enough to have already called the bank. He knows the account's closed."

She shut her eyes. Yes, the man was extremely clever and likely had telephoned the bank. With startling clarity, she abruptly knew how to apprehend the reverend. Time was of the essence.

Just as she formed the words in her mind, they melted away into a sea of blackness.

CHAPTER 42

JACK—SUNDAY, APRIL 24, 1910, 12:00 P.M.

*J*ack gave his particulars to the nurse at the reception desk and pushed open the door marked: "Severe Trauma Ward: Authorized Visitors Only."

He'd told a fib to gain access and was pushing his luck even more to visit not one but two patients. The young woman beaten at Lexie Calhoun's lay in a bed near the door, head and face heavily bandaged. The nurse said she would recover but was heavily sedated.

He stood over the bed, and by the look in her eyes, knew she recognized him. "Hello again. I know your jaw's busted, so don't bother trying to talk."

She blinked at him slowly.

"I want you to know the guy who hurt you won't do it to anybody else. He's dead." Jack saw the story in the morning paper: police detective Terrance O'Toole, fearing for his life, had been forced to kill "the notoriously violent hoodlum known as 'Pretty Boy,'" shooting him six times. The account didn't detail where Pretty Boy was hit, but Jack would lay odds most of the shots were in the back.

The young woman remained still under the bedclothes.

"This is for you." He handed over the money taken from

Stack and Pretty Boy, along with most of what was left from what Sarah had given him last week. "It doesn't begin to make up for what happened to you. But it's enough for a new start. Just promise me one thing—that you'll stay away from Lexie Calhoun and others like her."

She nodded and took the cash.

Jack continued down the ward and saw a nurse slowly unwinding loops of white bandage from Sarah's head. When the final layer came off, a stitched, two-inch cut on the back of her head came into view. The wound stood out clearly, as the surrounding hair had been clipped short.

"Your special someone is here, madam," said the nurse.

"Quite a bump," said Jack as he strolled up.

"Nurse, you will leave us," said Sarah.

"I'm sorry, madam, but I need to dress the wound first. But don't worry. There will still be plenty of time afterward for your husband to be sweet to you."

"I have no husband."

The nurse caught her breath and looked up. "Sir, you claimed to be a married couple. Only spouses can visit this ward."

"Just a bit of confusion," said Jack with a wave of his hand. He had hoped to keep his lie a secret from Sarah, but no such luck.

"This will really hurt, sorry." Sarah's face remained blank as the nurse applied a liberal dose of disinfectant to the injury.

"She seems a lot better," said Jack.

"She's expected to make a full recovery, although rest is essential." The nurse began rewrapping the wound. "The patient can go home at noon tomorrow but must stay in bed for a week. There—all finished."

"Nurse, I request that you depart immediately. I have something urgent to discuss with—"

"With your non-husband." The nurse glowered. "I'm going to talk with the floor supervisor. We'll be right back." She hurried away.

"I am aghast—and horrified—that you lied about our relationship."

"Had to. It was the only way to be with you." He knew she was a stickler for the truth, but that didn't explain the bright red, full-faced blush under her snowy white gauze crown. "Sorry if it bothers you. Must be terrible to have people think you'd marry a loser like me."

"I am weary of your nonsense." She sat up higher in the bed. "I have important things to tell you."

"Whatever you say, wifey." Jack smiled and took the chair next to the bed. For some reason, it felt right—and strangely exciting—to tease her in this way.

"Any more of that and I will insist that you leave. Is that understood?"

"Got it." He tapped his forehead.

"I have two pieces of information." Her eyes flicked to his face and then around the room. "First, you must no longer worry about immediate action on the part of the Black Cat Creeper."

"Yeah, I guess the whole thing was a sick joke."

"It was entirely serious, but the assassin's plot was foiled. He has temporarily left the city."

He knitted his brow, worried the head injury was causing her to babble again.

"Second, is Reverend Smartwell still in police custody?"

"Yeah, but the grapevine says charges will be dropped before his arraignment tomorrow at 2:00 p.m. Cops don't have the evidence to charge him." Jack heard brisk, purposeful footsteps approaching.

"You must act quickly, then. I suspect that he will—"

"Sir." The head nurse marched up, wearing a heavily starched white uniform and a sour look. "Only legally wedded spouses are allowed to visit patients in the severe trauma ward." The woman bore an uncanny resemblance to Jack's boyhood teacher, who ruled his one-room schoolhouse with terror in the form of a long hickory paddle. His backside twitched at the memory.

"We're talking about catching a killer, lady," he said. "How about if I leave in ten minutes?"

The nurse glared at him with small, grim eyes. "You will leave immediately and not return. They are here to escort you." She pointed at two big orderlies behind her.

"Retrieve me after I am discharged tomorrow," said Sarah. "We urgently need to complete our discussion."

"You will leave, young man," said the head nurse. "Now."

Jack stood. "Okay—see you tomorrow, Sarah. I'd better go before I'm dragged out by my ear."

WALKING AWAY FROM THE HOSPITAL, JACK STOPPED AT the intersection with Albemarle Street. This was the spot where that motor truck—with the Black Cat Creeper at the wheel, no doubt—had almost hit him. Didn't the Creeper peg yesterday as Jack's last on Earth? A speeding automobile approached, headlights glowing like a hellhound. The machine slowed, and the driver cursed as he glided past. Jack gave the guy a friendly wave and continued on.

The Creeper supposedly commanded a hefty fee, more than enough to ensure the job was finished. Why was Jack still drawing breath? And who would pay enough to put a big-time assassin on him in the first place?

With a jolt, the answer hit him. Bob Foster said the Creeper worked out of New York City—the place where Pete Nelson, his army buddy killed in the Philippines at Bud Dajo, was from. Pete claimed his father ran crime rackets in the Bowery. Pete had also said his father expected Jack to take care of his son—and that his father hated to be disappointed.

After four years of searching, the elder Nelson had finally

tracked Jack down. The Creeper was meant to make him pay for Pete's death. Payment in torment and, ultimately, death.

Sarah had said "the assassin's plot was foiled" and "he has temporarily left the city." How could she know that? Surely she hadn't confronted a professional killer. What would she have done, hit him with her purse and send him scampering away?

He thought about it hard while staring into the dirty water of the harbor at the foot of Fell Street before concluding there was only one answer, incredible as it was. Sarah must have faced down the killer and granted Jack a short-term reprieve.

A luxury steam launch puttered by with three young girls on deck, all waving at him energetically. He waved back, and the girls all screamed in unison, long and shrill, before giggling madly.

The screams drew an instant torrent of flop sweat down his face as his body began tremoring. His Moro ghosts were seconds away from appearing, trying their damndest to drive him insane.

Lydia claimed to know how to get rid of the ghosts. Jack didn't trust the woman but was so desperate for relief he decided to follow her instructions. He closed his eyes and pictured the ghost of the Moro woman and her baby in his mind. "I am sorry for what happened on Bud Dajo mountain," he spoke slowly and firmly. "I am sorry innocent people were killed. Woman with the baby who has haunted me, I am sorry you and your child were murdered. It was wrong. It was evil. I wish I could have stopped it from happening."

He opened his eyes. Nothing had changed. He still felt the apparitions could appear at any time. Strolling to the edge of the harbor, he pulled out the Colt revolver. It was the only thing left from his army days, and it had saved his ass more than once since. Maybe Lydia just guessed he'd used it to kill a Moro warrior before the massacre. Maybe he was just a sucker for a good story.

The gun made a big splash when it hit the water.

CHAPTER 43

*S*he waited for Jack in the hospital lobby. He smiled broadly as he approached and was issuing a greeting when she interrupted.

"Notify Mrs. Lanvale's bank that Reverend Smartwell may fraudulently attempt to withdraw her funds."

He looked baffled. "Are you okay?"

"I am in full possession of my faculties. Notify the bank immediately. Have them contact the police when he appears. I will explain why later."

Jack trotted to a telephone booth and made the call.

Her head hurt too much to speak during the ride home in the hansom cab. The trip went smoothly, and soon Jack was lightly grasping her arm as he escorted her into her house. The housekeeper was waiting in the entry hall.

"I want to rest in the library," said Sarah.

"Everything is arranged," said the housekeeper. "Mr. Harden moved a bed for you."

With Jack's help, Sarah moved slowly into the room. She stood over the freshly turned-down bed and lifted the hat perched on top of her bandaging. The millinery was destined for the floor, but the housekeeper nimbly took custody.

"Do you want me to help you lay down?" asked Jack.

She unzipped her skirt and let it drop to the floor. She was pulling off her petticoat as Jack hurriedly left, eyes averted. Looking down at her twisted garters and torn silk stockings, she was glad he departed—she did not want him to see her looking so unkempt. The housekeeper helped her finish undressing, put on a nightdress and dressing gown, and get into bed.

After a light knock, Jack reappeared. "Comfortable?" He pulled up a chair.

"What is Reverend Smartwell's status?"

"The cops have let him go, as predicted. I used your telephone just now to find out."

"Very well, then. If my hypothesis is correct, he will be in police custody again soon." She had a sixty percent confidence level in her conjecture, which she had repeatedly reviewed in the hospital.

Jack pulled the chair closer to the bed. "While we wait, let's go over the case from the top. It starts with Judge Barnabas Lanvale's gambling problem. He went into debt with a loan shark, and Mrs. Lanvale wouldn't or couldn't pay it off from her own funds. So mother and son hatched a plan to steal money from Lydia Nightingale. Lydia was supposedly fresh off a big inheritance, and the Lanvales thought she would be easy pickings."

"Barnabas Lanvale seduced Lydia's secretary, Anna Gilbert, as part of the scheme," said Sarah. "He knew she handled Lydia's finances and thought he could use her to obtain the banking details and withdraw the funds."

Jack nodded. "It was a good plan. Lydia claimed to talk to dead people, and it would be easy to build a guardianship case claiming she was crazy. There was a wrinkle, though. Lydia wanted to hire detective Sarah Kennecott, and Mrs. Lanvale, eager to please, agreed to help. Anna wasn't really missing, though—Lydia just wanted an excuse to meet with her daughter without letting on that she was the mother."

Sarah chewed on her lip. "I should have recognized Lydia immediately."

"Don't be so hard on yourself. Anyway, Anna must have told Judge Lanvale that Lydia was your mother. He worried that you might gum up the fraud, so he hired Ralph Stack to chase you out of town. One thing Anna didn't give the judge was the Boston bank details—maybe she was waiting for after the wedding to let on that Lydia was broke."

"Meanwhile, Reverend Smartwell developed his own plan to defraud Lydia," said Sarah. She shook her head, marveling that people could devote so much time and mental energy to a criminal enterprise.

"Smartwell knew the Lanvales were crooked and guessed they would try for a phony guardianship. He had his partner, George Funston, get a job as Judge Lanvale's clerk. Apparently, Funston was better at forgery than comedy."

"To complete the fraud, Reverend Smartwell duped Anna Gilbert to get Lydia's bank information," said Sarah. "But he knew that any attempt to remove funds from the Boston bank would cause the establishment to contact first Anna Gilbert, then Lucinda Pike, both of whom handled Lydia's finances. That is why he murdered the two women."

"Smartwell bribed Chance McCall to use a secret staircase in the hotel to go to and from Anna's room," said Jack. "But McCall found a receipt and tried blackmail, so Smartwell killed him, too."

"What if Reverend Smartwell, after learning that Lydia's account was closed, decided to defraud another person?"

Jack put his hand on the bed's metal headboard and drummed his fingers.

"Please cease that noise. I find it bothersome."

He stopped. "You think Funston could have forged another guardianship order for Mrs. Lanvale."

"Correct."

Jack rubbed his chin. "But we heard Mrs. Lanvale never

shared her bank account details. Smartwell would need that information to get her money."

"You suspect George Funston, posing as a municipal inspector, had free access to the Lanvale residence for a time. Perhaps, along with his other unlawful actions in the dwelling, he stole her bank information as well."

Jack stood. "That's why you wanted Mrs. Lanvale's bank notified about Smartwell."

"After his release from custody, and assuming he still has the forged guardianship order, Reverend Smartwell could attempt to carry out the fraud. But there are two barriers. One is that the bank might wish to contact Barnabas Lanvale about a withdrawal from his mother's account. The other is that publicity from Reverend Smartwell's arrest could give the bank pause in dealing with him."

"Those aren't problems," said Jack with a grin. "No sane bank manager is going to call hot-headed Judge Lanvale to ask if he really meant to approve a document saying his mother had lost her marbles. And while Smartwell couldn't bribe his way out of an arrest, he did pay off the cops to keep it out of the newspapers."

Sarah nodded. After factoring in Jack's information, she increased the confidence level in her hypothesis to seventy-five percent. "Allow me to ask your opinion about another matter." She pressed her fingertips into the bedclothes.

"Sure."

"Is there evidence implicating my mother—Lydia—in a crime?"

"There's no evidence that I know of." Jack sat back in his chair. "Lydia denied any role in her Boston benefactor's death and claims to have gotten next to nothing from the estate. I'm inclined to believe her."

Sarah relaxed her fingers slightly.

"I did wonder if she was trying to pull a reverse con on Mrs. Lanvale, but in the end, I don't think so. Lydia called herself a leech—she said mediums have to rely on rich patrons to support them. It's a voluntary arrangement all around, and that's a lot safer than pulling a risky scam."

"That is a plausible explanation." A burden of worry lifted. It was troubling enough that Lydia was an atrocious mother. Knowing she was a criminal would have made the situation far worse.

"There's one more thing you need to know about Lydia." Jack smoothed his necktie in a quick, nervous motion. "I think she cured me of my ghosts."

"Are you stating that your mental distress in connection with the massacre you witnessed overseas has eased?" She blinked with excitement.

"Lydia told me what my main ghost wanted—for me to apologize and to get rid of my Colt pistol. I did both and feel like a new man. No shakes, no craziness, no ghosts. Lydia must have been right."

"I am pleased your condition has improved." The words were pitifully inadequate. This was more than she could have ever hoped for—Jack overcoming his trauma with her mother's help. If he was better, it did not matter one whit if Lydia's intervention had a basis in psychology or the supernatural.

"Mr. Harden, sir," said the housekeeper from the doorway. "A gentleman has called on the telephone and is requesting to speak with you."

"Be right back." He dashed from the room.

Alone at last, Sarah noticed great tension in her neck, shoulders, and back. They were familiar symptoms of anxiety brought on by perception of a threat. But what threat? She was safe at home with the housekeeper and Jack.

Jack was the threat. Not the man himself, but her feelings for him. Emotions that threatened the familiar solitary orientation of her life, the self-reliance she depended on for day-to-day stability and planning for the future. She shuddered when recalling how disorienting it had felt to hear him referred to as her husband. The experience had been a bewildering mix of panic, elation, and dread.

She drew a breath and squashed her feelings into a tiny ball for storage in the back of her consciousness. She must focus on more straightforward, resolvable matters.

"Bingo," said Jack as he bounded through the door. "A bank teller I know confirmed that Smartwell showed up with a bogus guardianship document, intending to loot Mrs. Lanvale's account. The cops arrested him. And get this—Smartwell had a syringe and several vials of chemicals packed in his luggage. Want to bet the stuff is our untraceable poison?"

"If the vials contain a mix of adrenaline and potassium chloride, they are compelling evidence. Enough, I hope, to convict Reverend Smartwell of murder."

"He's going to pay for his crimes because you're so smart," said Jack with a grin.

"I merely constructed a hypothesis. Your role in solving the case was more important than mine."

"Cut the modesty. You put your life on the line. Speaking of which, we need to visit New York City. As soon as you're better."

"For what purpose?"

"To track down the Black Cat Creeper. Before he comes back here to finish with us."

She drew in a sharp breath. "You know."

"Let's leave it at that," said Jack as he prepared to stand. "You need to rest."

"Wait." She took hold of his sleeve. "I want you to kiss me." She looked directly into his eyes.

He leaned down. When their lips touched, every nerve in her body vibrated, a sensation that grew almost unbearably exciting as the kiss deepened. When he started to move away, she rose with him, her mouth working on his fervently. He returned her passion as his hand moved first to her neck and then under her nightgown to her bare shoulder. Abruptly, he pulled away. She pushed her face into the pillow, desperately trying not to sob or say anything foolish.

"Sarah, I want more than anything to—" he stopped short and said nothing for a long moment. "We have to, umm, talk when you feel better."

She kept her face in the pillow, not daring to respond.

He cleared his throat. "We need a blunt talk."

She couldn't be sure, but his voice sounded thicker, more nervous than usual. "Take care of yourself. I'll check back tomorrow." He stroked her arm gently and left.

She relived their kiss repeatedly while floating in an ecstatic daze. After what might have been minutes or much longer, she relaxed and analyzed what had happened. It occurred to her that perhaps he had only kissed her as a show of sympathy rather than a profession of emotional attachment.

After a twinge of upset, she told herself that would not necessarily be a bad thing. They would resume detecting soon. She needed to do so. She must focus on concrete issues rather than give rein to wild emotion.

Sarah noticed the housekeeper had thoughtfully placed a stack of her favorite books next to the bed. She picked up the first book: *Alice's Adventures in Wonderland.* A girl finds herself in a strange world populated with illogical creatures who defy easy understanding. She ultimately prevails with pluck and intelligence. It was Sarah's favorite story.

But she was in the mood for something else. She reached for the next volume and retrieved *Poems by Emily Dickinson.* Turning to a random page, she read:

Hope is the thing with feathers
That perches in the soul,
And sings the tune without the words,
And never stops at all,

And sweetest in the gale is heard;
And sore must be the storm
That could abash the little bird
That kept so many warm.

I've heard it in the chillest land.
And on the strangest sea;
Yet never in extremity,
It asked a crumb of me.

A bird. Solitary, free. Floating above the muddy ground and singing out in the worst possible weather. Forever praising the virtue of human desire. And keeping alive the possibility, no matter how faint, of finding true happiness.

AUTHOR'S NOTE

SPIRITUALISM

As Sarah reads in Chapter 5, the spiritualism movement began with the Fox sisters in 1848. Soon after they claimed to communicate with spirits, a host of other so-called mediums made similar claims. Fraud ran rampant among the ranks of mediums and psychics, and many well-known practitioners were exposed. That did nothing to stop people from flocking to séances and believing in the supernatural.

The late nineteenth and early twentieth centuries were an age of discovery: electric lighting, the telephone, a plethora of new medical knowledge. Some wondered if psychic phenomena might also have a basis in science, and eminent researchers studied the topic. This work led to no definitive conclusion, and as far as I am aware, there is no scientifically authoritative evidence for premonitions, communicating with the dead, or other psychic matters. But there are plenty of examples (self-reported, to be sure) of sober, rational people having experience with something that can be termed supernatural. Abraham Lincoln supposedly dreamed about his assassination beforehand, and the psychologist Carl Jung had a vision of World War

I one year before it started. Jung later used this experience to form his idea about a "collective unconsciousness" shared by all humans.

Sarah can't make sense of her experience with her dead sister Grace in Chapter 1. It comes down to the mystery of our dreams. As *Psychology Today* puts it:

> How can we relate to the dreams that pursue us? Are they simply the result of complex neurological activity and without real meaning, just as we know the moon is no enchanted sphere but a mere rock in space? What might we miss if we cast our lot with a viewpoint based wholly on the material world? Is it possible to consider the two worlds as being equally meaningful, the world of science and—to borrow the phrase John Keats used to characterize adventurers on the threshold of a new frontier—the world of "wild surmise"? Can we think of ourselves as vessels open to receiving wisdom through non-ordinary means? Can we be our own shamans?

- "Can Dreams Be Prophetic?" https://www.psychologytoday.com/us/blog/transcending-the-past/202002/can-dreams-be-prophetic.
- *Ghost Hunters: William James and the Search for Scientific Proof of Life After Death*, Deborah Blum, 2006.
- *Talking to the Dead: Kate and Maggie Fox and the Rise of Spiritualism*, Barbara Weisberg, 2004.

EMILY DICKINSON POEMS

Sarah is, of course, correct in recognizing Emily Dickinson as the author of the poems that Lydia Nightingale quotes.

Only a handful of Dickinson's poems were published during her lifetime. The history of her posthumously published work is complex. Her manuscripts were split between two custodians.

The first published compendium of her poems appeared in 1890, significantly edited and altered from their original handwritten manuscript versions. Some lines were rewritten, and punctuation and capitalizations were changed. Other editorial changes included omitting the poet's frequent dashes and idiosyncratic spellings. Previously unpublished Dickinson poems appeared in print as late as 1945. In 1998, The Harvard University Press published what is currently regarded as the most definitive edition of Dickinson's poetry.

Harvard owns the copyright for poems published after 1926, as well as for the later editions of her work. I wished to include the definitive rendition of "One need not be a chamber to be haunted" for the epigraph. I also used the definitive version of "The whole of it came not at once" in chapter 36. These two poems are licensed from Harvard, and so the format of both is in line with the latest HUP edition of Dickinson's poetry. The other poems used are from public domain (pre-1926) editions, and so omit Dickinson's dashes, odd spellings, and so forth. This is the format the public would have known in 1910.

A complete list of poem first lines is below (in some cases, I used fragments).

- Epigraph: One need not be a chamber to be haunted.
- Chapter 7: I measure every grief I meet.
- Chapter 10: I heard a fly buzz when I died.
- Chapter 10: My life closed twice before its close.
- Chapter 20: The reticent volcano keeps.
- Chapter 27: I'm nobody! Who are you?
- Chapter 36: The whole of it came not at once.
- Chapter 43: Hope is the thing with feathers.

Lydia also recites lines from Dickinson's correspondence in Chapter 10, as published in pre-1926 sources.

THE BUD DAJO MASSACRE

The First Battle of Bud Dajo, also known as the Moro Crater Massacre, came about due to U.S. Army action against a group of insurgent Moro natives on Jolo Island in the southern Philippines. U.S. forces were present as a consequence of victory in the Spanish-American war, which resulted in the occupation of the Philippines. The indigenous Moro people were accustomed to independence and fought against American efforts to interfere with their culture. Army units (including Jack's cavalry regiment) fought many battles against Moro warriors. In March 1906, a band of Moros stole livestock from a farmer at the base of Bud Dajo, an extinct volcano. The raiders fled to the top of the mountain. Army units were ordered to punish the offenders.

The resulting engagement was hardly a battle. Despite American claims of a glorious victory, the press published details about the many women and children killed. Mark Twain wrote: "It has no resemblance to a battle . . . [American forces went about] butchering these helpless people . . . we abolished them utterly, leaving not even a baby alive to cry for its dead mother." About 800 to 1,000 Moros were killed at Bud Dajo; American casualties were 21 killed, 75 wounded. Moro corpses were said to be piled five feet deep. Negative press led the Secretary of War to demand an explanation from the military for the "wanton slaughter" of women and children. But the controversy soon died down, and no one was held accountable for the massacre.

- *The Moro War: How America Battled a Muslim Insurgency in the Philippine Jungle, 1902-1913*, James R. Arnold, 2011.

CHILD LABOR

In 1910, America was just starting to grapple with regulating the use of children in the workplace. It was left to the individual states to pass laws regarding the practice. Maryland, like many other states, moved slowly to deal with the issue. In 1906, the law forbade employment of anyone under twelve in Baltimore City. But lax enforcement led to Maryland vegetable canneries violating the law as late as 1925. Meanwhile, muckraking journalists and others worked to document and publicize the perils of child labor. Lewis W. Hines was one of the most effective advocates against child labor. Hines took scores of photographs of child workers, including many in 1909 Baltimore oyster packing plants.

- "Child Labor in the American South: Maryland Cannery Workers," by Eytan Kaplowitz https://bit.ly/37VlacD.

PUBLIC LIBRARY RULES FOR SHARING USER INFORMATION

In chapter 25, Ralph Stack confronts Sarah with a list of books she had accessed in a public library. Stack would never get such information today, as librarians are ethically bound to protect user privacy, but this stance is relatively recent. It was not until 1938 that the ALA Code of Ethics for Librarians compelled librarians to treat patron information as confidential. Little evidence exists before this time of concern regarding patron privacy. In 1910, a man flashing a badge would have had little trouble accessing a library patron's list of books.

- *Library Privacy Guidelines for Library Management Systems,* http://www.ala.org/advocacy/privacy/guidelines/library-management-systems.
- "'A More Cooperative Clerk': The Confidentiality of Library Records," by Bruce S. Johnson https://bit.ly/3pWxwY1 [paywall].

SONG LYRICS

I have used edited lyrics from two songs:

- Chapter 12: "Sarah Dear," lyrics by Henry Jackson, music by Scott Joplin, 1905
- Chapter 39: "Swanee," lyrics by Irving Caesar, music by George Gershwin, 1919 (nine years too early for the story—and 10 years before Al Jolson made the song famous—but used via poetic license).

ABOUT THE AUTHOR

Bill LeFurgy is a professional historian and archivist who has studied the seamy underbelly of urban life, including drugs, crime, and prostitution, as well as more workaday matters such as streets, buildings, wires, and wharves. He has put his many years of research experience into writing gritty historical fiction about Baltimore, where he lived for over a decade. It remains his favorite city.

Bill has graduate degrees from the University of Maryland and has worked at the Maryland Historical Society, Baltimore City Archives, National Archives and Records Administration, and the Library of Congress. He has learned much from his family, including patience, emotional connection, and the need to appreciate different perspectives from those on the autism spectrum and with other personality traits that are undiagnosed, misdiagnosed, or unexplained.

Subscribe to my email newsletter: http://eepurl.com/gUf6CD

BillLeFurgy.com